Walks and Talks about London

SALZWASSER
VERLAG

John Timbs

Walks and Talks about London

Reprint of the original, first published in 1865.

1st Edition 2022 | ISBN: 978-3-75259-086-9

Verlag (Publisher): Salzwasser Verlag GmbH, Zeilweg 44, 60439 Frankfurt, Deutschland
Vertretungsberechtigt (Authorized to represent): E. Roepke, Zeilweg 44, 60439 Frankfurt, Deutschland
Druck (Print): Books on Demand GmbH, In de Tarpen 42, 22848 Norderstedt, Deutschland

WALKS AND TALKS

ABOUT

LONDON.

By JOHN TIMBS, F.S.A.

O Mister Timbs—oh, F.S.A.!
  One of five hundred Fellows,
To organise and make us hay
  Who rake, and blow the bellows;
Who do recall things great and small—
  The past, who will make pleasant;
What is pulled down in this our Town
  Your London makes most pleasant.

T. CROFTON CROKER, F.S.A.

LONDON

1865.

TO THE READER.

LONDON has so many aspects, that it has been well described as a subject always new. That hearty lover of our metropolis, Dr. Johnson, sitting in Bolt-court, said: "the happiness of London is not to be conceived but by those who have been in it. I will venture to say, there is more learning and science within the circumference of ten miles from where we now sit, than in all the rest of the kingdom." Again, Johnson says: "how different a place London is to different people," each person viewing it through the medium of one particular pursuit: "but the intellectual man is struck with it as comprehending the whole of human life in all its variety, the contemplation of which is inexhaustible."

The *isolation* of London is well conveyed in Horace Walpole's experience, that there is no being alone but in a metropolis; and it is said—the old Dramatist's truism—that "the next-door neighbours don't know each other."

The immensity of London has led to its being termed *a province covered with houses:* or, as Burke phrased it, "an endless addition of littleness to littleness, extending itself over a great tract of land." Johnson's definition is still more to the point: "if you wish to have a just notion of the magnitude of this city, you must not be satisfied with seeing its great streets and squares, but must survey the innumerable little lanes and courts. It is not in the showy evolutions of buildings, but in the multiplicity of human habitations which are crowded together, that the wonderful immensity of London consists." And many years ago, when Southey began to study the Map of London, he was dismayed at the sight of its prodigious extent.

To the man of a reflective turn of mind—

> to see the stir of the great Babel,
> And not feel the crowd,

is endlessly suggestive. As you enjoy this sort of *Mind-walk*, you can scarcely fail to be struck with the beautiful imagery of the poet of Cooper's Hill, in picturing this aspect of the Town:

> Where, with like haste, through several ways they run,
> Some to undo, and some to be undone;
> While luxury and wealth, like war and peace,
> Are each the other's ruin and increase;
> As rivers lost in seas, some secret vein
> Thence reconveys, there to be lost again.

Now, these WALKS AND TALKS have not been taken under either of these influences exclusively, but in a vein compounded of all of these; seeking to record Scenes and Impressions of the Past and Present in this our *Book-walk* and Table Talk, and thus show what has been lost and gained by modern change.

At the present moment our Metropolis is in this transition state: many an old place which we described in our CURIOSITIES OF LONDON* some ten years ago, no longer exists. To sketch a few of the leading changes consequent upon these removals, and that more discursively than was compatible with the plan of the CURIOSITIES, is the main object of the present volume, which has more of the character of personal observation than had its predecessor. Reminiscences of Persons, Places, and Events form the staple of the WALKS AND TALKS: which, though complete in themselves, may be received as indications of the character of the autobiographic volume of COLLECTIONS AND RECOLLECTIONS, which we intend to publish at no very distant period.

In conclusion, it is hoped that the present Work will be received with such indulgence as you have been pleased to accord to the productions of the same studious, though not unerring, hand.

I. T.

* Of the CURIOSITIES OF LONDON, sometime out of print, and scarce, a new, enlarged, and improved Edition is now in the press.

CONTENTS.

WALKS AND TALKS ABOUT LONDON.

A LITTLE TALK ABOUT LYON'S INN.

FOUR hundred and fifty years is a tolerable stretch of existence, even in antiquarian record. A piece of old London of this date—a long-neglected, out-of-the-way nook and corner—disappeared early in 1863, after having been threatened with destruction for nearly half a century. This old, degenerate place had, however, been a spot of note—one of the nurseries of our great lawyers—an Inn of Chancery, attached to the parent inn, the Inner Temple. Such was Lyon's Inn: the upper portion of the old block of buildings, a sort of middle-row between Wych-street, part of the "Via de Aldwych" north, and Holywell-street south; facing Newcastle-street west, narrowing to a wedgelike form east, and extending from St. Clement's churchyard nearly to the church of St. Mary-le-Strand. One of Strype's annotators describes it as "commonly called the Back-side of St. Clement's: the street runs up to the Maypole in the Strand." Wych-street is one of the oldest remaining portions of the metropolis. Here is New Inn, as old as Lyon's Inn; and the opposite face of the street retains a few picturesque house-fronts. Holywell-street, too, has a few lofty, gabled, and bayed dwellings, but nothing to remind us of Fitzstephen's description of this spot—"sweete, wholesome, and cleere; and much frequented by schollers and youths of the citie in summer evenings, when they walke forth to take the aire." This street was, in Strype's time, inhabited by divers salesmen and piece-brokers. Bodice- and stay-makers kept shop here within recollection, as did also silk-mercers, one of whom removed thither to the more courtly Bond-street. Here remained, to our time, two mercers' signs: "The Indian Queen," said to have been painted by Catton, R.A.; and a boldly-carved crescent-moon, exhibiting the old conventional face in the centre. Jews, who dealt in old clothes and lent masquerade finery, also dwelt here; a family of which class attained great length of days even in this grimy thoroughfare, where, in 1846, died one Harris, a clothesman, who had lived in the street more than seventy years. His wife died a few years before him, at the age of ninety-three; and his eldest son was seventy-three at the time of his father's death. The silk-mercers and stay-makers were succeeded by keepers of book-stalls, and venders of cheap periodicals; and the wares of some disreputable dealers being brought "under Lord Campbell's Act," the name of the street has been changed to Booksellers'-row. On the north side of the street was the oldest portion of Lyon's Inn; and here was the original entrance, blocked up many years since. It had a pair of boldly-sculptured lions' heads: opposite is a low-pitched court, with a corner-post carved with a lion's head and paws, serving as a corbel to support a very old house; this court being the entrance to Lyon's Inn from the Strand. The other entrance, in Newcastle-street, which was built and named after John Holles, Duke of Newcastle, who died 1711, rendered the Inn a thoroughfare; and after the blocking up of the original entrance, that in Newcastle-street remained the only gate.

The history of the Inn is briefly told. Sir George Buc, in Howes, edition 1631, says: "Lyon's Inn was a guest-inn or hostelry, held at the sign of the Lyon, and purchased by gentlemen, professors, and students in the law in the raigne of King Henry the Eighth, and converted to an Inn of Chancery." Hatton describes the Inn, nearly eighty years later, as follows:

Lyon's Inn, an Inn of Chancery, situate on the Sh. side of Witch Str. It has been such an Inn since Anno 1420, or sooner. It is governed by a Treasurer and 12 Ancients; those of this House are 3 weeks in Michaelmas Term, other Terms 2 in Commons; and pay 5*s*. for the Reading Weeks, for others 2*s*. 6*d*. Here are Mootings once in 4 Terms, and they sell their chambers for 1 or 2 Lives. Their Armorial Ensigns are Chequy Or and Azure, a Lyon Rampant Sable. They have a handsome Hall, built in the year 1700.—*New View of London*, 1708.

Herbert, in his *Antiquities of the Inns of Court and Chancery*, the materials for which he mostly derived from Dugdale's *Origines Juridiciales*, says: "It (Lyon's Inn) is known to be a place of considerable antiquity from the old books of the stewards' accounts, which contain entries made in the time of King Henry V. How long before that period it was an Inn of Chancery is uncertain."

We have referred to the Inn as a nursery of lawyers; and one of the most interesting records of its history is, that here was nurtured the incorruptible Sir Edward Coke, the founder of the independence of the Bench of England, and to whom his intriguing rival, Sir Francis Bacon, ascribed the praise of having preserved the vessel of the common law in a steady and consistent course. Sometime in the year after Coke's call to the Bar, *i.e.* in 1579, he having greatly distinguished himself in the *Mootings and Readings*, which constituted a necessary part of the education of an advocate in former times, the Society of the Inner Temple appointed him reader at Lyon's Inn; when the intelligence and learning displayed by him in the exercises raised for him a high reputation as a lawyer, and opened the way to that extensive practice at the Bar, which he acquired with a rapidity almost without parallel in the history of the profession. Lloyd, in his *State Worthies*, says that "his learned lecture so spread forth his fame, that crowds of clients came to him for counsel." In the next term after he was called to the Bar, he argued a case of much nicety and importance, known to lawyers by the name of Lord Cromwell's case, which he says, in his own report of it (4 Rep., 146), was the first cause that he moved in the King's Bench. Thenceforth, until he became Solicitor-General, his practice was enormous. In 1592 he became Recorder of the Inner Temple. It is curious to trace the start of our great constitutional lawyer from his readership at Lyon's Inn, and to picture the crowds of students who, in the days of Elizabeth, flocked to the old hall of the Inn, the hostelry of the Lancasterian time. Our several Inns of Court and Chancery have their illustrious names emblazoned upon their roofs and walls and windows; but neither of them eclipses in rank and interest that of Coke, from his readings in the small Strand inn, to his energetic coöperation in framing the celebrated Bill of Rights, and defending the constitutional privileges of the people of England—and this in his seventy-ninth year. We get an indication of the Inn buildings in 1543 (some years before Coke's time) from Van den Wyngrerde's View of London, in the Sutherland Collection in the Bodleian: beyond the Strand, all is open ground.

On entering the Inn from Newcastle-street, on the right, in the south-west corner of the court, was the hall, built in 1700,—a substantial brick edifice, with a small lantern on the roof; the east end had a stone-framed pediment, and the armorial lion sculptured in the tympanum; beneath was a handsome doorway of stone, with Doric columns; and under the windows were festoons of flowers, carved in stone. This entrance, with a flight of steps, is shown in prints of 1800 and 1804; but it had long been blocked up. The hall was a large, unadorned room; adjoining was "the parliament-chamber;" and beneath the entire edifice was a kitchen of cryptal spaciousness, with other offices. The kitchen had not been used for many years. Upon the last occasion, the clothes of the cook caught fire while she was attending to her viands. The flames overpowered her, unaided as she was, and the poor creature is said to have been burnt to a cinder.

We remember a few roughly-painted portraits of legal worthies upon the walls of the hall. It had been, for many years, let for Law Lectures, and for meetings of Architectural and other artistic societies.

The oldest portion of the Inn was the south side, fronting Holywell-street, a portion of which had four stories, and bay-windows; the upper chambers were of very low pitch, and access to them was by two spiral flights, reminding one of the corkscrew-staircase, oddly said to have been invented before the use of fermented liquors was rightly understood.

The northern and eastern sides of the square were of red brick, with two inscription-stones, the oldest of which bore the date of 1683. Small as was the court, it had within memory a few trees, and that almost invariable adjunct to an Inn of Court or Chancery, a sun-dial; this, however, so long ago as 1828, had lost its gnomon and figures, and was falling to pieces. Upon a gusty day in autumn, curious it was to watch the little hurricane, as the wind swept into corners and up open staircases the withered leaves, the rustle of which broke the silence of this strange old place.

We are not aware of the period at which the law-tenants left the Inn, and the little that is remembered of its subsequent occupiers is of comparatively modern date; nevertheless, these records tell of a few noteworthy persons and circumstances. In the old chambers a laborious student of Jeremy Bentham, through days and nights, and months and years, of hard reading, stored up information to qualify himself for the arduous duties of an officer of the Poor-Law Commission: indeed, here the primal measures of the new law may be said to have been framed; and never did public servant or confidential services merit higher recognition than their author. Thence he became a hard worker in the wide field of Sanitary Science.

Next door, in second-floor chambers, which, from their low pitch and small windows, resembled the cabin of a ship, there dwelt a ripe classic scholar, who, by way of relief, wrote in the *Weekly Dispatch* newspaper the spirited leaders signed "D.," which became a sort of mint-mark in that journal. He was succeeded in the tenancy by a hard-working author, one of whose toilsome feats was to have made an index of 2000 references in one night, by the aid of potations of strong green-tea!

The next noteworthiness is of considerably less enviable notoriety. In chambers of the south-east corner of the Inn lived the gambler William Weare, who was murdered by Thurtell at Elstree, in Hertfordshire, some forty-two years since, as commemorated in a ballad of the time, attributed to Theodore Hook:

They cut his throat from ear to ear,
His brains they battered in;
His name was Mr. William Weare,
He dwelt in Lyon's Inn.

He left his chambers on the afternoon of October 24, 1823, for Elstree, whence he never returned alive.

Next door, in the attics, through toilsome days and nights, was annually collected the *Post-Office Directory;* and from these labours may be dated the progressive completeness of the *Directory*, which has agglomerated into the very bulky volume that comes in with the Christmas turkeys, and has almost outgrown the Post-Office itself.

In the double set of chambers beneath lived Philip Absolon, the antiquary and genealogist, who greatly assisted E. W. Brayley in his best work, *The History of Westminster Abbey.* Absolon had his rooms filled with a valuable library, and almost endless stores of prints and drawings and articles of *virtù;* he was, moreover, an amateur herald-painter, and filled his windows with armorial glass of his own handiwork. He set a high value upon heraldry, but rated lowly Egyptian antiquities! When Salt's celebrated collection was about to be sold, Absolon received a catalogue, which he threw aside with disdain; the vain old herald-painter declaring the worthlessness of Egyptian antiquities as "stuff," prefixing a profane superlative, which we had rather not repeat.

Next door, northward, lived Captain Holland, the *littérateur*, during his editorship of the *Monthly Magazine*, in which were printed the earliest of Mr. Charles Dickens's "Sketches by Boz." One of these papers Holland had consigned to "the rejected" basket, from which limbo it was rescued by a dropper-in, whose attention was drawn to the somewhat mystical handwriting. He drew up the paper, which proved to be "The Bloomsbury

Christening," one of the raciest of the author's early sketches, and familiar to playgoers: every editorship has such mischances. Holland wrote some sound volumes for Lardner's *Cyclopædia.* In the chambers above resided a well-read man of the law, who has since distinguished himself as a topographer of the very interesting parish of Lambeth. And on the opposite side of the Inn lived Murphy, architect of the chapel in Stamford-street with a noble Doric portico.

Such are the associations, legal, literary, and artistic, of old Lyon's Inn. A few navy-agents lingered here to the last, as did some of the officers of the now defunct Insolvent Debtors' Court, which in no way relieved the seediness of the place. One of the messengers was a stalwart man, who, in his long service, must have almost walked round the world, scattering notices—in most cases unnoticed—or consummations of bad debts, which might have been left to their natural oblivion. What an amount of ill-news must this Mercury of insolvency have sown broadcast in his time! but his occupation's gone. A few of the oldest inhabitants of this mouldy Inn had almost *grown to the spot,* so wedded do men become by habit and circumstance to loopholes of retreat from the din and roar of the great Babel by which they are surrounded. An aged man of the law was heard to say that he was born there, and there he should wish to die; and his neighbour in the garret took such delight in his window-gardens, that he sighed not for bowers or fields, though they had been Elysian. Here he lived to a great age, at a rent of fewer pounds than months in the year; and he left with a pang the seedy old place, where he had dwelt so long "in measureless content." He was the last to quit old Lyon's Inn.

THE LAST DAYS OF DOWNING-STREET.

IT is hard to imagine the seat of the Government of the greatest country in the world being fixed for many score years in a *cul-de-sac* of old Westminster; yet such has been the case for two centuries past, or since 1667, when a time-serving baronet, Sir George Downing, a political "sider with all times and changes," after serving Cromwell, became Secretary to the Treasury, under Charles II. At the Revolution, the street was part of the forfeited property of Lee, Lord Lichfield, who retired with James II., to whom he was Master of the Horse. It is described, about 1698, as "a pretty, open place, especially at the upper end, where are four or five very large and well-built houses, fit for persons of honour and quality, each house having a pleasant prospect into St. James's Park, with a tarras-walk" (R. B., in Strype). And in the *Daily Courant*, Feb. 26th, 1722, four of these houses are advertised to be let—"Inquire of Charles Downing, Esq." Among the eminent inhabitants of the street were Aubrey de Vere, the last Earl of Oxford, who died here March 16th, 1702-3. In 1733 John Boyle, Earl of Orrery, the friend of Swift, and contributor to the *World* and *Connoisseur*, lived here; as did James Boswell, the biographer of Johnson, in 1760. Gibbon, the historian, was frequently the guest here of Lord Sheffield. Hatton describes Downing-street, "between King-street, E., and no thorow fair, West;" in other words, a *cul-de-sac.*

All this time, "Downing-street" had been used as a sort of phrase for Government; and "Downing-street influence" had become synonymous with something like political corruption. Originally, the First Lord of the Treasury alone had his official residence here. It had been given by King George I. to Baron Bothmar, the Hanoverian Minister, for life. On his death, George II. offered it to Sir Robert Walpole; but he would only accept it for his office of First Lord of the Treasury, to which post he got it annexed for ever, taking up his abode there in 1735. Seven years later, there was a destructive fire in the street. Horace Walpole tells us that, hearing of the fire, he hastened to Whitehall, but could not get to the end of the street in his chariot for the crowd. When he got out, the first thing he heard was a man enjoying himself: "Well, if it lasts two hours longer, Sir Robert Walpole's house will be burnt to the ground." This was a very comfortable hearing; but Horace found the fire was on the opposite side of the way, and at a good distance. "By degrees," says Cunningham, "one house was bought after another: first the Foreign Office, increased afterwards by three other houses; then the Colonial Office; then the house in the north corner, which was the Judge Advocate's, since added to the Colonial Office; then a house for the Chancellor of the Exchequer; and, lastly, a whole row of lodging-houses, chiefly for Scotch and Irish members." Here the great Lord Chatham was carried to a messenger's house, Mr. Sargent's, after his fatal swoon in the House of Lords.

Some amusing incidents are related of Lord North's ministerial sojourn here. It was from Downing-street that the easy-going Premier wrote his laconic dismissal to Fox: "His Majesty has thought proper to order a new Commission of Treasury to be made out, in which I do not see your name.—NORTH." Fox was much annoyed; his character being so frail, that the scandalous mob believed he was turned out for robbing the Treasury.

When North was elected Knight of the Garter, he practised the charity enjoined by the rules of chivalry by a dole, or distribution, every Sunday morning at the door of his residence in Downing-street, of broken victuals, and 5*s.* 3*d.* to each of twenty poor persons, there assembled by order.

When the rioters, in 1780, had nearly filled the little square at the end of Downing-street, and Lord North and his friends in the minister's residence were debating how the noisy mob should be treated, Mr. St. John held a pistol in his hand, and was much excited; Lord North, who never lost an opportunity of jesting, exclaimed: "I am not half so much afraid of the mob as of Jack St. John's pistol."

When, a few years later (1783), Lord North descended from the post of First Minister to Secretary of State, he jested on the change. His apartments at the Treasury being situated on the second-floor, he experienced some fatigue in ascending so many steps. Frequently, from the effect of long habit, or from absence of mind, forgetting his official descent, he went straight to the Treasury chambers, on the first-floor. These accidents, which would have distressed more irritable men, never externally discomposed good-humoured Lord North.

Prime Ministers have variously affected Downing-street. Pitt's laborious habits of work kept him much at his office. A curious piece of Parliamentary work, in his administration, —a genuine Downing-street record,—has turned up. When, in 1783, Mr. Pitt introduced his bill for regulating fees, perquisites, and other emoluments in public offices, he pointed out one of the charges of previous administrations, specifying a sum of 340*l.* paid to the Secretary of the Treasury for the article of *whipcord.* Some sort of explanation was given in Parliament, which diverted more than it satisfied its hearers. (See Sir N. W. Wraxall's *Historical Memoirs*, vol. ii. p. 361.) Has not this *whipcord* charge something to do with the Treasury *whipper-in?*

Haydon once asked Lord Melbourne if he occupied Downing-street. His lordship said "No," with hesitation; but he was fond of leisure, and, by keeping at his house in South-street, he was out of the way of bore till business-hours. Lord Grey was always in it; and Haydon, in his picture of his lordship ruminating by the fireside after a great Reform debate, has minutely painted the Premier's private room.

In the Colonial Office, No. 14 in the street, in a small waiting-room on the right-hand as you entered, the Duke of Wellington—then Sir Arthur Wellesley—and Lord Nelson, both waiting to see the Secretary of State, met,—the only time in their lives. The Duke knew Nelson from his pictures; Lord Nelson did not know the Duke, but was so struck with his conversation, that he stepped out of the room to inquire who he was. Mr. Cunningham relates this meeting, which has been painted and engraved.

Downing-street may be said to have formed one side of the Treasury buildings, which, on the north, front St. James's Park, and communicated with the old ministerial street by a vaulted passage. Here is still preserved the royal throne, or chair, at the head of the Treasury table. In this range of buildings was the Cockpit of the palace at Whitehall, which, after the fire in 1697, was altered into the Privy Council Office—a conversion which has provoked many a lively sally. Hatton describes the Cockpit as "between the gate into King-street, Westminster, and the gate by the banqueting-house;" the former was designed by Holbein, and known as the Cockpit-gate. The old place had some interesting historical associations. Philip Herbert, Earl of Pembroke and Montgomery, from a window of his apartments in the Cockpit, saw his sovereign, Charles I., walk from St. James's to the scaffold. Monk, Duke of Albemarle, died here, 1669-70; and Villiers, Duke of Buckingham, 1673. And here, in the council-chamber, Guiscard stabbed Harley, Earl of Oxford. The old place retained its original name long after the change in its uses. Mr. Cunningham says: "The Treasury Minutes, circ. 1780, are headed 'Cockpit;'" the *Picture of London*, edit. 1806 and 1810, refers to the Council-chamber as "commonly called the Cockpit;" and we remember to have read at the foot of a printed proclamation at Whitehall, "Given at the Cockpit," &c.

Downing-street was doomed to demolition half a century since: the clearance was begun so long ago as 1828, when was taken down the south side of Downing-street; at the corner, next King-street, was the noted Cap and Bagpipes, used as a chop-house in early life by George Rose, subsequently Secretary to the Treasury, and one of the earliest promoters of savings-banks. Soane had already commenced his classic front of the Government Offices in Whitehall, and forming part of the north side of Downing-street; and it was then proposed to extend the elevation southward; but this has been delayed five-and-thirty years, while the public business has been carried on in various locations, resembling second-class lodging-houses. Soane's façade was harshly handled, a Roman temple being inappropriate for a British Council Office; but the interior, especially the Council-chamber, shows the skill and taste of the architect. It occupies the site of the royal tennis-court. In 1846-8, Soane's exterior was altered, a portion of the old York-place front taken down, and the façade completed by Barry, as we now see it.

In 1863, the foundations of the new offices were laid in "solid concrete;" and on the quadrangle formed by Downing-street and Charles-street, and St. James's Park and King-street, are to be erected the Foreign Office, the Indian Office, the Colonial Office, and the Pay Office. In the clearance for these buildings, whole centuries of associations have been swept away.

We have first to deal with a narrow old thoroughfare—King-street—which it is difficult to picture as once the principal street of the city of Westminster; yet such it was. In the reign of Henry VIII. it had gardens or meadow-land on the east side, reaching down to the river; the Cockpit-gate was at the north end, and the High-gate of Richard II. at the southern extremity. This was the only road for the passage of the royal carriages when the king went to Parliament, and fagots were usually thrown into the ruts to amend this royal way. At the opening of the Session of 1597, "divers people were smothered and crushed to death," pressing in this narrow street to see Queen Elizabeth and her nobility riding to Parliament. Through this narrow street Charles I. was conveyed from Whitehall to Westminster Hall, in a chair or sedan, to his trial.

A few years after, a strange incident is recorded of the street. Cromwell, then in the flush of his temporary power, was passing in his state carriage, on his way to Parliament, when the coach was kept stationary, and separated from the guard of halberdiers, by the pressure of the crowd, which blocked up the road. Suddenly, Lord Broghill, who accompanied Oliver, observed the door of a cobbler's stall repeatedly open and shut, and saw something bright glistening behind it. He immediately struck the door with his scabbard, when out sprang a tall man, armed with a sword, and made his escape. He was, probably, some offended officer in the Irish army. Cromwell never again rode through King-street.*

Pepys records a sad catastrophe in 1660, when, "a great stop of coaches" occurring, a drayman and Lord Chesterfield's coachman quarrelled, and one of the footmen was killed. Nearly a century and three-quarters ago, it was proposed to rebuild the street. Evelyn was told by the Marquis of Normanby that "King Charles had a design to buy all King-street, and build it nobly," and that this might have been done for 50,000*l.* However, the old street remained a perilous passage for law-makers until the formation of Parliament-street, towards the end of the reign of George II. About a century previously, Hatton described King-street as "the most spacious street, and principal for trade, in Westminster." Within half a century of the above relief of the traffic, the houses were ancient; for not a house in it was built of brick until that of Dudley, the second Lord North, about 1646, and that was the only brick house in the street for many years.

Among the memories of the street are its having contained the abodes of the poets Spenser, Sackville Lord Buckhurst, the Earl of Dorset, and Carew the courtier. In an obscure lodging here, Spenser died "for lake of bread."

On the west side of the street lived Oliver Cromwell, in a house the precise situation of which is thus preserved in a Ms. communication to Cunningham's *Handbook of London*, 1850:

* Walcott's *Memorials of Westminster*, p. 69.

Shortly before the great Trial, in 1838, between the parish of St. Margaret and the inhabitants of Privy-gardens, a very rigid examination of the old parochial rate-books took place; and in one of them Lieutenant-General Oliver Cromwell was found rated for a house in King-street, which was ascertained, with as much certainty as the extensive alterations in the vicinity would admit, to be one of two very ancient tenements lying between the north side of the gateway entrance to Blue Boar's Head-yard and the wall of Rams'-mews; and there was strong ground for believing that the two ancient tenements had originally been one. These tenements, as well as the Blue Boar's Head public-house, situated on the south side of the gateway, and a portion of the stable-yard behind, for a distance of about two or three hundred feet from King-street, are the property of one of the colleges at Oxford. The public-house (Blue Boar's Head), as rebuilt about 1750, is now (1850) standing.—*George H. Malone.*

It was at this house that, in July 1649, Cromwell, Lord Lieutenant of Ireland, "began his journey, by way of Windsore, and so to Bristol;" he went forth in "a coach, with six gallant Flanders mares, divers coaches accompanying him, and very many great officers of the army; his life-guard, consisting of eighty gallant men, the meanest whereof a commander or esquire in stately habit, with trumpets sounding almost to the shaking of Charing-cross, had it been now standing" (it had been taken down two years). And in the Cole Mss. in the British Museum is a copy of a letter of Cromwell to his wife from Dunbar, Sept. 4, 1650, addressed to her in this street. In a house on the site of Rams'-mews lived Sydenham, the celebrated physician. Here, too, is Gardener's-lane, described in 1650 as "a pretty, handsome place." Amid its present squalor we cannot forget that Hollar, the engraver, died here in 1677, while an execution was in his house. Farther down the street was Thieving-lane; "so called, for that thieves were led that way to the Gate-house, while the Sanctuary continued to be in force." Hard by is now the Gardener's-lane police-station.

In clearing the site, Fludyer-street and Crown-street disappeared. Fludyer-street was a quiet thoroughfare, with a gate opening into St. James's Park. It occupied the site of Axe-yard, named from the Axe brewhouse, referred to in a document temp. Henry VIII. Here lived Sir William Davenant, the poet-laureate; and Pepys, when young and unknown. Colonel Mansel lodged here when he had been nearly entrapped by Dangerfield into the Meal-tub Plot. The street, built in 1766, when Axe-yard disappeared, was named from Sir Samuel Fludyer, Bart., the ground-landlord; and who, when Lord Mayor, entertained George III. and Queen Charlotte at Guildhall. Fludyer was godfather to Sir Samuel Romilly, who, when young, was to have had a clerkship in the house of the Fludyers, who were clothiers; but the death of both partners put an end to the scheme. Crown-street was named from Rose-and-Crown-court and a tavern of that sign. Here died Dr. Kippis, the Nonconformist minister, editor of the *Biographia Britannica*, and projector of the *New Annual Register*.

At the north end of Duke-street, the flight of steps which led into the Parade, St. James's Park, and the State-Paper Office, have been removed. The latter was Soane's latest work, was unlike his other designs, and resembled an Italian *palazzo*: it had scarcely been built thirty years. It would have mortified the architect's vanity, had he lived to witness the short existence of his latest building; and, at a street's distance, his classic façade of the Treasury transformed by another hand within twenty years.

Hereafter, the new Government Offices will form a portion of one side of King-street; and the block of houses opposite will be removed, throwing open to view, among other noble objects, the new mansion of the Duke of Buccleuch, Whitehall, with its lofty Mansard-roof, to supply what the low-lying site denied.

WALKS AND TALKS IN VAUXHALL-GARDENS.

OLD and young—mankind in all their seven ages—every one—loved Vauxhall; which is best proved by its two centuries of existence as a place of amusement in our fickle climate. It is a pleasant place for old folks to talk of; and there is so much agreeable anecdote associated with the Gardens, that it is impossible not to be charmed with their name. You dream of their most palmy periods—of the *Spectator* and Sir Roger de Coverley on their voyage to the Gardens; of old Jonathan Tyers, and the paintings in the pavilions and boxes by Hogarth and Hayman; of Horace Walpole, and his fine connections in one of the bowers; and of Fielding's sketches in his *Amelia*. Then, by aid of a well-known bird's-eye view, you see the Vauxhall of a century and a quarter since,—the dowdy orchestra; the sweeping semicircles of arcades; the long walks, with their lofty festal arches; the masses of trees, between which the company promenaded without other shelter: not a house was then to be seen near the Gardens, beyond which, in the print, are fields and trees, with an undulated distance. The land is common and unenclosed; all that appears of culture is in the strip, apparently of kitchen-garden, on the right side of the Gardens, where the salads were grown.

The reader need hardly be told, these Gardens were in the parish of Lambeth, just below Vauxhall-bridge,—where, however, he may now look for them in vain: even the Water-gate, at which the company who came by river were landed, has disappeared.

There is a popular error, attributing the name of Vauxhall to Guy Faux—our old firework friend—which it may be as well to correct at starting. We must go back to a remoter age than that of James I. to solve the question.

"La Sale Faukes," in South Lambeth, is mentioned in the

Charter of Isabella de Fortibus, Countess of Aumale and Devon, and Lady of the Isle of Wight, dated in 1293, by which she sold her possessions to King Edward I. Thus we must try earlier than the close of the thirteenth century for its derivation. In the *Testa de Nevill* we read, under Surrey: "Baldwin, son and heir of the Earl of the Isle, is in the custody of Fulke de Breauté; he should be in the ward of the lord the king; also his lands in the hundred of Brixton, and they are worth 18*l.* per annum." Fulke de Breauté, the celebrated mercenary follower of King John, married Margaret, Earl Baldwin's mother, and thus obtained the wardship of her son. He appears to have built a hall, or mansion-house, in the manor of South Lambeth, during his tenure of it; and from this time it was called indifferently Faukeshall, or South Lambeth, and is so termed in the tenth year of Edward I. The capital messuage, with its garden, named "Faukeshall," was valued in the twentieth of the same reign at 2*s.* yearly. We have, therefore, satisfactory evidence that Vauxhall owes its origin and name to an obscure Norman adventurer, who became suddenly rich during the turbulent reign of John, and was ignominiously driven from the country in the minority of Henry III. (*Archæological Journal*, vol. iv.). The land on which Fulke erected his hall now belongs to Canterbury Cathedral. The manor of Fulkeshall fell, by attainder, to the Crown. It was successively held by the Despencers and the Damories; but the latter exchanged it with Edward III. for an estate in Suffolk; and the manor was conferred on Edward the Black Prince, who piously left it to the Church of Canterbury; and the bequest was spared by Henry VIII. to the Dean and Chapter.

The old manor-house has a darker history than the Gardens: its name of Faukeshall was changed to Copped, or Copt, Hall. Here Lady Arabella Stuart was held captive, under the guardianship of Sir Thomas Barry. The tradition that it ever belonged to Guido or Guy Fawkes only rests upon the coincidence of names. The estate, in the manors of Lambeth and Kennington, belonged to a family named Faucke, or Vaux, in the reigns of Elizabeth and James I.; and, in 1615, Jane Vaux, widow, held property of that description here, and the mansion-house connected with it. Mr. Nichols, in his *History of Lambeth Parish*, mistakenly affirms that Guy Vaux had a mansion here, and that it was named from him Vauxhall: he then conjectures that Jane Vaux was the relict of the infamous Guy, who was executed the 31st of January 1606; but, as Mr. Bray, who was a lawyer as well as the county historian, remarks, Guy Vaux could not have been the owner of the copyhold belonging to Jane Vaux in 1615; for if she had been his widow, it would have been forfeited as the estate of a traitor. Besides, his father's name was Fawkes, and had long spent his estate; and Jane was the widow of a much better man—John Vaux, an honest vintner of London, who bequeathed property for the erection of seven almshouses in this parish. Nevertheless, the house in which the conspirators stored their powder and other combustibles, during the digging of the mine, was certainly at Lambeth, and near the river-side; but that house did not belong to any one of them, it being merely hired for the purpose in the summer of 1604. Neither history nor tradition has recorded the exact site of the conspirators' storehouse; but we have the following evidence of its destruction by fire. In an anniversary sermon, preached at Lambeth Church by Dr. Featley, on November 5, 1635, is this passage: "You have heard the miracles of God's providence in the discovery of this powder-plot: behold now the mirrour of His justice. The first contriver of the fire-workes first feeleth the flame; his powder-sin upbraids him, and fleeth in his face." It is added, in a note: "This last yeare, the house where Catesby plotted this treason in Lambeth was casually burnt downe to the ground by powder."—*Featley's Clavis Mystica*, p. 824; 1636.

The earliest notice specifically assignable to Vauxhall Gardens is by Evelyn, in his *Diary*, 2d July 1661: "I went to see the *New Spring Garden* at Lambeth; a pretty contrived plantation. Sometimes they would have music, and sit on barges on the water." With this agrees the mention of *Les*

Jardins du Prin-temps at Lambeth by Balthasar Monconys, a French traveller, who visited England early in the reign of Charles II. He describes the Garden as much frequented in 1633, and "having grass and sand walks, dividing squares of twenty or thirty yards, which were enclosed with hedges of gooseberries, within which were roses, beans, and asparagus."

Lysons, upon the authority of an enrolment in the Duchy of Cornwall Office, states that Sir Samuel Morland, in 1675, "obtained a lease of Vauxhall-house, made it his residence, and considerably improved the premises." Morland had already shown his inventive turn, and King Charles had made him Master of Mechanics to his Majesty. Aubrey tells us, that some years before, Morland had built "a fine room at Vauxhall, *anno* 1667, the inside all of looking-glass, and fountains very pleasant to behold, which is much visited by strangers; it stands in the middle of the garden." And Mr. Bray was informed by one of the proprietors of Vauxhall in 1813 of a circumstance which shows that the dwelling-house then connected with the garden once belonged to Sir S. Morland. From the back-kitchen of the house, a lead-pump was removed about the year 1794, bearing the mark

I · S		6
9	M	4

The room mentioned by Aubrey as having been erected by Morland is believed to have stood where the orchestra was afterwards built; and grave old Mr. Bray hints at the probability of the room having been erected by Sir Samuel for the reception of Charles II., when he visited this place with his ladies. Now, the embellishments of the Gardens, from very early date to our time, consisted of whimsical proofs of skill in mechanics, such as Morland indulged in. The model-pictures in the Gardens had to our day their mechanism of an artificial cascade, a water-mill, and a bridge with a mail-coach and a Greenwich long-stage passing over; an animated cottage-scene, with figures drinking and smoking by machinery, were in existence in 1820; bushes and subterranean musical sounds were among the attractions; the tinkling of the streams of the block-tin water-fall is in our ears:

all partaking of Morland's taste, which in the present day would be termed polytechnic; so that Charles II.'s *Master of Mechanics* may have originally set the fashion of the curiosities of Vauxhall Gardens, which existed in character more than a century and a half after Morland's death.

Pepys, an excellent authority upon the gaieties of his day, has in his *Diary* entries, in 1665-8, of his visits to Fox-hall and the Spring Garden; and of "the humours of the citizens, pulling off cherries, and God knows what; to hear the nightingale and the birds, and here fiddlers, and there a harp, and here a Jew's trump, and here laughing, and there fine people walking, is mighty divertising." Pepys also tells of "supper in an arbor;" ladies walking "with their *masks* on," &c.; and, "July 27, 1688.—So over the water, with my wife and Deb and Mercer, to Spring Garden, and there eat and walked; and observe how rude some of the young gallants of the town are become, to go into people's arbors, where there are not men, and almost force the women; which troubled me to see the confidence of the vice of the age; and so we away by water, with much pleasure, home." Tom Brown, a dozen years later, speaks of the close walks and little wildernesses, which "are so intricate, that the most experienced mothers have often lost themselves in looking for their daughters."

The Gardens flourished in the reign of Queen Anne, when Addison carried Sir Roger de Coverley to spend an evening there. The reader will remember (*Spectator*, No. 383; May 20, 1712) the passage by water, from the Temple-stairs to Spring Garden, "which is exquisitely pleasant at this time of year," and indicates this to be the fashionable way of going to the Gardens, still called Spring Garden; by which name the license was granted annually so long as the place lasted. But the mask tapping Sir Roger on the shoulder, and asking him to drink a bottle of mead with her, and the *Spectator's* rhapsody upon "the fragrancy of the walks and bowers, with the choirs of birds that sing upon the trees, and the loose tribe of people that walked under their shades;" and his comparison of the place to "a sort of Mahometan paradise,"—all bear out the motto of "a beauteous garden, but by vice maintained." A glass of Burton ale and a slice of hung-beef was the supper of that period; cheese-cakes and syllabub were earlier fare in Wycherley's day; and punch and ham are not yet heard of.

The place, however, resembled a tea-garden of our early days till the year 1728, when Spring Gardens were leased for thirty years to Jonathan Tyers, of Denbies, in Surrey, at the yearly rent of 250*l.* The lease enumerates the Dark Room, Ham Room, Milk House, and Pantry Room; and among the arbours, lined and paved with tiles, are the names of Checker, King's Head, Dragon, Oak, Royal Arbour, York, Queen's Head, Royal George, Ship, Globe, Phœnix, Swan, Eagle, and the Barge. The hatch at the Water-gate was of Tyers's time: he, on the 7th. of June 1732, opened the season with a *Ridotto al fresco*, instrumental music, and a masquerade. Among the visitors were Frederick Prince of Wales, and his attendant nobles. About 400 persons were present, in masks, dominos, and lawyers' gowns; to keep whom in order, one hundred Foot-Guards were posted about the Gardens. The admission-ticket (one guinea) was designed by the younger Laguerre. The *Ridotto* was repeated with such success, as to induce Tyers to open the Gardens with music every evening during the summer: he decorated the grounds with paintings; engaged a band of excellent musicians; issued silver season-tickets of admission, at a guinea each; set up an organ in the music-house; and, in 1738, placed in the Gardens a fine statue, by Roubiliac, of Handel, as Orpheus playing on his lyre. Here was also a statue of Milton, by Roubiliac, cast in lead, and painted stone-colour. The sculptor is said to have owed his introduction to his first patron, Sir Edward Walpole, to an advertisement Roubiliac put forth of his having found, on his way home from Vauxhall, a pocket-book containing bank-notes and papers of consequence to their owner, Sir Edward Walpole. The statue of Handel was Roubiliac's first work in England: it was sold in 1854 to the Sacred Harmonic Society for 200*l.*, and is now in their committee-room, Exeter Hall, Strand.

The Vauxhall season of 1739 was for three months, and the admission only by silver tickets, at 25*s.* each, to admit two persons. These silver tickets were struck from designs by Hogarth: the obverse bore the number, name of the holder, and date; and the reverse, a figure of Euterpe, Erato, or Thalia. Hogarth was at this time in summer-lodgings at Lambeth-terrace; and the house, and a vine which he planted there, are pointed out. He had grown intimate with Tyers, whom he recommended to embellish the Gardens with paintings; and for the pavilions which Tyers had built, Hogarth drew "The Four Times of the Day," which were copied by Hayman, who, when young, was a scene-painter at Drury-lane Theatre. Hogarth painted for the vestibule portraits of Henry VIII. and Anne Boleyn—said to be Frederick Prince of Wales, and Lady Vane. The print bears the lines, by Allan Ramsay:

'Here struts old pious Harry, &c.;

a proof has been sold for 13*l.* 2*s.* 6*d.* For this assistanc Tyers presented Hogarth with a gold ticket of perpetual admission for six persons, or "one coach." It bears on its obverse "Hogarth," and beneath it, "*In perpetuam benificii memoriam;*" on the reverse are two figures, encircled with the motto, "*Virtus voluptas felices una.*" After Hogarth's decease, the gold ticket remained in the hands of his widow, and was by her bequeathed to a relative. It was last used in the season of 1836, and is now in the possession of Mr. Frederick Gye, who purchased it for 20*l.*

From Dr. Burney we learn that Tyers, in the summer of 1745, added, for the first time, *vocal* to his instrumental performances; on which occasion, Mrs. Arne—who, before her marriage, had studied under Geminiani—was engaged as principal singer; and her husband, afterwards Dr. Arne, began to compose ballads, duets, and other pieces for the Gardens; Lowe and the elder Reinhold were also engaged to sing; and Wornam as organist. Beard, also, was one of the early singers, and he loved to annoy Jonathan Tyers by asking him when the Gardens would be opened for the season, in order that he might order of his tailor a great-coat; for then would rain certainly set in: one of the months of the season—July—is the rainiest of the year.

Fielding, in *Amelia*, which he wrote in 1751, describes the Vauxhall of that date: "The coaches being come to the water-side, they all alighted, and, getting into one boat, proceeded to Vauxhall. The extreme beauty and elegance of the place is well known to almost every one of my readers; and happy is it for me that it is so, since to give an adequate idea of it would exceed my power of description."

In 1752, Tyers purchased a moiety of the estate for 3800*l.*; and a few years afterwards, as Lysons informs us from the records in the Duchy of Cornwall Office, "he bought the remainder,"—probably at the expiration of his original lease, in 1758.

In 1751, the walks are described as illuminated with above 1000 lamps; but the print of this date shows glass vase-shaped lamps on posts, and suspended in the music-house, though in no great profusion. The walks are wide and open; the straggling groups of company are in happy ease: the ladies in their hoops, sacques, and caps, as they appeared in their own drawing-rooms; and the gentlemen in their grotesque hats, and wearing swords and bags.

Horace Walpole, in a letter to Montague, has a piquant account of the frolics of a fashionable party at the Gardens in the June of 1750, which we give in his own words: "I had a card from Lady Caroline Petersham to go with her to Vauxhall. I went accordingly to her house, and found her and the little Ashe—or the Pollard Ashe, as they call her: they had just finished their last layer of red, and looked as handsome as crimson could make them. . . . . . We marched to our barge, with a boat of French horns attending, and little Ashe singing. We paraded some time up the river, and at last debarked at Vauxhall. . . . . Here we picked up Lord Granby, arrived very drunk from Jenny Whim's" (a tavern between Chelsea and Pimlico). "At last we assembled in our booth, Lady Caroline in the front, with the visor of her hat erect, and looking gloriously handsome. She had fetched my brother Orford from the next box, where he was enjoying himself with his *petite partie*, to help us to mince chickens. We minced seven chickens into a china dish, which Lady Caroline stewed over a lamp, with three pats of butter and a flagon of water, stirring and rattling and laughing, and we every minute expecting the dish to fly about our ears.' She had brought Betty, the fruit-girl, with hampers of strawberries and cherries, from Rogers's, and made her wait upon us, and then made her sup by herself at a little table. . . . . In short, the air of our party was sufficient, as you will easily imagine, to take up the whole attention of the Gardens; so much so, that from eleven o'clock to half an hour after one, we had the whole concourse round our booth. At last they came into the little gardens of each booth on the sides of ours, till Harry Vane took up a bumper, and drank their healths, and was proceeding to treat them with still greater freedom. It was three o'clock before we got home."

Five years later (1755), we find the *Connoisseur* making merry with the imitative finery: "At Vauxhall the artificial ruins are repaired, the cascade is made to spout with several additional streams of block-tin, and they have touched up all the pictures which were damaged last season by the fingering of those curious connoisseurs who could not be satisfied without feeling whether the figures were alive." Then follows the story of a parsimonious old citizen going there with his wife and daughters, and grumbling at the dearness of the provisions and the wafer-like thinness of the slices of ham. At every mouthful the old fellow exclaims: "There goes twopence! there goes threepence! there goes a groat!" Then there is the old joke of the wafery slices of ham, and the expert carver who undertook to cover the Gardens — eleven acres — with slices from one ham!

The suppers long maintained their light character, and consisted of

> Lilliput chickens boiled,
> Bucellas warm, from Vauxhall ice,
> And hams that flit in airy slice,
> And salads scarcely soil'd.—*Lond. Mag.*, Sept. 1824.

It is curious to find Sir John Fielding commending the Garden of 1757 for "its elegant eatables and drinkables, in which particular Vauxhall differs widely from the prudish and abstemious Ranelagh, where one is confined to tea and coffee."

Goldsmith, in the *Citizen of the World*, is enraptured with "the lights glimmering through scarcely moving trees; the full-bodied concert bursting on the stillness of night; the natural concert of the birds in the more retired part of the grove, vying with that which was formed by art; the company gaily dressed, looking satisfied; and the tables, spread with various delicacies,—all conspired to fill my imagination with the visionary happiness of the Arabian lawgiver, and lifted me into an ecstasy of admiration. 'Head of Confucius!' cried I to my friend, 'this is fine! This unites rural beauty with courtly magnificence.'" The last gay scene in Goldsmith's life was his accompanying Sir Joshua Reynolds to Vauxhall.

Tyers died in 1767. So great was the delight that he took in his place, that, possessing his faculties to the last, he caused himself to be carried into the Gardens a few hours before his death, to *take a last look at them!* Jonathan was of a moody turn; for at his seat Denbies, over against Dorking, he formed a sort of anti-Vauxhall in a wood, which he named "Il Penseroso;" where was a temple, with reflective inscriptions; a clock which struck every minute; besides life-size figures of a Christian and unbeliever in their last moments; Truth treading on a mask; and a male and female skull, with poetical inscriptions in lugubrious verse, said to have been written by Soame Jenyns. Tyers left the Vauxhall property to his four children, of whom Jonathan, the youngest son, conducted the Gardens until his own decease in 1792. The property remained in Tyers's family until it was sold, in 1821, to Bish, Gye, and Hughes, who retained it till 1840. Their most profitable season was 1823: 133,279 visitors; 29,590*l.* receipts. In 1827, Charles Farley, of Covent-garden Theatre, produced in the Gardens a representation of the Battle of Waterloo, with set-scenes of La Belle Alliance and the wood and *château* of Hougomont; also horse and foot soldiers, artillery, ammunition-wagons, &c. The greatest number of visitors in one night was August 2, 1833, shilling admission, when 27,137 persons paid. In July 1841, the estate (about eleven acres), with its buildings, timber, covered walks, &c., was offered for sale by auction, but bought in at 20,200*l.* The Gardens were open from 1732 to 1840 without intermission; in the latter year they were closed, but were reopened in 1841. At the close of this season there was a sale of movable property, when twenty-four pictures by Hogarth and Hayman produced small sums: they had mostly been upon the premises since 1742; the canvas was nailed to boards, and much obscured by dirt.

Among these pictures were:—By Hogarth: Drunken Man, 4*l.* 4*s.*; a Woman pulling out an Old Man's Gray Hairs, 3*l.* 3*s.*; Jobson and Nell in the *Devil to pay*, 4*l.* 4*s.*; the Happy Family, 3*l.* 15*s.*; Children at Play, 4*l.* 11*s.* 6*d.* By Hayman: Children Birds'-nesting, 5*l.* 10*s.*; Minstrels, 3*l.*; the Enraged Husband, 4*l.* 4*s.*; the Bridal Day, 6*l.* 6*s.*; Blindman's Buff, 3*l.* 8*s.*; Prince Henry and Falstaff, 7*l.*; Scene from the Rake's Progress, 9*l.* 15*s.*; Merry-making, 1*l.* 12*s.*; the Jealous Husband, 4*l.*; Card-party, 6*l.*; Children's Party, 4*l.* 15*s.*; Battledore and Shuttlecock, 1*l.* 10*s.*; the Doctor, 4*l.* 14*s.* 6*d.*; Cherry-bob, 2*l.* 15*s.*; the Storming of Seringapatam, 8*l.* 10*s.*; Neptune and Britannia, 8*l.* 15*s.* Four busts of Simpson, the celebrated Master of the Ceremonies, were sold for 10*s.*; and a bust of his royal shipmate, William IV., 19*s.*

The Gardens were finally closed July 25, 1859; and in the following month were sold the theatre, orchestra, dancing-platform, firework-gallery, fountains, statues, vases, paintings, &c., which brought small sums. The most attractive lot was the

Gothic orchestra, built by a carpenter named Maidman, and which, in 1738, had replaced Tyers's rustic music-house. This Gothic orchestra was circular in form, with pinnacles, cupola roof, a gallery, shell sounding-board, looking-glass panels, &c., and produced 99*l.*

The price of admission to the Gardens was 1*s.* until 1792; except on particular nights, as on the celebration of the fiftieth anniversary, when it was 10*s.* 6*d.* After 1792 the admission was raised to 2*s.*, including tea and coffee; in 1809 to 3*s.* 6*d.*; in 1850 reduced to 1*s.*; and since various. At the Vittoria *fête*, July 1814 (admission one guinea), 1350 visitors dined in the rotunda, the Duke of York presiding. There were also present the Dukes of Clarence, Kent, Sussex, and Gloucester; the Princess of Wales, and the Duchess of York. The fireworks were by Colonel Congreve, of rocket celebrity. Fireworks were first occasionally exhibited here in 1798.

Among the Vauxhall composers were Arne, Boyce, Carter, Mountain, Hook (organist upwards of forty years; father of Theodore Hook, and uncle of Dr. Hook, Dean of Chichester), and Signor Storace. Male singers: Beard, Lowe, Webb, Dignum, Vernon, Incledon, Braham, Pyne, Sinclair, Tinney, Robinson, Bedford, and Sharp; females: Miss Brent, Mrs. Wrighten, Mrs. Weischel (mother of Mrs. Billington), Mrs. Mountain, Signora Storace, Mrs. Crouch, Mrs. Bland, Miss Tryrer (afterwards Mrs. Liston), Miss Graddon, Miss Love, Miss Tunstall, &c. Italian operas were performed here in 1829. The band were the last to wear the semicircular, or cocked, hat:

> By that high dome, that trembling glows
> With lamps, cock'd hats, and shiv'ring bows,
> How many hearts are shook!
> A feathered chorister is there,
> Warbling some tender grove-like air,
> Composed by Mr. Hook.—*London Magazine*, 1824.

The Gardens are minutely described in the *Ambulator*, 12th edit., 1820, where the paintings in the supper pavilions, by Hogarth and Hayman, are enumerated. Very little alteration in the arrangement of the walks or the position of the buildings had been made since they were originally laid out or constructed by the elder Tyers, as may be seen by comparing the different views of the Gardens. One of the earliest representations, dated 1737, shows the seats and supper-tables in the quadrangle surrounding the orchestra, together with a perspective of the Long Walk, and an Herculean statue at its extremity. About sixty visitors are seen; and in front of the orchestral band is a prominent figure, wearing a cocked hat and playing the trumpet, supposed to be intended for the celebrated Valentine Snow (afterwards sergeant-trumpeter), of whom Dr. Burney says, he was "justly a favourite here, where his silver sounds in the open air, by having to expand, never arrived at the ears of the audience in a manner too powerful or piercing."

The general plan of the Gardens was a quadrangular grove, with the orchestra near its centre, surrounded by broad covered walks, from the roofing of which were suspended, by wires, illumination "bucket-lamps:" the earlier lamps resembled the street-lamps of the last century. At the head of the quadrangle was the Prince's Pavilion, originally built for the accommodation of Frederick Prince of Wales. To the right and left of the grove were semicircular sweeps of supper-boxes. The rotunda, seventy feet in diameter, had part of its area enclosed as a ride for equestrian performances. At some distance northward of the quadrangle was the theatre, where for many years were exhibited a mechanical cascade, water-mill, and moving figures; but latterly this theatre had been used for ballets and dramatic pieces.

The number of lamps upon extra gala-nights exceeded 20,000. The fireworks were discharged from a lofty tower, at the end of a long walk; whence Madame Saqui descended along a rope several hundred feet in length in a shower of fire, or Il Diavolo Antonio swung by one foot on the slack-rope, pealing from a silver trumpet as he slung the overture to *Lodoiska;* or—

See! the large, silent, pale blue-light
Flares, to lead all to where the bright,
Loud rockets rush on high,
Like a long comet roaring through
The night, then melting into blue,
And starring the dark sky;
And Catherine-wheels, and crowns, and names
Of great men, whizzing in blue flames;
Lights, like the smiles of hope;
And radiant, fiery palaces,
Showing the tops of all the trees;
And Blackmore on the rope.

London Magazine, 1824.

Balloons were celebrated exhibitions of late. The first ascent was made from the Gardens in 1802. Green made several ascents from here, the most memorable of which was his voyage from Vauxhall to Weilburg, in the Duchy of Nassau, in 1836, in the stupendous balloon constructed in the Gardens, at the cost of 2100*l.*: height, 80 feet; circumference, 157 feet. This balloon was subsequently sold to Green for 500*l.*

The old place retained its plan to the last; but the lamps had long fallen off in their golden fires; the punch got weaker, the admission-money less; and the company fell in a like ratio of respectability, and grew dingy, not to say raffish—a sorry falling-off from the Vauxhall crowd of a century since, when it numbered princes and ambassadors, "and on its tide and torrent of fashion floated all the beauty of the time; and through its lighted avenues of trees glided cabinet-ministers and their daughters, royal dukes and their wives, and all the red-heeled macaronies."* Even fifty years ago, the evening-dress of the company was elegant; and head-dresses of flowers and feathers were seen in the promenade, and the entire place sparkled as did no other place of public amusement. But low prices brought low company. The conventional wax-lights got fewer; the punch gave way to fiery brandy or doctored stout; though the semblance of Vauxhall was still preserved in the orchestra printed upon the plates and mugs. The old firework-bell

* Forster's *Life and Adventures of Oliver Goldsmith*, p. 675.

tinkled as gaily as ever; but matters grew more seedy; the place seemed literally worn out, and even the very trees were scrubby and singed,—

> Here nut-brown trees, instead of green,
> With oily trunks and branches lean,
> Cling to nine yellow leaves;
> Like aged misers, that all day
> Hang o'er their gold and their decay,
> Till death of both bereaves;—

it was high time to say, in letters of lamps, "Farewell for ever!"

It would be unpolite, nay, unpardonable, to leave Vauxhall without saying a word of Mr. Simpson, M.C., who, by his bowing, kept the Gardens in order; his blandness acting like oil upon many an angry ebullition of punch and punctilio. He was a sort of guard-of-honour to "the royal property."

The site has been cleared; the old pleasure-haunt has been swept away, and a church dedicated to St. Peter has been built upon a portion of the ground. It is memorable as the first example in London, in the present revival, of a church vaulted throughout. There is, however, a wonderful vitality in some localities and their associations; and the place we have been picturing to the reader appears to be gifted with this lasting character. We remember its many "last nights," and its countless "farewell galas;" but *stat nominis umbra*—in the "Vauxhall-Gardens Estate," a portion of which has been sold "in lots, suitable for the erection of shops, residences for operatives, factories, and business premises:" Vulcan in the Elysian fields, with a witness! However, the recollection of our "Spring Garden" is preserved in the names of the site, which, we are told, "comprises a considerable portion of the site of the late Royal Vauxhall Gardens, and having frontages upon Kennington-lane, Vauxhall-walk, and several new roads and streets, called Auckland-street, Burnett-street, Brunel-street, Leopold-street, Gye-street, and Italian-walk."

THE LAST OF THE OLD BRIDEWELL OF LONDON.

THE disappearance of prisons from our metropolis is a change for congratulation, although these social plague-spots be but removed to reappear elsewhere. The bracing northern air of Holloway must be healthier than the atmosphere of old Blackfriars; and Horace's *mens sana in corpore sano* may be imported into our prison discipline with advantage. The migration to which we have just referred has led to the removal of the old Bridewell of London, thus clearing one of the oldest historic sites in the metropolis. Here stood the ancient royal palace of Bridewell, which extended nearly from Fleet-street to the Thames at Blackfriars, and was founded upon the remains of a building supposed to be Roman, and inhabited by the kings of England previous to the Conquest. Here our Norman kings held their courts. Henry I. gave stone towards rebuilding the palace; and in 1847, in excavating the site of Cogers' Hall, in Bride-lane, was discovered a vault, with Norman pellet-moulding, and other remains of the same date. The palace was much neglected until, upon the site of the old Tower of Mountfiquit, Henry VIII. built "a stately and beautiful house, giving it to name Bridewell, of the parish and well there." This house was erected for the reception of Charles V. of Spain, though only his nobles were lodged here, "a gallery being made out of the house over the water (the Fleet), and through the wall of the City into the Emperor's lodgings in the Blackfriars." Subsequently, here was constructed over the Fleet Bridewell stone bridge, which was painted by Hayman, and engraved by Grignion as the frontispiece to the third volume of the *Dunciad*. The whole third act of Shakspeare's *Henry VIII.* is laid in "the palace at Bridewell," which is historically correct. The capricious king, taking a dislike to the palace, let it fall to decay. The "wide, large, empty house" was next presented to the City of London by Edward VI., after a sermon by Bishop Ridley, who begged it of the king as a workhouse for the poor, and a house of correction; also as a provision for "sturdy rogues," and as "the fittest hospital for those cripples whose legs are lame through their own laziness." The gift was confirmed by charter only ten days before the death of the king. Nearly two years elapsed before Queen Mary confirmed her brother's gift; and in February 1555, the Mayor and Aldermen entered Bridewell, and took possession, with seven hundred marks, land, and all the bedding and other furniture of the house of the Savoy. But the house soon proved costly and inconvenient to the citizens, by attracting thither idle and abandoned people from the outskirts of London, when the Common Council issued acts against "the resort of masterless men." In 1608 the City erected here twelve large granaries for corn and two storehouses for coals; and in 1620 the ancient chapel was enlarged. In Aggas's Plan of London, the buildings and gardens of the Hospital extend from the present site to the Thames, on the bank of which a large castellated mansion is represented; as also in Van der Wyngrerde's (1543) View, in the Bodleian Library; but in Hollar's View, *after* the Great Fire, most of the buildings are consumed.

Hatton thus minutely describes the Hospital in 1708:

> It is a prison and house of correction for idle vagrants, loose and disorderly servants, night-wakers, &c. These are set to hard labour, and have correction according to their deserts; but have their clothes and diet during their imprisonment at the charge of the house.
>
> It is also an hospital for indigent persons, and where twenty art-masters (as they are called), being decayed traders,—as shoemakers, taylors, flax-drapers, &c.,—have houses, and their servants or apprentices (being about 140 in all) have clothes at the house charge, and their masters, having the profit of their work, do often advance by this means their own fortunes. And these boys, having served their time faithfully, have not only their freedom, but also 10*l.* each towards carrying on their respective trades; and many have even arrived from nothing to be governors.

The Hospital was rebuilt, as represented in Kip's View of 1720, in two quadrangles, the principal of which fronted the Fleet River, now a vast sewer under the middle of Bridge-street. Within the present century were built the committee-room and prisons; the chapel was also rebuilt, and the whole latterly formed only one large quadrangle, with a handsome entrance from Bridge-street; the keystone of the archway being sculptured with the head of King Edward VI.

The Bridewell boys were distinguished by a particular dress, and attended fires with an engine belonging to the Hospital. In 1755 the lads had, however, grown unruly, and so turbulent in the streets as to be a great annoyance to peaceable citizens. Their peculiar costume was then laid aside, and they became more orderly. The flogging at Bridewell for offences committed without the prison is described by Ward in his *London Spy:* both men and women were whipped on their naked backs before the Court of Governors. The president sat with his hammer in his hand, and the culprit was taken from the post when the hammer fell. Hogarth, in his "Harlot's Progress," gives this peculiar feature of the place. In the Fourth Plate, men and women are beating hemp under the eye of a savage taskmaster; and a lad, too idle to work, is seen standing on tiptoe to reach the stocks, in which his hands are fixed; while over his head is written, "Better to work than stand thus." When Howard visited Bridewell, he found the building damp and unhealthy, and the rooms, cells, and corridors confined and dark, and altogether a bad specimen of a prison.

"Lob's Pound" was a cant name for Bridewell, the origin of which so puzzled Archdeacon Nares, that he said: "Who Lob was, is as little known as the site of Lipsbury Pinfold." In *Hudibras* the term is employed as a name for the stocks into which the Knight put Crowdero:

> Crowdero, whom, in irons bound,
> Thou basely threw'st into Lob's Pound.

Miss Baker suggests, in her *Northamptonshire Glossary*, that the name originated from "lob," a looby or clown, rather than any specific individual,—Bridewell being the place of correction for the petty offences of that class.

Bridewell was, until of late years, used as a receptacle for vagrants committed by the Lord Mayor and sitting Aldermen; as a temporary lodging for persons, previous to their being sent home to their respective parishes; and a certain number of boys were brought up to different trades. The male prisoners sentenced to and fit for hard labour were put upon the tread-wheel, by which ccrn was ground for the supply of Bridewell, Bethlehem, and the House of Occupations. The younger prisoners, or those not sentenced to hard labour, were employed in picking junk and cleaning the wards. The females were set to work in washing, mending, and getting up the linen and bedding of the prisoners, or in picking junk and cleaning the prison. The punishments for breaches of prison-rules were, diminution of food, solitary confinement, and irons, as the case might be. In 1842 were confined here 1324 persons, of whom 233 were under seventeen, and 466 were known or reputed thieves. In 1818 no employment was furnished to the prisoners. The Seventh Report of the Inspectors of Prisons returned Bridewell as answering no one object of improvement except that of safe custody; it did not correct, deter, or reform; and nothing could be worse than the association to which all but the City apprentices were subjected. However, in 1829, there was built, adjoining Bethlehem Hospital, in Lambeth, a "House of Occupations," whither young prisoners were thenceforth sent from Bridewell to be taught useful trades.

The demolition of the prison of Bridewell is therefore a salutary measure. The committals are now made to the City Prison at Holloway, which, notwithstanding its large extent,—once thought by alarmists to be needlessly vast,—soon became nearly full of prisoners. Meanwhile, a portion of Bridewell Hospital is reserved for the detention and reformation of incorrigible City apprentices committed here by the Chamberlain from time to time; this jurisdiction being preserved by the Court of Chancery in dealing with the matters which concern the disposal of the building and the estates of the Governor of the Hospital. Reformatory schools are also to be built from the revenue of the hospital, stated at 12,000*l.* per annum. At the Social Science Congress in 1862, the worthy Chamberlain read a paper on the peculiar jurisdiction of his Court, which is a valuable contribution to the transactions of the Society. It should be added that, under the former discipline of the prison, special care was taken to prevent the apprentices making the acquaintance of the low vagrants and misdemeanants who ordinarily occupied the building. The apprentices were placed in small cells, closed in with double doors, which shut out sound as effectually as sight; communication was therefore nearly impossible. Henceforth, only the apprentices will be confined here. The number of committals rarely exceeds twenty-five annually; and, on our visit to the Bridewell in June 1863, we found but one apprentice confined there. Although the annual number is so small, the power of committal, which the Chamberlain has most praiseworthily asserted, and successfully maintains, acts as a terror to evil-doers, by keeping in restraint 3000 of these lads of the City.

The vacated buildings, though satisfactory in one sense, were, at our visit, a gloomy scene: it is scarcely possible to visit a prison, even when its cells are empty, without saddening thoughts of wasted and perverted life, sorrow and suffering, through lack of a homely but rare virtue—common honesty. Here was a piece of ground, leased for the burial-place of Bridewell Precinct, wherein Robert Levett, the old and faithful friend of Dr. Johnson, and an inmate of his house, was buried in 1732. Not a vestige of the ancient Bridewell remained. The noblest feature of the later building was the Court-room, 85 ft. 4 in. by 29 ft. 8 in., wainscoted, and hung with the great picture, erroneously attributed to Holbein, of Edward VI. granting the Royal Charter of Endowment to the Mayor. Beneath was the cartoon of "The Good Samaritan," by the youthful artist, Dadd. The other pictures were a fine full-length of Charles II., by Sir Peter Lely; and portraits of the Presidents, including Sir William Withers, 1708—a very large equestrian portrait, with St. Paul's in the background. But the most valuable embellishments were the tables of benefactions, ranging from 500*l.* to 50*l.*, "depensilled in gold characters." In this hall the Governors dined annually, each steward contributing 15*l.* towards the expenses; the dinner being dressed in the spacious kitchen beneath, only used for this purpose. The hall and kitchen were taken down at the close of 1862.

In the entrance-corridor from Bridge-street are the old chapel-gates, of remarkably fine ironwork, presented by Sir William Withers; and on the staircase is a bust of the venerable Chamberlain Clark, who died in his ninety-third year.

At parting with the old place we are sorry to have to strip one of its boasts of much of its value. The great picture of Edward VI. transferring Bridewell Palace to the City of London, which was engraved by Vertue in 1750, and afterwards adopted into the series of historical prints published by the Society of Antiquaries, it is only necessary to observe, represents an occurrence which took place in 1553, ten years after Holbein's death. Consequently, it is simply impossible that he could have painted it, notwithstanding that one of the figures in the background was asserted by Vertue and by Walpole to be Holbein's own portrait. Upon this picture, Mr. J. Gough Nichols remarked, in 1859, that "it is not now regarded as Holbein's work, as it bears no comparison with his capital picture at Barber-Surgeons' Hall of King Henry VIII. granting his charter to that Company." "But," adds Mr. Nichols, "after all, though not a masterly work of art, it is a valuable item among a very few historical pictures, and it would be desirable to recover its real history, of which we literally know nothing."—*Archæologia*, xxxix. 21.

Mr. W. H. Black, F.S.A., in a communication to the Society of Antiquaries, also says: "The discovery of Holbein's Will (proving him to have died eleven years before the alleged and commonly received time of the painter's death) cannot fail to draw after it some interesting consequences, as affecting the genuineness of works of art ascribed to this great master. The principal of these is the celebrated picture at Bridewell Hospital, commemorating a noble public act of charity, in the gift of the royal Palace of Bridewell, at the very end of the reign of King Edward VI., viz. 10th April 1553. The long-pending controversy about the authorship of that picture is now for ever set at rest, so far as regards the painter to whom it has been hitherto ascribed."—*Archæologia*, xxxix. 276.

An interesting fact, of another complexion, in connection with Bridewell remains to be noticed. In 1863, Mr. Lemon, of the State-Paper Office, called the attention of the Rev. Dr. Waddington to a manuscript which he had found in that depository, showing that in the old Bridewell were imprisoned the members of the Congregational Church first formed after the accession of Elizabeth. On the evening of the 20th of June 1567, the gates of the old prison were opened to receive a company of Christian men and women, who were committed to the custody of the gaoler for an indefinite term, at the pleasure of the authorities who consigned them to his care. A word of recantation would have saved them. The Lord Mayor of London, in pity for their condition, urged them to make the required acknowledgment; but conscience rendered them proof against all threatening, and firm against all prevarication. In that company of prisoners, led to their respective cells, were men, unknown to fame, who discovered the long-neglected principles of Church government in the New Testament, which have since wrought in silence such mighty and beneficial changes. It is, no doubt, to this company that Bishop Grindal refers in his letter to Bullinger, July 11, 1568: "Some London citizens," he says, "with four or five ministers, have openly separated from us, and sometimes in private houses, sometimes in fields, and occasionally even in ships, they have held meetings and administered the sacraments. Besides this, they have ordained ministers, elders, and deacons after their own way. The number of the sect is about two hundred, but consisting of more women than men. The Privy Council have lately committed the heads of this faction to prison, and are now using means to put a timely stop to the sect."

Dr. Waddington has also discovered some papers written by the members of this Church in the Bridewell, signed chiefly by Christian women, together with a document containing a brief statement of their principles, by Richard Fitz, their pastor. It appears from these records—which have been kept, though in a loose form, for nearly three hundred years—that Richard Fitz, their minister, Thomas Rowland, deacon, Partridge, and Giles Fowler, died in prison. From the enlarged proportions the Congregational denomination has since reached in Great Britain and America, considerable interest is attached to Bridewell because of these associations. Dr. Waddington, following the current of history from this hidden source, shows, by indisputable evidence from original papers in the public archives, that the succession of Congregational Churches from this period is continuous. The Bridewell may thus be regarded as the starting-point of Congregationalism after the Reformation, as Plymouth Rock is considered to be the corner-stone of America.

Brief and fragmentary as are these touching and simple memorials, it is as satisfactory as it is remarkable that they should have been preserved by the Metropolitan Bishop, and finally transferred to the royal archives. The name of Fitz was known to the Christian exiles in Holland associated with the Pilgrim Fathers. Henry Ainsworth speaks of "that separated Church, whereof Mr. Fitz was pastor, in the beginning of Queen Elizabeth's reign." It was reserved for us to identify him in his relation to the "Flock of Slaughter," suffering bonds and imprisonment in the Bridewell. These original papers enable us with certainty to trace the origin of the first voluntary Church in England after the Marian persecution, as contemporaneous with the Anglican movement.—See *Historical Papers: No.* 1, *Richard Fitz.*

THE FAIR OF MAY FAIR.

THE streetology of London is full of anomalies; but few are so striking as the old rural names still applied to quarters which present no other trace of their former appropriation. The histories in little of these places are so many "green spots" in the account of the great town itself; and to show the changes of the tenants of such places, as well as the transformations of their surfaces, is one of the most amusing and instructive studies in the painting of London life. Disraeli fully appreciates the interest of the subject, as well as the best mode of doing justice to it, when he observes that, in carrying out Lord Orford's project for a book-walk through the streets of the metropolis—"it would be first necessary to obtain the *original names*, or their meaning, of our streets, free from the disguise in which time has concealed them. We shall otherwise lose many characters of persons, and many remarkable events, of which their original denominations would remind the historian of our streets."

One of the most attractive spots for working the plan which Disraeli has here chalked out is May Fair, named from its having been the site of a low metropolitan carnival, but known at present as "a seat of the most elegant population." It lies north of Piccadilly, between Park-lane and Devonshire House, and was originally called Brook-field, from its being close to the brook or burn, Tyburn. Here, in 1688, was appointed to be held, by royal grant, a cattle and horse market twice a week. After the suppression of the annual fair held in St. James's Park, it was revived in Brook-field, as early as the reign of Charles II. Pepys, in 1660, still calls it St. James's Fair; and the name was not changed till after James II., in the fourth year of his reign (1688), granted the Fair to commence on the 1st of May, and continue fifteen days after it, yearly, for ever; and it was specified that "multitudes of the booths were not for trade and merchandise, but for musick, shows, drinking, gaming, raffling, lotteries, stage-plays, and drolls."

In the *Postman*, No. 597, April 1699, the Fair was advertised to begin on the 1st of May, at the east end of Hyde Park, near Bartlet House, and continue for fifteen days after; "the two first days of which will be for Leather and Live Cattle; and care is and will be taken to make the ways leading to it, as well as the ground on which it is kept, much more convenient than formerly for persons of quality that are pleased to resort thither."

Next year, by an advertisement in the London journals of 27th April, we learn: "In Brook-field Market-place, at the east corner, is a Fair to be kept for the space of sixteen days, beginning with the 1st of May; the first three days for Live Cattle and Leather, with the same entertainments as at Bartholomew Fair; where there are shops to be let ready built for all manner of tradesmen that usually keep fairs, and so to continue yearly at the same place."

The Fair of the next year, 1701, is thus admirably described in a letter of Brian Fairfax, in Nichols's *Tatler*, i. 418: "I wish you had been at May Fair, where the rope-dancing would have recompensed your labour. All the nobility in town were there; and I am sure even you, at your years, must have had your youthful wishes to have beheld the beauty, shape, and activity of Lady Mary when she danced. Pray ask my Lord Fairfax after her, who, though not the only lord by twenty, was every night an admirer of her while the Fair lasted. There was the city of Amsterdam, well worth your seeing: every street, every individual house was carved in wood, in exact proportion one to another; the Stadthouse was as big as your hand; the whole, though an irregular figure, yet that you may guess, about ten yards' diameter. Here was a boy to be seen, that within one of his eyes had DEUS MEUS in capital letters, as GULIELMUS is on half-a-crown; round the other he had a Hebrew inscription; but this you must take, as I did, upon trust.* I am now drinking your health at Lockett's; therefore do me justice in Yorkshire."

The May Fair of 1702, though it opened merrily, did not close without a tragedy. There was Mr. Miller's booth over against Mr. Barnes, the rope-dancer's, where was "presented an excellent droll, called Crispin Crispianus, or a Shoemaker a Prince, with the best machines, swinging and dancing, ever yet in the Fair." The pickpockets and other rogues, however, flocked there in such numbers, that the magistrates interfered, and some soldiers taking part with the mob against the constables, a Mr. John Cooper, a peace-officer, was killed; he was buried in St. James's Church, and his funeral-sermon was preached by Dr. Wedgewood, before the Justices, High Constable, &c. of Westminster. The above riot led to an agitation to put down the Fair, when the *Observator* said: "Oh, the piety of some people about the Queen (Anne), who can suffer things of this nature to go undiscovered to her Majesty, and consequently unpunished! Can any rational man imagine that her Majesty would permit so much lewdness as is committed at May Fair for so many days together, so near her royal palace, if she knew any thing of the matter? I do not believe the patent for that Fair allows the patentees the liberty of setting up the devil's shops, and exposing his merchandise to sale; nor was there ever one fair or market in England constituted for this purpose. But this Fair is kept contrary to law, and in defiance of justice: for the last Fair, when the civil magistrates came to keep the Queen's peace there, one constable was killed, and three others were wounded." One Cork,

* This *sight* reminds us that a similar wonder was exhibited at the Bazaar (now Princess' Theatre), in Oxford-street, in the autumn of 1828; when a little girl was shown there with "Napoleon Empereur" on the iris of her left eye, and "Empereur Napoleon" on the iris of the right eye; attempted to be explained by the child's mother intently looking, during her pregnancy, at a five-franc piece of Napoleon's, which had been given to her by her brother previous to a long absence. It is hard to say whether the marvel of 1701 or that of 1828 is most credible.

a butcher, was executed at Tyburn for the murder; but the Fair was not abolished.

Here are a few specimens of the May-Fair bills of entertainment: "At John Sleep's Musick Booths (from Turnmill-street), in Brook-field Market, at the sign of the Star Musick Booth, during the Sixteen Days of May Fair, Gentlefolks and others will be entertained with variety of all sorts of Musick, Singing, Dancing, and other pleasant Pastimes. *Vivat Regina!*"

In the next bill, Miller, of the Loyal Association Booth, flies at higher game: "An excellent Droll, called King William's Happy Deliverance and Glorious Triumph over his Enemies, or the Consultation of the Pope, Devil, French King, and the Grand Turk, with the whole form of the Siege of Namur, and the Humours of a Renegade French-Man and Brandy Jean, with the Conceits of Scaramouch and Harlequin, together with the best Singing and Dancing that was ever seen in a Fair; also a Dialogue Song. *Vivat Rex!*"

Next was "Husband's Booth," with "an excellent Droll, called, The Fairy Queen, or Love for Love, and the Humours of the Hungry Clown; together with that excellent Art of Vaulting on the Managed Horse· performed by Thomas Simpson, the famous Vaulting Master of England."

And lastly was "a Droll, intermingled with a most delightful merry Comedy, after the manner of an Opera, with extraordinary varieties of Singing and Dancing, by his Grace the Duke of Southampton's Servants. *Vivat Regina!*"

From the above, and other May-Fair bills of the same period, it appears that Sorias as Scaramouch, Baxter as Harlequin, and Evans as an Equestrian, were the favourite performers.

The enormities of the Fair appear to have but little abated; for Strype describes it as a place "where young people did use to resort, and, by the temptation they met with here, commit much sin and disorder. Here they spent their time and money in drunkenness, fornication, gaming, and lewdness, whereby were occasioned oftentimes quarrels, tumults, and shedding of blood." Therefore, in November 1708, the grand jury of Westminster made a presentment of "the public enormities and inconveniences; and, being encouraged by the example of the worthy magistracy of the City of London in their late proceedings against Bartholomew Fair, did present, as a public nuisance and inconvenience, the yearly riotous and tumultuous assembly" called May Fair; "in which place many loose, idle, and disorderly persons did rendezvous, draw and allure young persons, servants, and others, to meet there to game," &c. The subject was taken up strongly in a tract, now scarce, entitled, "Reasons for suppressing the yearly Fair in Brook-field, Westminster, commonly called May Fair, recommended to the consideration of all persons of Honour and Virtue" (8vo, Lond., 1709; 43 pages). The Fair was then discontinued; for in the *Tatler*, April 18, 1709, we read: "Advices from the upper end of Piccadilly say that May Fair is utterly abolished; and we hear that Mr. Pinkethman has removed his ingenious company of strollers to Greenwich." And in the *Tatler*, May 24, we read that "the Fair is now broke; but it is allowed still to sell animals there. Therefore, if any lady or gentleman have occasion for a tame elephant, let him inquire of Mr. Pinkethman, who has one to dispose of at a reasonable rate. The downfall of May Fair has quite sunk the price of this noble creature, as well as of many other curiosities of nature. And great is the desolation among the gentlemen and ladies who were the ornaments of the town, and used to shine in plumes and diadems,—the heroes being most of them pressed, and the queens beating hemp. Mrs. Saraband, so famous for her ingenious puppet-show, has set up a shop in the Exchange, where she sells her little troop under the term of 'jointed babies.'" It is added, by the way, that the "rake-hell Punch," by his loose life and conversation, did not a little contribute to the ruin of the Fair.

The Fair of 1708 was the last for several years. It was subsequently renewed, as we see from a coloured drawing* of the May Fair of 1716, when the men wore all sorts of cocked-hats to give a little life to their sagacity. Here we have the Maypole, with its flying rope; the mountebank on his platform; the preparation for the ass-race; the house on the right has its show-cloth of Adam and Eve; beyond it is the sign of the Dog

* Engraved in *London Society*, No. 24, in illustration of a Paper entitled, "May Fair a Hundred Years ago;" here reprinted (with additions) by the courtesy of the proprietors of the above popular work.

and Duck,—for duck-hunting was a prime sport here, especially for the butchers of the market; and in the distance is May-Fair Chapel. The rural aspect of the place—its gabled houses, backed by lofty trees—should be noticed; for these were soon doomed to change. However, the Fair survived; for the newspapers of 1736 inform us that "an ass-race attracted vast crowds to May Fair;" and in 1744 the grand jury of Middlesex, among several gaming-houses and places frequented by people of bad character, presented Hallam's New Theatre, at May Fair, for its great meetings of idle and disorderly persons.

The Fair was held principally on the site of what is now Curzon-street, Hertford-street, and Chesterfield House and Gardens. John Thomas Smith, in his *Streets of London*, tells us that "the ground between the back of Lord Coventry's, No. 106 (Piccadilly), and the south wall of the Earl of Chesterfield's garden in Curzon-street, was, in 1722, an irregular space; 'May Fair-row' and 'Hay-hill-row' being, at that time, the only regular buildings. There was, within memory, on the western portion, partly on the site of Hertford-street, an old wooden public-house, one of the original signs of the Dog and Duck, behind which, towards the north, was a stream of clear water, nearly 200 feet square, surrounded by a gravel-walk, boarded up knee-high, and shaded all round by willows." This pond was notorious for the cruel sport of duck-hunting. Here is one of its characteristic announcements:

June 25, 1748.—At May Fair Ducking Pond, on Monday next, the 27th inst., Mr. Hooton's Dog Nero (ten years old, with hardly a tooth in his head to hold a duck, but well known for his *goodness* to all that have seen him hunt) hunts six ducks for a guinea, against the bitch called the Flying Spaniel, from the Ducking Pond on the other side of the water, who has beat all she has hunted against, except Mr. Hooton's Good-Blood. To begin at two o'clock.

Mr. Hooton begs his customers won't take it amiss to pay Twopence admittance at the gate, and take a ticket, which will be allowed *as Cash* in their reckoning. No person admitted without a ticket, that such as are not liked may be kept out.

Note.—Right Lincoln Ale.

Duck-hunting was held in such high repute in the reign of

Charles II., that the king and many of his prime nobility often witnessed it, and with their dogs joined in the sport. In Mrs. Behn's play of *Sir Patrick Fancy*, a Sir Credulous Easy talks about a cobbler, his dog-tutor, and his expectation of soon becoming "the Duke of Ducking-pond."

In Maitland's *London*, 1756, May Fair is mentioned as still annually celebrated ; and of its humours, some ten years later, we have a curious picture by that painstaking antiquary, John Carter, who, writing in 1816, says :

Fifty years have passed away since this place of amusement was at its height of attraction : the spot where the Fair was held still retains the name of May Fair, and exists in much the same state as at the above period : for instance, Shepherd's Market, and houses surrounding it on the north and east sides ; and White Horse-street, Shepherd's-court, Sun-court, and Market-court. Westward : an open space, extending to Tyburn (now Park) lane, since built upon as Chapel-street, Shepherd-street, Market-street, Hertford-street, &c. Southward : the noted Ducking-pond, house, and gardens ; in a large riding-school, Carrington-street, the residence of the noted Kitty Fisher (about 1779). The market-house consisted of two stories : first story, a long and cross aisle for butchers' shops, and, externally, other shops connected with culinary purposes ; second story, used as a theatre at Fair-time for dramatic performances. My recollection serves to raise before me the representation of the *Revenge*, of which the only object left in remembrance is "the black man" Zanga. Below, the butchers gave place to toymen and gingerbread-bakers. At present, the upper story is unfloored, the lower nearly deserted by the butchers, and their shops occupied by needy peddling dealers in small wares ; in truth, a most deplorable contrast to what once was such a point of allurement. In the area encompassing the market-building were booths for jugglers, prize-fighters both at cudgels and back-swords, boxing-matches, and wild-beasts. The sports not under cover were mountebanks, fire-eaters, ass-racing, sausage-tables, dice-ditto, up-and-downs, merry-go-rounds, bull-baiting, grinning for a hat, running for a shift, hasty-pudding eaters, eel-divers, and an infinite variety of other similar pastimes.

This account may be relied on, as Carter was born and passed his youthful days in Piccadilly (at "Carter's Statuary"), two doors from the south end of White Horse-street.

Another of the Fair attractions was in a front one-pair room in Sun-court (on the south side of Curzon-street), where a Frenchman exhibited "the astonishing strength of the *Strong Woman*, his wife," which John Carter has very minutely described and authenticated: he tells us, a blacksmith's anvil being procured from White Horse-street, with three of the men, they brought it up, and placed it on the floor. The woman was short, but most beautifully and delicately formed, and of a most lovely countenance. She first let down her hair (a light auburn), of a length descending to her knees, which she twisted round the projecting part of the anvil, and then, with seeming ease, lifted the ponderous weight some inches from the floor. After this, a bed was placed in the middle of the room, when, reclining on her neck, and uncovering her bosom, the husband ordered the smiths to place thereon the anvil, and forge upon it a horse-shoe. This they obeyed, by taking from the fire a red-hot piece of iron, and with their forging-hammers completing the shoe with the same might and indifference as when in the shop in their constant labour. The prostrate fair one seemed to endure this with the greatest composure, talking and singing during the whole process; then with an effort, which to the bystanders appeared supernatural, she cast the anvil from off her body, jumping up at the same moment with extreme gaiety, and without the least discomposure of her dress or person. That there was no trick or collusion was obvious from this evidence of Mr. Carter's: "The spectators stood about the room, our family and friends; the smiths were strangers to the Frenchman, but known to us." The *Strong Woman** next put her naked feet on a red-hot salamander, which feat, by the way, did not surprise the narrator.

Another celebrity of the Fair was the celebrated gingerbread-vender, dressed in laced cocked-hat and feather, embroidered coat, ruffles, and white-silk stockings, but better known by his cry of "Tiddy-diddy, Doll-loll, loll-loll." There was also a satiric exhibition of puppets beheading puppets in a coal-shed,

* Mr. Daniel thinks the Strong Woman to have been Mrs. Allchorne, who died in Drury-lane in 1817, at a very advanced age. Madame performed at Bartholomew Fair in 1752.—See *Merrie England*, &c.

in allusion to the recent decapitation of the Scotch chieftain, Lord Lovat.

Pennant, who died in 1797, remembered the last celebrations of May Fair: "The place was covered with booths, temporary theatres, and every enticement to low pleasure." The nuisance was finally discontinued at the instance of George, sixth Earl of Coventry, who, disturbed with the riot and uproar of the place in the rear of his house in Piccadilly, procured the abolition of the Fair: his lordship died in 1809.

We now part with the history of the Fair, and turn to the period at which the site became a fashionable quarter. Much of the ground was built upon as early as 1704, when certain individuals, living in a place called "May Fair," are rated for the first time to the poor of the parish of St. Martin's-in-the-Fields. In the same books, under the year 1708, is the following entry: "Mr. Sheppard, for the ground-rent of the Faire, market, and one house, 1*l.* 1*s.*" And in the year 1709 a rate is paid to the poor by "Christopher Reeves, for the play-house in the fair."

In the *London Journal*, 27th May 1721, it is stated: "The ground on which May Fair formerly stood is marked out for a large square, and several fine streets and houses are built upon it."

From the above Sheppard, Shepherd's Market derives its name.* He built and resided in the long white garden-house, on the north side of Curzon-street, "for many years inhabited by Lady Fane, and afterwards by Lady Reade, who died in it." In 1750, Mr. Sheppard offered to sell the above freehold house and garden for the small sum of 500*l.*; and after the death of Lady Reade, the property was purchased by Lord Carhampton for that sum. His lordship, having greatly improved the house, sold it, with the garden, to Mr. Stuart Wortley, afterwards Lord Wharncliffe, for 12,000*l.* (*J. T. Smith*).

* In the now bygone farce of *The Lady and the Devil*, one of the characters, in a far-off country, sits down to write home "to his dear love, Sal Hartshorn, in Shepherd's Market."

Over against this property is Curzon Chapel, within ten yards of which was "Keith's Chapel," a place of great notoriety. The Rev. Alexander Keith, the proprietor of this small chapel, was a disgrace to his cloth, and was indifferent to all objects but money and notoriety; by his conduct subjecting himself to ecclesiastical censure, and, in 1742, to a public excommunication. Keith, however, excommunicated in return the bishop of the diocese; Dr. Andrews, the judge; and Dr. Trebeck, the rector of St. George's, Hanover-square. Keith's principal vocation was the performance of secret marriages at a minute's notice: they became almost as notorious as the Fleet marriages—6000 in one year; the busiest period of this illicit trade being Fair-time. The cunning with which this May-Fair parson contrived to advertise this traffic in connection with a domestic bereavement is ingenious.

"We are informed," says the *Daily Advertiser*, Jan. 23d, 1750, "that Mrs. Keith's corpse was removed from her husband's house in May Fair, the middle of October last, to an apothecary's in South Audley-street, where she lies in a room hung with mourning, and is to continue there till Mr. Keith can attend her funeral. The way to Mr. Keith's chapel is through Piccadilly, by the end of St. James's-street, and down Clarges-street, and turn on the left. The marriages (together with a license on a five-shilling stamp and certificate) are carried on for a guinea, as usual, any time till four in the afternoon, by another regular clergyman, at Mr. Keith's little chapel in May Fair, near Hyde Park Corner, opposite the great chapel, and within ten yards of it; there is a porch at the door like a country church-porch."

In Horace Walpole's Letters is some amusing gossip about Keith. Here we find the story of Handsome Tracy, who was inveigled into marrying the butter-woman's daughter, of Craven-street. Tracy consented to dine with her: "The mother," says Walpole, "borrowed some silver to buy a leg of mutton, and they kept the eager lover drinking till twelve at night, when a chosen committee waited on the faithful pair to the minister of May Fair. The doctor was in bed, and swore he would not get up to marry the king; but he had a brother over the way who perhaps would, and who did." Of

Keith's preaching it is told that in his sermon on the death of Frederick Prince of Wales, he said, "He had no great parts, but he had great virtues—indeed, they degenerated into vices; he was very generous, but I hear his generosity has ruined a great many people; and then his condescension was such, that he kept very bad company." And when Keith, "the marriage-broker," was told the bishops would hinder his marrying, he replied, "Well, let 'em;" but he would be revenged, and buy two or three acres of ground, and "underbury them all!"

In this chapel, James, fourth Duke of Hamilton, was married to the youngest of the beautiful Miss Gunnings. The Duke fell in love with her at a masquerade, and determined to wed her in the spring. Walpole, writing to Sir Horace Mann, Feb. 27th, 1752, says:

> About a fortnight since, at an immense assembly at my Lord Chesterfield's, made to show the house, which is really most magnificent, Duke Hamilton made violent love at one end of the room, while he was playing at Pharaoh at the other end; that is, he neither saw the bank nor his own cards, which were of three hundred pounds each; he soon lost a thousand. I own I was so little a professor in love, that I thought all this parade looked ill for the poor girl; and could not conceive, if he was so much engaged with his mistress as to disregard such sums, why he played at all. However, two nights afterwards, being left alone with her while her mother and sister were at Bedford House, he found himself so impatient, that he sent for a parson. The doctor refused to perform the ceremony without license or ring; the Duke swore he would send for the Archbishop; at last they were married with a ring of the bed-curtain, at half an hour after twelve at night, at May-Fair Chapel.

Within two years, in 1754, the Marriage Act put an end to Keith's vocation: the records are carefully preserved; for the registers of the May Fair marriages, in three folio volumes, closely and clearly written, are kept with the parish-books of St. George's, Hanover-square.

Curzon-street is named after the ground-landlord, George Augustus Curzon, third Viscount Howe. Mr. Cunningham relates an interesting association of the street—that Sir Francis Chantrey, when a young man and undistinguished, lived in an attic in No. 24; and that here he modelled his Head of Satan, and his bust of Earl St. Vincent. At this period of his life he derived his chief support from a Mrs. D'Oyley, who lived at No. 21. In the large house, No. 16, for many years resided Sir Henry Halford, the celebrated Court physician under George III., George IV., William IV., and Queen Victoria. Sir Henry was twenty years President of the College of Physicians, and contributed much valuable information to the literature of his profession. In 1862 the above mansion was for sale, when the sum asked was 15,000*l.*, subject to a considerable ground-rent.

Chesterfield House and garden has been already incidentally mentioned. This magnificent mansion was built by Isaac Ware, for Philip, fourth Earl of Chesterfield, author of the celebrated Letters to his Son: his boudoir he calls the gayest and most cheerful room in England, and his library the best, and his garden a scene of verdure and flowers not common in London. The columns and the grand staircase were brought from Canons, the seat of the Duke of Chandos; hence Lord Chesterfield called the latter the Canonical pillars of his house. And the large copper-gilt lantern, for 18 candles, was bought by Lord Chesterfield at the sale at Houghton, the seat of Sir Robert Walpole. There is in the house some of the finest *papier-mâché* in London.

In the *Quarterly Review*, No. 152, is this nicely-written description of the famous house:

In the magnificent mansion which the Earl erected in Audley-street, you may still see his favourite apartments, furnished and decorated as he left them,—among the rest, what he boasted of as the "finest room in London,"—and perhaps even now it remains unsurpassed; his spacious and beautiful library, looking on the finest private garden in London. The walls are covered half-way up with rich and classical stores of literature; above the cases are, in close series, the portraits of eminent authors, French and English, with most of whom he had conversed; over these, and immediately under the massive cornice, extend all round, in foot-long capitals, the Horatian lines:

"NUNC . VETERUM . LIBRIS . NUNC . SOMNO . ET . INERTIBUS . HORIS .
DUCERE . SOLICITÆ . JUCUNDA . OBLIVIA . VITÆ."

On the mantelpieces and cabinets stand busts of old orators, interspersed with voluptuous vases and bronzes, antique or Italian, and airy statuettes, in marble or alabaster, of nude or semi-nude Opera nymphs. We shall never recall that princely room without fancying Chesterfield receiving in it a visit of his only child's mother; while probably some new favourite was sheltered in the dim, mysterious little boudoir, which still remains, also in its original blue damask and fretted gold-work, as described to Madame de Monconseil.

It is hard to trace the gay voluptuary in Lord Hervey's whole length of him—"very short, disproportionate, thick, and clumsily made; having a broad, rough-featured, ugly face, with black teeth, and a head big enough for a Polyphemus."

In Mr. Kirwan's very pleasant table-book, *Host and Guest*, we are reminded that Lord Chesterfield was the first nobleman who made the most strenuous efforts to introduce French cookery. He engaged as his cook La Chapelle, a descendant of the famous cook of Louis XIV. La Chapelle published, in 1733, a treatise on cookery, in three volumes, which is now rarely met with. Like Alexis Soyer's books, La Chapelle's *Modern Cook* was printed for the author, and sold by Nicholas Prévost, a Frenchman, over against Southampton-street, in the Strand. About this period, Lord Chesterfield was Lord Steward of the Household to George II. His dinners and suppers were deemed perfection; and these entertainments were among the few items in which his expenditure was liberal. Lord Chesterfield lived till 1773; and, says Mr. Kirwan, "I more than once heard the late Earl of Essex say, more than thirty years ago, at Brookes's Club, that he remembered, as a boy of fourteen or fifteen, seeing the Earl seated on a rustic seat outside the courtyard of his house in May Fair. Chesterfield House was, ninety-one years ago, at the very extremity of London, and all beyond it was an expanse of green fields."

The Earl also built Stanhope-street, the street leading from his mansion into Park-lane. The ground belonged to the Dean and Chapter of Westminster, with whom the Earl considered he had a hard bargain, as appears by the following clause in his will, with Lord Mahon's comment thereon :

> In case my said godson, Philip Stanhope, shall, at any time hereafter, keep, or be concerned in keeping of, any race-horses or pack of hounds; or reside one night in Newmarket, that infamous seminary of iniquity and ill-manners, during the course of races there; or shall resort to the said races; or shall lose, in any one day, at any game or bet whatsoever, the sum of 500*l.*,—then, in any of the cases aforesaid, it is my express will that he, my said godson, shall forfeit and pay out of my estate the sum of 5000*l.*, for the use of the Dean and Chapter of Westminster.

The Earl had doubtless found the Chapter of Westminster of that day exorbitant and grasping in their negotiation with him for the land; "and he declared, that he now inserted their names in his will, because he felt sure that, if the penalty should be incurred, they would not be remiss in claiming it."

Chesterfield's declining years, though now and then brightened by flashes of wit and merriment, were clouded by sickness and despondency. His ruling passion was ruffled in his last moments, when his only expressed anxiety related to his friend Dayrolles being in the room without a chair to sit down upon. The Earl died in Chesterfield House, 24th of March 1773; desiring, by will, that his remains might be buried in the next burying-place where he should die, and that the expense of his funeral might not exceed 100*l.* He was accordingly interred in Grosvenor Chapel, South Audley-street; but his remains were afterwards removed to Thetford, Notts.

In Chesterfield-street, almost within the shade of Chesterfield House, lived George Selwyn, the brilliant wit; and in the same street Beau Brummel took a house, just after he had come into possession of his fortune—some thirty thousand pounds. He soon became famed for the excellence of his dinners, and the Prince of Wales was more than once his guest. Brummel was not a mere coxcomb, but already a man of great shrewdness and observation and satirical spirit. Madame de Staël felt having failed to please him as her greatest misfortune, and placed the Prince of Wales's neglect of her as a minor misfortune. Hard by, in Charles-street, at No. 27—a very small house, looking over the north wall upon the garden of Chesterfield House—lived Mr. Beckford, the author of *Vathek*, in just such a loophole of retreat as delighted this man of taste and knowledge, "run to seed in the gratification of extravagant freaks." From the drawing-room—which has a ceiling of florid plaster-work—you look into "the finest private garden in London;" while a few rooks in the lofty trees sing their *carmen autumnale* upon the site of the Fair of May Fair.

At No. 16, in Charles-street, the family mansion of Earl Craven, is a suite of five drawing-rooms, fitted up in the magnificent styles of Louis XIV. and XV., and numbering among its art-treasures a few costly items from a palace of Cardinal Richelieu.

At the east end of the street, some five-and-twenty years since, lived Sir Edward Lytton Bulwer, in a house of moderate size, on the north side, a few doors from Berkeley-square. Sir Edward had the house embellished after his own taste: one of the drawing-rooms was a facsimile of a chamber which Bulwer had visited at Pompeii; vases, candelabra, chairs, tables, to correspond. James Smith humorously describes his dining here: "Our host lighted a perfumed pastille modelled from Vesuvius. As soon as the cone of the mountain began to blaze, I found myself an inhabitant of the devoted city; and, as Pliny the elder, thus addressed Bulwer, my supposed nephew: 'Our fate is accomplished, nephew! Hand me yonder volume! I shall die as a student in my vocation. Do thou hasten to take refuge on board the fleet at Misenum; yonder cloud of hot ashes chides thy longer delay. Feel no alarm for me: I shall live in story; the author of *Pelham* will rescue my name from oblivion.' Pliny the younger made me a low bow," &c. Sir Edward's dining-room was furnished in the old English style, carved chairs, tables, and sideboard, which drew from a visitor the judicious remark, that "such furniture is all right in old baronial halls, but to encounter it in a small house in a London street is too startling a transition." In his ancestral seat, Knebworth, Sir Bulwer Lytton is at home.

FROM HICKS'S HALL TO CAMPDEN HOUSE.

NOW that the steam-horse is undermining and overriding our great city, a four-horse coach has almost become a phenomenon, or nearly as great a rarity as the *lapis milliaris* in Cannon-street called "the London stone." Camden believed this relic to be part of the great central milestone from which the British high-roads radiated, and the distances on them were reckoned. When this practice was discontinued, we leave the British itineraries or road-books to settle. It is better known that, in later times, their measurements were made from the verge of London in various directions: thus, perchance, a few of the milestones on the great north road may to this day proclaim their distances "from the spot where Hicks's Hall formerly stood," this being the northern starting-point. Many a traveller has doubtless wondered why Hicks's Hall should have been fixed on; who Hicks was, and why his name should be entitled to this distinction. The old Roman road-stations were named after emperors; but Hicks has nothing of imperial dignity to warrant the adoption. Many years ago, Mr. Charles Knight wrote a very pleasant paper upon the special wonder as to the identification of Hicks, reminding one of Swift's Mrs. Harris of other days. The humour of Mr. Knight's paper is very genial; he has there described the *locus in quo* of the noted Hicks's Hall. There can be no doubt as to its site. In a wide part of St. John-street, Clerkenwell, some two hundred yards from Smithfield, anciently the town-green, an inscription on a public-house states that Hicks's Hall *there* formerly stood. It was built some two hundred and fifty years since—the year in which the New River was brought into London. St. John-street then extended by the side of the Priory of St. John of Jerusalem (of which the gate remains) to the Monastery of Clerkenwell and Cow-cross, which opened into the fields. It may be added, that the site of Hicks's Hall is now almost crossed by a railway.

The builder of the Hall was Baptist Hicks, according to his epitaph in Campden church, Gloucestershire, born in 1551, "of a worthy family in the city of London." He was the youngest son of a silk-mercer, who kept shop in Cheapside, "at Soper-lane end, at the White Bear." This part of the street was termed the Mercery; but, before the Great Fire, according to Strype, there were here "but sheds or shops, with terraces over them, as of late some remained at Soper-lane end, where a woman sold roots and herbs." Young Hicks was brought up to his father's business; and, having extensive dealings at Court, so greatly increased his fortune, that he became one of the most affluent citizens of his time. This is partly attributed to his ability to give credit, "after the coming of King James, with his bare Scotch nobility and gentry;" and "he got a great estate by supplying the court with silks and mercery wares." In 1603, he was sworn the king's servant, and knighted; but, from still continuing to "keep his shop" after obtaining that honour, he greatly offended some of the Aldermen Knights, with whom it appears to have been customary to "lay aside their trade after knighthood." In reply to some objections made in 1607, in which year the question of *precedency* between Sir Baptist and the Aldermen Knights was brought before the Lords Commissioners for the office of Earl Marshal, he stated that "his servants kept the shop, though he had a regard to the special credit thereof; and that, had two of his servants kept their promise and articles concluded between them and him, he had been free of his shop two years past, and did then but seek fit opportunity to leave the same."

It is curious to find this dispute for precedency agitating the whole City, and to contrast the stringency of the objection to aldermen traders with the laxity of our times, when a City baronet kept shop as a retail trader opposite the Mansion House which he had for a year tenanted as Lord Mayor. The real question in Sir Baptist Hicks's case was, whether a Knight *Commoner* was entitled to precede a Knight *Alderman*, on the ground of *seniority* of date in respect to his knighthood,—"the Aldermen Knights and their wives striving for precedency, and Sir Baptist and his lady sometimes, for peace sake, granting it." The difference became so warm, that at length, on the petition of the Lord Mayor and the Knights Aldermen to the King, the case was heard by the Lords Commissioners in the Marshal's Court at Whitehall; but finally decided against the Commoners, it being decreed that the Aldermen Knights should "take place and superiority in precedency within the City, before the Knights Commoners." Thus ended this solemnly-argued and long-protracted contest. Four years after, Sir Baptist could have taken the superior rank, he being, in 1611, elected Alderman of Bread-street Ward; but, doubtless in dudgeon, he was discharged on paying 500*l.* At the express desire of the King, Hicks had been appointed justice of the county; and now liberally built the Hall, for the meeting of the magistrates, which we have already referred to. Strype says, it cost about 900*l.*, or thereabouts; elsewhere, he states 600*l.* Howes thus describes the building, and the naming of it:

> Sir Baptist Hicks, Knight, one of the justices of the county, builded a very stately Session House of brick and stone, with all offices thereunto belonging, at his own proper charge; and upon Wednesday, the 13th of January, this yere, 1612, by which time this house was fully finished, there assembled twenty-six justices of the county, being the first day of their meeting in that place, when they were all feasted by Sir Baptist Hicks; and then they all, with one consent, gave it a proper name, and called it Hicks's Hall, after the name of the founder, who then freely gave the same house to them and their successors for ever. Until this time, the Justices of Middlesex held their usual meeting in a common inn, called the Castle (near Smithfield Bars).

Hicks's Hall had other celebrity besides its milestone distinction. It occurs in *Hudibras*, part iii. canto 3:

> And old, droll sot, who told the clock
> For many years at Bridewell Dock,

At Westminster and Hicks's Hall,
And hiccius-doctius played in all.

In Hicks's Hall, William Lord Russell, the patriot, was condemned to death for high treason, July 14, 1683; here, too, Count Koningsmarck, the real, though not the actual, assassin of Mr. Thynne, was tried and acquitted; and, in March 1765, a bill of indictment was found at the Sessions here against the Count de Guerchy for the absurd charge of a conspiracy to murder the Chevalier d'Eon.

Hicks's Hall, we gather from a view of it in the collection of Mr. W. Hobart Wilson, of Brompton, scarcely reaches Howes's description; it was not large, had a bay-window on the first-floor, and above it a gable. The Sessions were held here until late in the last century, when, the Hall getting out of repair, and much impeding the thoroughfare, a new Sessions House was erected on Clerkenwell-green, and completed in 1782: long after which, however, this new edifice was called "Hicks's Hall." The architect, Rogers, removed here from the old hall a fine Jacobean chimney-piece; and here is preserved also a portrait of Sir Baptist Hicks, believed to have been never engraved; it hung in the dining-room at the first Sessions House. The old Hall was taken down; and hence the milestone puzzle.

In the same year that Hicks built for the county his patronymic Hall, he also purchased an estate upon the high ground of Kensington; or, according to a tradition in the parish, Sir Baptist won the property from Sir Walter Cope "at some game of chance." Old Bowack describes the site—"being upon a hill makes it extreme healthful and pleasant." The original approach to the mansion from the town of Kensington was through an avenue of elms, which extended nearly to the High-street. Holland House had then been built a few years for Sir Walter Cope, of whom Sir Baptist Hicks is said to have won the ground upon which he built a mansion for himself, and which adjoins the Holland House estate. The architectural fashion of that time was termed Jacobean; and the mansion consisted of turrets surmounted with cupolas; bays, with large windows; ornamented entrance-porch, open parapets, and roofs with dormer-windows. In this respect, Hicks's mansion bore a general resemblance to his neighbour Cope's, but was much smaller. It was built of brick, with stone door and window cases and finishings; two square end turrets, with conical roofs, and flanking three bays, and an enriched central porch. In 1620, Sir Baptist was created a baronet; and in 1628, was raised to the peerage as Baron Hicks of Ilmington, in the county of Warwick, and Viscount Campden, in Gloucestershire. Henceforth, the mansion at Kensington was named Campden House, and the adjoining ground Campden-hill, which is now thickly covered with villas. The Campden arms were now sculptured upon the central bay of the mansion. The year after Sir Baptist had been raised to the peerage, he died at his house in the Old Jewry, and was buried at Campden, where his epitaph tells us that his life was spent "religiously, virtuously, and generously;" and, of his riches, "he disposed to charitable uses a large portion, to the value of 10,000*l.*," besides the numerous bequests made by his will, of which gifts Strype has given a long enumeration. The same writer records these verses in "memorial" of his virtues:

Reader, know,
  Whoe'er thou be,
Here lies Faith, Hope,
  And Charitie.

Faith true, Hope firm,
  Charity free;
Baptist Lord Campden
  Was these three.

Faith in God,
  Charity to brother,
Hope for himself:
  What ought he other?

Faith is no more ;
Charity is crowned ;
'Tis only Hope
Is under ground.

Sir Baptist Hicks had also been a distinguished member of the Mercers' Company, to which his widow made liberal bequests; one object was to assist young freemen beginning business as shopkeepers with the gratuitous loan of 1000*l.* Sir Baptist had two daughters, co-heiresses, who are reputed to have had 100,000*l.* each for their fortune. His title devolved to his son-in-law, Edward, Lord Noel, who was married to Juliana, his eldest daughter. Mary, his youngest, married Sir Charles Morrison, of Cashiobury, in Hertfordshire, Knt. and Bart., whose monument, with their effigies, finely executed by Nicholas Stone, is in Watford church. The arms of Sir Baptist, with the date 1612, and the arms of his two sons-in-law, were in a large bay-window in the front of the mansion. Baptist, the third Lord Campden, who was a zealous Royalist, lost much of his property during the Civil Wars; but was permitted to keep his estates by paying the sum of 9000*l.*, as a composition, and making a settlement of 150*l.* per annum on the Commonwealth ministry. He resided chiefly at Campden House during the Protectorate; and the Committee for Sequestrations held their meetings here. Charles II. honoured Lord Campden with special notice, and supped with him at Campden House about a fortnight after his restoration. In 1662, an Act was passed for settling the mansion upon this nobleman and his heirs for ever; in July 1666, his son-in-law, Montague Bertie, Earl of Lindsey, who so nobly distinguished himself by his filial piety at the battle of Edge Hill, and who was wounded at Naseby, died in Campden House.

In 1661 the mansion was hired of the Noel family by Anne Princess of Denmark, who resided there for about five years with her son, William Duke of Gloucester, then heir presumptive to the throne. The adjoining house is said to have been built at this time, for the accommodation of the Princess' household; it was named Little Campden House, and subsequently The Elms. It was, for some time, tenanted by the Right Hon. William Pitt, the minister.

At Campden House the young Duke's amusements were chiefly *playing at soldiers;* and at a very early age he formed a regiment of boys, chiefly from Kensington, who were on constant duty here. He was placed under the care of the Earl of Marlborough and of Bishop Burnet. When King William gave him into the hands of the former, "Teach him to be what you are," said the king, "and my nephew cannot want accomplishments." Bishop Burnet, who had superintended his education for ten years, characterises him as an amiable and accomplished prince. The last thing the bishop explained to him was the Gothic constitution, and the beneficiary and feudal laws, of which Burnet talked, at different times, nearly three hours a day! The king's chief ministers came once a quarter to examine the progress the Prince had made, and were astonished at his proficiency. He was, however, of weak constitution; and the day after keeping his birthday—24th of July 1700—he was seized with malignant fever, and died at Windsor on the fourth day of his illness; he was the only remaining child of seventeen that the Princess had borne. Burnet says: "His death gave great alarm to the whole nation. The Jacobites grew insolent upon it, and said, now the chief difficulty was removed out of the way of the Prince of Wales's succession." Mr. Shippen, who then resided at Holland House, wrote the following lines upon the young Prince's death:

> So, by the course of the revolving spheres,
> Whene'er a new-discovered star appears,
> Astronomers, with pleasure and amaze,
> Upon the infant luminary gaze.
> They find their heaven's enlarged, and wait from thence
> Some blest, some more than common influence;
> But suddenly, alas! the fleeting light,
> Retiring, leaves their hopes involved in endless night.

In 1704, Campden House was in the occupation of the

Dowager Countess of Burlington, and of her son the architect-Earl, then in his ninth year. Late in Queen Anne's reign, Campden House was sold to Nicholas Lechmere, the eminent lawyer, who, in 1721, was created a peer. Between his lordship, who then occupied the mansion, and Sir John Guise there sprang up a pretty quarrel, which gave rise to Swift's ballad of "Duke upon Duke." Here are three of its thirty-seven stanzas:

Back in the dark, by Brompton Park,
He turned up through the Gore,
So slunk to Campden House so nigh
All in his coach-and-four.

The Duke in wrath called for his steeds,
And fiercely drove them on;
Lord! Lord! how rattled then thy stones,
O kingly Kensington!

...

Meanwhile, Duke Guise did fret and fume:
A sight it was to see,
Benumbed beneath the evening-dew,
Under the greenwood tree.

Swift had lodged at Kensington, and well knew the locality.

At the close of the last century, the land in front of Campden House was planted with trees, which nearly cut off the view from Kensington; and, at the same time, a new road was made eastward, planted with a shrubbery. The garden, in the rear of the mansion, must have been a complete one: Lysons describes a caper-tree, which had flourished here for more than a century. Miller refers to it in the first edition of his *Gardener's Dictionary:* the tree was sheltered from the west, having a south-east aspect; and though not within the reach of any artificial heat, it produced capers every year. The southern avenue of elms was now removed; and upon the two piers of the old gateway were placed two finely-sculptured dogs, the supporters of the Campden arms.

The old mansion of the ennobled citizen of the reign of James I., and the residence of the Princess Anne, and where was nursed the heir to the British throne, was now doomed to neglect. With that marked fatality which attends large old houses that lose status in their tenancy, "Queen Anne's Palace," as Campden House was popularly called, was occupied for more than sixty years as a boarding-school for ladies. In such cases, the "delightful task" very properly occupies more attention than keeping up the old house; and we have known more than one well-appointed mansion, with its "Queen Anne staircase," its lofty suites of rooms, its carved door-case and marble floors, spacious court and garden, and other appurtenances, let at a less rent than that of a small modern villa. In such cases, the decorative portions are mostly left to decay.

A view in Faulkner's book about Kensington shows Campden House, in 1820, to have been then a very dowdy pile; the principal front has lost most of its ornaments, and is covered with stucco; the turrets have lost their cupolas; the parapet is gone, and with it the picturesque roof: still the entrance-hall then had its original panelling, and archway leading to the grand staircase. The great dining-room, in which Charles II. supped with Lord Campden, was richly carved in oak; and the stuccoed ceiling was emblazoned with the arms of the Campden family. But the glory of this apartment was the tabernacle oak mantelpiece, of six Corinthian columns supporting a pediment, grotesque devices filling the intercolumniations, and two finely-carved caryatid figures supporting the whole. The *state apartments*, on the first-floor, were three large rooms facing the south; that on the east, "Queen Anne's bedchamber," had an enriched plaster ceiling, with pendants; and the walls were then hung with red-damask tapestry, of foliage pattern. The large bay-window of the central apartment was filled with armorial glass. The eastern wing, on the first-floor, contained "the globe-room," which Faulkner thought to have been originally a chapel; others set it down as a theatre for puppets, to amuse the young Duke of Gloucester; it communicated by a flight of steps with a terrace in the garden. The adjoining apartment had its plaster ceiling enriched with arms, and a mantelpiece of various marbles. Such was the mansion in which the Princess Anne held her little court, in the cold shade of "kingly Kensington;" for, during the reign of William, she appears to have lived in much discomfort, neglected by his sister, and treated very coolly by the King. The old place must have afforded some fine schoolrooms for the later occupants. Some fourteen years since, it was let to a tenant who expended considerable sums upon re-embellishment and refurnishing; and a theatre was fitted up for amateur performances. In the spring of 1862, however, by a conflagration of remarkable rapidity, Campden House was reduced to a few blackened and windowless walls; and in it was consumed property which had cost many thousands of pounds. The historic interest of the place had, nevertheless, ceased some sixty years before. The name of Campden has been given to the high ground about here—one of the most charming sites in the environs of the metropolis; it adjoins the park of Holland House, the upper apartments of which are on a level with the stone gallery of St. Paul's Cathedral. Thus, we have Campden Hill and Grove; consisting of elegant villas and lines of well-appointed houses, where painters do love to dwell. In Campden House-road is the Observatory of Sir James South; among the working instruments is a 7-feet transit, a 4-feet transit circle, and one of the equatorials with which Sir James South, in conjunction with Sir John Herschel, made a catalogue of 380 double stars.

TALK ABOUT THE TEMPLE, PAST AND PRESENT.

THAT the grave decisions of her Majesty's Privy Council should be "given at the Cockpit at Westminster," or rather upon the site of that ancient institution, is not a whit more strange than that, for nearly five centuries, some of the leading practisers of the laws should have been settled upon the spot where the lawless Knights Templars long held sway. It is curious to observe how, in this transition from sacred to secular purposes, some of the holier influences have been saved. The circular church and appurtenances, which were leased for an annual fee-farm rent of 10*l.* to "a society of students of the common lawe," has been preserved to our time, and *restored* by its higher artistic taste. The preacher is styled Master of the Temple, as was the lord paramount of the Templars; the early lawyers had their pillars in the church and cloisters—a falling off from their spiritual predecessors; and the Middle Temple still bears the arms of the Knights Templars—Arg. on a cross gu., a paschal lamb or, carrying a banner of the first, charged with a cross of the second, such as we see in university towns lowered to the Lamb and Flag public-house sign; whilst Pegasus salient of the Inner Temple long enjoyed a similar distinction in becoming a popular London sign. This winged horse, with the motto "Volat ad æthera virtus," was substituted by the Inner Temple for the Holy Lamb early in the reign of Elizabeth. There has been much amusing speculation upon the cause of the change: it is thought to have been intended to signify—in allusion to the fable of Pegasus forming the fountain of Hippocrene by striking the rock—that the lawyers aspired to become poets. This assumption of the winged horse by the one society, and the retention of the ancient Christian symbol by the other, gave origin to the following lines, which Archdeacon Nares tells us were chalked upon one of the Temple gates:

> As by the Templars' hold you go,
> The *Horse and Lamb* display'd,
> In emblematic figures show
> The merits of their trade.
>
> The clients may infer from thence
> How just is their profession,—
> The Lamb sets forth their innocence,
> The Horse their expedition.
>
> O happy Britons! happy Isle!
> Let foreign nations say,
> Where you get Justice without guile,
> And Law without delay.

The Law Societies seem very prudently to have repudiated the ancient seal of the Templars—two mounted upon one horse; which, according to the scandal of Matthew Paris, pointed to the time when they lived upon alms—being so poor that *one horse served two of them!*

Many of the rules and usages of the military brotherhood were, however, adopted by the legal fraternity. The ancient ceremony of the admission into the privileged brethren of the latter closely resembled that of the brethren into the monastic order of the Temple. The coif is said to have descended from the *fratres servientes;* and many observances of the Templars prevailed to our times in the common Hall of the Temple, though its paved courts no longer echoed the tread of the military monks. The manciple, or purveyor of provisions to the lawyers, is referred to by Chaucer, who says, that functionary had of masters more

> than thrice ten,
> That were of lawe expert and curious.

This is presumed to be the oldest mention of the Temple as a place for lawyers.

In the reign of Edward I., when the practice of the common law first became a distinct profession, and the new legal societies were originated, the white-robed Templars were building their monastery on the Thames bank; and they had not long completed their famous round church, which seems to have given the name of the New Temple to their great convent. Here sovereigns were subsequently their guests, councils assembled, and the military friars dispensed a royal hospitality in their great Hall, which seems to have occupied the site of the present Inner Temple Hall, and to have been built at or about 1240, when they added to the round the oblong portion, or choir, of the Temple Church. The several buildings, connected by cloisters, were enclosed by walls, which on the north fronted the King's Highway (now Fleet Street); from the gardens of the Bishop of Exeter's town house or inn on the west, and the lands of the White Friars on the east. But before the year 1310 the Templars had been seized, and their order suppressed; and three years later the New Temple was given by Edward II. to Aymer de Valence, Earl of Pembroke, whose tomb will be remembered as one of the finest sculptured ornaments of the choir of Westminster Abbey. At the Earl's death, the property passed to the Knights of St. John of Jerusalem (the gate of whose monastery in Clerkenwell still remains), and by them was leased to the students of the common law; and the Outer Temple to Walter Stapleton, Bishop of Exeter and Lord Treasurer, beheaded by the citizens of London in 1326. This latter statement rests upon the authority of Sir George Buc, which Mr. Foss has shown may be reasonably doubted; and he is of opinion that the Bishop's mansion was the western boundary of the New Temple, but never formed any part of it.

The above change of occupation, as well as the character of the buildings, is thus alluded to by Spenser, in his beautiful *Prothalamion*:

> Those bricky towers,
> The which on Thames' broad aged back doe ride,
> Where now the studious lawyers have their bowers,
> There whilom wont the Templar Knights to hide,
> Till they decayed through pride;

and old Fuller remarks, that here the professors of the law

were thenceforth to use learning and eloquence for the purpose of defending Christians from each other, as the soldiers of the Cross had used the sword to defend the Holy Places from the unbeliever.

The division of the Temple is referred to the reign of Henry VI.,—the palmy days in which Chief-Justice Fortescue wrote his celebrated treatise in praise of the laws of England; when the knights and barons, with other grandees and nobles of the realm, were accustomed to place their sons in the Inns of Court and Inns of Chancery, although their parents might not desire that they should become profoundly learned in the law, or get their living by its practice. At that time there were about 2000 students in the several Inns, all of whom, Fortescue says, were gentlemen by birth; and he sets down the annual expense of each student at 78*l.*, a sum equivalent, perhaps, to 450*l.* of our money.

The situation of the Temple, between the great artery of Fleet-street and the busy Thames, has ever been suggestive of poetic comparison of the stillness of its venerable church, its halls, libraries, its many courts and nooks and corners, with the roar of the full tide in the adjoining highway. Not only in sound but in sight are the gardens of the Temple refreshing as "green spots" in this London existence. We agree with Mr. Pearce: "the view from these gardens—when the eye ranged to the opposite side of the river, over the green marshes and gradually-rising ground, to the Surrey hills, and the rich oak and beech woods that clothed them—must, centuries ago, have been very beautiful, but is now lost."

The Temple then stood in the suburbs of London: the monastery and gardens of Whitefriars lay on the east; there was a great water-gate to the Temple Gardens, through which the King's clerks and justices were wont to pass to Westminster; and to the west the river-bank was occupied by episcopal residences, their gardens, and water-gates. The nearest of these, the inn of the Bishop of Exeter, afterwards became Essex House, which, with its surrounding grounds, was bought by the Society of the Temple soon after the Restoration. The water-gate of Essex House remains, built into the modern houses at the bottom of Essex-street; it is a lofty arch, flanked by two Corinthian pilasters; and "in a view of the Thames, showing the Frost Fair in the reign of Charles II., the king, queen, and court are seen coming down the Temple-garden stairs to witness the sports on the ice; and in part of the background is the archway, and beyond the archway are the gables and other parts of Essex House. A garden with terraces is between the arch and the river."—*The Builder*, 1861.

What a change is here from the water-gates and gaily-decorated barges of prelates and nobles, to the steamboat-pier and its cheap steamboats for the convenience and recreation of the million!

No alteration took place when the Temple property passed to the Crown at the dissolution of religious houses in the reign of Henry VIII.; and the students of the two Inns of Court remained the tenants of the Crown, paying the fee-farm rent of 10*l.* for the lands till 1608, when James I. granted them at the accustomed rent of 10*l.* paid by each Society out of the property "for the entertainment and education of the students and of the profession of the law residing in the inns of the Inner and Middle Temple for ever;" and the Templars upon this occasion presented the King with a cup of pure gold, weighing 200 ounces. The old fee-farm rent continued to be paid to the Crown until the time of Charles II., when it was purchased by the Societies.

Except the Church, not any portion remains of the edifices belonging to the Knights Templars. The Inner Temple Hall occupies the site of a hall of the time of Edward III. The Middle Temple Hall was built about midway in the reign of Elizabeth, in whose time also were erected most of the narrow courts and rows, almost wholly of brick. The greater part of the Inner Temple was, however, destroyed in the Great Fire of 1666, the flames stopping within a very few yards of the Temple Church; and we read in Lord Clarendon's Life, "that some gentlemen of the Inner Temple would not endeavour to preserve the goods which were in the lodgings of absent persons, nor suffer others to do it, 'because,' they said, 'it was against the law to break up any man's chamber.'" Lord Clarendon, in his *Autobiography*, has this minute record of the conflagration: "The Fire (of London) decreased, having burned all on the Thames side to the new buildings of the Inner Temple, next to Whitefriars; and, having consumed them, was stopped by that vacancy from proceeding further into that house, but laid hold of some old buildings which joined to Ram-alley, and swept all those into Fleet-street."

Ram-alley here mentioned, leading from Mitre-court to the Inner Temple, was, in the above days, noted, among other things, for "many a worthy lawyer's chamber." It is often mentioned in seventeenth-century plays; and Pepys repeats Tom Killigrew's scandalous story of the Lord Chancellor (Jeffreys) having been bred in Ram-alley, and bound 'prentice to Lord Cottington.

After a fire, in 1695, were rebuilt the cloisters and chambers above, westward of the Church. Hatton describes the Church as at the north end of the Cloister (which is in the Middle Temple), and at the south end of the Inner Temple-lane, so that it is very commodiously situated for the joint use of the two houses of the Inner and Middle Temple. Before us is a print of the Temple-buildings in Hatton's time, which shows them nearly as they existed for a century. The river-walk was then recessed, and not straight, as at present.

THE INNER TEMPLE.

Before stepping southward from Fleet-street by the gateway, of plain Jacobean architecture, semicircular, with the Pegasus in the spandrils, built in 1609, let us note, on the east side, house No. 17, interesting as a specimen of olden street architecture, though not of the age of the inscription—"Formerly the palace of Henry VIII. and Cardinal Wolsey." Sexagenarian readers may recollect this house as the last depository of the Waxwork of Mrs. Salmon, who in her advertisements, with more probability, styled the house as "once the palace of Henry Prince of Wales, son of King James I." The first-floor front-room has an enriched plaster ceiling, inscribed P. (triple plume) H., which, with part of the wainscoting, denotes the structure to be of the time of James I. Still, we do not find in the lives of Prince Henry any identification of this house as a royal palace. It appears, however, that the house, though never the residence of Prince Henry, was the *office in which the Council for the Management of the Duchy of Cornwall Estates held their sittings;* and in the Calendar of State Papers, edited by Mrs. Green, is the following entry of the time of Charles, created Prince of Wales four years after the death of Henry: "1619, Feb. 25; Prince's *Council Chamber, Fleet-street.*—Council of the Prince of Wales to the Keepers of Brancepeth, Raby, and Barnard Castles: The trees blown down are only to be used for mending the pales, and no wood to be cut for firewood, nor browse for the deer." Other entries occur to the same effect; thus settling the appropriation of the old house in Fleet-street, but stripping it of about a century of its boasted antiquity. It was, for some time, Nando's Coffee-house, much frequented by Lord Chancellor Thurlow, when a young man looking out for briefs. The house, No. 16, at the opposite corner of the gateway, was "the Cross-keys," tenanted, between 1717 and 1736, by Bernard Lintot, the original publisher of Pope's *Homer.* The house next became a confectioner's, and has so continued: it was rebuilt, in a more embellished style, in 1857.

We now enter the Inner Temple, where, upon the west side of the gateway, leading down the lane, was the shop of Jacob Robinson, the publisher of Pope and Warburton, who first met here, and plighted their faith to each other: the shop was last tenanted by Mr. Pheney, a law-bookseller, some thirty years since.

At No. 1, in the lane, Dr. Johnson resided in chambers on the first-floor, from 1760 to 1765. His library was contained in two garrets. Here Boswell first called upon Johnson;

here the Doctor received a visit from Mdme. de Boufflers; and Boswell tells us how, on her departure, Johnson forgot to accompany her to her coach; when, recollecting his want of gallantry, he hurried down the staircase, and overtook Boswell and the lady before they reached the Temple gate, seized her hand, and conducted her to her carriage. "His dress," says Boswell, "was a rusty-brown morning suit, a pair of old shoes by way of slippers, a little shrivelled wig sticking on the top of his head, and the sleeves of his shirt and the knees of his breeches hanging loose." The house was inscribed "Dr. Johnson's Staircase:" it and the adjoining houses were taken down in 1857, and upon the site have been erected lofty and handsome stone-fronted chambers. "Dr. Johnson's Staircase" was withdrawn from the sale of the materials; the Benchers having determined to retain possession of it. The boarded and timber floor, on which the learned Doctor and his literary friends had so often walked, with the windows, doors, moulded panel partition, &c., sold for 10*l.* 5*s.* At the bottom of the lane, in Farrar's-buildings, Boswell had his chambers, to be near Dr. Johnson. Charles Lamb lived at No. 4. "Two rooms on the third-floor, and five rooms above," he writes to Coleridge, "with an inner staircase to myself, and all new-painted, &c., for 30*l.* a year. The rooms are delicious; the best look backwards, into Hare-court, where there is a pump always going—just now it is dry. Hare-court's trees come in at the window, so that it's like living in a garden." This court was named after Nicholas Hare, Master of the Rolls in the reign of Mary. The pump of which Lamb speaks has long been famous for its water, though Garth disparagingly compares it "with Aganippe's streams."

We have now another great literary association in the lane. Thither came Oliver Goldsmith, when he removed from Gray's Inn; he took chambers on the then library-staircase of the Inner Temple, which he shared with one Jeffs, butler to the Society. His neighbour, Johnson, soon paid him a visit, and went prying about the rooms—Goldsmith grew fidgety, and, apprehending a disposition to find fault, exclaimed, with the air of a man who had money in both pockets,—"I shall soon be in better chambers than these!" which harmless bravado drew from Johnson four Latin words, implying—"It is only yourself that need be looked for." Happy would it have been for Goldsmith had he borne in mind this consolatory compliment, and squared his expenses accordingly!

Upon the east side of the lane, the old chambers of Churchyard-court have been taken down, and a noble stone-fronted structure erected in their place; and to this and the opposite new lines have been given the honoured names of Johnson and Goldsmith's Buildings.

The famous old Church has been thrown open to view, unencumbered by mean buildings; and in removing the house over the porch, a western wheel-window was exposed in the Norman Round. Its northern side has been thoroughly *restored* —not faced with smoothly-dressed stone, like the southern side, but the original character retained. The western Norman porch has likewise been restored, and covered with a leaded gable roof; the effect is glorious. Additional characterisation has been given to the Round: the smooth parapet has been removed from the upper part, and the renovated ashlar-work carried throughout. A new cone or spire has been placed on the top of the Round, in place of the former roof; it terminates in a large gilt vane—the bird is strictly medieval; the dormer-lights are less successful. By the clearance of buildings, a sort of new location is given to the Norman Round and porch: it is unmatched in our church architecture.

Whoever compares its present appearance with its outline in the print of 1720, will at once see with what artistic skill and feeling the repairs and restorations of the last forty years have been conducted. Two years before the date of Hatton's *New View* (1708), "the Church was wholly new whitewashed, gilt and painted within, and the pillars of the round tower wainscoted, with a new battlement and buttresses on the south side, and other parts of the outside were well repaired; also the figures of the Knights Templars new cleaned and painted, and the iron-work enclosing them painted and gilt with gold."

The architecture is midway between Romanesque and Early English Gothic; the great western door very fine. The choir, in pure Lancet style, was almost rebuilt by Savage and Sydney Smirke in 1840-2: it has externally three high gables with crosses, and the bell is hung in a new stone turret on the north side. The Romanesque windows of the clerestory, filled with brilliant stained glass, the Saracenic ceiling, the sculptured heads by Sir R. Smirke, and the beautifully-carved choir stalls and benches, and the altar, divide attention with the characteristic features of the Church—the cross-legged effigies of the Knights Templars and the rude effigies of the Kings, painted on the west end of the chancel, in which a brief history of the Templars in England, and of this Church, may be read. To the left of the altar is the marble tablet to the learned Selden, who lies beneath in a deep-bricked grave, the coffin enclosed within slabs of marble, arches of brick being turned over the grave, and upon that lies the earth. In the triforium, ascended by a narrow staircase, are the tombs of Plowden, the jurist; Martin, to whom Ben Jonson dedicated his *Poetaster;* Howell, the letter-writer; and Edmund Gibbon, of whose family arms his kinsman, the great historian, gives a curious account. Among the recent memorials is a portrait-bust of Hooker, the learned Master; and a marble tablet to Oliver Goldsmith, who is buried in the ground east of the choir. The organ, by Schmydt, has quarter-tones, and competed with an organ by Harris: strangely enough, the award was given by Judge Jeffreys, and was one of the mildest decisions of his life of ill repute. In so solemn a place as the Round, we can hardly imagine lawyers receiving clients as merchants on 'Change; yet so they did—

> Retain all sorts of witnesses,
> That ply i' the Temple under trees,
> Or walk the Round with knights of the posts,
> About the cross-legg'd knights, their hosts.
>
> *Hudibras,* part iii. c. 3.

Ben Jonson speaks of "meeting in the Temple Church," and walking the Round; and Otway of "the peripatetic philosophers of the Temple Walk." This custom was kept up in the Cloisters, which were rebuilt for that purpose after the Great Fire. North-east of the choir is the house of the Master of the Temple, fronted by a garden, beneath which is the Benchers' vault. The place has an air of solemn seclusion; the garden blooming upon the place of sepulture is impressive. In March 1862, during an excavation in Lamb-buildings, at a short distance south of the Round of the Church, were found some pillars and part of the basement of St. Anne's Chapel, which connected the convent of the Temple with the church. The chapel was taken down in 1827: here Almeric de Montfort, the Pope's chaplain, who was imprisoned by Edward I., was set at liberty at the instance of the Roman Pontiff.

Crossing Lamb-building,—denoted by a gilt lamb over a doorway,—we reach the Terrace, where are the Library and Chapel, Parliament Chamber and Hall—Smirke's Tudor, of some five-and-thirty years since, as told in the inscriptions. The Library, a magnificent room, is on the second-floor; the end of the building has a fine oriel window; upon this spot was an old brick house, against which was a sun-dial, with the quaint "Begone about your business"—an old Temple memorial.

Over the entrance to the Library is the bust of the learned William Pettyt, the founder of the Library: it includes 400 Mss., parliamentary statutes and common law, ecclesiastical records, year-books; Hoveden, Higden, and other English historians; letters and papers, with signs-manual of Kings and Queens of England; and Bacon's *History of the Alienation Office*, in manuscript.

The Hall is comparatively small; its chief ornaments are the portraits of Coke and Littleton: Coke, when a student here, lit his own fire every morning at three o'clock in the winter. The Temple, by the way, has been irreverently called "My Lord Coke's Shop." Here, too, is Pegasus, from the brush of Sir James Thornhill.

Of the festivities in the Hall we must say a few words. Here dinner is served to the members of the Inn daily during term-time; the masters of the bench dining on the state or daïs, and the barristers and students at long tables extending down the Hall to the carved screen at the western end. On grand days are present the judges, who dine in succession with each of the four Inns of Court. To the Parliament Chamber, adjoining the Hall, the Benchers repair after dinner to exercise the *argumentum ad Bacculinum* in term-time. The loving-cups, used on certain grand occasions, are huge silver goblets, which are passed down the table, filled with a delicious composition, immemorially termed *sack*, consisting of sweetened and exquisitely-flavoured white wine. The butler attends the progress of the cup to replenish it, and each student is restricted to a *sip*. Yet it is recorded that once, though the number present fell short of seventy, thirty-six quarts of the liquid were consumed.

The gentlemen of the Inner Temple were of old famed for their plays, masques, and revels, and sumptuous entertainments. Christmas, Hallowe'en, Candlemas, and Ascension-day, were anciently kept with great splendour in the Hall. When Sir Heneage Finch (afterwards Lord Chancellor Nottingham) was Reader of the Society, King Charles II. dined with him in the Hall,—an honour, it is said, never before granted by a king in this country. Charles was received with *twenty violins*, dinner being served by fifty gentlemen of the Society in their gowns. Next year the Duke of York and Prince Rupert were admitted members. For these feasts the Master of the Revels arranged the dancing and music; after the play, a barrister sang a *song* to the Judges and Sergeants, and dancing was commenced by the Judges and Benchers round the sea-coal fire; as satirised in Buckingham's witty play of *The Rehearsal*, ridiculed by Dr. Donne in his *Satires*, Prior in his *Alma*, and Pope in *The Dunciad:*

> The Judge to dance, his brother Sergeant calls.

Sir Christopher Hatton, with four other students of the

Inner Temple, wrote the play of *Tancred and Gismund*, which, in 1568, was acted by that Society before Queen Elizabeth; and there is a copy (1592) among the Garrick Plays in the British Museum.

In this Hall, in honour of Mr. Talbot, a Bencher, receiving the Great Seal, was held, Feb. 2, 1733, the last revel in any Inn of Court. A gallery was built for ladies above the screen. After dinner were acted *Love for Love*, by Congreve, a Templar; and *The Devil to Pay*, by actors from the Haymarket. The Master of the Revels formed a ring, and danced, or rather walked, round the fireplace three times; the old song of "Round about the Coal Fire," with music, being sung by Toby Aston, dressed in a bar-gown. Dancing followed, in which the ladies from the gallery joined; then a collation, and more dancing. The Prince of Wales was present in the music-gallery, *incog.*

At the Inner Temple, on May 29, a gold cup of sack is handed to each member, who drinks to the happy restoration of Charles II. The Hall waiters are called *panniers*, from the *pannarii* who attended the Knights Templars.

Eastward of the Terrace is a fine open area—the red-brick house-fronts cheerfully contrasting with the green of the lime-trees and sycamores. In Crown Office-row, westward, Charles Lamb was born, in 1775, and passed the first seven years of his life. The Temple was his home and recreation—"the most elegant spot in the metropolis: what a cheerful, liberal look hath that portion of it which from three sides overlooks the greater garden, that goodly pile

Of building strong, albeit of Paper hight,

confronting with massy contrast the lighter, older, more fantastically-shrouded one named of Harcourt, with the cheerful Crown Office-row (place of my kindly engender), right opposite the stately stream, which washes the garden foot with her yet scarcely trade-polluted waters, and seems but just weaned from her Twickenham Naiades." But here have been many changes since Lamb's boyhood. He complained of the Gothicising the entrance to the Inner Temple Hall and Library front. "What is become," he asks, "of the winged horse that stood over the former?—a stately arms. And who has removed those frescoes of the Virtues which Italianised the end of the Paper-buildings?—my first hint of allegory. They must account to me for these things, which I miss so greatly." The Paper-buildings have been reërected since the great fire here in 1838; they are of red brick and stone, by Sydney Smirke, with overhanging oriels and angle turrets, assimilating to continental examples of the Tudor style, and reminding us of Spenser's "bricky towers." King's Bench-walk has also been in part rebuilt. At No. 5 the Earl of Mansfeld, when Mr. Murray, had chambers:

> To number 5 direct your doves,
> There spread round Murray all your blooming loves.
>
> Pope, *To Venus, from Horace.*

A second compliment to this great man occasioned a famous parody:

> Graced as thou art with all thy power of words,
> So known, so honoured, at the House of Lords.
>
> Pope (*of Lord Mansfield*).

> Persuasion tips his tongue whene'er he talks,
> And he has chambers in the King's Bench-walks.
>
> *Parody*, by Cibber.

Samuel Lysons the topographer, and Jekyll the wit, had chambers at No. 6; and we remember the brothers Roscoe living here when they published their piquant anecdote-book, *Law and Lawyers.*

Nor can we forget Charles Lamb's charming sketches of "The Old Benchers of the Inner Temple," who had the Terrace almost sacred to themselves, in the fore-part of the day at least. Who does not remember "the roguish eye of Jekyll, ever ready to be delivered of a jest;" Thomas Coventry, "whose person was a quadrate, his step massy and elephantine, his face square as the lion's, his gait peremptory and path-keeping, indivertible from his way as a moving column, the scarecrow of his inferiors, the browbeater of equals and superiors, who made a solitude of children wherever he came; for they fled his insufferable presence as they would have shunned an Elisha bear? His growl was as thunder in their ears; whether he spoke to them in mirth or in rebuke, clouds of snuff, aggravating the natural terrors of his speech, broke forth from each majestic nostril, darkening the air. . . . And so he passed the terrace." Coventry was master of four or five hundred thousand pounds—a hoarder rather than a miser; but he gave away 30,000*l.* once in his lifetime to a blind charity. He kept the table of a gentleman, and his kitchen-chimney was never suffered to freeze.

Then there was the pensive gentility of Samuel Salt, and his man, the quick little fellow Lovel, at once his clerk, his good servant, his dresser, his flapper, his guide, auditory, treasurer. Lamb had access to Salt's Library, and thus he was "tumbled in a spacious closet of good old English reading, where he browsed at will upon that fair and wholesome pasturage."

With Coventry and with Salt, in their walks upon the Terrace, most commonly would join them Peter Pierson, a benevolent man, but with a face implying an incapacity of being happy. Contemporary with these was Daines Barrington, another oddity, who walked burly and square. In the account of his year's treasurership was—"Item, disbursed Mr. Allen, the gardener, twenty shillings for stuff to poison the sparrows, by my orders; which charge was unanimously disallowed by the Bench." Next to him was old Barton—a jolly negation, who took upon him the ordering of the bills of fare for the Parliament Chamber, where the Benchers dine. Then Read and Twopeny—Read, good-humoured and personable; Twopeny, good-humoured, but thin, and felicitous in jests upon his own figure. If T was thin, Wharry was attenuated and fleeting, with spiteful features. Of this period was the omniscient Jackson: he was the Friar Bacon of the less literate portion of the Temple, and decided how the cook should write down *edge*-bone of beef in his bill of commons. Mingay, with his iron hand—he had lost his right hand, and supplied it with a grappling-hook—was somewhat later. "Baron Maseres, who walks (or did till very lately, says Lamb) in the costume of the reign of George II., closes my imperfect recollections of the Old Benchers of the Inner Temple. Fantastic forms, whither are ye fled? Or, if the like of you exist, why exist they no more for me?" Then with what exquisite humour he invokes the New Benchers!—"So may the Winged Horse, your ancient badge and cognisance, still flourish; so may future Hookers and Seldens illustrate your church and chambers; so may the sparrows, in default of more melodious quiresters, unpoisoned, hop about your walks; so may the fresh-coloured and cleanly nurserymaid, who by leave airs her playful charge in your stately gardens, drop her prettiest blushing curtsy as ye pass, reductive of juvenescent emotion; so may the younkers of this generation eye you, pacing your stately terrace, with the same superstitious veneration with which the child Elia gazed on the Old Worthies that solemnised the parade before you!"*

We must here say a little of the earlier students of the Inn. Chaucer is said to have been of it, but upon slight evidence. The name has been seen on the record, but it is not unfrequent in records under the Norman dynasty. Thynne, in his *Animaderversions* of Speght's edition of Chaucer, says, "It is most certain to be gathered by circumstances of records that the lawyers were not in the Temple until towards the latter part of the reign of King Edward III., at which time Chaucer was a grave man, holden in great credit, and employed in embassy. So that methinketh," adds the writer, "he should not be of that house." The first English tragedy of any merit, *Gordobuc*, was written in the Temple by Thomas Norton and Thomas Sackville. Of the Inner Temple also were Littleton (the famous Judge), Sir Edward Coke, Sir Christopher Hatton, Lord Buckhurst (Lord High Treasurer), Heneage Finch, Judge Jeffreys, Francis Beaumont (Beaumont and Fletcher), and

* *Essays of Elia.*

William Browne, author of *Britannia's Pastorals.* The "studious lawyers" were not, however, always so quiet as Spenser pictures them. In Henry VIII.'s time, the gentlemen of the Temple were addicted to "shove and slip groats" (games played with halfpence), which became forbidden them under a penalty; and encounters were then so frequent, that Templars were prohibited from carrying any other weapon into the Hall (the dining-room) than the dagger or carving-knife, which it was customary to carry about the person in those days for the mutton.

From the Terrace we enter the Inner Temple Garden through some good old ironwork, dated 1730, in which the winged horse is not forgotten. It is about three acres in extent. Shakspeare has made this the place in which the distinctive badges (the white rose and the red rose) of the houses of York and Lancaster were first assumed by their respective partisans (see *First Part of Henry VI.*, act ii. sc. 4). The identity of this dramatic locality is not, however, so well attested as the depopulation of half the country by the Wars of the Roses. In the centre of the grass-plot is a sun-dial, on a pedestal of good design, the inscription states, by "Henricus Wynne, Londini, A.D. 1770." A little to the east of this dial is a venerable sycamore, which died about fifteen years since, and is now carefully railed in. Under the shade of this sycamore it is said that Dr. Johnson and Oliver Goldsmith loved to sit by the river-side for hours in the summer months. Johnson had no prevision of steamboats, but he foretold that London would be one day lighted with smoke as he saw the man relight by its smoke a half-extinguished wick. "Though this tree," says a correspondent of the *Builder*, "might not have flourished at the time of the supposed incident of plucking the red and white roses, no doubt this picturesque object was there in Shakspeare's days. A print of the Gardens, reëngraved in 1770 from an older one of the date of 1671, shows three trees on the site of the present one; and the gardener states that in digging he has come to the roots of two more similarly placed to the full-grown ones in the old print. In this print is shown a brick-terrace, faced with stones, with flights of steps running along the north side, where the chrysanthemums now are. This terrace is probably still remaining, filled with earth, which slopes to the Thames. A little distance towards the river, from the dial, a part of this grass, not so well grown as the rest, marks the old river wall, which has, since the year 1670, been encroached on in parts fifty or sixty yards. A portion of this was exposed at the time of the reëdification of Paper-buildings a few years ago, and was of great strength.

It must have been pleasant to hear your gardener prate of his whereabout, especially in his own garden, from the time "when Adam dolve." Mr. Broome, who has been gardener to the Inner Temple a quarter of a century, tells us that at that distance the Temple Garden was very celebrated for white and red roses—the old Provens cabbage and maiden-blush blooming here beautifully. There were then only two steamboats on the river; but their great increase, and the growth of the factory chimney-stalks, vomiting clouds of smoke, made all the vegetation in the garden dwindle, *except chrysanthemums;* and some fine old lime-trees ceased to bloom. But the science which in some measure made the smoke, has contrived means to abate it: the roses again blow, the stocks are again fine, and even hawthorns flower vigorously. Mr. Broome exhibited, in 1864, to the Central Horticultural Society, 24 trusses of roses grown in this ground, which speaks well for the management and capabilities of a garden in the heart of London; and Mr. Broome thinks the olden celebrity of the Garden for roses may have led Shakspeare to lay here the scene of the Red and White Rose brawl. In the flower-beds next the main walk the gardener manages to secure four successive crops of flowers: the pompones are very gorgeous; but the great autumnal boast is the chrysanthemums of the northern border. The trees suffer less from coal-smoke than from the penalty of Adam—the "churlish chiding of the winter's wind." The limes in Temple Garden, which are sheltered by Paper-buildings, are in perfect health; but those trees which are exposed to the cold currents of wind across the Garden suffer severely, and are generally disfigured with dead wood; the trees also decrease in size as they are nearer the river: some of the finest are planes, with noble heads and abundant leafage. With these and the limes contrasts, in its dark hue, the wych-elm, which thrives here, notwithstanding the causes which have injured the other trees. But the Temple lost some other rural tenants, which it has never regained. There were formerly rooks in the trees —a colony brought by Sir William Northey from Woodcote Green, Epsom; here the rooks continued to build, in defiance of noise and smoke: but all the birds left many years since. About 200 families enjoy this Garden throughout the year; and the public are admitted in fine weather, of which some 10,000 persons—the majority poor little sickly-looking creatures—take advantage: rarely is a flower plucked or a branch injured. Such a scene would have softened the heart of child-hating Coventry!

THE MIDDLE TEMPLE.

The entrance from Fleet-street is by a red-brick and stone-fronted gatehouse, built by Wren in 1684, "in the style of Inigo Jones, and very far from inelegant." It occupies the site of the structure erected by Sir Amias Paulet while Wolsey's prisoner in the gatehouse of the Temple, which was very sumptuously furnished with cardinals' hats and arms. Between this gate and Temple Bar, in 1583, young Francis Bacon stood among his brother-barristers to welcome Queen Elizabeth into the City. Within the gate are shops, in one of which lived Benjamin Motte, the publisher of the works of Pope and Swift; his imprint being, "At the Middle Temple-gate." In the Lane lived Elias Ashmole, the antiquary and herald, after he had left the astrologers and alchemists; he was called to the Bar, in Middle Temple Hall, in 1660: on January 26, 1679, by a fire which broke out in chambers adjoining those in which Ashmole resided, he lost the greater part of his library, a cabinet of coins, besides seals, charters, and other antiquities, and a collection of engraved portraits.

The Lane leads to the Temple-stairs, formerly the Water-gate. On the left are Plowden-buildings, named after the great jurist; but a nobler memorial of his treasurership is the Middle Temple Hall, built 1562-72: the east window is dated 1570. It has a splendid interior, of the Renaissance and Elizabethan style; it is 100 ft. long by 40 wide, and upwards of 60 ft. in height. The roof is of dark oak, and one of the most scientifically constructed in England,—omitting the principal arched rib, and multiplying the pendants and smaller curves; it contains a vast quantity of timber. There is also a Renaissance carved screen and music-gallery, garnished with Elizabethan armour and weapons. The screen is said to have been formed in exact imitation of the Strand front of old Somerset House; but, according to Mr. Cunningham, this is a vulgar error, like the tradition which relates that it was made of the spoils of the Spanish Armada, the records of the Society proving that it was set up thirteen years before the Armada put to sea. This screen is of the Tuscan and Ionic orders, with arched entrances and columns; caryatides, grotesque figures, statuettes in niches, and carvings of fruits and flowers, pierced arches, and fine panel-work, complete this curious example of olden art.

On the windows are emblazoned the arms of eminent members. As the nucleus of the royal portraits here is Charles I., passing through an arch, attended by an equerry, M. de St. Antoine: this majestic picture is claimed to be Vandyke's original, as are also the same portraits at Hampton Court and Warwick Castle. Above the oak-panelling are imitative bronze busts of the twelve Cæsars; and on the dais are marble busts of Lords Eldon and Stowell, both members of the Inn. The shields of arms in the wainscoting are effective. The massive tables and seats are some of them probably as old as the Hall itself. In the roof is a louvre (now glazed) through which the smoke ascended from the great central fireplace, which at Easter-time was decked with shrubs and flowers: upon the large stone hearth is a circular iron grate for the consumption of charcoal.

The rude dinner state in olden times may be imagined from the members having "cut their meat on wooden trenchers," and drunk in cups of ashen wood, until the reign of Elizabeth, when green earthen pots were substituted. Fragments of these green pots were dug up on the site of Paper-buildings in 1849. The Hall dinner is to this day a ceremonious scene. The barristers, students, and other members, in their gowns, having assembled in the Hall, the Benchers enter in procession to the dais; the steward strikes the table with his hammer three times, grace is said by the Treasurer or senior Bencher present, and the dinner commences. The old call to dinner was by sounding a horn kept for the purpose; and the drum and fife, trumpets, violins, sackbuts, recorders, and cornets, played at every course. The Benchers observe somewhat more style at their table than the other members at theirs. The general dinner is a tureen of soup, a joint of meat, a tart, and cheese; and to each mess of four is allowed a bottle of port wine. The dinner over, the Benchers, after grace, retire to the Parliament Chamber. At both Temples the form of dinner resembles the repasts of the military monks—the Benchers on the dais representing the Knights; the barristers the *Frères*, or Brethren; and the students the Novices.

Complaints are made of the neglect of certain old customs at the Middle Temple Hall dinners. Formerly, when the attendant placed the wine upon the table, he mentioned one of the Masters of the Bench in whose name it was that day given. The mess of four members before whom the bottle was placed stood up and bowed to him, the Bencher named also standing in his place on the dais, and returning the salute. During the oyster-season two barrels of oysters were brought into the Hall every Friday in term, an hour before that of dinner; napkins and oyster-knives were provided, and the members helped themselves. When but one Bencher dined, on leaving the Hall he invited the senior Bar-mess to take wine with him in the Parliament Chamber (W. J. Bernhard Smith, *Notes and Queries*, 2d S., No. 106). These things are not attended to at the Middle Temple. The Benchers' invitation and the oyster whet are exercised at the Inner Temple, where the dinners are excellent. The loving-cup ceremony, which we have noticed as rife in 1836, has long ceased, and the cup is now used to hold tooth-picks! The former salads have been wittily scandalised as "like eating a gravel-walk, and meeting with an occasional weed."

In the two Temples, for the *Calves'-head Roll*, every Bencher is taxed yearly 2*s*., every barrister 1*s*. 6*d*., and every gentleman under the Bar 1*s*., to the cook and other officers of the house, for a dinner of calves'-heads in Easter Term; but the *dinner* is *nominis umbra*.

We read of strange scenes at the Hall dinners. Sir John Davys was expelled the Society of the Middle Temple for thrashing his friend, Mr. Richard Martin, also a Bencher of the Inn, during dinner-time in the Hall. Davys was afterwards, on proper submission, readmitted; and Martin is still remembered, not by his thrashing, but by Ben Jonson's noble dedication to him of his *Poetaster*. It deserves to be mentioned, in illustration of the revels at Christmas in the Hall, that in taking up the floor, about the year 1764, near one hundred pairs of dice were found, which had been dropped on different occasions through the chinks of the boards, the dice being then very small—at least one-third less than those now in use (Cunningham's *London*). Sir Symonds d'Ewes tells us how, in 1623, after supper in the Hall, he argued a moot at the Bench; "two gentleman, under the Bar, arguing first in law—French bareheaded, as I did myself before I was called to the Bar at the cupboard."

The readings in the Hall were revived in 1861, when Dr. Phillimore, the Reader for the Lent season, inaugurated his election by reading here a paper "On Minority and Majority in England and Abroad."

In this noble Hall was performed, soon after its production, Shakspeare's *Twelfth Night;* thus recorded in the table-book of

John Manningham, a student of the Middle Temple: "Feb. 2, 1601-2.—At our feast we had a play called 'Twelfth Night; or, what You will.'" "So that," says Mr. Knight, "there is one locality remaining where a play of Shakspeare was listened to by his contemporaries."

The Middle Temple feasts were very sumptuous. Evelyn describes that of 1688—"so very extravagant and great, as the like had not been seen at any time." He was elected one of the comptrollers of the Middle Temple revellers, "as ye fashion of the young students and gentlemen was, the Christmas being kept this yeare with great solemnity;" but he soon resigned his staff of office. Again, in 1688, he records: "Went to see the revels at the Middle Temple, which is an old but riotous custom, and has relation neither to virtue nor policy." Aubrey was admitted in 1646, and "enjoyed here the greatest felicity" of his life; but, among his "accidents," on St. John's Night, 1673, he was "in danger of being run through with a sword by a young Templar at Burges's chamber in the Middle Temple."

Sir Henry Herbert tells of the Prince d'Amours, in 1635, giving a masque to the Prince Elector and his brother in Middle Temple Hall, when the Queen, Henrietta Maria, disguised as a citizen, sat amongst her subjects a spectator of the gay scene.

We find among the members many men of rank and learning, notwithstanding the old taunt—

The Inner Temple for the rich,
The Middle for the poor.

Treasurer Plowden has been already named. Sir Walter Raleigh studied here, but probably as the guest of a friend, or renting chambers of his own, for his name does not appear on the books of the Society; though his commendatory verses to Gascoigne's "Steele Glass" are stated to be by "Walter Rawley, of the Middle Temple."

Of this Inn, also, were Sir Thomas Overbury, known by his graphic skill in delineating character; John Ford, the early dramatist; Sir Edward Bramston, who had for his chamber-fellow Mr. Edward Hyde (Lord Clarendon), admitted when his uncle, Sir Nicholas Hyde, was Treasurer. The future Chancellor devoted the forenoon to the business of the Courts, the evenings to taking instructions and other legal employment. It was not his habit to dine in the Hall, as most of the other students were accustomed to do.*

Bulstrode Whitelock was of this Inn, as also Ireton, Cromwell's son-in-law; John Evelyn, Lord Keeper Guildford, and Lord Chancellor Somers. Wycherley is said to have received here visits from the Duchess of Cleveland, in the disguise of a milliner. Shadwell, Southern, and Congreve studied here; and certain wits were satirised as "pert Templars" by Pope, partly because none of the reigning wits, with the exception of Congreve, had received a Temple education:

> Three College sophs and three pert Templars came,
> The same their talents, and their tastes the same;
> Each prompt to query, answer, and debate,
> And smit with love of poetry and prate.—*Dunciad*, book ii.

Edmund Burke was entered at the Middle Temple in 1747, and came to keep his terms in 1750, when the heads and limbs of the Rebels were stuck upon Temple Bar. In 1756 we find him in two-pair chambers at the "Pope's Head," the shop of Jacob Robinson, the poet's publisher, just within the Inner Temple gateway. Burke never liked law studies, and was not called to the Bar.

Richard Brinsley Sheridan, a few days before his marriage with Miss Linley, entered his name on the Middle Temple books; but he never gave one serious hour to the law. Thomas Moore, the poet, was of the Inn. Sir William Blackstone had chambers in Brick-court: when he entered, he wrote "The

* We need not detail the admission to the Inns, and Calls to the Bar, but merely add that, once admitted, the student has the use of the library, and is entitled to a seat in the church or chapel of the Inn, and to have his name set down for chambers. He is then required to keep *commons*, by dining in the Hall for twelve terms, four in each year; on commencing which, he must deposit with the Treasurer 100*l.*, to be retained, with interest, until he is *called;* but members of the Universities are exempt from this deposit. The student must also sign a bond, with sureties, for the payment of his commons and term-fees.

Lawyer's Farewell to his Muse;" though he "loved to live in the suburbs of her graces," if we may judge from his critical notes on Shakspeare.

Dunning, Lord Ashburton, was induced by the then Master of the Rolls to study for the Bar: he entered the Middle Temple May 8, 1752, and was called, according to the Temple books, July 2, 1756. He used often to dine at a little eating-house near Chancery-lane, for sevenpence halfpenny. Thurlow, who was of the Inner Temple, described Dunning as "like the knave of clubs." Cowper, who had Thurlow for his fellow-clerk in a solicitor's office, was of the Middle Temple, where he resided eleven years, neglecting the law, but dallying with literature. While here Cowper made love to his cousin Theodora, the sister of his correspondent, Lady Hesketh. He frequented Dick's (then Richard's) Coffee-house; and while at breakfast here, he read a letter in the newspaper which he imagined to be written to drive him to self-destruction.

The most recent addition to the Middle Temple is the erection of a Library in the garden fronting the Thames—a picturesque pile; H. R. Abraham, architect. It is in character collegiate Gothic, 15th century; it has two floors of chambers beneath the Library, and a lofty roof, with crestings, and ornamental louvre; and an octagonal staircase turret at the north-east angle. The Library is a noble room, 96 feet long, 42 wide, and 70 feet high; the roof reminds one of Westminster Hall, but is two-centred: it is of American pitch-pine. There is a stained-glass window at each end; the oriel, south, has the arms of the royal princes from the time of Richard Cœur de Lion down to the present Prince of Wales; and the northern window has the shields of all who have been Benchers during the erection of the building: there are five windows of silvered glass on each side. Over the door is hung the portrait of the founder of the Library, Robert Ashley, a collateral ancestor of the Earl of Shaftesbury. The books number between 15,000 and 16,000: strong in civil, canon, and international law-books; English, Scotch, Irish, and American reports; divinity, and ecclesiastical history; proclamations and other documents of the Civil War. The Library was formally opened October 13, 1861, by the Prince of Wales, who had been enrolled a Bencher. After the opening, there was a special service at the Temple Church; and a sumptuous banquet to 750 guests. The entire edifice is of fine Bath stone, and cost under 14,000*l.*, while part of the site cost the Benchers 13,000*l.*

The Garden is more secluded than that of the Middle Temple: the Hall and new Library contribute much to the picturesqueness of the spot; while from the Library oriel, the Thames, with its bridges, Somerset House, and the Houses of Parliament, is very striking. In the garden is an aged memorial-tree, a *catalpa syringifolia*, related to have been planted by Sir Matthew Hale, —who, however, was not of the Temple, but Lincoln's Inn. The plants are effectually graduated, and the flowers well sheltered. On the lawn is a large table sun-dial, elaborately gilt and embellished.

The other Inns of Court have not been so careful of their fountain as the Middle Temple, which has now played for more than a century and a half. Hatton describes it as forcing its stream "to a vast and almost incredible altitude." A more ornamental group has been substituted; the effect of the sound and ripple of the water in this corner is very refreshing, and has been commemorated by Miss Landor in a descriptive poem, of pensive beauty,—opening with:

> The fountain's low singing is heard on the wind,
> Like a melody bringing sweet fancies to mind;
> Some to grieve, some to gladden: around them they cast
> The hopes of the morrow, the dreams of the past;
> Away in the distance is heard the vast sound,
> From the streets of the city, that compass it round,
> Like the echo of fountains, or ocean's deep call:
> Yet that fountain's low singing is heard over all.

In Garden-court, to which we descend from Fountain-court, Oliver Goldsmith removed from Inner Temple Library Staircase, to what the rich old Dr. Scott describes as a miserable garret; Goldy, nevertheless, would not accept the Doctor's proposal that he should write for the Administration. Here Goldsmith passed many happy hours at his window, looking over the Garden at the old Temple rookery, watching the habits of the rooks, which he has so well described in his *Animated Nature*. It was while living here that Goldsmith hired a man-servant (a Patlander, of course), and was metamorphosed into a smart physician, with a professional wig and cane, purple-silk small-clothes, and a scarlet rocquelaire buttoned to the chin; but he soon grew tired of the profession, and small amount of fees. In 1768, Oliver, with the profits of his comedy the *Good-natured Man*, purchased chambers in Brick-court, Middle Temple, for which he gave 400*l.*; they were No. 2, second-floor, right of the staircase. He furnished them handsomely; and then came waste and debt and difficulties, which he never got over. Mr. Forster tells us, in his admirable *Life* of the poet, that Goldy borrowed money of Mr. Edmund Bett, a barrister, who occupied the opposite rooms, who remained very intimate with him for the rest of his life, and whose *Poor-Law Treatise* is supposed to have received revision and improvement from him.

Under Goldsmith's were the chambers of Mr. Blackstone, then finishing the fourth volume of his *Commentaries*. He used to complain of the racket made overhead; and a Mr Children, who succeeded him, made the same complaint. And how could it be otherwise? for here Goldsmith gave dinners to Johnson, Reynolds, Barry, Bickerstaff, and other friends; and supper-parties to young folks of both sexes. These last were preceded by noisy round games at cards, followed up by blindman's-buff, and romping games of forfeits, and uproarious singing and dancing. Sometimes a "former friend" called most inopportunely, as was the case one evening, when the Doctor was drinking wine with Topham Beauclerc and General Oglethorpe. The caller was half-tipsy; he sat down with the fine connections, and all at once took from his pocket a quarter of a pound of tea and half a pound of sugar, which he offered Goldsmith, as he could not repay two guineas which the Doctor had lent him. This was too much even for Goldy's good-nature, and the intruder was turned out with his tea and sugar.

In these chambers Goldsmith breathed his last. He was asked, "Is your mind at ease?" "No; it is not," were the last-recorded words of Oliver Goldsmith. He grew too weak to talk, and scarcely took any notice of what was said to him. He sank into a deep sleep; he awoke, but in strong convulsions, which continued without intermission until he expired, on the 4th of April 1774, at five o'clock in the morning, in the forty-sixth year of his age. On the stairs of his chambers there were the lamentations of the old and infirm, and the sobbing of women—poor objects of his charity, to whom he had never turned a deaf ear, even when himself struggling with poverty.

There was some talk of a public funeral; but, as the poor poet had died 2000*l.* in debt, the idea was relinquished. Five days after his death, at five o'clock of the evening of April 9, he was privately interred in the burial-ground of the Temple Church. Burke and Reynolds superintended the arrangements; but the chief mourner was Sir Joshua's nephew. The poet rests at a short distance from the brick-wall on the north side of the burial-ground, and his grave is covered with a memorial-stone, inscribed, "Here lies Oliver Goldsmith." Formerly a tree shaded the spot.

In Essex-court, Middle Temple, lived another errant man of letters, Richard Porson, whose irregularities were of a more reckless cast than those of poor Noll. Porson probably chose this abode to be near his friend Perry, the editor and proprietor of the *Morning Chronicle*, and whose sister he married. Perry's house was in Lancaster-court, in the Strand; hence Porson facetiously called him "My Lord of Lancaster." Many a time at early morn must Porson have staggered to his chambers in Essex-court from his old haunt, the Cyder Cellar, in Maiden-lane, where he scarcely ever failed to pass some hours, after spending the evening at the deanery of Westminster, at Perry's, or elsewhere. It is related of him, upon better authority than most of the stories told to his discredit, that one night, or rather morning, Gurney (the Baron), who had chambers in Essex-court under Porson, was awakened by a tremendous thump in the chambers above. Porson had just come home dead-drunk, and had fallen on the floor. Having extinguished the candle in the fall, he presently staggered down-stairs to relight it; and Gurney heard him keep dodging and poking with the candle at the staircase-lamp for about five minutes, and all the while very lustily cursing the nature of things. It is a grievous thing to be awaked out of one's sleep by such a noise as Porson's fall must have made; but the laugh which Gurney must have enjoyed at the scholar's perplexity, and his learned way of meeting it, was worth the aforesaid endurance.

We read, also, of Porson's shutting himself up in these chambers for three or four days together, admitting no visitors. One morning his friend Rogers went to call, having ascertained from the barber's hard by that Porson was at home, but had not been seen by any one for two days. Rogers proceeded to his chambers, and knocked at the door more than once: he would not open it, and Rogers came down-stairs; but as he was crossing the court, Porson opened the window, and stopped him. He was then busy about the Grenville Homer, for which he collated the Harleian Ms. of the *Odyssey*, and received for his labour but 50*l.* and a large-paper copy. His chambers must have presented a strange scene; for he used his books most cruelly, whether they were his own or belonged to others. He said that he possessed more *bad* copies of *good* books than any private gentleman in England.

With a few changes in Temple customs and fashions, we conclude. The Temple was formerly guarded by its own servants in livery, by certain of whom the hour was cried at night, and whose duty it was, moreover, to ascend each staircase at certain hours, to see that all was safe. These duties are now performed by the metropolitan police. The Temple is not so much a place of residence as formerly. Morning visits are not made in black-silk gowns and powdered wigs; and the

Chief-Justices of our Courts have ceased to wear fans, as Sir Edward Coke was in the habit of doing.

Dr. Dibdin thus describes the Garden-walks of the last century: "Towards evening it was the fashion for the leading counsel to promenade during the summer months in the Temple Gardens. Cocked-hats and ruffles, with satin small-clothes and silk stockings, at this time constituted the usual evening-dress. Lord Erskine, though a good deal shorter than his brethren, somehow always seemed to take the lead both in place and in discourse, and shouts of laughter would frequently follow his dicta."

Wig-shops are few; but Lord Chancellor Campbell has left us some amusing gossip about Dick Danby's, in the Cloisters; and in Essex-court, at Albin's, a full-bottomed wig for a Q.C. may occasionally be seen in progress; here the scratch-wig of Johnson, and the more ornamental wig of Goldsmith, may have been often dressed.

Throughout the Temple the Latin inscriptions recording the repairs and restorations of the buildings remind you of the *genius loci*; and where time is so valuable, it is fit we should take note of it at every turn. Accordingly, the sun-dials were formerly very numerous. Three remain, with mottoes: Temple-lane, "Pereunt et imputantur;" Essex-court, "Vestigia nulla retrorsum;" Brick-court, "Time and tide tarry for no man." In Pump-court and Garden-court are two dials without mottoes. The pillar-dials in the Gardens have been named. The Inner-Temple dial, removed in 1828, obtained its quaint inscription, "Begone about your business," as the story goes, through the answer of a crabbed old Bencher to the painter who importuned him for a motto for the newly-painted dial. With this kind of repair, by the way, we venture to suggest that the original dates of the dials should be kept, instead of the date of each repainting being recorded upon them. In these days of archæological revivalism, this is worth consideration.*

* Reprinted, with many additions, from the *Illustrated London News.*

RECOLLECTIONS OF SIR RICHARD PHILLIPS.

THIS popular *littérateur*, who has been fairly characterised as "a man remarkable for his activity and originality," was born in London, in December 1767. He was educated first at a school in Soho-square; and then at Chiswick, where he soon indicated a genius for English composition and the science of numbers, rather than a taste for classical studies; to which cause may be referred the singularly vernacular style of his writing, and the entire absence of classical embellishment in his felicitous illustrations for the largest class of readers. Of his school-days he has left a vivid picture,* the mainspring being the author's accidentally hearing, when he had grown to manhood, the bells of Chiswick church: "The recurring tones," he observes, "produced corresponding vibrations on my nerves, and I felt myself played upon like a concordant musical instrument. Presently, however, it occurred to me that I was not an entire stranger to the tones of those bells, and that part of their fascination arose from an association between them and some of the earliest and dearest objects in my remembrance. 'Surely,' I exclaimed, 'they are Chiswick bells!' the very bells under the sound of which I received part of my education, and, as a schoolboy, passed the happiest days of my life! Well may their tones vibrate to my inmost soul, and kindle uncommon sympathies! I now recollect that the winding of the river Thames must have brought me nearer to that simple and primitive village than the profusion of wood had permitted me to perceive; and my nerves had been unconsciously acted upon by tones which served as keys to all the associations connected with these bells, their church, and the village of Chiswick. I listened again, and now discriminated the identical sounds which I had heard during a period of more than thirty years.

* From *A Morning's Walk from London to Kew*, pp. 211-214.

In fancy, I became a schoolboy. 'Yes,' said I, 'the six bells repeat the village legend, and tell me that *my dun cow has just calved,*' exactly as they did above thirty years since! Did the reader ever encounter a similar key-note, leading to a multitude of early and vivid impressions? for in like manner these sympathetic tones brought before my imagination numberless incidents and personages no longer important, or no longer in existence. My scattered and once-loved schoolmates, their characters, and their various fortunes, passed in rapid review before me; my schoolmaster, his wife, and all the gentry, and heads of families, whose orderly attendance at Divine Service on Sundays, while those well-remembered bells were chiming for church (but now departed, and mouldering in the adjoining graves), were rapidly presented to my recollection. With what pomp and form they used to enter and depart from their house of God! I saw, with the mind's eye, the widow Hogarth, and her maiden relative Richardson, walking up the aisle, dressed in their silken sacs, their raised head-dresses, their black calashes, their lace ruffles, and their high crook'd canes, preceded by their aged servant, Samuel; who, after he had wheeled his mistress to church in her Bath-chair, carried the Prayer-books up the aisle, and opened and shut the pew!

"There, too, was the portly Dr. Griffiths, of the *Monthly Review*, with his literary wife, in her neat and elevated wire-winged cap; and, ofttimes, the vivacious and angelic Duchess of Devonshire, whose bloom had not then suffered from the canker-worm of pecuniary distress, created by the luxury of charity! Nor could I forget the humble distinction of the aged sexton, Mortefee, whose skill in psalmody enabled him to lead that wretched group of singers, whom Hogarth has so happily portrayed, whose performance with the tuning-fork excited so much wonder in little boys; and whose gesticulations and contortions of head, hand, and body, in beating time, were not outdone by Joah Bates, in the Commemoration of Handel! Yes, simple and happy villagers! I remember scores of you.

How fortunately ye had escaped the contagion of the metropolitan vices, though distant but five miles; and how many of you I have conversed with who, at an adult age, had never beheld the degrading assemblage of its knaveries and miseries!"

Richard Phillips was brought up in the large establishment of an uncle, proprietor of the Lion Brewery, in Soho, to which property he was heir. This prospective fortune, however, did not overcome his distaste for his uncle's business; but a passion for literature, and especially for mathematics and experimental philosophy, in which predilection he was thwarted, led him, at the age of seventeen, to detach himself from his family connections, and seek his own fortunes. He imagined that the time had arrived to emancipate South America from the Spanish yoke, and left London, in 1785, with an intention to embark at Liverpool for Spanish America; but, being deceived by the ship's captain, he settled as a schoolmaster, first at Chester, and afterwards at Leicester, in the year 1788.

At Leicester he opened a bookseller's shop, and commenced a newspaper, marked by its strong tone of political independence. Here he first became acquainted with Mr. William Gardiner, the musical amateur, and author of *Music and Friends*. With Mr. Phillips he established a Philosophical Society; and as electricity was the novel science of that day, the president, Phillips, and the members entered into a variety of experiments; and, like Franklin, erected on the top of the Society's rooms a lofty pole, in the form of a spear, and drew the electricity from the clouds. The members also studied astronomy, and made a notable observation of a transit of Mercury over the Sun.

At this time broke out the French Revolution, 1789, when the young philosophers became obnoxious to the loyal party, who considered the people knew too much already, and that their philosophical discussions might take a political turn; so the Society was broken up. Meanwhile, Phillips advocated in his journal, the *Leicester Herald*, the principles of civil and religious liberty: he was closely watched by the Corporation, and at length entrapped in selling Paine's *Rights of Man*, for which he was brought to trial, and sentenced to eighteen months' imprisonment in Leicester Gaol. Here he was harshly treated, though visited by Lord Moira, the Duke of Norfolk, and other partisans of distinction.

Soon after Phillips's release, a dire calamity befell him: a fire broke out at his neighbour's, which spread to his dwelling-house, and burned it to the ground, with his printing-office, his books and papers, the library and pamphlet-room. He then removed to London, where his first effort was an attempt to establish a Sunday newspaper on a more literary plan than the *Craftsman* and *Monitor*, the then Sunday newspapers. While making his arrangements, he was sought by Mr. John Bell, to whom he developed his plan, with a view to partnership; but the terms not being agreed on, Bell by himself started the paper: hence the origin of *Bell's Messenger*, which still flourishes. In his next speculation, Mr. Phillips was less communicative, but more successful. At this time, 1795, the principal magazines published monthly in London were the *Gentleman's* and the *Universal*, in neither of which was a sufficient tone of political and philosophical inquiry to satisfy the demands of the age; at least, such was Mr. Phillips's inference, when he projected the *Monthly Magazine*, which was admitted to be as original a design as the *Gentleman's Magazine* itself, when compared with the periodical publications which preceded it.

It may here be mentioned, that Phillips's aptitude for business was not confined to teaching or bookselling. In 1792, he was instrumental in setting afloat many canals: he used to relate that he bought and sold the first canal-share that ever was transferred, in the winter of 1791. His success led him to become a general buyer and seller of canal-shares: as the speculative mania increased, no room of any inn at Leicester, nor even the Town-hall, could accommodate the eager thousands; and the meeting was adjourned to a field, the chairman taking his station under a tree. Persons abandoned their usual occupations, and galloped over the country to meetings called to originate new canals; and it often happened that ten times the sums required were subscribed in a few hours. Phillips, the originator, cleared some thousands in a few months, and others became, on a sudden, really or nominally rich; but the political alarm of 1792 dashed these golden dreams to the ground: shares fell from 200*l.* premium to 5*l.* Hundreds of persons were ruined; the law gave the speculators no respite; and the result, though disastrous to many, was the formation of at least sixty new canals. Phillips also embarked in the hosiery business, through his Leicester connections, upon his first settling in the metropolis.

At the commencement of the *Monthly Magazine*, Mr. Phillips lodged and boarded at the Chapter Coffee-house, in Paternoster-row; and at this celebrated resort of men of letters, he was on a keen look-out for recruits. He relates that he knew the characters of "the Chapter," from the voracious glutton in politics, who waited for the wet papers in the morning twilight, to the comfortless bachelor, who sat till the fire was raked-out at half-past twelve at night; all of whom took their successive stations, like figures in a magic-lantern. Our projector's means were, however, but limited; for he used to relate that he came to London from Leicester with little property beyond a check for 38*l.*, which he placed in the hands of Mr. Johnson, on the north side of St. Paul's-churchyard, the first publisher of the *Monthly Magazine*, as security for the expenses of the first number. Its announcement was not by advertisement in the newspapers, but by circulars, addressed to the most active persons, political as well as literary, in the Opposition interest; which circulars, to save heavy postage, were enclosed in commercial parcels. The demand for the first number astounded the booksellers, many of whom scarcely knew of the announcement of the magazine; and Phillips, calling on his publisher about the fifth day of the month, received back his check, with the gratifying assurance from Johnson that the success of the *Monthly* was certain. It was sold at one shilling; and its politico-literary character was a novelty, or rather a phenomenon, in periodical literature. Phillips was the conductor of the political portion of the magazine; its literary editor being Dr. Aikin. This arrangement continued for ten years, when Aikin seceded, and set up a rival magazine, called the *Athenæum*, which he edited throughout its publication, two years and a half. Another imitation of Phillips's magazine was the *New Monthly Magazine*, started by Henry Colburn,—in form, contents, and arrangement, a counterpart of the *Monthly Magazine*, save in its politics, which were of the Tory school. Colburn used naïvely to express his surprise at Phillips's hostility. And, in the *Biographical Dictionary of Living Authors*, 1816, though published by Colburn, the *Monthly Magazine* was traduced as "the common sewer of virulent politics and infidelity." The *New Monthly Magazine* was, subsequently, with the aid of Thomas Campbell, recast into a purely literary journal.

Phillips's own testimony as to the sale of magazines, which has been generally exaggerated, may be here quoted. He tells us, that "The *Gentleman's Magazine*, in its days of popular extracts, never rose above 10,000; and, after it became more decidedly antiquarian, it fell in sale, and continued for many years at 3000. There was also a lighter work called the *European Magazine*, and one, better selected, called the *Universal Magazine;* both of which sold also to the latter extent. These were the periodicals with which I had to contend when I began the *Monthly Magazine*, in 1795: but till 1824, when I sold that work, the average regular sale never exceeded 3500, or 3750; and the last two fell in sale, from various causes, till discontinued."

One of the most striking contributions to the *Monthly Magazine* was a series of articles, entitled "Stephensiana," which appeared between 1821 and 1824; they were mostly from the papers of Alexander Stephens, of Park House, Chelsea, who collected anecdotes of his contemporaries, and generally entered them day by day. After Stephens's death, these papers were purchased of his widow by Phillips; they were in all sorts of forms, from the memoir to the slightest memorandum, all in the most illegible hand, or rather scrawl, ever seen,—in deciphering which, Phillips employed his own reminiscences: the account of the old Chapter Coffee-house, and its Wittinagemot Club, is principally Phillips's contribution. A Correspondent of *Notes and Queries* rates the merit of these *ana* highly: "They contain," he says, "many profound thoughts and just observations, and also a great many anecdotes of celebrated men. The author was a philosopher and a scholar, evidently of considerable mark; and holding liberal views when Toryism was rampant, and Reform at a discount. He was on terms of intimacy with the most noted men of his time, whether as statesmen, philosophers, or authors; and a great number of the anecdotes which are to be found in his 'Stephensiana,' I have not seen any where else."

At Leicester, Mr. Phillips was a collector of local antiquities; though in after-life we know him to have treated the study of antiquarianism as puerile and trifling gravity. He was, we believe, the first person to popularise the circumstances attending the death of Richard III.; and to relate the history of the Blue Boar Inn at Leicester, where Richard slept the night before the battle of Bosworth; as well as the story of the massive oak bedstead, whereon the King slept, the discovery in it of gold coin, &c.—which narratives have been repeated in hundreds of anecdote-books. Mr. Phillips likewise procured a few fragments of Wolsey's stone-coffin, after it had been taken out of St. Margaret's Church, Leicester, the remains turned out, and a portion of the coffin used as a horse-trough at the White Horse Inn. In 1789, the bones of Wolsey were exhibited for some weeks on a bench in a garden at Leicester; when Mr. Phillips bought the skull for a shilling of the gardener, and kept it until it was destroyed in the fire at his house.

In 1806, Mr. Phillips visited the spot in the New Forest where William Rufus was killed by the glancing of an arrow from a tree. In a cottage about 100 yards distant, Phillips found a family named Purkis, the same as that of the charcoal-burner who, in 1100, lived on the same spot, and conveyed the

King's body in his cart to Winchester. On further inquiry, he learnt that the same family had, from that time, not only lived on the same site, but to that day followed the same occupation of making charcoal, and conveying it by a cart to Southampton and other towns. They still possessed the bridle which was on the King's horse, and which, on Rufus's fall, and the flight of Tyrrel and his attendants, came into the hands of Purkis; but as the then master of the dwelling had endeavoured to destroy it, his wife had concealed it, and described it as lost. The bridle had been for centuries shown to monarchs and other visitors, when it was purchased by Mr. Phillips: it is a true Norman bridle, and of the same fashion as the ornamented bridles still in use in the northern provinces of France. At Lyndhurst, in the King's House, or Lord Warden's Lodge, is preserved an ancient stirrup, said to have been used by Rufus at the time he was shot. With respect to Purkis—

> Still, so runs our forest creed,
> Flourish that pious yeoman's seed,
> E'en in the selfsame spot;
> One horse and cart their little store,
> Like their forefathers'—neither more
> Nor less the children's lot.—*W. S. Rose.*

The name may still be found at Minstead. Mr. Lower says, the *name* is certainly not older than the 13th or 14th century, being a corruption of Perkins, through Perkiss.

There had previously appeared in the *Monthly Magazine* a series of anecdotes, remarks, letters, &c., by Horace Walpole; which Phillips reprinted as "a little lounging miscellany," entitled *Walpoliana*, and published at 71 St. Paul's-churchyard. He also issued companion volumes from Addison, Swift, and Brooke, and the French *Anas*; besides Memoirs of Samuel Foote, Lee Lewes, Mrs. Robinson, Lady Mary Wortley Montague, John Wilkes, and the Life and Correspondence of Samuel Richardson; likewise, for several years, a volume of memoirs of "Public Characters;" also, Histories of England, Universal History, &c. He introduced Sydney Owenson, afterwards Lady

Morgan; Mr. Surr (Phillips's brother-in-law), with the *Winter in London*, in which the author had sketched the beautiful Duchess of Devonshire with unintentional identity; Mr. Godwin's *Life of Chaucer;* and *Caleb Williams* and *Fleetwood*, the same author; Travels, by Holcroft, Sir John Carr, &c. Another popular work was the publisher's *Picture of London*, 1803, remarkable for the adaptation and completeness of its information. The *Ambulator*, and the *Guide to all the Watering-Places*, we also owe to Phillips's able appreciation of the public requirements.

Miss Owenson's first novel, *The Novice of St. Dominick*, appeared in 1805, for which she coaxed Mr. Phillips out of a considerable sum. "He was not a loser by the bargain, for a lady novelist was then a rarer bird than now, and an Irish subject was also less hackneyed. But on the strength of this, when her next work was ready, Miss Owenson insisted on a higher price, and played against Mr. Phillips a rival publisher, of whom he was jealous, until she got her own terms."*

Mr. Phillips now removed to New Bridge-street. In 1807-8 he served the office of Sheriff of London and Middlesex, performing the duties with great *éclat*. He effected several reforms in the City prisons: to him we owe the sanitary measure of frequently lime-washing the wards of Newgate; and, in conjunction with his colleague, Mr. Smith, Mr. Phillips established the Sheriffs' Fund for the daily distribution of food to the poor prisoners; which Fund is maintained to this day. He also rejoiced that, during his shrievalty there was not a single execution—a rare event in the then severity of our criminal code. Phillips received knighthood on presenting to the King an Address in favour of Ministers, a distinction which his colleague declined. This drew upon the Knight the censure of his strong political party, though the Administration was a liberal one; and such disapprobation is not to be rated above the honour of the Sheriff and his lady being drawn up Ludgate-hill in their state-chariot by a party of the crowd on Lord Mayor's Day.

* *Times* review of Lady Morgan's *Memoirs.*

In this year Sir Richard Phillips wrote his *Letter to the Livery of London*, which has not only been the guide of successive Sheriffs, but of the Legislature, in reforms of our criminal jurisprudence. The book is thoroughly practical; not the production of a professed author, lawyer, or politician, but of a man of business. The abuses which it exposes, in its picture of Newgate of some fifty years since, are scarcely credible; and the extortions of sheriffs' officers and lock-up houses, in connection with the 24,000 writs then annually addressed to the Sheriffs, are of like enormity: the Tables of Rates and Fees were modified in this year; and the Letter concludes with a list of abuses, each specification commencing with "It cannot be denied," &c. Of course the humane Sheriff had innumerable oppositions; and the Recorder, Silvester, contrived to embroil the two Sheriffs, upon a point of form, stating in good set terms, that he would never consent to a certain alteration in the practice of the Court, and as long as he lived it should continue as it then was! In the Appendix to the Letter are some details of the expenses of the Sheriffs' state and hospitality; usually upwards of 2000 guineas each: state chariot, horses, and state liveries; the inauguration dinner; a fourth of the Guildhall dinner, Nov. 9; the Old Bailey dinners; meat at the City prisons, &c. The Letter was followed by Sir Richard's *Treatise on the Powers and Duties of Juries*, a work which has been translated into the continental languages.

Sir Richard used to relate some odd incidents of his shrievalty. It was an unprofitable year for the executioner, as no execution took place in London; and "Jack Ketch" grew so discontented, that on some culprits being ordered to be whipped, he plainly told the Sheriff he might whip the rogues himself, as the situation was made "worth nothing at all." He was paid weekly a guinea by the under-sheriffs, half of which he paid his assistant; an altercation ensued, which ended in the Sheriff raising the salary to a guinea and a half. The barbarous punishment of the pillory was then common; and the Sheriff, on more than one occasion, endeavoured to stem the excesses of the mob by keeping them at a distance, and suffered much abuse for his humane feeling.

The *personnel* of the two sheriffs presented a strange contrast. Smith (who served as Lord Mayor in 1818) loved aldermanic cheer, but was pale and cadaverous in complexion; whilst Phillips, who never ate animal food, was rosy and healthful in appearance. One day, when the Sheriffs were in full state, the procession was stopped by an obstruction in the street traffic; when droll were the mistakes of the mob: to Smith they cried, "Here's Old Water-gruel!" to Phillips, "Here's Roast-Beef; something like an Englishman!"

When Phillips was indicted at Leicester, in 1793, for selling Paine's *Rights of Man*, Spencer Perceval, then at the Bar, was retained as counsel against him, this being his first cause in behalf of Government. His triumph was easy: Phillips was sentenced to eighteen months' imprisonment, and Perceval pursued his career of promotion. Phillips, soon after his release, removed to London, and a prosperous trade enabled him to keep a country-house at Belsize, Hampstead, and he had for his neighbour Perceval, then Attorney-General, and afterwards Chancellor of the Exchequer. Phillips and Perceval frequently saw each other, but never spoke. The one became Sheriff, the other First Lord of the Treasury. They necessarily met at Court, but still looked shy at each other: at length, when George III. knighted Phillips at the *levée*, immediately on his retiring from the King's presence, he was saluted in the ear, in a pompous tone, with, "I congratulate Sir Richard Phillips." The latter turned his face, and met that of Perceval, and replied, "I am astonished and gratified by this coincidence; it is, sir, our first *rencontre* since we met at Leicester." "Well," said Perceval, "I am pleased to see in Mr. Phillips Sir Richard Phillips, Sheriff of London; altered, I hope, as much in principles as in situation." "No," rejoined the other, "my principles are the same; and will, I trust, always continue unchanged." Perceval looked disappointed; and though the parties bowed and smiled when they met, Phillips always found himself crossed by the influence of the Minister, till, some four years after, Perceval was shot by Bellingham; and it so happened that Phillips, coming into the House of Commons at the instant, was one of those who assisted in removing the lifeless body of his old opponent.

Sir Richard did not advance in civic life beyond his shrievalty: he maintained a long unbroken friendship with his neighbour, Waithman, for whom he framed many Resolutions for the Common Council and Common Hall. At the funeral of Queen Caroline, in 1821, Sir Richard accompanied Sheriff Waithman, when a bullet passed through the carriage-window as the *cortège* passed through Hyde Park.

A year of commercial reverses followed Phillips's shrievalty; the publishing establishment in Bridge-street was broken up, and Sir Richard withdrew from public life for a time, which he sedulously employed in writing some elementary educational books. So long ago as 1798, he had commenced the reform of school-books, then in a low state; and, as the general result, we may state that, with his own hand, he wrote or compiled above 200 elementary books, chiefly in subservience to a system developed in 1816, now well known in schools, called "Interrogative, or Questions and Exercises for the Study of Pupils." As political feelings ran high in the season of Sir Richard's activity, and he would never compromise his principles, to protect his books against prejudices he adopted the names of Blair, Goldsmith, Mavor, Barrow, Bossuet, Adair, Pelham, &c. Goldsmith's *Geography*, Mavor's *Spelling-Book*, Blair's *Catechisms* and *Preceptor*, were among the most successful results: for the renewal of the copyright of Blair's *Mother's Catechism*, Sir Richard received from the then proprietor, in 1842, the large sum of 850*l*.

Amidst Sir Richard's pressing business pursuits, he found time to identify himself with several inquiries of public interest, in the *Monthly Magazine* and elsewhere. He relates, that the exposure of the Duke of York and Mrs. Clarke had for its immediate cause the resentment of one M'Callum against Sir

Thomas Picton, who, as Governor of Trinidad, had, among other arbitrary acts, imprisoned M'Callum in an underground dungeon. On getting to England, he sought justice; but finding himself baffled, he first published his Travels in Trinidad, to expose Picton; he then ferreted out charges against the War Office; and, through Colonel Wardle, brought forward the notorious great-coat contract. This being negatived by a ministerial majority, he then traced Mrs. Clarke, and arranged the whole of the exposure for Wardle and others. To effect this in the teeth of power, he wrought night and day for months, though destitute of resources. He lodged in a garret in Hungerford Market, and often did not taste food for twenty-four hours: he lived just to see the Duke of York dismissed from office, and to publish a short narrative, and then died of exhaustion and want.

Sir Richard had also his story of the amour of George III. and Hannah Lightfoot, which was as follows: About the year 1756, there lived, at the corner of Market-street, St. James's, a linendraper named Wheeler, a Quaker, who had a beautiful niece, named Hannah Lightfoot, known as "the fair Quakeress," from serving in her uncle's shop. The lady caught the eye of Prince George in his walks and rides from Leicester House to St. James's Palace, and she soon returned the attentions of such a lover. The acquaintance alarming the royal family, it was contrived to marry the Quaker to a young grocer and former admirer, of the name of Axford, of Ludgate-hill; the marriage ceremony, according to a manuscript before us, being performed by Dr. Wilmot. The Prince grew inconsolable; and a few weeks after, as Axford was one evening from home, a royal carriage came to the door, and the lady was hurried into it by the attendants, and carried off at full speed. Where she was taken to, or what became of her, was never known. Some reported that she survived her lover; others, that she died in 1765, after having had three sons, since general officers. Her death disturbed the royal mind. Axford, broken-hearted, retired to Warminster, set up a grocer's shop, married again, and had a family: he died in old age, about 1810, but not without having sought clamorously for information about his wife, at Weymouth and other places. [We remember a grocer of the above name and family at Ludgate-hill; and on the north side of Fleet-street, between 1822 and 1826.]

Of Mrs. Robinson, distinguished as a writer in verse and prose, as well as by her exquisite beauty and personal misfortunes, Sir Richard used to relate: She was the daughter of a merchant at Bristol, named Darby, who failing in business, and dying soon after, his widow took her lovely daughter to London, where, at sixteen, she was induced to marry a young attorney, of specious appearance, named Robinson. Her husband soon after falling into difficulties, Garrick encouraged her to try the stage for subsistence; and at nineteen she performed several parts with success: she first appeared as Juliet, in 1776. Her beauty had already become known to the Prince of Wales; and one night, after she had played the part of Perdita in the *Winter's Tale*, she received from the hands of Lord Malden a lock of his royal highness's hair, enclosed in a billet, with these words—"To the ever-adorable Perdita—Florizel—to be redeemed"—in the Prince's handwriting. The vanity of a young woman in her situation rendered her an easy prey, and she soon after became the mistress of the Prince, and lived in a style of splendour. The connection produced much uneasiness to the King; the sum of 5000*l.* is stated to have been paid to Mrs. Robinson for giving up the Prince's letters, &c.; and the intrigue was broken up. However, the habits of luxury which Mrs. Robinson had acquired during her royal connection could not be shaken off. Her attachments were of a romantic cast: on the return of the celebrated trooper, Colonel Tarleton, from his guerilla warfare in the backwoods of America, she fell desperately in love with him; in a journey by night, to render him a personal service, she caught cold, followed by fever, and lost the use of the sinews of her knees, being then only twenty-two. This affliction she never overcame, and was unable to stand upright or walk during the remainder of her life. She now devoted herself to literature, and many of her poetical pieces are of highly-wrought sentiment. She maintained her personal fascinations, and she was considered as one of the loveliest women in England till her forty-second year, when her sedentary life brought on dropsy of the chest, of which she died, in 1800, neglected and poor, at Englefield Green, and was interred at Old Windsor. Her papers, with the lock of hair and billet of the Prince of Wales, were purchased by Sir Richard Phillips, by whom her Memoirs, as far as she had written them, were published. Her portrait was more than once painted; her favourite attitude being with her head resting upon her upraised arm, which was of beautiful form.

Sir Richard Phillips, more than half a century ago, agitated in the *Monthly Magazine* the question of a memorial to Shakspeare, but unsuccessfully. He was well acquainted with the Irelands, father and son, and thus related the circumstances of their notorious Shakspeare forgeries. Mr. Samuel Ireland, originally a silk-merchant in Spitalfields, was led by his taste for literary antiquities to abandon trade for those pursuits, and published several Tours. In an excursion upon the river Avon, he explored every locality associated with Shakspeare. His son, a youth of sixteen, who accompanied him, perceiving the eagerness with which he sought for any of the poet's Ms. remains, conceived that it would not be difficult to gratify his father; and in 1793, being then in his eighteenth year, he produced some Mss. asserted to be in the handwriting of Shakspeare, which, he said, had been given him by a gentleman possessed of many other old papers. Young Ireland, who was articled to a solicitor in Chancery, fabricated, in the first instance, the deed of mortgage from Shakspeare to Michael Frazer. The ecstasy expressed by his father urged him to the fabrication of other documents, represented to come from the same quarter; and at length he announced the discovery of an original drama, under the title of *Vortigern*, which he exhibited act by act, written in the period of two months. Having provided the paper resembling that of the period (the fly-leaves of old books), and with ink prepared by a bookbinder, no suspicion was entertained of the deception. The father, who was a maniac upon such subjects, gave such *éclat* to the supposed discovery, that his house in Norfolk-street, Strand, was daily crowded to excess by persons of the highest rank, as well as by men of letters. The Mss., being mostly decreed genuine, were considered to be of inestimable worth. Some conceited amateurs in literature at length sounded an alarm; notwithstanding which, Mr. Sheridan agreed to give 600*l.* for permission to play *Vortigern* at Drury-lane Theatre. The house was crowded. The predetermined malcontents began an opposition from the outset; some ill-cast characters converted grave scenes into ridicule, and there ensued between the believers and sceptics a contest which endangered the property. The piece was accordingly withdrawn.

The young author was now so beset for information, that he found it necessary to abscond from his father's house; and then, to put an end to the ferment which his ingenuity had created, he published a pamphlet, wherein he confessed the entire fabrication. Besides *Vortigern*, young Ireland also produced a play of *Henry II.*; and, although there were in both such incongruities as were not consistent with Shakspeare's age, both dramas contain passages of considerable beauty and originality.

Mr. Ireland was the dupe of his zeal upon such subjects; and the son never contemplated at the outset the unfortunate effect which the reaction would have upon his father's health and fortune. Such was the enthusiasm of certain admirers of Shakspeare (among them, Drs. Parr and Warton), that they fell upon their knees before the Mss.; and, by their idolatry, inspired hundreds of others with similar enthusiasm.

Mr. Ireland died about 1802. His son, William Henry, long survived him; but the forgeries blighted his literary reputation for ever, and he died in straitened circumstances.

Sir Richard Phillips also took especial interest in memorials of Shakspeare, and made more than one attempt to raise a fund for erecting a Shakspeare monument, but failed. In 1817, at Tewkesbury, he was led by a reputed inscription on the tombstone of a John Harte, buried there in 1800, which described him as a sixth descendant of the poet Shakspeare, to inquire whether there lived in that town any survivors of the family. After much search, he discovered a son of this Harte, who had been christened by the name of William Shakspeare, and who was a journeyman chairmaker. The contour of his countenance strikingly resembled the portrait of the poet in the first folio edition.

Sir Richard gave poor Harte a guinea, and appealed to the public for him in the *Monthly Magazine*, wherein it appears that Harte's father held the property in Shakspeare's two houses at Stratford, but they had long been under mortgage; and his mother sold them by auction, deriving a balance, after paying the mortgage and expenses, of only 30*l.* The family pedigree Harte had preserved; but had no other relict of the great poet save a long walking-stick, which had been given to him by his father as one which had belonged to Shakspeare.

Between the years 1813 and 1816, Sir Richard wrote in the *Monthly Magazine* a very attractive narrative, which he subsequently reprinted in a library volume, entitled *A Morning's Walk from London to Kew*: the Preface is dated from Holloway, 1817, where Sir Richard and his family resided in a villa, named the Pavilion, in that then rural suburb. The *Walk* has little of antiquities or topography, but is full of lively observation and suggestive remark, and is dedicated to "The free and honest searchers after Moral, Political, Natural Truth; the votaries of Common Sense, the patients of their Natural Sensibilities; all who are neither too old, too powerful, nor too wise; and finally, all those who pass their lives in search of Happiness, and who are not unwilling to be pleased, in whatsoever form, or by whomsoever the attempt may be made." We have already (at p. 94) quoted from this very entertaining volume the author's reflections on the bells of Chiswick Church. His accounts of the Kit-Kat Club and its Pictures, and the Mayor of Garratt, are curious; but the originality of the *Walk* is best characterised in the following striking suggestion of the author for uniting Railway Communication into a "System," as connecting lines are now called. On reaching the Surrey Iron Railway, at Wandsworth, where a train of carriages was drawn by one horse, Sir Richard says: "I thought of the millions which have been spent at Malta, four or five of which might have been the means of extending *double lines of iron railway* from London to Edinburgh, Glasgow, Holyhead, Milford, Falmouth, Yarmouth, Dover, and Portsmouth. A reward of a single thousand would have supplied coaches and other vehicles, of various degrees of speed, with the best tackle for readily turning out; and we might, ere this, have witnessed our mail-coaches running at the rate of ten miles an hour, drawn by a single horse, or *impelled fifteen miles an hour by Blenkinsop's steam-engine.*" This suggestion first appeared in 1813. It is not a little curious, that Sir Richard Phillips published, some ten years later, the first *Treatise on Railways*, by Nicholas Wood, of Killingworth, wherein the writer deprecates any attempt at a greater speed than fourteen miles an hour upon railways.

Sir Richard Phillips next remodelled his publishing establishment at Bridge-street: he had retained his *Monthly Magazine*, and soon created a new stock. Here, as became a literary publisher, Sir Richard formed a collection of original portraits of English authors and artists, including Chaucer, Dryden, Locke, Prior, Pope, Addison, Steele, Fielding, Churchill, and Richardson; Hogarth, Garrick, Wolcot, and Lady Mary Wortley Montague; besides a curious picture of the Great Fire of London; and a drawing of old Tunbridge Wells, engraved in Richardson's Correspondence; also a set of drawings of houses of celebrated men of letters, by Sam. Ireland; and a host of minor curiosities. One of the *penates* was a bronze cast of Canova's colossal bust of Napoleon I. at Apsley House.

The portrait of Chaucer was discovered by Sir Richard, in 1802, in a garret in the house in which Cromwell was born, at Huntingdon; the picture is thought to have been painted in the Low Countries, about twenty years before Chaucer's death;

the celebrated collector, Count Truchsess, conceived it to have been first painted in water-colours, and oiled afterwards for preservation; and he certified that the name Chaucer, in the background, was laid on with the painting. The drawing of old Tunbridge Wells is by Logan, the celebrated fan-painter; it has forty-seven portraits—of Dr. Johnson, Richardson, and their contemporaries, and is the only drawing of the artist's thought to be in existence. Logan was originally dwarf to the Prince of Wales.

It is now time to advert to a class of works which Sir Richard Phillips wrote and published from time to time, and in which he aspired to be known as the originator of a reformed system of Natural Philosophy, substituting matter and motion in place of what he termed "the superstitions and fancies" of attraction and repulsion, universal gravitation, caloric, fluids *per se*, &c. He was, in truth, so stanch an anti-Newtonian as to attack the conferring of three pensions by the Government merely because the recipients were advocates of the Newtonian philosophy. Thus, in 1835, he wrote to M. Arago: "A Cambridge professor last year published an elaborate volume in illustration of *Gravitation*, and on him has been conferred a pension of 300*l.* per annum. A lady has written a light popular view of the Newtonian dogmas, and she has been complimented by a pension of 200*l.* per annum. And another writer, who has recently published a volume to prove that the only true philosophy is that of Moses, has been endowed with a pension of 200*l.* per annum."

The volumes, pamphlets, and papers in which Sir Richard promulgated his views, seemed to be his relaxation from the cares of business; just as mathematics have proved the recreation of more than one of our learned masters of law. His protests, dialogues, and aphorisms showed his indomitable courage and honesty of purpose; and although he made few converts, he sought discussion with all thinkers—from the President of the Royal Society to the last seeker of perpetual motion. He was discredited in most quarters. Upon one of his text-books, *Essays on the Proximate Mechanical Causes of the General Phenomena of the Universe*, he was severely taken to task in the *Quarterly Review*, 1818. The chapter on Geological Changes in this work is most attractively written.

Among the controversialists of the great *Junius* question was Sir Richard Phillips, who at one period believed the *Letters* to have been written in Lansdowne House. It is, however, better established that oxygen was discovered here in August 1774, by Dr. Priestley, then librarian to the Earl of Shelburne, who is thought by some theorists to have written the famous *Letters* in conjunction with John Dunning afterwards Lord Ashburton, and Lieutenant-Colonel Barré. The late Mr. Britton believed in this joint authorship; and that a William Greatrakes, of Youghal, in Ireland, was the actual amanuensis. Mr. Britton published this "elucidation" of the enigma, with a mezzotint, after Sir Joshua Reynolds's three portraits, in one group, of Barré, Lord Shelburne, and Dunning; besides a vignette exhibiting, beneath the "mask" of "Junius," the face of Colonel Barré. The picture was painted for Sir Francis Baring, by Sir Joshua, in 1784-5, and is by some regarded as evidence of the joint authorship. However, Mr. Britton did little more than add to the number of speculators. Sir Richard Phillips, to our knowledge, wrote the following evidence in the *Anecdote Library*, published in 1822: "If any man of the time was in the secret, it was the first Marquis of Lansdowne; and he told Sir Richard Phillips, within a fortnight of his death, that, if he survived, he would publish all about it, and that the true author had never been named. Almon, said he, talks of Boyd; but what says Almon to Maclean? Now, it so happened that Lauchlin Maclean was, at one time, secretary to the Earl of Shelburne; was an active partisan of Wilkes (to whom he lent the sum of 600*l.*); was an able political writer; and, during a previous residence in America, had written some letters in a Philadelphia paper, in the identical style of Junius, though at the time alluded to he had never been named. Soon after Junius ceased to write, Maclean obtained an appointment in

India, and took his passage in a ship which was lost, with all on board; hence the secret of Junius and all the proofs were buried in the ocean." This reminds one of Theodore Hook putting an end to one of his stories by "an unexpected meeting"—a railway collision. To return to Junius. Only a week before his death, the Marquis of Lansdowne was personally appealed to on the authorship by Sir Richard Phillips. In conversation, his lordship said: "No, no; I am not equal to Junius; I could not be the author; but the grounds of secrecy are now so far removed by death" (Dunning and Barré were at the time dead) "and change of circumstances, that it is unnecessary the author of *Junius* should much longer be unknown. The world is curious about him, and I could make a very interesting publication upon the subject. I knew Junius, and I *know all about* the writing and production of these Letters." The Marquis added, "If I live over the summer, which, however, I don't expect, I promise you a very interesting pamphlet about Junius. I will put my name to it; I will set the question at rest for ever." The Marquis, however, died in May 1805. Some years later, in a letter to the *Monthly Magazine*, July 1813, the third Marquis of Lansdowne wrote: "It is not impossible my father may have been acquainted with the fact, but perhaps he was under some obligation of secrecy, as he never made any communication to me on the subject."

Sir Richard, however, was subsequently induced to alter his opinion, and to enlist in the belief of Dr. Wilmot having written the *Letters*, as maintained in the work published by Mrs. Elizabeth Wilmot Serres; for among Phillips's papers we find, in his handwriting: "Having seen a paper in the hand of the great John Dunning, in which he gives Dr. Wilmot permission to print, with Dr. W.'s *Junius*, his 'Letters of Philo-Junius,' I can have no doubt on the subject." This paper is accompanied by a pen-and-ink sketch of "the house, formerly St. John's Monastery (near Brampton), inhabited by Dr. Wilmot." Sir Richard also possessed a Ms. poem, *The Vices: a Satire*,—which was published by his son, Horatio Phillips, at

No. 3 Charing Cross, about 1829, as by the author of *Junius.* It bore, for a frontispiece, an engraved stanza from the Ms., and a portion of the *Junius* Ms., to prove the identity of the handwriting.

Sir Richard was a sexagenarian, when, in his own emphatic manner, he compared himself to "a burnt-out volcano;" and in 1823, after writing, editing, and supervising innumerable books, he disposed of a third share of his principal literary property, and retired, on a moderate competency, to Brighton, hoping there to pass the evening of his life, at least, in ease. Sir Richard, however, found "of making of books there is no end:" he projected fifteen volumes of Ana, which were delegated to five authors; while Phillips sat down to produce a *Dictionary of Facts and Knowledge;* and, in conjunction with Dr. Birkbeck, to announce two serial works of great extent, to be published by a "Society for the Diffusion of Useful Knowledge," 1825—this being the first announcement of such Society. Meanwhile, he had commenced his "Book of Facts," a volume of many hundred pages of small type, the success of which has given rise to scores of dictionaries and books of reference. The *Million of Facts* was first published in 1829, and is continued to the present day: a firm of Parisian *editeurs*, in 1842, produced *Un Million des Faits,* and have in its preface most ungratefully abused the work from which they had unblushingly stolen their title!

In 1826, Sir Richard published his *Golden Rules of Social Philosophy;* including those Rules for Magistrates, Sheriffs, Electors, Jurors, and Parish Priests,—which had been for many years before the public: of the Rules for Electors and Jurymen, half a million copies had been distributed. To these were now added, Golden Rules for Sovereign Princes and Members of the British Legislature; of Civil and Religious Liberty; for discriminating Truth in Human Inquiries; for Political and Social Economy; for Journalists, Bankers, Young Shopkeepers, and Instructors of Youth: in short, the Social Science of forty years ago. In his preface, the author points to the philosophers as the least tractable class. The book is full of speculation and practice, and is dedicated to "Simon Bolivar, the Liberator;" the author not having lost the feeling which led him, at the age of twenty, to sigh for the regeneration of Spanish America:

E'en in our ashes live their wonted fires.

Sir Richard evidently had bestowed much care and thought upon his *Social Philosophy.* He wrote to a friend at Paris, even amid the turmoil of the Panic: "Send l'Abbé Grégoire my *Social Philosophy.* It was for such men that I wrote the book; *not* for the mercenary scribblers of my own country, &c. Drop a tear for me on the tomb of my friend Volney, in the Père la Chaise; and I must come to Paris to die, that I may lie near him. How superior is the profession of letters in France to its condition in England! there it is for glory—here for pelf."

Sir Richard had scarcely finished this volume, when the social earthquake—the panic of 1826—gravely affected his fortunes: two banking-houses, with which he was connected, stopped on the same day; and, to complete the disaster, one of his agents was involved in the common ruin. Sir Richard hastened to London, and found it a pandemonium. Several opulent banks had been run down by the public frenzy on that day; and commercial houses of established credit had stopped payment by scores. The panic spread over the nation; and the stoppage of fourscore country banking establishments ruined or paralysed traders, agriculturists, and manufacturers. He proceeded to the Bank of England, and suggested measures to its directors; he wrote to the Minister, pressing the issue of Exchequer-bills, —but all in vain. He lost by this revulsion between 40,000*l.* and 50,000*l.*; but he bore his reverse of fortune with equanimity, and blamed not his debtors, but the Ministry and Parliament of the time.

At Brighton Sir Richard found much congenial society, as a relief to his literary toil; for he was now actively engaged in revising his constantly-printed elementary books; his *Million of Facts,* and other works. One of his connections was Richard Ironmonger, the old friend of Sheridan: he had long resided at Brighton, and was an active magistrate. He was returned to Parliament for Stafford, but did not live to take his seat; and it is remarkable that Sheridan's election-defeat at Stafford unquestionably hastened his death. Mr. Ironmonger had promised Sir Richard Phillips some information for the Life of Sheridan, which Mr. Moore was just about completing; the poet, accordingly, proceeded by appointment to Brighton, which Ironmonger had quitted on the same day for London: Moore was hospitably received by Phillips; but, in his *Diary*, probably annoyed by Ironmonger's absence, he exhibits ungenerous feelings towards his host, who had been equally disappointed.

In the summer of 1828, Sir Richard, considering, like a namesake, that

> He who by the plough would thrive,
> Himself must either hold or drive,

started upon a tour through the United Kingdom, to introduce to preceptors and preceptresses his interrogative system of teaching without answers: his reception was extremely gratifying; and the Journal of his Tour, as far as published, presents the social aspects of the counties through which he journeyed, in a manner at once entertaining and useful for its information, collected with manifest advantages. The work was published by the author's younger son, who had commenced business at Charing Cross, with promise of support from the Useful Knowledge Society, but which was not realised. Incidental to his Tour, Sir Richard collected much curious information; as in his visit to the house, formerly John's Monastery, inhabited by Dr. Wilmot (Junius), who, it is stated in a Ms. found among Sir Richard's papers, married Prince George, in 1759, to the Fair Quakeress; and, in 1767, Wilmot married Henry Frederick, Duke of Cumberland, though much against his will, to his own daughter. Wilmot was born in 1714, and had been an associate of Bolingbroke, Glover, Thomson, Mallet, Hammond, and others in the Court of Frederick, at whose funeral, in 1751, Wilmot was chief-mourner. We have already alluded to Sir Richard's having seen Dunning's written permission to Dr. Wilmot to print with his (Dr. W.'s) *Junius* the "Letters of Philo-Junius." The mystery about the *Junius* Ms., says Phillips, is solvable by considering that Dr. Wilmot had an accomplished sister, wife of Captain Payne, who wrote just such a neat character as that in which *Junius* is penned; and that Wilmot's own hand had been spoiled by scribbling school-exercises, &c. He wrote verse as well as prose: the Ms. of the Preface to the *Heroic Epistle to Sir William Chambers* (which Sir Richard possessed) is in the handwriting of Dr. Wilmot; while a list of persons to whom presentation-copies were to be sent is in a character, not of *Junius*, but more like it. Wilmot is stated to have called upon Almon, the publisher, with the Ms. of the Epistle, at night, in a mask. Almon could not trace him; but, as he was of clerical mien, the publisher fixed on Dr. Mason, one of the King's chaplains: hence the Heroic Epistle was attributed to Mason, author of the *English Garden*, &c. Ten thousand copies of the Epistle were sold in a month; and who but a man of Junius's feelings could have kept the secret? In Wilmot's tall, commanding person we recognise the tall clergyman who put the Letter of *Junius* into Woodfall's letter-box, as well as the same person in the interview with Almon. And, in Wilmot's connection with the Duke of Cumberland, Lord Chatham, and Wilkes, we trace the means of his accurate information and perfect political views. Sir Richard learned at Warwick that Wilmot had been blind seven years before his death, but that his mind was vigorous to the last. Shortly before he died (aged ninety-two), he caused a cart-load of letters and papers to be burnt by his servants; a few he confided to Lord Warwick, and others to his grand-daughter; but still, in the spirit of *Junius*, sealed, and not to be opened till after the death of George III. Phillips examined these papers, which he maintained should have been brought before Parliament; but they were "written down."

Sir Richard continued in literary activity almost to his last year; he retained much of his copyright property, especially his educational books, which, to this day, are used in many schools. His aptitude as a *raconteur* was very remarkable: he would walk about his dining-room by the hour, dictating to his amanuensis with such regularity and sequence of detail, that his narrative scarcely required any correction in printing; with most persons, dictation begets an involved manner, a sort of parenthetical habit, which is any thing but perspicuous: he had, moreover, an amanuensis who paid special attention to punctuation, which Sir Richard himself could not reduce to practice. To his talent as a *raconteur* we owe the first account which appeared of Andrew Crosse's experiences at Fyne Court, on the Quantock Hills, in Somersetshire. He worked alone in this retreat until 1836, when, at the Meeting of the British Association at Bristol, he was induced to explain his experiments, and gave to the Meeting a general invitation to Fyne Court; one of the first to accept which was Sir Richard Phillips, who, on his return to Brighton, described in a very attractive manner, at the Sussex Institution, Mr. Crosse's experiments and apparatus; a long report of which being communicated to the *Brighton Herald*, it was quoted in the *Literary Gazette*, and thence copied generally into the newspapers of the day. Sir Richard described Crosse's apparatus for measuring, collecting, and operating with atmospheric electricity; he collected it by wires, extended from pole to pole, or tree to tree, in his grounds and park, the wires being insulated by glass tubes, and connected with a controlling apparatus. Sometimes the current was so great as to charge and discharge the great battery of 50 jars, and 73 square feet of coating, twenty times in a minute, with reports as loud as cannon.

In the spring of 1838, Sir Richard wrote to John Britton, another hard worker in the field of letters: "Your friendly letter was a ray of sunshine on a very dull day. You struck out for yourself a path of literary renown, and I am quite sure you have reached the summit. For my own part, my pursuits have been so diversified for the last twenty years, that I had almost forgotten one of my literary children, *The Walk to Kew*. Your approbation I value, because on such a subject you are a first-rate judge. You must have read fifty such works; I never read one: therefore, in my mind, there is no element of comparison. I had no design of the book when I took the walk, and my notes were very scanty."

In the autumn of 1839, we last called upon Sir Richard at Brighton. We found the old bookmaker—he always maintained that Euclid was but a bookmaker—full of years and memories, but infirm in health. We talked over various matters; and he summed up his long life, saying he was "past crying for the cake." There was the old study, well filled with books and papers; but the master seemed to have done his work. * * * * He died in the spring following, in his seventy-second year, attended by his devoted wife and family. His remains were interred near the north-west corner of the old church at Brighton, whence they have been removed to the new cemetery, with the altar-tomb, which bears the following inscription:

Here rest the Remains of
SIR RICHARD PHILLIPS, KNT.,
Born December 13, 1767; died April 2, 1840.

He lived through an age of memorable events and changes, and was an active and anxious contemporary. He was Sheriff of London and Middlesex in 1807-8, and an effective ameliorator of a stern and uncharitable Criminal Code. He was, in 1798, the inventor and promulgator of the Interrogative System of Education, by which new impulses were given to the intelligence of society. He also placed Natural Philosophy on the basis of common sense, and developed the laws of Nature on immutable principles, which will always be coextensive with the respect of mankind for truth. In the promotion of these objects, and a multitude of others, he wrote and published more original works than any of his contemporaries; and in all of these advocated Civil Liberty, General Benevolence, Ascendency of Justice, and the Improvement of the Human Race.

As a Son, Husband, Father, and Friend, he was also an example for imitation; and left a mourning family little to inherit besides his good name.

There is a fine gallery-portrait of Sir Richard Phillips in his Sheriff's robes, painted by Saxon; and his bust by Turnerelli, which is engraved on the frontispiece to the *Million of Facts.*

With a few miscellaneous details, we conclude.

In his twelfth year, Sir Richard conceived an abhorrence to

the slaughter of animals; and from that period lived entirely on vegetable products, enjoying such robust health that no stranger could have suspected his studious and sedentary habits. He has published his "Reasons for not eating Animal Food."* It has been jocosely said of him, that although he would not eat animal food, he was addicted to gravy over his potatoes. Sometimes the Pythagorean principle was more strongly enunciated; as, when about to take his seat at a supper-party, perceiving a lobster on the table, he strongly denounced the cruelty of his friends sitting down to eat a creature which had been boiled alive; and the offensive dish had to be removed.

Notwithstanding Sir Richard's discrimination, and usually true estimate of the public taste, he missed several prizes in the publishers' wheel-of-fortune. He used to relate his interview with Lord Byron with a view to the publication of his early poems; the offer of the copyright of *Waverley*, from a connection of Sir Walter Scott; he was one of the many publishers who refused Bloomfield's *Farmer's Boy*, offered to him by the author for a dozen copies; and he declined O'Meara's *Napoleon in Exile*, of which several editions were sold within twelve months. Nevertheless, Sir Richard was considerate to young authors; and the writer of these Recollections was mainly indebted to his "lines of fair encouragement," at a period which proved the turning-point of his course of life. That our publisher was often made the dupe of ingratitude and dishonesty should not be forgotten in estimating his help to men of letters.

Among Sir Richard's papers, we find an account of his acquaintance with S. T. Coleridge, whom he first heard of as a political lecturer at Birmingham and other places, in 1795. On the same day that the first number of the *Monthly Magazine* appeared, Coleridge also commenced his *Friend:* the antagonism was disagreeable; for, says Phillips, the *Friend* "absorbed the papers and poetry of several persons who might have been useful to me." Of the *Monthly Magazine*, No. 1, there were sold 3000

* The "Reasons" are twenty-two in number, and occupy ten pages of the *Social Philosophy*.

copies; of the *Friend*, 100 or 200. The rival editors met at a dinner-party at Bristol, where Coleridge's harangues were so persistent, that, in five or six hours, the rest of the company only edged in occasionally for a few minutes, while the orator took breath. Some three years afterwards, Coleridge undertook to prepare, by Phillips's suggestion, Specimens of the English Poets, prefaced by original critiques, for which the writer was to receive 100*l.*, two-thirds of which were paid in advance. The copy of the work was not supplied: in two years, after law proceedings, the money was refunded through Dr. Stoddart, and the *Specimens* were then announced for publication by Longman and Co., by Robert Southey, brother-in-law of Coleridge, and residing with him in Cumberland. In twenty-five years more, Phillips and Coleridge met at Highgate; and after some recrimination, Sir Richard visited Samuel Taylor at Mr. Gilman's; where, the *Social Philosophy* being named, as Phillips was leaving, Coleridge bawled out—"Was it written under the grace of God?" The one estimated the frothy harangues and metaphysics of the other at a very low rate; and his poetry Phillips valued at a like level, the best piece being, in his opinion, the Ode to Pitt, containing the line—

Letters four do spell his name.

We have already alluded to the Useful Knowledge Society, to the plan of which Sir Richard lays claim in the following statement, found among his papers, in his own handwriting:

"During my tour, I frequently found on chairs and tables the Sixpenny Tracts of the Society, which has assumed the office of propagator of Useful Knowledge. There was a plausibility in the idea which conferred credit on its labours; and a list of the Committee, including many of the most intelligent men in the kingdom, has added to the plausibility. The idea of such sixpennyworths of knowledge, and of a Society to give them sanction, and, above all, as a security from the craft of trade, was *all my own.* I communicated it, in July 1825, to Mr. Brougham; and it was afterwards formed under circumstances which conferred on him the applause of certain flatterers, of whom he and I think alike. This little knot concocted the Society, and, in spite of the array of Committees, have since conducted it."*

Sir Richard also stoutly maintained that the very successful *Percy Anecdotes* originated in a suggestion made by him to Dr. Tilloch and Mr. Mayne,—to select the anecdotes from the many years' files of the *Star* newspaper, of which Dr. Tilloch was then editor, and Mr. Thomas Byerley (the Reuben Percy of the authorship) was assistant-editor; and to the latter overhearing the suggestion, Phillips contended, might the *Percy Anecdotes* be traced. Byerley died in 1824; he was the first editor of the *Mirror*, commenced by John Limbird in 1822. Sholto Percy was Joseph Clinton Robertson, who died in 1852; he was the projector and editor throughout of the *Mechanics' Magazine.* The name of the collection of anecdotes was not taken from the popularity of the *Percy Reliques*, but from the Percy Coffee-house, in Rathbone-place, where Byerley and Robertson were accustomed to meet to talk over their joint work. The *Star* was then an evening paper, notable for its anecdotic gossip.

Sir Richard Phillips left, in manuscript, a Memoir of his Life, brought up to a period within twenty years of his decease. This incomplete Memoir has not been printed. Sir Richard also left miscellaneous papers, principally relating to his "Personal Tour," which are in the possession of his grandson and representative, Mr. Bacon Phillips, of Brighton.

* This hasty note must not be understood to convey any reflection upon the conduct of Mr. Brougham in the above arrangement. The date, 1825, corresponds with the first announcement of the Society, named at page 115.

CURIOSITIES OF FISHMONGERS' HALL.

MANY a pleasant page is to be gleaned from the wide field of the history of our great City, in which the Guilds and Companies were formerly the lords paramount. In the present day we hear most of these Companies through the extension of their festivities to public men:

> Implentur veteris Bacchi, pinguisque ferinæ;

and in the plenitude of the Present the interest of the Past is lost sight of; reminding us that "they who care nothing for their ancestors, care little for their posterity—indeed, little for any thing but themselves." It must not, however, be forgotten that, the chief motives for the establishment of the City Companies were, the due regulation of trade; the combination of individuals for the protection of their rights; the charitable relief of distressed members; the cultivation of social intercourse; and the observance of religious rites for the benefit of the souls of deceased members and their families. Five centuries have rolled away since the Fishmongers, now one of the oldest and wealthiest of the Twelve Great Companies, of which it is fourth in rank, were incorporated. The Fishmongers were, however, among the earliest guilds. Two centuries previously we trace them by amercement in the reign of Henry II. A charter was granted them by Edward I. in his first year, this being the earliest statute relative to fish: it prohibited partnership in fish with foreigners, and ordained that none should store it up in cellars to retail afterwards at exorbitant rates, or buy before the King's purveyors had made their choice; and no fish were to be kept after the second day, on pain of losing the fish, or being fined at the King's pleasure. The fishmonger's profit allowed was one penny in the shilling. No fish was to be sold in-doors, nor watered a second time. For the first and second offences the fishmonger was to be fined, and for the third "jugyd to a pair of stockys openly in the market-place." In Edward's reign he fined the Fishmongers 500 marks for forestalling; which led to a fresh rule—that no fish was to be sold before being landed, and only to be sold after mass, and salt-fish after first bell. The Guild grew rich; and upon the return of Edward I., after his victory over the Scots, they eclipsed other trades in the passage of the King through the City; the Fishmongers having in their show gilt sturgeons and silver salmon, and a thousand armed knights on horseback.

The reign of Edward II. proved troublesome to the Fishmongers, notwithstanding the good services of Walworth, their distinguished member. In 1332, Parliament enacted that "no Fishmonger should be admitted Mayor of this City;" but this prohibition was removed next year, and they were allowed to sell fish in Stock Fish-row, now first mentioned.

In the time of Edward III., 1363, the Fishmongers proved their relative importance by giving to the King 40*l.* towards carrying on his French wars; the Mercers, the highest company, only giving 41*l.*; and, in 1365, the Mercers and the Fishmongers gave the same sum of ten marks. By the Great Charter of five hundred years ago, the Fishmongers were incorporated anew, under the title of the Mystery of the Fishmongers of London; and to them was given the right of overseeing the crying and selling of fish, which was only to be sold in three places—Bridge-street (now Fish-street-hill); Old Fish-street, near St. Paul's; and a place called "The Stocks," now the site of the Mansion House: no one might meddle with the fish-trade unless he was free of the Fishmongers' Company, and was also of the "Fish Inquest;" and all fish must be sold between Billingsgate and London-bridge; or, if above Bridge, between Dribble Wharf and Fresh Fish Wharf, to be warehoused by clear day and not by night; and not sold, excepting before a Fishmonger, in order that the King might be served at proper price.

It should here be explained, that there were originally two guilds, Salt Fishmongers and Stock Fishmongers, and they continued separate for many years; but were united in the reign of Henry VI., severed in the reign of Henry VII., and finally reunited in the reign of Henry VIII., and have so continued to the present time. At the last-named period, they agreed that so long as the name of Stock Fishmongers should last, two of them should be admitted Joint Wardens with the four Wardens of the Fishmongers, thus accounting for the present number of six Wardens in the united Company. The indenture of Henry VIII. enumerates a yearly payment of 40*s.* for the distribution of coals among the poor of the two Companies; and 3*l.* to be spent in recreation or feasting for both. The preamble recites the clause obliging Fishmongers to follow their own trade; because all sorts of people, freemen as well as aliens, and freemen of other Mysteries, went with the Fishmongers to buy up fish at fairs, and so greatly raised its price that they could not deal; and nothing could, in consequence, be bought or sold at reasonable rates.

Curious are these details of the trade and mystery, and the regulations extending even to the crying of fish. The old rules provide that the apprentices "shall not suffer their hair to grow long," and "shall wear gowns in the fish-market, but not out of it." Henry III., to increase the Queen's custom at Queenhithe, ordered all fish to be landed at that port; and this led to the establishment of the great London fish-market in Bread-street Ward. It is described by Stow as commencing with movable stalls, set out with fish on market-days, whence they grew to shops, and to tall houses, three and four storeys in height; a Fishmonger Mayor had here, in 1349, two shops, one rented at 3*s.* and the other at 4*s.*; this market occupying a plot of ground lengthwise, along Old Fish-street, from Bread-street to the Church opposite, St. Mary Magdalen. Knightrider-street was, in these early times, famous for fish and fish-dinners; and Friday-street, from fishmongers dwelling there, and serving the Friday market of Roman Catholic times. Sir William Davenant, who was a boy when Shakspeare lived, describes Old Fish-street as so narrow that neighbours could shake hands from the garret-windows across the street. This street was noted for its taverns and signs; and tokens exist of the sign of Henry VII., and Will Somers, Henry VIII.'s jester. Another tavern had the head of Wolsey for a sign; and Aubrey says, the Cardinal had here a stately cellar for his wines. In the reign of Edward II., some of the principal dealers removed to Bridge-street, which market communicated with Billingsgate; but they occupied other stations, as Fish Wharf, Oyster-gate Wharf, Stock-fish-row, and Eastcheap. In Bridge-street, at one time, lived "the topping men and merchants of the trade." The interments of wealthy Fishmongers are numerous in the registers of St. Magnus, and St. Botolph, Billingsgate. St. Michael's was a general burial-place of Stock Fishmongers: the church was founded and enlarged by Lovekyn and Walworth, Mayors, who are buried here.

Thus we see that the Company of Fishmongers was formerly one of the most numerous and powerful of the ancient Liveries of London. As early as the days of Edward III., it equalled the Goldsmiths in riches, and the Mercers in numbers; and carried on a keen rivalry with the Skinners, whom the then fashion of wearing costly furs had brought into what the old Fishmongers thought a premature and undeserved importance. This rivalry led to serious results; for in one little difficulty as to precedence, in Cheapside, many of both Companies were killed outright, and many more executed afterwards for their share in the desperate affray. Indeed, so bitter was the feud, that even the lubricating influence of dinners, by making the Companies dine together alternately, was tried in vain; and it was not till the Fishmongers carried their point, and were allowed their places "in Paul's, next the Grocers, towards the image of our Lady of Grace," that the matter was finally settled. Such haughty independence was not altogether unbecoming in a Company which virtually made the laws that preserved and kept the shoals of fish with which the Thames then teemed; and who had to see that "no fish-spears nor angle-rods with more than two hooks" were used, nor nets allowed nearer London Bridge than the Old Swan Inn on the north side, and St. Mary Overey's on the south, whereby both salmon and other fish may not be hindered from swimming upwards."

The Company, five centuries ago, were not unmindful of the value of records, when they conferred an honorary membership upon Andrew Horn, citizen and Fishmonger, the compiler of the famous Guildhall muniment, *Liber Horn.* He rose to the rank of Chamberlain of the City; was a scholar, antiquary, and book-collector to no small extent, for the fourteenth century. He died in 1328, and bequeathed to the Corporation of the City six great volumes of history, laws, and civic antiquities, denoting the patriotic and archæological zeal of this literary Fishmonger of the days of Edward III. A portion of the *Liber Horn* has been translated and edited by Mr. H. T. Riley, M.A.

The admirable order in which the records of the Company are kept at the Hall to the present day, and the good taste shown in the preservation of the memorials of the Fishmongers, show them to have inherited the regard with which their ancient fellow-citizen, Horn, viewed such matters.

The Companies of the Salt Fish-and Stock Fish-mongers were anciently possessed of as many as six Halls—one for each Company, in New Fish-street, Old Fish-street, and Thames-street. These, however, were all united in the year 1536, the 28th of Henry VIII.; after which, they had but one Hall, namely, the House given them by Sir John Cornwall, in 1427, the 6th year of Henry VI.: to this the Fishmongers attached other erections, forming a quadrangle, with a Tudor embattled front to the river; the dining-hall crossing the quadrangle had a high roof like that of Westminster Hall, whence was suspended the largest pageant, as shown in Hollar's View "before the Fire." Stow describes it as standing about midway between the Bridge-foot and Ebgate, or Old Swan-lane. This Hall was almost entirely destroyed in the Great Fire, when

> A key of fire ran all along the shore,
> And frighten'd all the river with a blaze.

We see the actual damage in Hollar's Long View of the City, immediately after the conflagration. A new Hall was built by

Jarman, surveyor to the Company, and not by Sir Christopher Wren, as stated by Elmes, and others; which misstatement may have arisen from its being "according to Wren's splendid plan for adorning the banks of the Thames." Jarman's claim as the architect is confirmed by the Fishmongers' Court-books, from which we gather that the Hall was completely finished in June 1671; and Alderman Lawes, who was then Prime Warden, having just been elected one of the sheriffs, was voted the use of the Hall "for the service of his shrievalty." It was a long red-brick edifice, with stone window-cases; a grand double flight of stone steps led from the river-bank to the chief apartments; the door-way was decorated with Ionic columns, a pediment, and shield of the Company's arms, which were repeated in the large pediment in the centre of the edifice. Such was the river-front. The cellars were let as "Wine Shades," from the year 1697, the entrance being from the quay: here "the citizens drank their genuine old port and sherry, drawn from the casks, and viewed the bridge-shooters and boat-racers."

The principal entrance to the edifice was by a gateway in Thames-street, over which were boldly sculptured in stone the Company's arms: the Hall extended nearly the whole length of the building; its ceiling, as well as that of the adjoining Court-room, was fine old plaster-work. The state chambers were hung with rare paintings of fish, and rich chandeliers. We remember in the upper end of the Hall, in a niche, was the full-sized statue, carved in wood by Edward Pierce, of Sir William Walworth, Fishmonger and Mayor, who stabbed Wat Tyler, the rebel, with a dagger, said to be that in the hand of the statue; though a publican of Islington pretended to possess the actual weapon, and, in 1731, lent it to be exhibited at Bartholomew Fair. Beneath the statue was an inscription, certifying Richard II. having given "the dagger to the City arms;" where, however, it represented, long before the time of Sir William Walworth, the sword of St. Paul, the patron saint of the Corporation. The dagger formerly in the hand of the statue, without its guard, is preserved by the Company; the workmanship is of Walworth's period. Upon the rebuilding of London Bridge, the Hall was taken down, the Corporation paying 20,000*l.* to the Company. We remember the dismantling of the premises: the long dining-tables, which had so long groaned beneath the weight of civic fare; the high-backed chairs of the court-room, which had held many a portly citizen—nay, the huge dripping-pans, the soup-kettles, and venison-dishes—all passed under the noisy ordeal of the auction hammer. The "Wine Shades" was then removed to the premises of Alderman Garratt, who, as Lord Mayor, in 1825, laid the first stone of the new bridge.

Nearly upon the same site, with the addition of a piece of ground purchased at the rate of 630,000*l.* per acre, was erected the present Hall, from a design by Roberts, 1830-3. It is a stately edifice, raised upon a lofty basement, and has the finest situation in the metropolis. The view of the Thames eastward, with its forest of shipping, is eminently suggestive of the source of our country's greatness.

The entrance-hall has polished Aberdeen granite columns. Upon the staircase is the statue of Walworth, already described, which, when in the former hall, was gaudily coloured; it is now tinted to imitate stone, and the dagger it carries is of wood. Above this statue is a gilt figure of St. Peter, the patron saint of the Company; it was formerly placed at the head of their barge. Here also are whole-length portraits of William III. and his Queen, by Murray; and George II. and Queen, by Shackleton. In the spacious room northward is a large portrait of the Margrave of Anspach, who was a member of the Company; and opposite is that of the Margravine of Anspach. The banqueting-hall has Sienna scagliola Corinthian pilasters, between which are emblazoned the arms of the benefactors and past Prime Wardens of the Company. At one end of the Hall are the royal arms, and opposite those of the Fishmongers, in stained glass. On the front of the music-gallery are emblazoned the arms of the City and twelve great Companies; and in the centre are judiciously placed the elaborately-carved arms and insignia, removed from the Company's barge when their river state was given up. Here also are portraits of the Duke of Kent (freeman of the Company), by Beechey; and Queen Victoria, by Herbert Smith, presented by the influence of the late Prince Consort, who was also a freeman. The heraldic insignia, though novel in a Grecian hall, are very striking, especially when the room is lighted up by gas.

In the southern ante-room is a fine portrait of Earl St. Vincent (the Admiral, and a freeman), by Beechey; and among the banners of the Company is preserved the old flag presented to Lord St. Vincent by the crew of the *Ville de Paris;* the shot-holes in the flag have been darned over and repaired. In the Court dining-room is a splendid silver chandelier, weighing 1330 ounces. This beautiful work has a little history, which is recorded in the minutes of the Company. It appears that a silver chandelier was first manufactured for the Fishmongers, which, through the information of one of the workmen, was found to be *loaded* inside the scroll-work of the branches, &c. with *copper:* this, as the work was charged by weight, was a fraud, of which the minutes record the detection—how first one scroll was examined, then another, and at length the entire chandelier assayed by the Goldsmiths' Company; and, eventually, another chandelier of the same design was made entirely of silver, in place of the copper-loaded one. This is a very fine piece of metal-work of the year 1754.

The Curiosities in the several apartments are specially interesting, as a sort of pictorial museum of the history of the Company. In a glass-case is the dagger of Sir William Walworth. Similarly encased is the funeral-pall of Walworth: the sides are worked in gold, with the Saviour giving the keys to St. Peter; and at the ends are the Deity and ministering angels. This pall, or hearse-cloth, is finely engraved by Shaw, and described by Miss Lambert in her volume on Needlework. Above the pall hangs an original drawing of a portion of the pageant exhibited by the Company, Oct. 29, 1616, when Sir John Leman, a Fishmonger, entered on the office of Lord Mayor. The groups and objects, grotesque as well as picturesque, in this procession, show our present realisation of a Lord Mayor's Show to be but a very frigid and formal business. Beneath the picture hangs a drawing of the Company's state barge, whose "golden glister" on the fishful river now exists but in memory. Here, too, are eight curious pictures of fish, by Spiridione Roma, skilfully grouped and correctly coloured; also, are paintings, by Scott, of Old London Bridge and the Custom-house Quay, about a century since; besides drawings of the old and present London Bridge; engravings and drawings of Gresham's School at Holt (lately rebuilt); and the Company's almshouses, St. Peter's Hospital, at Newington and Wandsworth—all interesting memorials of the Fishmongers' munificence, past and present; and here appropriately is placed a portrait of the octogenarian Mr. Towse, thus honoured for his many years' faithful service as clerk to the Company.

The presidential chair of the Prime Warden (the Fishmongers have not a Master) is a relic of Old London Bridge, and commemorative of the new one; bridge piers form the angles, arches support the seats, and across the back are carved the old and present London Bridges and other Thames bridges. The story of the chair is thus told on a silver plate in the back: "This chair was made by J. Ovenston, 72 Great Titchfield-street, London, from a design given by the Rev. William Jolliffe, Curate of Colmer, in Hampshire; and it was made entirely from the wood and stone taken up from the foundation of Old London Bridge, in July 1832, having remained there 656 years; being put down, in June 1176, by the builder, Peter, a priest, who was Vicar of Colechurch; and 'tis rather curious that a priest should begin the bridge, and, after so long a period, that a parson should clear it entirely away." Upon the seat of the chair is incised: "I am part of the first stone that was put down for the foundation of Old London Bridge, in June 1176, by a priest named Peter, who was Vicar of Colechurch, in London; and I remained there undisturbed, safe on the same oak piles this chair is made from, till the Rev. William John Jolliffe, Curate of Colmer,

Hampshire, took me up in July 1832, when clearing away the old Bridge, after new London Bridge was completed."

St. Peter's Hospital, at Newington, was founded about two centuries and a half since; it had a handsome dining-hall, richly emblazoned with arms. Well do we remember its formal gardens, the statue in the grounds adjoining, the little chapel, the snug almshouses, and the old almspeople in the walks; the site is now partly occupied by Mr. Spurgeon's Tabernacle.

These are but a few of the illustrations of the history of the Fishmongers' Company. Too much praise can scarcely be awarded for the care taken of the antiquities as well as the commemorations of the more distinguished members of the Company; their heraldic honours shine in every direction. Although, in the long vista of years at which we have glanced, times and customs have strangely changed, and trade is no longer fettered by regulations formerly indispensable, the Fishmongers' statutes have not entirely fallen into desuetude: they had power, in early times, "to enter and seize bad fish;" and to this day, two inspectors are employed by the Company, and report to the Court the number of unwholesome fish destroyed. The Charter by which the Company is now governed was granted in the reign of James I. The property of the Fishmongers has, by bequests and judicious management, greatly increased in value; and it is gratifying to add, that the Charity Commissioners, at their latest visitation, bore testimony to the excellent administration of the funds of the Company. Curious it is to look back at the empty enactment of 500 years since, "that no Fishmonger be Lord Mayor of this City," and contrast it with the records which show that more than fifty of the Company have been Lord Mayors. Stow tells us of "these Fishmongers having been jolly citizens, and six Mayors of their Company in the space of twenty-four years;" and in our time, Sir Matthew Wood and Mr. W. Cubitt, Fishmongers, each filled the civic chair twice.

On Feb. 12, 1863, the Prince of Wales took the first step towards becoming a member of the Corporation of the City of London by taking up his freedom of the Worshipful Company of Fishmongers, of which his Royal Highness' father and grandfather were also freemen. On July 10, 1864, the Company had been incorporated 500 years: the day was Sunday; and on Tuesday following, the event was celebrated by a festival at Fishmongers' Hall, when the Prime Warden, James Spicer, Esq., narrated to the party an interesting *précis* of the history of the Company, showing them to have grown in wealth, and alike maintained their dignity and state, and ministered to the support of their less fortunate brethren; so that the fifth century of the Company's existence was a fit event for commemoration.

We have described the Old Fish Market; and it may be interesting to add, that in the autumn of 1854 was discovered, in the house at the corner of Lambeth-hill, at the west end of the above street, a curious relic of its ancient fishful appropriation. During some alterations in the house, the rubbish of many years, accumulated in the cellar, was cleared out, and a quantity of the earth removed, when some vaulting was found. Its existence had been long talked of: the former tenant of the house called it "a chapel," although he used the place as a cellar; and here it should be remarked, that the trade of the old fishmongers in this part of the town was often carried on in *cellar-shops*. The place thus discovered consisted of a suite of vaulted chambers, communicating with each other, one of which contained a raised seat, canopied, and in part perfect; in the side recesses were stone slabs, fixed with strong iron clamps; and in one was a marble trough, which, from its peculiar form, suggested that it was used for the total immersion of the infant in baptism. The roof was curiously vaulted, and, with the walls and canopied seat, was richly decorated with polished marine shells, fragments of old glass; and pieces of quartz crystal and calcareous spar, cut into patterns or devices. The place resembled a grotto in the *rococo* taste of the last century; but tradition points to the appropriation of the vault at a much earlier period. Bishop Bonner is said to have lived in the house; probably from the suspicion that the vault was a secret chapel of the bigoted prelate.

Some elucidation has been suggested from the following passage in a volume entitled, *The Antiquities of London and Westminster*: "Upon Paul's-wharf-hill, within a great gate, and belonging to that gate next to Doctors' Commons, are many fair tenements, that in the leases went by the name of 'Camera Dianæ,' or 'Diana's Chamber'—so denominated from a spacious building that, in the time of Henry II., stood in Ship-place. In this *camera*, or arched and vaulted structure, full of intricate ways and windings, Henry II., as sometimes he did at Woodstock, kept (or was supposed to have kept) that jewel of his heart, Fair Rosamond—she whom there he called 'Rosa mundi;' and here Diana, and hence had this house that title. To this day are remains and some evident testifications of tedious turnings and windings; as also a passage underground to Castle Baynard, which was, no doubt, the King's way to his Camera Dianæ." Now, a passage has been traced into an adjoining vault, in the direction where Baynard Castle formerly stood. The walls of this adjoining portion are of great thickness and strength. We are compelled to add, that "Fair Rosamond" is even a more speculative guess than "Bishop Bonner," as the tenant of this fantastic place; but the above quotation is not without its value. We rather incline to the opinion expressed in the *Literary Gazette* at the time of the *find*—that these vaults were the scene of Roman-Catholic rites, when the priests of the old religion were proscribed, and people were forbidden to harbour them under heavy penalties. The decoration of the roof and walls may be of later date; or, probably, some devoutly-disposed Fishmonger of the Roman-Catholic times may have executed the shell-work designs, the materials for which lay at hand, or he had ready means of procuring. Be this as it may, the place is curious and suggestive, especially when we recollect that there scarcely exists in the metropolis a more interesting locality than the above spot.

There is a pleasing episode in the Fishmongers' history, which should not be passed over; such is—

THE STORY OF DOGGET, HIS COAT AND BADGE.

The first of August has been *a red-letter day* on the Thames for nearly a century and a half, or since the first Anniversary of the Accession of King George I.—when Thomas Dogget, "a Whig up to head and ears," in demonstration of his loyalty to the House of Hanover, first gave a waterman's orange-coloured coat, and silver badge of the Hanoverian horse, to be rowed for by six young watermen, whose apprenticeship on the Thames expired the year before. Dogget, a loyal Irishman, was born in Castle-street, Dublin, date uncertain (Cunningham says, 1670). He is described as "a little, lively, spract man, who danced the *Cheshire Round* full as well as the famous Captain George, but with more nature and nimbleness." He made his first appearance at the Dublin Theatre; thence he "strolled" into the provinces, came to England, and rose to be manager of a company, when each member wore a brocaded waistcoat, and kept his own horse, on which he rode from town to town. Dogget made his first bow in London at Bartholomew Fair, by the bill, "at Barker and Dogget's booth, near Hosier-lane end," in "a new droll, called Friar Bacon, or the Country Justice; with the Humours of Tollfree, the Miller, and his Son Ralph, acted by Mr. Dogget. With variety of scenes, machines, songs, and dances. *Vivat Rex!* 1691" (Dr. Rimbault; *Notes and Queries*, 2d S., No. 177).

Dogget was first brought into notice by his clever performance of Solon, in D'Urfey's comedy of *The Marriage-hater Match'd*, acted in 1692. He must have been a capital low-comedy actor; for old Downes, the prompter, informs us that Dogget "wore a farce in his face." Cibber's *Apology* tells of him as an actor and manager previous to the last seven years of his life. Dogget wrote one comedy, the *Country Wake*, of his performance in which Steele says, in the *Spectator:* "There is something so miraculously pleasant in Dogget's acting the awkward triumph and comic sorrow of Hob, in different circumstances, that I shall not be able to stay away whenever it is acted." By a paper of Addison's, also in the *Spectator*, Dogget would appear to have excelled in grave or elderly men—as aldermen, knights and baronets, country squires, and justices of the quorum. He was, in stage phrase, an *excellent dresser:* he could be extremely ridiculous, but knew exactly when and where to stop the current of his jokes. He could paint his face to resemble any age, from manhood to extreme senility, which caused Sir Godfrey Kneller to say that Dogget excelled him in his own art; for *he* could only copy nature from the originals before him, while the actor could vary them at pleasure, and yet always preserve a true resemblance. Congreve was a great admirer of Dogget, and wrote for him the characters of Fondlewife in the *Old Bachelor;* and Ben, the sailor, in *Love for Love.* He became patentee and manager, with Wilks and Gibbon, of Drury-lane Theatre; but on Booth joining the management, in 1712, Dogget retired, with 1600*l.* for his share,—a piece of trickery worked by a letter written by Booth to Coke, the Vice-Chamberlain. Our old comedian has had many celebrations of his loyalty and good-fellowship, but none written with more heartiness than the following lines on a window-pane at Lambeth, dated Aug. 1, 1736:

> Tom Dogget, the greatest sly drole in his parts,
> In acting was certain a master of arts;
> A monument left,—no herald is fuller,—
> His praise is sung yearly by many a sculler.
> Ten thousand years hence, if the world lasts so long,
> Tom Dogget will still be the theme of their song;
> When old Noll, with great Lewis and Bourbon are forgot,
> And when numberless kings in oblivion shall rot.

The last line, we suspect, would have been too strong in the nostrils for Tom's loyalty. There is a small print representing Dogget dancing the Cheshire Round, with the motto, *Ne sutor ultra crepidam.* His portrait is also in the collection of the Garrick Club.

Dogget grew rich, and became a member of the Fishmongers' Company. He died September 22, 1721, and was buried at

Eltham, in Kent. He had continued to give the Coat-and-Badge prize yearly, and bequeathed a sum of money, the interest of which was to be appropriated to the same purpose annually, for ever, on August 1; and, with the minute attention to costume which distinguished him as an actor, as well as in political principle, he directed that the orange colour of the coat, and the white horse of Hanover badge, should be adhered to. The Company view the boats to be rowed in a short time previous to Aug. 1, when they hold a Court, to start the watermen for the Coat and Badge, which are presented to the winner after a banquet given at Fishmongers' Hall in the evening. The Company have added four money-prizes.

The bequest for a river contest may be explained by the olden association of the Thames with our theatres. According to Taylor, the Water-Poet, about 1596, 40,000 watermen mostly lived through "the players playing at the Bankside." Wren's theatre, in Dorset Gardens, had a handsome front towards the river, with a landing-place for playgoers by water. Vauxhall Gardens had their water-gate, and the proprietors gave a new wherry and a prize-cup to be rowed for annually; as did also old Philip Astley, the rider. Edmund Kean likewise gave a wherry to be annually rowed for; but neither of these prizes have been perpetuated by bequest, as in the instance of good and true Thomas Dogget. Long may his memory continue to be embalmed in the loving-cup of the Fishmongers' Company!

When, in 1863, the Prince of Wales visited Fishmongers' Hall, eighteen watermen who, since 1824, had at various periods been winners of Dogget's Coat and Badge, wearing this honorary garb, were substituted for the usual military guard of honour in the vestibule.

A MORNING IN SIR JOHN SOANE'S MUSEUM.

GENTLE Reader, if thou hast any taste for architecture, sculpture, painting, antiquities, or art-treasures, ancient or modern—and if thou hast neither of these likings, verily thou art in a parlous state—why, choose a fine bright morning, in April, May, or June, for a visit to the house of Sir John Soane, upon the north side of Lincoln's Inn Fields. Although one of the Free Exhibitions, or Sights, of the metropolis, this is not a "show-house," but a well-arranged collection, small in comparison with other museums; nevertheless, its inspection is a great treat for those who seek to understand and appreciate what they see.

More than thirty years have elapsed since Sir John Soane munificently made to the nation this gift of the results of a long and active professional lifetime. The full appreciation of the value of the bequest has been of slow growth; this, however, has been quickened of late by the increased attention paid to the culture of art, and its diffusion among all classes of the people. That the son of a Berkshire bricklayer or petty builder should by his own energies have raised himself from poverty and obscurity to a position of opulence and celebrity, is a memorable triumph of self-help. He was born at Whitchurch, in Oxfordshire, in the year 1755, according to John Britton, who had gone to the expense of obtaining a baptismal certificate to that effect. To the circumstance of Soane, when a boy, being taken as a messenger into the office of Dance, the architect, is to be attributed his following that profession. From an errand-boy he became a pupil, first of Dance and then of Holland, another eminent architect; with the latter Soane remained to the time of his being sent to Italy for three years, at the recommendation of Sir William Chambers, in consequence of Soane's design for a triumphal bridge having obtained the gold medal of the Royal Academy, whose pension of 60*l.* a year was then conferred upon him, that he might prosecute his studies in Rome; he diligently improved this privilege for a few years. That he was at Rome in his twenty-fourth year (1779), a portrait of him in his museum, painted by Hunneman in that year, and at Rome, is evidence. That what he saw was not lost upon him, we have ample proof in his own works and in the large collections he left behind him. After his return from Italy, he was elected architect and surveyor to the Bank of England. Another timely advantage was his succeeding to a very considerable fortune in right of his wife. "Soane," says Mr. Cunningham, "got his first footing within the charmed pale of the Royal Academy in November 1795. He was then in his fortieth year, and West was president. Nor was his rise from the lower class so rapid as he could have wished. His signed diploma as an R.A., or one of 'forty,' is dated the 8th of April 1802. Sir William Chambers was then dead." Advantageous appointments followed, including that of architect to the Houses of Parliament, of the destruction of which by fire he once uttered a sort of prevision. He was kept in constant occupation for many years, and became unrivalled in making estimates, in knowledge of the value and quality of materials, in directing sound construction, and in the skilful arrangement of plans, combined with study and taste in a remarkable degree. Subsequently he was elected Professor of Architecture to the Royal Academy, and in 1831 received the honour of knighthood.

A few years before his death Sir John Soane retired from his profession, and devoted himself to the completion of his house on the north side of Lincoln's Inn Fields, where he had resided since 1792, when he commenced the mansion for himself. Of its extent the elevation towards Lincoln's Inn Fields conveys but an imperfect idea, since its rear is of the width of the front and two adjoining houses. The former is faced with a stone screen, of pleasing design; and, having a southern aspect into a large open area, is well adapted to preserve the front rooms cool in summer and warm in winter: this embellishment was added in 1812. Sir John, having resolved to bequeath to the British nation his house and his Museum of Antiquities, his library of books and manuscripts, and the collection of pictures which it contains, with an endowment of 30,000*l.* and the freehold, for preserving the gift and keeping it free for public inspection, announced this determination at the end of his twelfth and last lecture at the Royal Academy, March 21, 1833. He sought the aid of Parliament for this purpose, when some opposition to the Bill was manifested; this feeling having arisen from Sir John disinheriting his only surviving son, George (who took to literature), to make this bequest to the country. Between father and son a most violent breach had existed for many years, notwithstanding many attempts at reconciliation. Mr. Cunningham "has seen a letter written, in 1824, by Dr. Croly, the poet, to the son on the subject. The father was willing to forgive and forget; Dr. Kitchiner interposed; and the offer of the father was made to the son through Kitchiner, and in these terms: 'Let my son keep to any decided or regular pursuit for two years, and I will be reconciled to him.' It is painful to think that the terms were never carried out, and that the reconciliation never took place." The Bill was ultimately passed, with a clause to enable Sir John Soane, at any time, to bequeath his valuable relics to the British Museum, instead of allowing them to remain in the house in Lincoln's Inn Fields; thus placing again in the donor's control the disposal of the 30,000*l.* and the mansion. Were the above clause carried into effect, and the relics merged into the British Museum collection, it would altogether defeat Soane's intentions: one of these was to preserve the entirety of the museum, to show his great *forte* in the contrivance of his own house, besides picturesque and perspective effects which depend upon arrangement and plan for the mode of admitting light in interiors.

Soane's alienation from his son inclined "friends" to look

forward to considerable legacies from him; but he did not realise such expectations. He expended large sums in engraving and printing two descriptions of his Museum; to one of which Mrs. Hofland contributed in prose and verse. Soane also gave large donations to public bodies, as well as to private individuals. When Nash, the architect, left his second wife a widow, she became a pensioner on Sir John Soane and some other friends. Advanced as he was in years, both his faculties and health remained unimpaired to the last; when, with scarcely a day's previous illness, he died, at his house in Lincoln's Inn Fields, Jan. 20, 1837.

The Act of Parliament now came into operation, and the Trustees were appointed to carry into effect the Will of the founder.

As we approach the house, No. 13, introduced in the stone-screen, we identify it by Gothic corbels (twelfth century), and terra-cotta canephoræ, copied from the caryatides of the Temple of Pandrosus at Athens, which are eminently characteristic embellishments. As you enter, you cannot fail to be struck with the multiplicity of the objects, and the ingenious contrivances by which a house of very moderate size has been made to contain so large an amount of curiosities and works of art, without altogether destroying its character as a private residence. The entrance-hall is decorated with casts in plaster, after the antique; medallions, reliefs, and other sculptures; and the door leading to the staircase has some fine specimens of ancient painted glass. The vestibule and staircase are coloured in the style of an Italian palace.

From the hall we enter the Dining-room and Library, some 40 feet long by 20 feet broad. The walls, soffits, and arches are of deep vermilion colour, in imitation of the walls at Herculaneum and Pompeii. The ceiling is decorated with elaborate moulding, and is gilt and coloured. In panels are paintings by the late Henry Howard, R.A., for which it is said about 2000*l.* were paid. These paintings by Howard represent Phœbus in his car, preceded by Aurora and the Morning Star, led on by the Hours:

> jocund to run
> His longitude through heaven's high road.

In the oblong compartment near the door are represented the Seasons (which were anciently supposed to be only three), diffusing their various productions; and in the corresponding compartment Night is advancing, with the Pleiades in his train. The other compartments are of a similar character. Here is a model, in cork, of part of Pompeii, showing the excavations; above are plaster models of ancient Greek and Roman buildings restored; and beneath, in a case, is a collection of prints and architectural drawings, including Kent's design for a new Parliament House, made about 1740; also, Sir William Chambers's drawings for Somerset House; while on each side are antique fictile vases, alabaster urns, and antique bronzes. On the east side, over the chimneypiece, is a portrait of Sir John Soane, 1829, almost the last picture painted by Sir Thomas Lawrence; beneath, on the chimneypiece, is a plaster model of the Board of Trade and Privy Council Offices, Whitehall, adapted by Soane in 1826. Upon the bookcases are, a large Greek painted vase from the Englefield Collection; a bronze jug from Rome, and a chopin (1593) from Bath; also Greek and Roman vases, Wedgwood's Etruscan pottery; and on the chimneypiece a highly-finished model of the remains of the temple of Jupiter Stator at Rome. Upon a pedestal is a Greek painted fictile vase, 2 ft. 8 in. high, from Lord Cawdor's Collection. Here the bookcases are surmounted with busts of Homer, Shakspeare, Ben Jonson, and Inigo Jones. To the right of the entrance-door is Sir Joshua Reynolds's "Snake in the Grass," purchased at the Marchioness of Thomond's sale, by Sir John Soane, for 510 guineas. The small walnut-tree and marble library-table formerly belonged to Sir Robert Walpole; and on this table is exhibited the magnificent Ms. Commentary on the Epistle of St. Paul, illustrated by Giulio Clovio, who died in 1578. "When the wonderful finish of these illuminations, by the way, is observed, it does not seem strange to find Vasari saying that Clovio spent nine years in executing twenty-six miniatures in a Breviary of the Virgin (now in the Royal Library at Naples), for the Cardinal Alessandro Farnese. Clovio was decidedly the king of illuminators" (*Builder*, No. 852). Among the print treasures is an illustrated Pennant's *London*, for which Sir John Soane gave 650 guineas. The *Builder* critic observes: "But in an architectural point of view, the chief feature in this apartment is a collection of twenty highly-finished models in plaster-of-Paris, restorations of ancient Greek and Roman buildings, by the late M. Fouquet, of Paris. These are really, although small, exquisite works; which are most valuable, not only to ordinary visitors, but also to students in architecture. [The architectural drawings by Kent and Chambers have been mentioned.] Here is a model of a monument erected over the family-vault in the burial-ground of St. Giles-in-the-Fields, in St. Pancras, in the year 1815, to the memory of Sir John Soane's wife, Elizabeth. In this tomb the remains of Sir John and his eldest son were also buried." The north window is enriched with subjects of sacred history, in ancient painted glass. The look-out through the screen windows upon the large garden of Lincoln's Inn Fields, and the picturesque Tudor group on the east side, is a charming scene.

We now enter the Little Study, north-eastward, which contains marble fragments of Greek and Roman sculpture, antique bronzes, and curious natural productions. Over the door is a plaster cast of the Apotheosis of Homer, from the original marble of Archelaus of Briene. The chimneypiece is decorated with fragments of an antique altar, marble cornices, bases of columns, candelabra, cinerary urns, &c.; and on the opposite side are sculptured fragments and bas-reliefs in wax; also, a large fungus, cornua ammonis, &c.

The antiquarian visitor should not fail to inquire for the Dressing-room, from which is seen the Monk's Yard, containing a collection of Gothic fragments from the ancient Palace of Westminster, arranged like a ruined cloister; and opposite is the Monument Court, containing architectural groups of various forms and nations. The Corridor has on its walls architectural ornaments, marble fragments, plaster-casts of grotesque heads and foliage; and a beautiful model of a Sleeping Girl, by T. Banks, R.A., being the original study, in 1793, for a monument to Miss Boothby, daughter of Sir Brooke Boothby, in the church of Ashbourne, in Derbyshire. In the Students' Room, in addition to numerous antique casts, is a large collection of models in wood of modern buildings, which were designed by Sir John Soane.

From the Corridor you enter the Picture-room, which is admirably lighted at the top through an enriched ceiling of arches canopied: it has, as it were, double walls, or at least movable planes; so that after you have examined, as you think, the whole contents of the room, the side wall, or shutter, is turned on its hinges, and two fresh surfaces are displayed. Here are Hogarth's four Election pictures, purchased of Hogarth by Garrick (under peculiar circumstances) for 200*l.*; and bought by Sir John Soane at the sale of Mrs. Garrick's effects, in 1823, for 1650 guineas.

The four pictures are—The Entertainment; Canvassing for Voters; Polling; and Chairing the Members. "The Entertainment," says a critic in the *Builder*, "in particular, is worthy of notice and study. In the criticism on the works of this great artist, while praise has been given to him for the originality and mental qualities of his numerous works, his manipulative skill has been too much overlooked. This picture is a rare example of rich and harmonious colouring: the details are admirably finished; the breadth of light and shadow, and skill shown in the composition, independently of other considerations, entitle this picture to a distinguished place among the works of the best painters." Here also are three views in Venice by Canaletto: one, the Great Canal, considered the *chef-d'œuvre* of the painter, and formerly in Alderman Beckford's Collection, is of marvellous power and brilliancy, glow of sunlight, and transparent depth of shadow. Here is the study of a head from one of Raphael's Cartoons—saved from the wreck of the lost Cartoons, which remained in the possession of the family of the weaver who originally worked them in tapestry; also copies of two other heads from the same, by Flaxman. Here are likewise pictures by Calcott, Jackson, Howard, Danby, Sir F. Bourgeois, Sir James Thornhill, Fuseli, and Bird. Among the drawings are fifteen views, in Indian ink, of the Temples of Pæstum, by Piranesi; seen from a little distance, they have the effect of most elaborate finish—an effect, however, produced by very slight means.

We now descend to the Monks' Parloir, which has its ceiling and walls mostly covered with fragments and casts of ecclesiastical and other structures, carvings in wood and ivory, and engraved brasses; vases found in ancient Peruvian tombs; painted glass, &c.; and a very fine Flemish carving, in wood, of the Crucifixion.

In the lower part of the Museum, the most noticeable items are—a bust of the First Napoleon; a mask of Mary Queen of Scots; a bust of General Paoli; bas-reliefs and other models, by Flaxman; a bust of J. P. Kemble, by Gibson; and a bas-relief, by T. Banks, R.A., of the Angel opening the Door of St. Peter's Prison.

Amongst the casts, is one of part of the monument to the celebrated Bernard Gilpin, in the church of Houghton-le-Spring, Durham, of which parish he was rector. The story is well told by the *Builder* critic. It displays a tree and boar. Gilpin attained a great reputation by the fearlessness with which he pursued his ministry, whether amongst the lawless inhabitants of the ruder parts of Northumberland, or in face of the threats of Queen Mary. Himself a bachelor, and with ample means, his hospitality was unbounded: every fortnight, it is said, forty bushels of corn, twenty bushels of malt, and a whole ox, were consumed in his house, besides provisions of many other kinds. This bit of plaster hanging against the wall there, does good service in preserving the memory of a brave heart. And so with scores of the busts, medals, casts, and drawings that surround us.

In the Sepulchral Chamber is the splendid ancient Egyptian sarcophagus of Oimenepthak I., discovered by Belzoni, in 1817, in a royal tomb in the valley of Biban el Malook, near Gournou, Thebes. It was bought by Sir John Soane of Mr. Salt, the traveller, in 1824, for the sum of 2000*l.* When first discovered, this sarcophagus was considered by Dr. Young to be the tomb of Psamnis. On May 10, 1864, Mr. Joseph Bonomi, the excellent Curator of the Soane Museum, illustrated to the Syro-Egyptian Society Belzoni's very animated description of this sarcophagus by a section and plan of the catacomb, which is excavated to a depth of one hundred yards into the solid rock. The sarcophagus is completely covered with hieroglyphics and 659 figures, all of which were originally filled in with a blue paste. The subjects on both sides are of a religious character, while that on the floor of the sarcophagus is personal. Two subjects of particular interest were pointed out, one as representing the ancient Cosmical philosophy, and the other as exhibiting in a very perfect manner the doctrine of the Metempsychosis. Mr. Bonomi also stated that the sarcophagus revealed two remarkable features which have not been seen in any other example: the first in the existence of two holes, at each end of the lid, for the admission of ropes to insure the gradual adjustment of the cover into its proper place; and the next, the evidence of a means of preserving the edges of the sarcophagus from fracture during the process of lowering, and affording the means of hermetically closing it. The sarcophagus is formed of a large mass of alabaster; the seventeen fragments which formed part of the cover have been put together; and nineteen plates of the whole, drawn by Mr. Bonomi, and described by Mr. S. Sharpe, have been published.

The subject of the pictures and inscriptions engraved upon this royal coffin is the passage of the soul of the deceased, in the boat of the sun, through the regions of the under-world, represented by a series of halls, on the outside, inside, and the lid, and inhabited by beings divine or diabolic. There are one or two other scenes represented; in the most curious of which,

Osiris is sitting as judge of the dead, the figure of the deceased standing before him bearing on his shoulder the balance in which his merits and demerits are to be weighed; while a cynocephalus in a boat carries away the sinful part of him in the shape of a hog. Among the personages who inhabit the halls through which the sun's boat passes, are evil-doers, scorched and consumed by the fiery breath of serpents; while the virtuous are rewarded with an easy existence, and abundance of food from the tables of the gods. The king for whom this elaborate sarcophagus was executed was Seti, surnamed Meri-en-Ptah, the father of Rameses the Great; his name is preserved by Manethe under the form of Sethos: he was the father of that king who passes for the persecuting Pharaoh famous in Israelitish history. On the wall of the Temple of Karnak, Seti is represented in his chariot, dragging his captives after him: the profile is slightly Jewish; he was not of pure Egyptian descent, but from a branch of the Shepherd Kings.*

Belzoni found this sarcophagus among the hills west of the Nile, in a richly-painted tomb, under eighteen feet of gravel and earth. The sarcophagus was empty, the body of the king having been abstracted. Belzoni brought away the huge receptacle, and made copies of the paintings on the walls: on arriving in London, he constructed a model of the tomb, which he exhibited at the Egyptian Hall, Piccadilly, in 1821: on the first day 1900 visitors paid half-a-crown each for admission.

Some of the brickwork of Soane's house had to be taken down in order to admit the sarcophagus, which is one piece of alabaster, between nine and ten feet in length. Viewed by lamp-light, the effect of the chamber is most impressive; and when Soane first obtained the sarcophagus, in 1825, he had the chamber lighted with lamps upon three evenings, during which large parties of persons of rank and talent, including many foreigners of distinction, were invited. A somewhat enthusiastic visitor says: "Seen by this medium, every surrounding object, however admirable in itself, becomes subservient to the

* Notice of Mr. Sharpe's Work, in the *Saturday Review.*

sarcophagus—the ancient, the splendid, the wonderful sarcophagus is before us, and all else are but accessories to its dignity and grandeur; a mingled sense of awe, admiration, and delight pervades our faculties, and is even oppressive in its intensity, yet endearing in its associations."

Affixed to the wall of this chamber is a marble tablet to the memory of the wife of Sir John Soane; and there is another below to the memory of John Soane, jun., who died in his thirty-seventh year. On the south side is a model of a colossal statue of Britannia, 230 feet high, submitted by Sir John, then Mr. Soane, in the year 1779, to the Committee for raising a naval pillar or monument on Greenwich Hill. Looking upon the models of tombs around him, a critic has well observed: "What a boon to the modern world the tombs of the ancient have been! Calculators have shown that the whole surface of the globe has been dug over 128 times to bury its dead; that 1283 human beings have been buried in each square rod of it, or about five persons to each square foot!"

We have not space to detail the fragments of antique sculpture and architectural ornaments which decorate the walls of this chamber; where, oddly enough, we find a head of Jupiter cheek-by-jowl with the bust of Heydegger, Master of the Revels to King George II.

Eastward is the Crypt, with several cork models of ancient tombs and sepulchral chambers from Sicily: in one tomb lie the remains of the deceased, amid paintings, vases, and other funereal accompaniments.

The Breakfast-room has some interesting prints, pictures, and drawings; a richly-mounted pistol, once belonging to Peter the Great and Napoleon I.: of whom the latter is a portrait in his twenty-eighth year, painted by Gorma, a Venetian artist, and valued by Josephine as an excellent likeness; also a miniature of Napoleon, painted at Elba, in 1814, by Isabey.

We now pass up the staircase to the South Drawing-room, where, on a screen, are Hogarth's eight paintings, the Rake's Progress, from Alderman Beckford's Collection, purchased by

Soane for 570 guineas. Among repulsive objects in these pictures, what types of pure English beauty do we meet with! Here are also the gold, silver, and bronze medals struck by the architects of England in honour of Soane; and a complete collection of the Napoleon medals. Here, too, are the ivory tables and four ivory chairs, formerly Tippoo Saib's. Amongst the drawings is one, by Rubens, of a design for an emblematical frame for the royal portrait of King Charles I.; also drawings by Stothard, Clerisseau, Pannini; and busts of James Wyatt, Thornton, the Marquis of Buckingham, and others.

The North Drawing-room contains a large collection of architectural drawings, chiefly of Soane's buildings; Van Tromp's Barges entering the Texel, by Turner, and several other paintings and sketches by modern masters. Upon tables are displayed several illuminated Mss., a Ms. Tasso, the first three editions of Shakspeare, sketch-books of Sir Joshua Reynolds, &c.

The Tivoli Recess is noticeable for its interesting casts and models, and the Morning Room for its paintings, drawings, and engravings: one item is a bust of Shakspeare, enriched by all the flowers mentioned in his works.

From the Model-room we get a fine view of Lincoln's Inn Gardens; Lindsey House, a work of Inigo Jones; the College of Surgeons, Lincoln's Inn Hall and Library, St. Paul's Cathedral, the Houses of Parliament, &c. Some of the models in this room are by Flaxman; the drawings by Soane are interesting memorials of his works.

Among what may be termed professional curiosities are the watch, measuring-rods, and compasses of Sir Christopher Wren. Among the drawings, those of Thorpe, the Elizabethan architect, are very fine. The antiquities and casts are as useful to artists and pattern-drawers as the new rooms in the Louvre, at Paris. The entire Collection cost Sir John Soane 50,000*l.* It is of great service for artistic study in architecture, sculpture, painting, and house-decoration.

On the staircase is a very fine water-colour drawing—a view

in the Vale of Chamouni—by Turner; here are also Chantrey's model of a Sleeping Child; bas-reliefs, by Flaxman; a bust of George Dance, the architect, by Rossi; painted glass; a sketch of a dog, by Rubens; and scores of other items.

Cunningham has these piquant notes on the presentments of Soane, which are not rare: "His looks are preserved to us by the hands of four of his contemporaries skilled in catching a likeness, and something more. Lawrence has refined upon his face with his customary delicacy; Owen has massed the features of the man of *forty-eight* with his usual breadth; Jackson has painted him when old and parsimonious, age-worn and anxious; Chantrey has caught him in all his moods: he is sagacious, querulous; thinking of Inigo and Wren, the Three per Cents, and the Belzoni Sarcophagus. The Chantrey bust bears the following inscription:

JOHN SOANE, Esq., R.A.
Presented, as a Token of Respect, by
FRANCIS CHANTREY, Sculptor. 1830.

This was a complimentary return for the exquisite little gallery which the architect designed for the studio of the illustrious sculptor. That Chantrey looked for more than an empty executorship from Soane was often hinted at the time, and not wholly without foundation."

There is an odd story of another portrait, yet not mentioned. Sir Francis Chantrey (one of Soane's executors) communicated laughingly to his "friend and assistant, Allan Cunningham," an entry in the bank-book of Sir John Soane of a payment to a well-known literary veteran, for what Soane considered "a good and acceptable service." The sum was 500*l*., and the service —the destruction, by "a well-known hand," of a portrait of Soane by Mr. Maclise. The portrait, hung in the rooms of the Literary Fund, was in no way a flattering likeness of the rich and able architect of the Bank of England.*

Sir John Soane was a man of irritable temper and overween-

* Mr. Peter Cunningham, in the *Builder*.

ing vanity: he once brought an action against a critic for abusing his works! His success raised up a large crop of envy, and cunning persons worried him so intensely, that we heard of his once shutting himself up in a villa on Richmond Hill, to get out of the way of his tormentors. Some of his works have had but a brief existence. "Soane's Corridor, and other work in the old Houses of Parliament, a famous fire destroyed; Barry paid no Burlington reverence to his Board of Trade, Whitehall; still more recently, Mr. Cockerell has altered his Bank of England; and only the other day his well-designed State-Paper Office was levelled to the ground. Yet his name will live among architects for his wonderful skill of giving breadth of effect and beauty within narrow limits, and, rarer still, well-considered and seldom-exceeded estimates."—*Cunningham.*

We have incidentally mentioned Sir John Soane's prevision of the burning of the Houses of Parliament. In his *Designs for Public Buildings*, 1828, he wrote: "In the year 1800, the Court of Requests was made into a House of Lords; and the old buildings of a slight character, several storeys in height, surrounding that substantial structure, were converted into accommodations for the officers of the House of Lords, and for the necessary communications." These old buildings were chiefly of timber, covered with plaster. "In such an extensive assemblage of combustible materials, should a fire happen, what would become of the Painted Chamber, the House of Commons, and Westminster Hall? Where would the progress of the fire be arrested? The want of security from fire, the narrow, gloomy, and unhealthy passages, and the insufficiency of accommodations in this building, are important objects, which call loudly for revision and speedy amendment." Sixteen years after this admonition, the conflagration took place: through the favourable direction of the wind, Soane's Parliamentary buildings, his Law Courts, and the Great Hall, were preserved; had the volumes of flame and flakes of fire been wafted towards the vast timber roof of the Hall, it must have been destroyed, with every building immediately connected with it.

A SITE OF SPECULATION.

TOWARDS the south-western termination of the Strand is a low-lying tract of ground, which, for nearly two centuries past, has been a focus of speculation, such as even in these speculative times has scarcely a parallel. Here it is curious to find, through generations, failure following failure; the speculators seeming to imitate desperate gamblers in following ill-luck. A sort of fatality has long hovered over the spot: it may be, from that much-abused and much-defended Francis Bacon having been born here—and was but barred dying here by his banishment from Court. Bacon himself was bold in speculation, though he may have borrowed much from his namesake the Friar; and great as have been the results of his philosophy, the ill-luck of the disgraced Chancellor would seem to have darkened the fortunes of the locality. Of the York-House estate the only relic is the picturesque Water-gate, long ascribed to Inigo Jones, but, by an account-book in the Soane Museum, proved to be the work of Nicholas Stone. We need scarcely remind the reader that at York House lived Sir Nicholas Bacon; and here was born his son, Francis Bacon, Jan. 22, 1560-1. Here he kept his sixtieth birthday, and here the Great Seal was taken from him. When importuned to part with the mansion, Bacon replied, "For this you will pardon me: York House is the house where my father died, and where I first breathed; and there will I yield my last breath, if so please God and the King." He did not, however, return to York House after his release from the Tower, being forbidden to come within the verge of the Court. Next, George Villiers, first Duke of Buckingham (the ill-fated favourite of two sovereigns, who was stabbed by Felton at Portsmouth), got possession of York House upon terms not scrupulously fulfilled; for Chamberlain writes to Carleton, "Visct. St. Albans has filed a bill in Chancery against Buckingham on account of the non-performance of his contract for taking York House" (Mrs. Green's *Calendar of State Papers*). How this matter was settled has not yet been explained. However, Buckingham having got possession, the King (James I.), after much trouble, persuaded the Archbishop of Canterbury to part with the freehold of the house (which had been the residence of the See) in exchange for other lands; and, in 1624, it was conveyed to Buckingham. He had the old mansion taken down, and commenced building a magnificent new one, in which Portland stone was extensively used; James I. paying 1800*l.* for 2000 tons of that material to be used in Buckingham's building (Mr. Bruce's State-Paper *Calendar of Charles I.*). This new fact in the history of York House does not correspond with the statement that Buckingham only built the Water-gate with stone near the middle of a long embattled wall fronting the Thames, the house being merely a temporary structure: Buckingham's "noble soul," Pepys tells us, appeared "in the door-cases and the windows." Cromwell seized the estate, and gave the house to General Fairfax, on the marriage of whose daughter and heiress to George, second Duke of Buckingham, the property was reconveyed to the Villiers family. The Duke resided here subsequent to the Restoration; but, in 1672, sold the estate for 30,000*l.*: the house was taken down, the gardens were cleared, and upon the site were erected York-buildings, which were afterwards severally named nearly as we now see them: *George* Street, *Villiers* Street, *Duke* Street, *Of* Alley, and *Buckingham* Street; the distinctive name and title of their former possessor being thus literally preserved.

A few persons of note came early to reside here. John Evelyn took a house in Villiers-street for the winter, in 1683. Pepys, the diarist, had a handsome mansion, the last on the west side of Buckingham-street, looking upon the Thames; and at the opposite corner was the house in which Peter, the Czar of Russia, lodged for a time. Harley, Earl of Oxford, was living here in 1708, the year in which he was removed from his secretaryship by Queen Anne; and in Villiers-street Sir Richard

Steele lived, after his wife's death, from 1721 to 1724: Mr. Peter Cunningham found, in the rate-books of St. Martin's, the word "gone" against Steele's name in 1725; he died in Wales in 1729. Sir Richard had one of the many schemes in this focus of speculations. Here he projected a sort of nursery for the stage, which required large premises; and possibly he may have fitted up some portion of Buckingham's reception-house, which had been spared. Here Steele gave to some two hundred guests a sumptuous entertainment, with dramatic recitations. Addison assisted, and wrote an epilogue for the occasion, in which we can relish the quiet humour of these lines:

> The Sage, whose guests you are to-night, is known
> To watch the public weal, though not his own.

It was in fitting up the theatre, which was opened with this entertainment, that Steele was outwitted by his carpenter. The theatre was nearly completed, when Sir Richard, anxious to try whether it was well adapted for hearing, placed himself at the back of the gallery, and begged the carpenter to speak up from the stage. The man did not know what to say, when Steele called out to him to say whatever was uppermost; and, after a moment, the carpenter began, in a voice perfectly audible: "Sir Richard Steele," he said, "for three months past me and my men has been a-working in this theatre, and we've never seen the colour of your honour's money. We will be very much obliged if you'll pay it directly; for until you do, we won't drive in another nail." Sir Richard said that his friend's elocution was perfect, but that he didn't like his subject much.

In Duke-street, "over against the Blew Posts," lodged Humphrey Wanley, the learned antiquary; and Shadwell, the dramatic poet's son, and a celebrated physician in his time, lived in the same street.

One of James's pictures at Hampton-Court Palace, painted in the reign of George II., is "The Thames, comprising Westminster-bridge, the Hall and Abbey, Whitehall, Hungerford-stairs, Adelphi, and the Water-works;" the latter a spire-like shaft of a veritable steam-engine, or "fire-engine," for supplying the west end of London with water. These waterworks were undertaken by a Company, incorporated by Act of Parliament, 1691. The works are described in the *Foreigner's Guide to London*, 1720; but the Company, extending its operations to purchasing estates, granting annuities, and assuring lives, was one of the bubbles of that year of wild speculation. The Company ceased to work this fire-engine in 1731; but it was afterwards shown for several years as a curiosity. "Its working by sea-coal," says the *London Daily Post*, 1741, "was attended with so much smoke, that it not only must pollute the air thereabouts, but spoil the furniture." The failure is burlesqued in a humorous ballad, printed by Mr. Thomas Wright in his *England under the House of Hanover*. The confused affairs of the Company, and the consequent disputes and lawsuits with its creditors and debtors, gave rise to a host of pamphlets, and even a political novel. The last of the property was sold in 1783. However, the spirit of the York-buildings speculations lingered here until our time; for, in Buckingham-street, in 1818, were "the Sea-water Baths," which were supplied by a vessel with water from below Southend. It may be curious to add, that however the smoke of the fire-engine of 1720 may have polluted the air and spoilt the furniture, in the upper chambers of the house adjoining, Etty, 120 years later, painted some of his finest flesh-pictures, amidst the smoke of the Thames steamers.

Adjoining York-buildings is a spot where failure seems to have commenced with the Hungerfords, of Farleigh Castle, Somerset, who had a mansion here, placed between York House and Suffolk, now Northumberland House. Sir Edward Hungerford, who was created a Knight of the Bath at the coronation of Charles II., is known as "the spendthrift;" he is said to have given 500 guineas for a wig to figure in at some ball; to keep up his foolish game, he sold, at one time, twenty-eight manors; and he pulled down part of his large town-house, and converted the other portion into tenements and a market, in the year 1650. In 1720, Strype described the market as "at first, in all probability, to have taken well, especially for fruit and herbs, as lying so convenient for the gardeners to land their goods at the stairs, without the charge and trouble of porters to carry them farther by land, as now to Covent Garden Market. But being baulked at first, it turns to little account, and that of Covent Garden hath got the start; which is much resorted unto, and well served with all fruits and herbs, good in their kind." However, the glory of the Hungerfords was not forgotten in the market-house; for, in a niche on the north side, was placed a bust of one of the family in a large wig—Sir Edward, in the 500-guinea wig! Beneath was this inscription:

> Forum utilitatæ publicæ per quam necessariam,
> Regis Caroli secundi inuente Majestatæ propriis
> Sumptibus erexit, perfecitque D. Edvardus
> Hungerford, Balnei Miles, Anno MDCLXXXII.

The market, "baulked at first," again proved a sorry failure: it was a strange medley, for over the market-house was a large room, called "the French Church." We read also of a disreputable hack scribbler lodging here.

The market had dwindled to a single row of stalls and shops, the hall had been let as stables, and the place was principally used as a thoroughfare to and from Hungerford Stairs, when a Company raised, in 100*l.* shares, some 200,000*l.*, purchased the estate and some adjoining ground,—altogether 3¼ acres,—and thereon, within two years, was erected a new market, adapted from a Roman market, which was publicly opened July 2d, 1833, but proved as unprofitable as the original Hungerford scheme. The opening was signalised by the ascent of a balloon: one of the aeronauts, being inexperienced, not long after lost his reason. A large exhibition-hall and bazaar were built in 1851, when Mr. Bouton produced here his dioramic views of Fribourg and Venice; the premises and the pictures were destroyed by fire, March 31, 1854. The fish-market, which, it was promised, should counteract the high price of fish at the west end of the town, failed before the magnates of Billingsgate. Still, the river-front became the great focus of the upper Thames steam-navigation, there being here a million of embarkations and landings annually. The market-scheme attempted too much, in trying to unite Leadenhall, Billingsgate, and Covent-Garden Markets. A foot suspension-bridge, constructed by the younger Brunel, from Hungerford Market, across the Thames, to Belvedere-road, Lambeth, and opened April 18, 1845, added to the failures: the bridge cost 110,000*l.*, and was sold for 226,000*l.*; but only the first instalment was paid, and the purchase was thus void: however, the bridge was taken down in 1863. The Italian piers, designed by Bunning, were the most graceful ornaments of the Thames bridges. The chains were carried to Clifton, for the suspension-bridge erecting there; and the rest of the Hungerford structure was employed in a bridge carrying the extension of the South Eastern Railway across the river to the Charing-Cross Terminus and Italian Hotel; the latter, with some 300 feet frontage to the Strand, in length, and five storeys high, designed by E. M. Barry, A.R.A. The bridge is but a poor substitute for the picturesque Hungerford Suspension-Bridge: as an engineering work, it is fine; and it was constructed with very little interference with the river traffic. It is a curious fact that the line of railway, though taken through one of the most densely-populated districts of London, has only, from first to last, removed 250 houses—a fact which says a good deal for the care with which its route had been marked out. Among the claims for compensation was that of the tenants of Hungerford Hall for the sale of ices, coffee, &c., who claimed upwards of 13,000*l.* for giving up their premises for the formation of the railway. The net profits were stated at 4000*l.* a year; the receipts in the previous year were 9552*l.*: the jury assessed the compensation to be paid by the Company at 7750*l.*

Among the buildings removed for the Strand improvements, in 1863, was the house built upon part of the site of York House, at the corner of Villiers-street, No. 31 Strand, where lived Richardson, well known to print-collectors of the last century; his business was continued by his son, who died about 1813, when the large stock of prints was sold by auction; the house had a large window projecting over Villiers-street. Another old house removed was No. 23 (Yeates, the confectioner's); with a wooden front, which must have been built in the seventeenth century. No. 18 was the birthplace of Charles Mathews the elder, comedian: his father was a bookseller; and his shop was the resort of Dr. Adam Clarke, Rowland Hill, and other Dissenting ministers. Old Mr. Mathews used to relate that he remembered Napoleon Bonaparte residing in London, for five weeks, in 1791 or 1792; that he lodged in a house in George-street, Adelphi; that he occasionally took his cup of chocolate at the Northumberland Coffee-house, opposite Northumberland House; that he there read much, and preserved a provoking taciturnity towards the frequenters of the coffee-room; though his manner was stern, his deportment was that of a gentlemen. It is added, that Napoleon was also fond of walking through the streets of the metropolis.* Near his lodging, in the Adelphi, was a place much resorted to by another ruler of France, Louis Philippe, who, between 1848 and 1850, was a frequent visitor at the Lowther Bazaar, in the Strand.

In Craven-street, on the west side, upper end, lived Mr. Denis O'Brien, who wrote in the *Morning Post* the impassioned appeal in behalf of his distressed friend, Sheridan, then upon his death-bed: "Prefer ministering in the chamber of sickness," said O'Brien, "to ministering at

The splendid sorrows that adorn the hearse.

I say, *life* and succour against Westminster Abbey and a funeral." O'Brien lived in a well-appointed house, where Sheridan had been a frequent visitor, and was at home in the host's convivial society; the latter held a colonial appointment, was employed in secret political service, and in frequent

* This story is from a letter in the *Birmingham Journal*, April 21, 1855, and is given upon the authority of one James Colman, living in St. Martin's parish, and then in his 106th year; he was born in Church-court, in the Strand.

communication with the Prince Regent, who, upon one occasion, presented him with a splendid silver tea and coffee service and salver; but O'Brien fell into the luckless fate of secret-service men, and was, at length, deserted by the party whom he had actively served; he died in great distress. O'Brien told Mr. Moore that Sheridan applied to him a short time before his death, when he sent him 100*l.*

We return to the Water-gate, at the foot of Buckingham-street, which, we learn, is to be removed, and rebuilt in the embankment of the Thames. The preservation of this picturesque gate has already been attended with difficulty. It is backed by an enclosed terrace, named Villiers-walk, planted with lime-trees: the stone-work was repaired, the iron-work renewed, and the gate roofed, in 1823, at a cost of 300*l.*, defrayed by a rate levied upon the inhabitants of York-buildings. To the terrace-walk, the residents in the neighbourhood had access by keys; and the walk was neatly kept by a person who lived in the lodge. For many years this duty was performed by the identical Hugh Strap whom Smollett has so prominently portrayed in his *Roderick Random.* His real name was Hugh Hewson, and for more than forty years he kept a hairdresser's shop in the parish of St. Martin-in-the-Fields. His shop was hung round with Latin quotations, and he would frequently point out to his customers and acquaintances the several scenes in *Roderick Random* pertaining to himself, which had their foundation, not in Smollett's inventive fancy, but in truth and reality. The meeting in the barber's shop at Newcastle, the subsequent mistake at the inn, their arrival together in London, and the assistance they received from Strap's friend, were all facts. Hewson left behind him an interlined copy of *Roderick Random,* showing how far we are indebted to the genius of the doctor, and to what extent the incidents were founded in reality. He died in the year 1809, at the age of eighty-five.

CHANGES IN COVENT GARDEN.

"WHICH is the most interesting portion of old London?" said a distinguished Fellow of the Society of Antiquaries to a friend, as they rode together home from a dinner-party of archæologists. "I can scarcely make up my mind to the locality," said the person thus interrogated. "Covent Garden," rejoined the F.S.A.; "because its celebrity is just old enough for us to be familiar with the lives of eminent persons who have rendered it so celebrated." This is reasonable; and may be proved from many pleasant volumes, which we shall occasionally quote, but shall rest chiefly upon our own recollection, for nearly forty years past, of what Sydney Smith has called "the amorous and herbivorous parish of Covent Garden."

Walter Savage Landor, in one of his delightful *Imaginary Conversations*, thus glances at the changes in Covent Garden: "The convent becomes a playhouse; monks and nuns turn actors and actresses. The garden, formal and quiet, where a salad was cut for a lady abbess, and flowers were gathered to adorn images, becomes a market, noisy and full of life, distributing thousands of fruits and flowers to a vicious metropolis." Although the Market dates from the reign of Charles II., in 1726, and later, it was called Convent Garden; and by the vulgar "Common Garden" (Sir John Fielding, 1776).

John Thomas Smith was minutely acquainted with old Covent Garden: he left a history of the quarter in manuscript, which has not been printed. Covent Garden, he says, was the first square inhabited by the great; for immediately upon the completion of the houses on the north and east sides, after Inigo Jones's design, they were *every one* of them inhabited by persons of the first title and rank, as appears by the parish-books of the rates at that time. The chambers occupied by Richard Wilson, now the Tavistock breakfast-rooms, were portions of the house successively inhabited by Sir Peter Lely, Sir Godfrey Kneller, and Sir James Thornhill.

Covent Garden, even so late as Pope's time, retained its fashion, as may be seen in the *Morning Advertiser*, March 6, 1730: "The Lady Wortley Montague, who has been greatly indisposed at her house in Covent Garden for some time, is now perfectly recovered, and takes the benefit of the air in Hyde Park every morning, by advice of her physicians."

Smith then refers to the parish of St. Paul's, as being at that time the only fashionable part of the town, and the residence of a great number of persons of rank and title, and artists of the first eminence; and also from the concourse of wits, literary characters, and other men of genius, who frequented the numerous coffee-houses, wine and cyder cellars, jelly-shops, &c., within its boundaries, the list of whom particularly includes the eminent names of Butler, Addison, Sir Richard Steele, Otway, Dryden, Pope, Warburton, Cibber, Fielding, Churchill, Bolingbroke, and Dr. Samuel Johnson; Rich, Woodward, Booth, Wilkes, Garrick, and Macklin; Kitty Clive, Peg Woffington, Mrs. Pritchard, the Duchess of Boton, Lady Derby, Lady Thurlow, and the Duchess of St. Alban's;* Sir Peter Lely, Sir Godfrey Kneller, and Sir James Thornhill; Vandevelde, Zincke, Lambert, Hogarth, Hayman, Wilson, Dance, Meyer, &c. The name of Samuel Foote should be added.

Smith, in *Nollekens and his Times*, tells of his meeting in Covent Garden Mrs. Elizabeth Carter, who had accompanied Mrs. Nollekens for the purpose of purchasing some roots of dandelion, an infusion of which had been strongly recommended to her husband by Dr. Jebb. Twigg, the fruiterer, procured for Mrs. Nollekens the roots she wanted from the "Simplers," who sat in the centre of the Garden. He was a talkative man, and was jocularly called the "Twig of the Garden:" he had been cook at the Shakspeare Tavern, and knew all the wits and

* In her theatrical times, Harriet Mellon, afterwards Duchess of St. Alban's, lodged in the first-floor of a house in Russell-street, opposite Brydges-street.

eccentric characters of his early days. He pointed out to Mrs. Carter the house in which lived Miss Reay, who was shot by the Rev. James Hackman: "it was that on the south-west corner of Tavistock-court, next to the one in which the famous William Vandevelde, the marine-painter, died;" the house was next occupied by Irish Johnstone, the delightful singer and excellent actor of the characters of Irishmen. At No. 13 lived Zincke, the celebrated enameller; next, Nathaniel Dance, the painter; and then Meyer, the famous miniature-painter; and, in the garrets, Peter Pindar (Dr. Walcot). The fruiterer said: "I recollect Old Joe, who was the first person who sold flowers in this Garden: his stand was at that corner within the enclosure, then called Primrose-hill (from primroses being sold there), opposite to Lowe's Hotel. Lowe had been a hairdresser in Tavistock-street, before he took that large house, which he established as a family-hotel, the earliest of that description in London, where he distributed medals, which procured him many lodgers." In reply to Mrs. Nollekens' inquiry for the house in James-street, where lived Charles Grignon, the engraver of the designs of Gravelot, Hayman, and Wale, Twigg replied: "No. 27. I recollect the old house when it was a shop, inhabited by two old Frenchwomen, who came over here to chew paper for the *papier-mâché* people." *Mrs. Nollekens:* "Ridiculous! I think Mr. Nollekens once told me that the elder Wilton, Lady Chambers's grandfather, was the person who employed people from France to work in the *papier-mâché* manufactory, which he established in Edward-street, Cavendish-square." *Twigg:* "I can assure you, madam, these women bought the paper-cuttings from the stationers and bookbinders, and produced it in that way, in order to keep it a secret, before they used our machine for mashing it." [This ridiculous story, we should think, originated in the *French* name given to this English manufacture.] *Mrs. Carter:* "I recollect, sir, when Mr. Garrick acted, hackney-chairs were so numerous, that they stood all round the Piazzas, down Southampton-street, and extended more than half-way along Maiden-lane, so much were they in requisition at that time. *Twigg:* "Then, I suppose, ma'am, you also recollect the shoe-blacks at every corner of the streets, whose cry was, 'Black your shoes, your Honour'?"—"Yes, sir, perfectly well; and the clergyman of our parish walking about and visiting the fruit-shops in the Garden in his canonicals; and I likewise remember a very portly woman, sitting at her fruit-stall in a dress of lace which, it was said, cost at least one hundred guineas, though a greater sum was often mentioned."

The Garden became infamous, in Smith's phrase, when its opulent inhabitants exchanged their residences for the newly-built mansions in Hanover, Grosvenor, and Cavendish squares; and Holles and the other streets adjacent. It was at that period that Mother Needham, Mother Douglass (*alias*, according to Foote's *Mirror*, Mother Cole), and Moll King, the tavern-keepers and the gamblers, took possession of the abdicated premises. Beneath the church-portico was "Tom King's Coffee-house," shown in Hogarth's print of Morning. It was a mere shed, as Murphy describes it—"well known to all gentlemen to whom beds are unknown." Upon the south side of the market-sheds was the noted "Finish," kept by Mrs. Butler, open all night, the last of the Garden taverns, and only cleared away in 1829. This house was originally the Queen's Head. Shuter was pot-boy here and elsewhere in the Garden; and, from carrying beer to the players behind the scenes, joined them as an actor.

At the Old Hummums, formerly a bagnio (in Arabic, "hammam"), died Parson Ford, who conspicuously figures in Hogarth's Midnight Modern Conversation. There is a capital ghost-story connected with his exit, thus told in Croker's edition of Boswell's *Life of Dr. Johnson:*

"*Boswell.*—Was there not a story of Parson Ford's ghost having appeared? *Johnson.*—Sir, it was believed. A waiter at the Hummums, in which house Ford died, had been absent for some time and returned, not knowing that Ford was dead. Going down to the cellar, according to the story, he met him; going down again, he met him a second time. When he came up, he asked some people of the house what Ford could be doing there. They told him Ford was dead. The waiter took a fever, in which he lay for, some time. When he recovered, he said he had a message to deliver to some woman from Ford; but he was not to tell them what or from whom. He walked out; he was followed; but somewhere about St. Paul's they lost him. He came back, and said he had delivered it; the woman exclaimed, 'Then we are all undone!' Dr. Pellet, who was not a credulous man, inquired into the truth of this story, and he said the evidence was irresistible. My wife went to the Hummums (it is a place where people get themselves cupped). I believe she went with the intention to hear about this story of Ford. At first they were unwilling to tell her; but after they had talked to her, she came away satisfied that it was true. To be sure, the man had a fever; and this vision may have been the beginning of it. But if the message to the woman, and their behaviour upon it, were true, as related, there was something supernatural. That rests upon his word, and there it remains."

The reader, we dare say, will recollect Horace Walpole's story of Sir Godfrey Kneller and Dr. Radcliffe being neighbours, and the servants of the latter gathering and destroying Kneller's fine flowers, and his threatening to shut up the gate. Radcliffe replied peevishly: "Tell him he may do any thing with it but paint it." "And I," answered Kneller, "can take any thing from him but his physic." Now, the house Sir Godfrey occupied was near the steps into Covent-Garden Theatre; he had a garden at the back, reaching as far as Dr. Radcliffe's, in Bow-street, —where, and not in Great Queen-street, the scene of the well-known anecdote must be laid: the merit of this unravelment is due to Mr. Cunningham.

Before the portico of St. Paul's Church is erected the hustings for the election of members of Parliament for Westminster. Contests are now restricted to one day; but in this political cockpit were fought many battles of Government and People, when "madman's holiday" extended to fifteen days; the defeat of the Tory party leading to the division of the Liberals into Whigs, Radicals, and Reformers.

The Market was a strange and shabby assemblage of shed and pent-house, rude stall and crazy tenement, coffee-house and gin-shop, intersected by narrow and ill-lit footways; until the site was cleared for a new Market in the year 1829. A sketcher of that date says: "Enter it from Russell-street: what can be more unsightly—with its piles of cabbages in the street, and basket-measures on the roofs of the shops—narrow alleys, wooden-buildings, rotting vegetables, *undique;* and swarms of Irish basket-women, who wander about like the ghosts on this side of the Styx; and who, in habits, features, and dialect, appear as if belonging to another world? Yet the Garden, like every garden, has its charms. I have lounged through it on a summer's day, mixing with pretty women, looking upon choice fruit, smelling delicious roses, with now and then an admixture of sundry disagreeables—such as a vigorous puff out of an ugly old woman's doodeen—to say nothing of the unpleasant odours arising from heaps of putrescent vegetables, or your hat being suddenly knocked off by contact with some Irish basket-woman, with cabbages piled on her head sufficient for a month's consumption at Williams's boiled-beef house in the Old Bailey.

"The narrow passages through this mart remind one of the Chinese streets, where all is shops, bustle, squeeze, and commerce. The lips of the fair promenaders, I collate (in my mind's eye, gentle reader) with the delicious cherry; and match their complexions with the peach, the nectarine, the rose, red or white, and even sometimes with the russet apple. Then, again, I lounge amidst chests of oranges and baskets of nuts, which, as boys, we relished in the playground, or, in maturer years, have enjoyed at the wine-feast! Here I can saunter in a greenhouse, among plants and heaths, studying botany and beauty. Facing me is a herb-shop, where old nurses, like Medeas of the day, obtain herbs for the sick and dying; and within a door or two flourishes a vender of the choicest fruits, with a rich display of every luxury to delight the living and the healthy."

We have viewed the Market from one of the windows of an adjoining hotel; and a more deplorable picture of wretchedness cannot be conceived than this ducal area presented: yet, at stated times, might be seen the collector descending from his curricle, to gather with outstretched hands the rents from stall-keepers. At length the site was cleared; and a new market commenced, from the designs of Fowler. In digging for the foundations was exhumed a quantity of human bones, on the north side of the area, supposed to have been the convent burial-ground. The market consists of a quadrangle, with two exterior colonnades of shops; and in the central building an avenue of shops for forced articles, the choice fruits, vegetables, &c. At the east end is a quadruple colonnade, with a terrace and two large conservatories, a fountain, emblematical sculpture, &c. At the west end are a colonnade, conservatory, and the Flower Market.

The market-buildings are perfectly fitted for their various uses, evince considerable architectural skill, and are so characteristic of the purpose for which the market has been erected, that it cannot be mistaken for any thing else but what it is; unless the inscription, "JOHN DUKE OF BEDFORD; erected MDCCCXXX.," over the east end, lead posterity to regard this as a patriotic act; whereas the Bedford family derive a large rental from the market, stated at 5000*l.* per annum. The area is three acres. The rent of some of the shops is from 400*l.* to 500*l.* per annum. The market is said to pay 10 per cent.

Some of the larger items of the market sales are exclusively of modern date, such as the 300,000 pines which come yearly into the port of London, or the hundreds of tons of rhubarb which are now sold in Covent Garden, in lieu of the original three bunches which found hesitating purchasers some forty years ago. According to the evidence of Mr. Maynwaring, one Boyce, of Maiden-lane, recollected when Covent Garden was let for 30*l.* a year. To the Horticultural Society of London much of this progress is due; and few persons of middle age, who take interest in the inquiry, can walk through Covent-Garden Market without acknowledging a debt of gratitude to the above Society. The supplies from the West of England, by railway, are very considerable: near Penzance, upwards of 1000 acres of brocoli are under cultivation. In short, the most luxuriant specimens of the finest vegetables and fruits which the skill of man and the earth can produce, are to be seen every day in Covent-Garden Market; and in variety and quantity, as well as excellence, surpass the products of all other countries.

Nevertheless, the days of extravagant desserts from Covent-Garden Market are numbered. Forced strawberries at two guineas a plate, and grapes at fabulous prices, are few and far between. Chaumontelle pears, it is true, were, in 1863, priced in the market at 15*s.* each—but these were of prodigious growth. The vast importations of foreign fruit have influenced this change; but foreign fruits are of inferior flavour to those which are grown in the British Isles.

It has been said, there is more certainty of being able to purchase a pine-apple here, every day in the year, than in Jamaica and Calcutta, where pines are indigenous. Of curious herbs for domestic medicines, distilleries, &c., upwards of 500 species may be procured at the shop of one herbalist.

Three millions sterling are said to be paid annually for fruits and vegetables sold in the market! In the middle avenue, hot-house grapes are priced at 25*s.* per pound, strawberries at 1*s.* per ounce, slender French beans at 3*s.* per hundred, peas at a guinea and even two guineas a quart, new potatoes at 4*s.* 6*d.* per pound, asparagus and rhubarb at 15*s.* the bundle; a moss-rose for half-a-crown, for the button-hole of the beau; and wedding bouquets of flowers at two guineas each.

Here, at the early market-hour, are stationed hawkers of account-books, dog-collars, whips, chains, curry-combs, pastry, ground spice, Everton toffy, money-bags, tissue-paper for the tops of strawberry-pottles, and horse-chestnut leaves for garnishing fruit-stalls; coffee-stalls, and stalls of pea-soup and pickled eels; basket-makers; women making up nosegays; and girls splitting huge bundles of water-cresses into little bunches.

In the summer of 1861, the spiritual wants of the market-people were provided for by the Bishop of London inaugurating a series of special Sunday Services in the market-place. A temporary rostrum was erected near the grand avenue, and upon this the Bishop took his stand, habited in his episcopal robes. Prayers and a short portion of Scripture were read by the Rector of the parish, and hymns were sung by the vast assembly from printed slips which were freely distributed amongst them. The Bishop then delivered an earnest address on the great duties of the Christian life. These and subsequent Services were promoted by the Home Mission: while they were being carried out, the majority of the London churches were only half filled; thus proving the movement a failure.

Inigo Jones's arcades, though masterpieces of architecture,—the proportions of the arches and piers, crossed with elliptical and semicircular arches into groins, are exquisitely beautiful,—have been unceremoniously treated; a portion at the north-east angle having been taken down to make room for a huge and almost useless iron and glass "Floral Hall." The premises removed were the Piazza Coffee-house, a favourite haunt of Sheridan, who sat here during the burning of Drury-lane Theatre; when a friend remarking on the calmness with which he bore his misfortune, Sheridan replied: "A man may surely be allowed to take a glass of wine *by his own fireside.*" And here Sheridan used to drink deeply with his manager, John Kemble: once, when the latter had written a "nervous flight" about the interests of the theatre, Sheridan replied: "Attributing your letter to a disorder which I know ought not to be indulged, I prescribe that thou shalt keep thine appointment at the Piazza Coffee-house to-morrow at five, and taking four bottles of claret instead of three, to which in sound health you might stint yourself, forget that you ever wrote the letter, as I shall that I ever received it."

Thackeray, who affected Covent Garden, has left this clever picture of it: "The two great national theatres on one side, a churchyard full of mouldy but undying celebrities on the other; a fringe of houses studded in every part with anecdote and history;

a colonnade, often more gloomy and deserted than a cathedral aisle; a rich cluster of brown old taverns—one of them filled with the counterfeit presentment of many actors long since silent, who scowl or smile once more from the canvas upon the grandsons of their dead admirers; a something in the air which breathes of old books, old pictures, old painters, and old authors; a place beyond all other places one would choose in which to hear the chimes at midnight; a crystal palace—the representative of the present—which peeps in timidly from a corner upon many things of the past; a withered bank, that has been sucked dry by a felonious clerk; a squat building, with a hundred columns and chapel-looking fronts, which always stands knee-deep in baskets, flowers, and scattered vegetables; a common centre into which Nature showers her choicest gifts, and where the kindly fruits of the earth often nearly choke the narrow thoroughfares; a population that never seems to sleep, and that does all in its power to prevent others sleeping; a place where the very latest suppers and the earliest breakfasts jostle each other on the footways—such is Covent-Garden Market, with some of its surrounding features."

The burnings of the two great Theatres are episodal changes, which it would occupy too much space to narrate.

It is some eighteen years since we lost the famous George Robins, of the Piazza; who, for fifty years, by his hammer, dispersed more property than any other man of his time. Lord Byron used to say his order could not go on long without George Robins to set their affairs right. He was beloved in literary and theatrical circles. Moore has described a dinner which Byron gave to Robins; at which Lord Kinnaird, Colman, and John Kemble were present. "I have seen Sheridan weep two or three times," writes Byron. "Once I saw him cry at Robins, the auctioneer's, after a splendid dinner, full of great names and high spirits." His auction-rooms were formerly the studio of Zoffany, who painted here Foote, in the character of Major Sturgeon. Hogarth's Marriage-à-la-Mode pictures were exhibited here gratis when the premises were Cocks's auction-rooms.

At the brave old mansion at the north-west angle of the Piazza there have been great changes within these ten years. The place has a long history. Sir Kenelm Digby lived here, and had his laboratory in the garden in the rear. The mansion was subsequently altered, if not rebuilt, for the Earl of Orford, better known by the name of Admiral Russell, who, in 1692, defeated Admiral de Tourville, near La Hogue, and ruined the French fleet. The house is built of fine red brick; and, before recent alterations, the façade was thought to resemble the forecastle of a ship. The fine old staircase is formed of part of the vessel Admiral Russell commanded at La Hogue, the *Britannia*, 100 guns. It has handsomely-carved anchors, ropes, and the coronet and initial letters of Lord Orford.

About 1794, when the premises were used as an hotel, Mrs. Hudson, the proprietor, advertised her house, "with stabling for one hundred noblemen and horses."

In the garden in the rear was formerly a small cottage, in which the Kembles, when in the zenith of their fame at Covent-Garden Theatre, occasionally took up their abode; and here, we are informed, was born the highly-gifted Fanny Kemble. It is interesting to recall Sir Kenelm Digby and his grave friends, with their empirical doings and Digby's "Sympathetic Powder" fame, airing themselves in this identical garden, reduced in our time to a receptacle for a few sooty shrubs.

At the beginning of the present century, and some years afterwards, the hotel was famous for its large dinner- and coffee-room. It was called the "Star," from the number of men of rank who frequented it. An anecdote of costly epicurism is related of this place. One day, a gentleman entered the dining-room, and ordered of the waiter two lamb-chops; at the same time inquiring, "John, have you a cucumber?" The waiter replied in the negative—it was so early in the season; but he would step into the market, and inquire if there were any. The waiter did so, and returned with—"There are a few, but they are half-a-guinea a-piece." "Half-a-guinea a-piece! are they small or large?" "Why, rather small." "Then buy two," was the reply. This incident has been related of various epicures; it occurred to Charles Duke of Norfolk, who died in 1815.

Evans, of Covent-Garden Theatre, removed here from the Cyder-Cellar in Maiden-lane, and, using the large dining-room for a singing-room, prospered until 1844, when he resigned the property to Mr. John Green. Meanwhile the great singing-room answered well its festal purposes, until the character of the entertainment, by the selection of music of a higher class than hitherto, brought so great an accession of visitors as to induce Mr. Green to extend his premises. He has accordingly built on the site of the old garden (Digby's garden) an extremely handsome hall, to which the former singing-room forms a sort of vestibule. The latter is hung with a collection of portraits of celebrated actors and actresses, mostly of our own time, which Mr. Green has collected; and a more appropriate gallery he could not have assembled for the gratification of his visitors. The new hall was opened in 1855; the architect was William Finch Hill.

The *spécialité* of this very agreeable place is the olden music, which is sung here with great intelligence and spirit; the visitors are of the better and more appreciative class, and often include amateurs of rank. The reserved gallery, by the way, is said to occupy part of the site of the cottage in which Fanny Kemble was born.

We now ascend from the Hall into King-street. At No. 35, in 1831, was instituted the Garrick Club, for bringing together the patrons of the drama and its professors; many leading comedians and active literary men are members. Here were the pictures collected by the late Charles Mathews, bequeathed to the Garrick by Mr. Durrant, now removed to the new club-house.

"Among the portraits were O'Neil's admirable likeness of Mr. Keeley, near Sir Edwin Landseer's portrait of Charles Young; Peg Woffington, Lee (the author of the *Bedlam Tragedy*, in nineteen acts), Mrs. Pritchard, and Mr. Garrick—an admirable illustration of

> Pritchard 's genteel, and Garrick six feet high ;

a most gentlemanly portrait of Pope, the actor; Garrick again as Macbeth, in the Court dress; two charming little paintings of Miss Poole, when a child-performer; the late Frederick Yates; Mrs. Davison (of rare beauty); and Miss Lydia Kelly. The smoking-room was adorned with gifts from artists, members of the Club. Mr. Stanfield has given a splendid sea-piece, with a wash of waves that sets one coveting an excursion; and Mr. David Roberts has given a large and noble painting of Baalbec, one of his finest works. Mrs. Stirling's bright face looked down upon the smokers; and here was a statuette of one who loved the room—the author of *Vanity Fair*.

"Next was a vast picture of Mr. Charles Kemble (long a member) as Macbeth; and a Miss O'Neil as Juliet. The coffee-room was devoted to the members' dinners; and Mr. Thackeray dined for the last time away from home at a table in a niche, in which hung the scene from the *Clandestine Marriage* where Lord Ogleby is preparing to join the ladies. Over the fireplace was another scene from the same play; and on the mantelpiece were Garrick's candlesticks, Kean's ring, and some other relics of interest. The paintings in this room were very valuable. There was Foote, by Reynolds; a Sheridan; John Kemble; Charles Kemble as Charles II. (under which picture he often sat in advanced life); Mrs. Charles Kemble, in male attire; Mrs. Fitzwilliam; Charles Mathews, *père;* a fine, roystering Woodward, reminding one of the rattling times of stage chivalry and "victorious Burgundy;" and in the morning-room was a delightful Kitty Clive, another Garrick, and, near the ceiling, a row of strong faces of by-gone days—Cooke the strongest.

"On the second-floor, in a front-room, were numerous small and very characteristic portraits; and in a press, full of large folios, was one of the completest and most valuable of collections of theatrical prints. In the card-room, behind this, were also some very quaint and curious likenesses; one of Mrs. Liston as Dollalolla. There was a sweet face of "the Prince's" Perdita, which excuses his infatuation and aggravates his treachery. When the visitor had seen these things, and a few busts, among them one of Justice Talfourd (an old member), he was informed that he had seen the collection."—This *résumé* is from a nicely-written paper in the *Illustrated London News*, July 16, 1864: we should add, an original portrait of Thomas Dogget, the comedian, which is stated not to have been engraved.

In the above month the Club removed to the house just built for them in the new Cranbourn-street; they having resolved to cling to the classic region round Covent Garden. The architect, Mr. Marrable, has adopted the Italian style; and the façade is handsome—not over-enriched.

Next door to the old Club-house in King-street lived Arne, the upholsterer; where lodged the Indian Kings, commemorated in the *Tatler* and the *Spectator*. Dr. Arne, the composer, and his sister Mrs. Cibber, the upholsterer's son and daughter, were born in this house. It has been many years tenanted by Mr. William Cribb, whose father published the magnificent mezzotint, by G. Clint, from Harlow's picture of the Trial of Queen Katherine. This celebrated painting (known as "the Kemble Family," from its introducing their portraits) was the last work of Harlow; whom his master, Sir Thomas Lawrence, characterised as "the most promising of all our painters." The picture, about 7 by 5 feet, is on mahogany-panel, 1½ inch thick, stated to have cost the painter 15*l.* It appears that Mr. T. Welsh first commissioned Harlow to paint for him a kitkat-sized portrait of Mrs. Siddons as Queen Katherine, introducing a few scenic accessories in the distance. It then occurred to Harlow to represent the whole Trial Scene; and most of the actors were prevailed on to sit for their portraits. The sum paid for the picture by Welsh was one hundred guineas; and a like sum by Cribb for Harlow's permission to engrave it: a first proof sometimes brings thirty guineas. To Mr. Cribb is due the credit of having been the first to appreciate the genius of Mr. Thomas Sydney Cooper, whose Cuyp-like pictures are so justly admired. The incident is agreeably told, by Miss Mitford, in her *Belford Regis:* Mr. Cribb was struck with a small cattle-piece by Cooper, which he saw in a shop-window in Soho; he sought out the young painter, and gave him his first commission; the painting was seen by artists and amateurs at Mr. Cribb's picture-room in King-street;, chiefly from this work commissions poured in, and the artist was on the road to fortune.

Mahogany was first used in England in this street: here Dr. Gibbons, the eminent physician, was building a house, when his brother, a West-India captain, brought over some mahogany as ballast; and thinking the wood might be of service to his brother the Doctor, he sent him a quantity of it; but the carpenters finding it too hard to work, it was laid aside. Soon after this, Mrs. Gibbons wanting a candle-box, the Doctor called upon his cabinet-maker in Long-acre, and asked him to make one of some wood which lay in his garden. Wollaston also complained that it was too hard; the Doctor said, he must get stronger tools. The candle-box was made and approved of; insomuch that the Doctor then had a bureau made of the same wood: the fine colour and polish were so pleasing, that he invited his friends to come and see the bureau; and among them was the Duchess of Buckingham. Her Grace begged some of the same wood of Dr. Gibbons, and employed Wollaston to make her a bureau also; on which the fame of mahogany and of Wollaston was much raised, and the wood came into general use. The doors of a few of the better class of old houses in King-street are of solid mahogany.

In King-street were the rooms of Paterson, the auctioneer, after he had left Essex House, Essex-street, in the Strand, formerly the residence of Sir Orlando Bridgman. He was the best book-catalogue maker of his time, and was the first auctioneer who sold books singly in lots. He had read most of the works he offered for sale in the English language; and often, in selling books, drew the attention of bidders to some book little known. Thus he pointed out to Dr. Lort, "at page 47" of a little book he was about to sell, a curious anecdote of Sir Edmondbury Godfrey, of which Paterson said he was not aware until he read it, while making his catalogue. The book was put up at 2*s.*; a strong competition arose, and it was sold for 1*l.* 5*s.*

Paterson had an impediment in his speech; yet he delivered, in his auction-rooms, a series of lectures upon Shakspeare's Plays; and had among his auditors George Steevens, Edward Malone; and Barry, the painter.

Upon Paterson leaving his room in King-street, it was taken by King, Collins, and Chapman, for the sale of books and prints, and occasionally let for the night. Here the veteran Collins gave his Evening Brush, or anecdotes of persons who had left this world before the birth of three-fourths of his audience. Here, too, Charles Dibdin commenced his London Amusement, and drew many tears by his pathetic and popular song of "Poor Jack." This song was in such requisition, that for months the printers could not produce it fast enough; and Dibdin hired a stall, "a bystander," similar to the stalls put up in front of the old Royal Exchange for the sale of newspapers; being large enough for Dibdin's man to stand in, and to deliver out the songs: the crowd and scramble, and even fights, to get "Poor Tom Bowling," or "Poll and my Partner Joe," were terrific.

One of the earliest of the recent improvements was the removal of a labyrinth of alleys at the west end of King-street, followed by the demolition of Rose-street, a dirty thoroughfare, with a curious literary history. Mr. Cunningham thus carefully narrates: "It was in this street (Dec. 18th, 1679) that Dryden, returning to his house in Long Acre, over-against Rose-street, was barbarously assaulted and wounded by three persons, hired for the purpose, as is now known, by Wilmot, Earl of Rochester. Fifty pounds were offered by the King for the discovery of the offenders, and a pardon in addition if a principal or accessory would come forward. But Rochester's 'Black Will with a cudgel' (the name he gives his bully) was bribed to silence, it is thought, by a better reward. Rochester took offence at a passage in Lord Mulgrave's Essay on Satire; an essay in which his Lordship received assistance from Dryden. There are many allusions to this Rose-alley Ambuscade, as it is called, in our old State poems. So famous, indeed, was the assault, that Mulgrave's poem was commonly called the Rose-alley Satire."

Samuel Butler, author of *Hudibras,* lived the latter part of his life in Rose-street, "in a studious, retired manner," and died there in 1680: he is said to have been buried at the expense of Mr. Longueville, though he did not die in debt. In the same street, Edmund Curll was living when he published *Mr. Pope's Literary Correspondence.* Saunders Welch, the well-known justice of the peace, once captured a rogue in Rose-street in a singular manner. At that time there was no flagged pavement, and the hackney-men could drive their coaches close to the very door. Welch had good information that a most notorious offender, who had for some time annoyed the Londoners in their walks through the green lanes to Mary-le-bone, and who had eluded the chase of several of his men, was in a first-floor of a house in Rose-street. After hiring the tallest hackney-coach he could select, he mounted the box with the coachman, and when he was close against the house, he ascended the roof of the coach, threw up the sash of a first-floor window, entered the room, and actually dragged the fellow from his bed out at the window by his hair, naked as he was, upon the top of the coach, and so carried him off.

Returning to King-street, we may note, that at the corner of Rose-street lived Mr. Setchel, the bookseller, whose daughter painted that very clever and popular picture, "The Momentous Question." Mr. Setchel and his father had kept shop here for seventy years. Among the changes in the street, is the erection of new offices for the Westminster Fire Office. In a house on this side lived Lenthall, Speaker of the House of Commons in the time of the Commonwealth (*Garrick Correspondence,* i. 83). We have heard, but not upon such good authority as the preceding, that in the old Garrick Club-house lived "Gentleman Lewis," the comedian; whose portrait, with 10,000*l.*, has been bequeathed to the nation. King-street would appear to have been for more than a century past noted for "book-auctioneers." Leigh was established here in 1744; from which time to the present, the priced catalogues, with the purchasers' names, are preserved by the present representatives of the firm, Sotheby and Wilkinson, in Wellington-street. In King-street, also, were the rooms of King and Lochee, who, in 1798, sold here Dr. Farmer's large library, extending over thirty-six days.

At the south-east corner of Bedford-street, the house where Clay sold his *papier-mâché* has been taken down, and loftier premises built for Mr. Moseley, the cutler and toolmaker. Clay was a pupil of Baskerville, of Birmingham, and first applied *papier-mâché* to tea-trays in 1760, by which he realised a fortune of 80,000*l.* Some of the finest of his trays were painted by early members of the Royal Academy, among whom was Wheatley.

In 1863, were taken down in Bedford-street Nos. 14, 15, and 16, on the west side, which, in Strype's time, was the best. At No. 15, facing Henrietta-street, lived Chief-Justice Richardson, a very companionable personage. He died in 1635, the year in which old Parr died. The exterior of his house was modern, but part of the interior was old, and of Richardson's time. Latterly it was tenanted by Mr. Joseph Lilly, the well-known bookseller, who removed thence to Nos. 17 and 18 New-street, Covent Garden, his large stock of old books, particularly rich in early English literature, and black-letter books in general.

In No. 16 lodged the father of Richard Brinsley Sheridan, as we gather from the following record in Whyte's *Miscellanea Nova.* "Mr. Sheridan one time lived in Bedford-street, opposite Henrietta-street, which ranges with the south side of Covent Garden, so that the prospect lies open the whole way, free of interruption. We were standing together at the drawing-room window, expecting Johnson, who was to dine there. Mr. Sheridan asked me, could I see the length of the Garden? 'No, sir'" (Mr. Whyte was shortsighted). "'Take out your opera-glass. Johnson is coming. You may know him by his gait.' I perceived him at a good distance, working along with a peculiar solemnity of deportment, and an awkward sort of measured step. At that time the broad flagging at each side of the street was not universally adopted, and stone posts were in fashion, to prevent the annoyance of carriages. Upon every post, as he passed along, I could observe he deliberately laid his hand; but, missing one of them, when he had got at some distance, he seemed suddenly to recollect himself, and, immediately returning back, carefully performed the accustomed ceremony, and resumed his former course, not omitting one till he gained the crossing. This, Mr. Sheridan assured me, however odd it might appear, was his constant practice; why or wherefore he could not inform me."

On the opposite side of the street, near the church-gate, was an old tavern, the Constitution (now rebuilt), noted as the resort of working men of letters, and for its late hours; indeed, the sittings here were perennial. Among other eccentric persons we remember to have seen here, was an accomplished scholar named Churchill, who had travelled much in the East, smoked and ate opium to excess, and was full of information. Of another grade were two friends who lived in the same house, and had for many years "turned night into day;" rising at eight o'clock in the evening, and going to bed at eight next morning. They had in common some astrological, alchemical, and *spiritual* notions, and often passed the night at the Constitution. This was the favourite haunt of Wilson, the landscape-painter, who then lived in the Garden; he could, at the Constitution, freely indulge in a pot of porter, and enjoy the fun of his brother-painter, Mortimer, who preferred this house, as it was near his own in Church-passage. He once made Dr. Arne, who had a very red face, with staring eyes, furiously angry by telling him that "his eyes looked like two oysters, just opened for sauce, put upon an oval side-dish of beetroot." Wilson had a model made in wood of a portion of the Piazza, measuring about six feet from the floor, including the stand. This he used as a receptacle for his painting implements; the rustic-work of the piers was divided into drawers, and the openings of the arches were filled with pencils and oil-bottles. When Wilson finally left London for Wales, he sold this model for about four pounds.

Crossing into Henrietta-street (called after Henrietta Maria,

Queen of Charles I.), here have been a few changes. The street, at first, was a place of high fashion: the last relic, in our time, was a first-rate hairdresser's at the east end; nearly opposite lodged, with her parents, the lovely Maria Foote, when in her theatrical career. In this street lived Kitty Clive, the actress; and Paul Whitehead, the poet. Other tenants, as Samuel Cooper, the miniature-painter, and M'Ardell and Sir Robert Strange, the distinguished engravers, have given the street artistic fame. Sir Joshua Reynolds used to declare that M'Ardell's prints (of his pictures) would immortalise him; and J. T. Smith estimated M'Ardell's print from Hogarth's picture of Captain Coram as surpassing any thing in mezzotinto now extant. Sir Robert Strange, originally a soldier in the rebel army of 1745, when Duke William put them to flight, saved his life by fleeing into a house, the door of which was open, and was there concealed under the hoop of a lady, with whom he fell in love, and married; he then became a loyal man, was pardoned by the King, and knighted. He ranks as "unquestionably the best engraver England ever produced;" his integrity in delivering subscription impressions was most scrupulous; he never took off more proofs than were really bespoke, and every name was put upon the print as it came out of the press, unless it were faulty, and then it was destroyed. Yet, many years after Sir Robert's death, his well-deserved reputation suffered by his defaced copper-plates being worked and sold, until the fraud was detected.

The street had the Castle Tavern, where Sheridan fought and disarmed Captain Mathews, his rival in Miss Linley's love. Here, too, was Rawthmell's Coffee-house, where the Society of Arts first met, March 29th, 1754, with Shipley, the drawing-master, for secretary; though Oliver Goldsmith had been a candidate for the office.

We now come to a tavern of our own day, No. 23, Offley's— which enjoyed great and deserved celebrity. It is sketched with a free hand n *Bentley's Miscellany*, March 1841, in *Horæ Offleana*. The supper-room was large and well-proportioned, and was, to our thinking, the best room of the kind in town; no pictures, placards, landscape paper-hangings, or vulgar coffee-room finery, to disturb one's relish of the good things there provided. Offley, according to this writer, was originally at Bellamy's, and, "as such, was privileged to watch, and occasionally admitted to assist, the presiding priestess of the gridiron at the exercise of her mysteries." Offley's chop was thick and substantial; the House of Commons' chop was small and thin, and honourable Members sometimes ate a dozen at a sitting. Offley's chop was served with shred shalots, warmed in gravy; and, accompanied by nips of Burton ale, was a delicious after-theatre supper. The large room at that hour was generally crowded with a higher class of men than are to be seen in taverns of the present day. There was excellent dining up-stairs, with wines really worth drinking—all with a sort of Quakerly plainness, but solid comfort. The fast men came to the great room, where the *spécialité* was singing by amateurs upon one evening of the week; and to prevent the chorus waking the dead in their cerements in the adjoining churchyard, the only window of the room was double. The "professionals" staid away. Francis Crew sang Moore's melodies, then in their zenith; sometimes, in a spirit of waggery, an amateur would sing "Chevy Chase" in full; and now and then Offley himself trolled out one of Captain Morris's lyrics. Such was this right joyously convivial place some five-and-forty years since upon the singing night. Upon other evenings, there came to a large round table (a sort of privileged place) a few well-to-do, substantial tradesmen from the neighbourhood; among whom was the renowned surgical-instrument maker from the Strand, who had the sagacity to buy the iron from off the piles of Old London Bridge (after it had lain for centuries under water), and convert it into some of the finest surgical instruments ever made. Offley's, however, declined: the singing was discontinued; time had thinned the ranks and groups of the bright and buoyant; the large room was frequented only by quiet, orderly persons, who kept good hours; the theatre-suppers grew few and far between; the merry old host departed,—when it was proposed to have his portrait painted—but in vain: success had ebbed away. The house was let to the Cambridge publishers, the Macmillans, who have since built for themselves a classically-fronted house in Bedford-street. By the way, in two houses opposite Offley's, Mr. Bohn, *père*, assembled his immense stock of books, to be outnumbered by his eldest son, Mr. Henry Bohn, in York-street,—thus maintaining the classic character of Covent Garden as a region of bibliopoles.

In Chandos-street the last silk-mercer's firm has disappeared: it was here that a large fortune was made from the famous mazarine-blue silk, the colour of the Cardinals' robes. Here lodged Humphrey Wanley, the antiquary, as we gather from a letter in the Harleian Mss. from the Rev. Thomas Baker, Cambridge, Oct. 16 (1718), addressed "To the worthy Mr. Wanley, at the Riding-hood Shop, the corner of Chandois and Bedford-streets, Covent Garden:" here we learn that the shop was also famed for its riding-hoods. The father of John Thelwall, the politician, was a silk-mercer in this street, where John was born, in 1764.

It is hardly worth extending our walk in Chandos-street, to record two of its olden notorieties, or rather infamies. Here, at the Hole-in-the-Wall Tavern, was arrested, in the reign of Charles II., the highwayman Duval. And, in an "improvement" clearance about 1830, was taken down, on the north side of Chandos-street, the large hotel known as "the Key," mentioned in scandalous chronicles of the present century as the resort of rakes, royal and noble, and their companions, for whose privacy coaches drove under the gateway, close to the hotel-door.

As you enter Maiden-lane from Bedford-street, it is hard to imagine Andrew Marvell lodging in a second-floor in this narrow place, when he sat in Parliament for Hull, and refused a Treasury order for 1000*l.*, brought to him by Lord Danby from the King. Nor can we fancy Voltaire lodging in this dull lane, at the White Peruke. More in character with the place is the Cyder Cellar, opened about 1730, and described as a "Midnight Concert-room," in *Adventures Underground*, 1750. Porson was a great lover of cyder, the patronymic drink for which the place was once famed: it became his nightly haunt; and he is even said to have passed his wedding-night here, and left at eight next morning. We remember the place not many years after Porson's death, when it was, as its name implied, a cellar, and the fittings were rude and rough: over the mantelpiece was a large mezzotint portrait of Porson, framed and glazed, which we take to be the missing portrait named by the Rev. Mr. Watson, in his lately published Life of the Professor. The Cyder Cellar was described in the *London Magazine*, by Charles Lamb, about 1823, as famous for political debates and discussions.

In the first-floor of the adjoining house was located, for a time, the Fielding Club—a society of authors and artists; prominent among whom was Albert Smith, ever ready with his lively and harmless rattle, without a grain of ill-nature in a whole night's patter and pleasant humour.

In the house, No. 26, nearly opposite, lived William Turner, who dressed wigs, shaved beards, and, in the days of queues, topknots, and hair-powder, waited on the gentlemen of the Garden at their own houses; when a hairdresser's was a more profitable trade than at the present day. A door under the arched passage on the right led to the shop, in the room above which was born, in the spring of 1775, Joseph Mallord William Turner, "the most prolific, the most varied, and the greatest landscape-painter the world ever saw;" he was baptised at St. Paul's, Covent Garden, on May 14, in the same year. At a very early age he took to drawing, and next coloured prints by John Raphael Smith, the crayon-painter and mezzotinto-engraver, who then lived in Maiden-lane. Another of Smith's colourers was Thomas Girtin, the founder of our English school of water-colour art; and from Girtin, Turner acquired his love for landscape-painting. Young Turner removed to apartments in Hand-court, next the above house, and, during his residence here, exhibited at the Royal Academy fifty-nine pictures. The great painter's natal house has been taken down, but the court, with the quaint school-house, remains.

Opposite the Cyder Cellar lodged Proctor, the painter and

sculptor, and a fellow-student with Flaxman: he was found here by West, in very reduced circumstances, and in a disturbed state of mind, arising from pecuniary embarrassment, and a most honourable wish to leave England for Rome, as a student of the Royal Academy, free of every debt. A friend of Proctor's went privately to a gentleman who held a note for money lent, and represented Proctor's distress; when the creditor put the note into the fire, and desired that the artist should make himself easy. Early next morning his friend hastened to Maiden-lane with the good news, but found that Proctor had died the preceding night. Thus, in two adjoining houses, how opposite was the fate of genius! Proctor's best work is Ixion on the Wheel.

Through Maiden-lane we pass to Southampton-street: near the foot stood Bedford House, principally built of wood; the garden extended northward, its wall bounding Covent-Garden Market. In Southampton-street is a bar-gate of the Duke of Bedford, who has power to erect walls and gates at the end of every thoroughfare on his estate. Here, in 1711, Bohea-tea was sold at 26*s.* per pound, at the sign of the Barber's Pole. At No. 27 lived David Garrick, before he removed to the Adelphi-terrace, No. 5, the new house which he had purchased.

No. 31, late Godfrey and Cooke's, was the oldest chemist's and druggist's shop in London; but was removed from here in 1863. *Here phosphorus was first manufactured in England;* the above premises having been the house, shop, and laboratory of Ambrose Godfrey Hanckwitz, who, immediately after the discovery of phosphorus by Brandt, the alchemist, under the instructions of the celebrated Robert Boyle, succeeded in preparing an ounce of the substance, and presented it to his master. Boyle's accounts of it, and his experiments, caused a demand for phosphorus; and Hanckwitz, working under Boyle's directions, commenced to manufacture it, and produced it in larger quantities than any other person. In his advertisement he says: "For the information of the curious, he is the only one in London who makes inflammable phosphorus, which can be preserved in water. Phosphorus of Bolognian stone, flowers of phosphorus, black phosphorus, and that made with acid oil, and other varieties. All unadulterated; every description of good drugs. He sells wholesale and retail.—N.B. He sells solid phosphorus, wholesale, fifty shillings an ounce, and retail, three pounds sterling the ounce."

Bedford House was taken down in 1704, and Southampton-street was then commenced: here, in 1706, Hanckwitz built his premises, the business of a chemist having been carried on by him in the neighbourhood since 1680. Jacob Bell, in his *Historical Sketch of the Progress of Pharmacy in Great Britain*, tells us that Hanckwitz "was a maker of phosphorus and other chemicals which were rare at that period, and which he sold in different parts of the country during his travels. His laboratory was a fashionable resort in the afternoon on certain occasions, when he performed popular experiments for the amusement of his friends. It opened with glass-doors into a garden, which extended as far as the Strand, but which is now built upon. Four curious old prints of the laboratory in its former state are in the possession of Messrs. Godfrey and Cooke (now of Knightsbridge); also a portrait of Hanckwitz, engraved by Vertue (1718), which he had distributed among his customers as a keepsake." Hanckwitz died in 1741. His successors, Godfrey and Cooke, maintained the date 1680 on their premises in Southampton-street; and upon a board, over the entrance to the laboratory, in Maiden-lane, where the seat of the important chemical manufacture is now a potato-store! We confess that we looked upon this change with a feeling of regret. Perchance some reader may say, "What care I about phosphorus!" Many a better-informed one will remember that to the utilisation of this elementary body we owe that domestic wonder—the Lucifer Match, accidentally discovered by a chemist and druggist of Stockton-upon-Tees some forty years ago, and brought into practice by Faraday.

With this brilliant *feu de chimie* we end our "Changes in Covent Garden."

THE LAST OF THE FLEET PRISON.

A Prison is a house of care,
  A place where none can thrive;
A touchstone true to try a friend,
  A grave for one alive:
Sometimes a place of right,
  Sometimes a place of wrong,
Sometimes a place of rogues and thieves,
  And honest men among.

Inscription on the Tolbooth, Edinburgh.

A PRISON in a crowded city is one of its waste places—a scene of stagnant life, yet where, in the lines of the nursery lyrist,

Satan finds some mischief still
For idle hands to do.

Such was the Prison of the Fleet; first built, some eight centuries since, upon the bank of a rapid stream, taking its rise in the rural heights of Hampstead,—fresh and clear in its early course,—but becoming foul and dark onward, through the pollution of the town; and passing the City wall,

To where Fleet-ditch, with disemboguing streams,
Rolls its large tribute of dead dogs to Thames.

Pope, *Dunciad.*

For nearly eight centuries had the Fleet been a place of security or confinement, and the terror of evil-doers of almost every grade. The disappearance of such a pile, certainly one of the most ancient foundations in the metropolis, should not pass without being made a note of; and, although the last building was little more than sixty years old, the *locus in quo* is storied with associations of more than ten times that date; during which its cells and dungeons were tenanted by political and religious martyrs, and men of more pliant consciences whom the law stigmatised as debtors. In whatever appropriation we regard the Fleet Prison, its entire removal indicates the reformed spirit of our jurisprudence, criminal and civil.

It appears, from various records, that "the Prison called the Fleet" was formerly held in conjunction with the manor of Leveland, in the county of Kent, and with "the King's houses at Westminster." The manor was part of the ancient possessions of the See of Canterbury, being held of the several Archbishops by knights' service. In the ninth of Richard I. (1198), Nathaniel de Leveland and Robert de Leveland, his son, were fined in sixty marks, to have the custody of the royal houses and of the prison, which, they stated, had been their inheritance ever since the Conquest.

Stow records that, in 1202, third of King John, the King granted the wardenship of the Fleet and the wardenship of the daughter and heir of Robert Leveland to Simon Fitz-Robert, Archdeacon of Wells. From 1206 to 1215, Robert de Leveland was warden; Margaret, his widow, carried the manor, &c., in marriage to Giles de Badlesmere; but he, having married her without the King's license, could not obtain his pardon till about three years previous to his death, and not then without great intercession. The early history of the Prison is, however, little better than a sealed book; the burning of the building by the followers of Wat Tyler being the only noticeable event. By the regulations of this period, the warden might arm the porters at the gates with halberts, bills, or other weapons.

Among the distinguished prisoners was the impetuous Henry Howard, Earl of Surrey, who was first committed here for sending a challenge: he was allowed in the prison two servants to wait upon him, but not permitted to entertain any of his friends at table. He made several applications for his release; pleaded to the Privy Council "the fury of reckless youth," and the inoffensiveness of his past life; and begged that, if he may not be liberated, he may at least be removed to a place of confinement in better air; he was then removed to Windsor, and in four days released. In 1543, Surrey was summoned before the Privy Council, at the instance of the City authorities, for having eaten flesh in Lent; and for having, with young Wyatt, the poet's son, and Pickering, gone about the streets at midnight, breaking windows with stone-bows. To the first charge he pleaded a license; submitting to sentence on the second, for which he was again sent to the Fleet. During his imprisonment, he wrote his Satire upon the Citizens, in which he pretends that he broke their windows to awaken them to a sense of their iniquities: it commences thus:

> London! hast thou accused me
> Of breach of laws? the root of strife,
> Within whose breast did boil to see,
> So fervent hot, thy dissolute life;
> That even the hate of sins that grow
> Within thy wicked walls so rife,
> For to break forth did convert so,
> That terror could it not repress.

Surrey's grave irony has misled the editor of his Poems, who states the poet's motive to have been a religious one; a very absurd defence of a vinous frolic of window-breaking.

Nash was imprisoned here for writing the satirical play of the *Isle of Dogs*, never printed: he died at the early age of thirty-five, having "prodigally conspired against good hours." Pope might well designate the Fleet "the Haunt of the Muses."

In the reigns of Edward VI. and Queen Mary, several victims of bigotry were committed here. Bishop Hooper was twice sentenced to the Fleet, which he only quitted, in 1555, for the stake and the fire at Gloucester: upon his way thither, he slept at the Angel Inn, St. Clement's, Strand. In the Fleet, his bed was "a little pad of straw, with a rotten covering;" his "chamber was vile and stinking."*

* At Gloucester, a statue of Bishop Hooper has been erected, at the cost of one hundred guineas; sculptor, Thornhill, of Dublin. It stands on a Gothic pedestal, surmounted by a canopy and a Gothic spire; which were built by the poorer inhabitants of Gloucester and its neighbourhood, at the expense of about 400*l.*, on the spot where the Bishop was burnt. This

The Sergeancy, or Wardenship of the Fleet, appears to have been early a "place," in the worst sense of the term. In 1586, it was underlet to two persons, whose cruelty and extortion were so heinous, that a Commission was issued to inquire into the matter of complaint.

At this time the Fleet was the prison for persons committed from the Court of Star Chamber. Bacon, in early life, held the office of Registrar of this infamous Court, worth about 1600*l.* per annum. In his *Life of King Henry VII.* he characterises this Court as "one of the sagest and noblest institutions of this kingdom;" "composed of good elements, for it consisteth of counsellors, peers, prelates, and chief judges."

From the reign of Elizabeth to the sixteenth of Charles I. (1641), the Star Chamber was in full activity. Among its political victims consigned to the Fleet were Prynne and Lilburne. Prynne was committed here for writing his *Histriomastix;* taken out of the prison, and, after suffering pillory, branding, mutilation of the nose, and loss of ears, was remanded to the Fleet. Lilburne, "Free-born John," and his printer, were committed to the Fleet for libel and sedition: the former was smartly whipped at the cart's-tail, from the prison to the pillory, placed between Westminster Hall and Star Chamber; and taken back doubly ironed into the prison-wards.

To Howel's imprisonment we owe his very entertaining *Familiar Letters,* several of which are dated from here. By "A Letter to the Earl of B., from the Fleet," Nov. 20, 1643, Howel was arrested "one morning betimes," by five men, armed with "swords, pistils, and bils," and some days after committed to the Fleet; and he adds, "As far as I see, I must lie at dead *anchor* in this *Fleet* a long time, unlesse some gentle *gale* blow thence to make me *launch* out." Then we find him consoling himself with the reflection that "the English peeple are in effect but prisoners, as all other islanders are." Other Letters by Howel date from the Fleet, 1645-6-7. Though

Memorial was inaugurated February 9th, 1863, the 308th anniversary of Hooper's martyrdom.

some of the Letters dated from various places abroad are believed to have been written in the prison, they bear internal evidence that Howel had visited these places.

In 1655, the Fleet and keeping of the Palace at Westminster were conveyed, for a consideration, to Jeremy Whichcote, Esq., of the Temple, barrister-at-law. At the request of Charles II., during his exile, Whichcote purchased the Wardenship, and, by officiating sometimes himself, sheltered the King's agents, and prevented a treacherous design against his person: for this he received a patent of baronetcy, dated Brussels, 2d April 1660; which title is borne at the present time by his descendant, Sir Thomas Whichcote, of Aswarby Park, Lincolnshire.

The Prison was burnt a second time on 4th September 1666, during the Great Fire; after which, Sir Jeremy Whichcote, the Warden, purchased Caron House and ten acres of land, in South Lambeth, for the safe keeping of the prisoners; the King appointed Caron House to be the prison of the Fleet; but it was rebuilt upon the old spot, and the prisoners were removed there.

After the abolition of the Star Chamber, in 1641, the Fleet became a prison for debtors, and for contempt of the Court of Chancery, Common Pleas, and Exchequer. It appears to have been used for the confinement of debtors from the thirteenth century, at least, by a petition from John Frauncey, a debtor in the Fleet, A.D. 1290.

Wycherley, the wit and dramatist, lay in the Fleet seven years, ruined through his Countess' settlement being disputed: he was thrown into prison, and is said to have been at last relieved by James II., who, having gone to see Wycherley's *Plain Dealer* acted, was so delighted, that he gave orders for the payment of the author's debts, and settling a pension of 200*l.* a year on him; but this history has an apocryphal air.

Sir Richard Baker, the chronicler, was one of the most unfortunate debtors confined here: he married in 1620, and soon after got into pecuniary difficulties, and was thrown into the

Fleet, where he spent the remaining years of his life, and died in 1644-5, in a state of extreme poverty. Mr. Cunningham, from the rate-books of St. Clement's Danes, tells us that Sir Richard lived in Milford-lane, Strand, from 1632 to 1639: possibly Lady Baker resided here. Sir Richard wrote his *Chronicle*, published 1641, and other works, as a means of subsistence, during his imprisonment. The *Chronicle* was for a century the popular book among the squires and ancient country gentlemen of the school of Sir Roger de Coverley. The author's residence in the Fleet was not very compatible with reference to authorities and antiquarian research; though full of errors, it has given more pleasure and diffused more acquaintance with history than works of higher pretensions: it is now little read; but we may remark, that in our time certain historical works which are most read are by no means the most accurate. Baker's *Chronicle* is certainly one of our most amusing "prison books," and has been treated with much unmerited ridicule. Sir Richard was interred in the nearest church, old St. Bride's, the burial-place of the Fleet Wardens. Francis Sandford, author of the *Genealogical History*, also died in the Fleet, in 1693.

We pass to another class of committals. Keys was sent here for marrying the Lady Mary Grey, the sister of Lady Jane Grey; Dr. Donne, for marrying Sir George More's daughter without her father's knowledge; Sir Robert Killigrew, for speaking to Sir Thomas Overbury as he came from visiting Sir Walter Raleigh; the Countess of Dorset, for pressing into the Privy Chamber, and importuning James I., "contrary to commandment;" and Lucius Carey, Viscount Falkland, for sending a challenge.

The abuses of the Wardenship did not disappear with the abolition of the Star Chamber; but the Warden still continued to exact enormous fees, by putting in irons and oppressing prisoners for debt, worse than in the time of the Star Chamber. In a little volume entitled the *Cries of the Oppressed*, published by Moses Pitt, in 1691, the enormities of the Fleet, where the author was imprisoned for debt, are unsparingly exposed; and a curious view of the place, its inmates and visitors, is given some of the latter wearing fashionable wigs, and carrying flowers to prevent "noisome smells" (then prevalent in the gaol) injuring their health. At the grated windows are destitute prisoners clamouring for charity, and a gentleman is contributing to the begging-box, which is handed to him; here are the turnkey with his huge key, visitors waiting to be let out, the grating in the door, formidable spikes upon the wall; and above it are seen the lofty hats of the persons walking in the opposite street.

In 1696, the Fleet cruelties and enormities were made public; but it was not until 1727 that a Committee of the House of Commons sat at the prison, and reported the Fleet to have been rebuilt by Sir Jeremy Whichcote, as a consideration for Charles II. having granted him the Wardenship and the keeping of the Palace at Westminster; the shops in Westminster Hall, certain tenements adjoining the Fleet, &c. But the Prison, being freehold, fell by descent or purchase into incapable hands, and the patent was set aside; and after a single life-grant, one Huggins, by giving 5000*l.* to Lord Clarendon, obtained the grant of the office for his own and his son's life. Huggins permitted numerous persons to escape from the prison and rules, among whom were two Crown debtors, of 4000*l.* and 10,000*l.*; in short, he confessed that so many persons escaped during his wardenship, that it was impossible to enumerate them. Charges of oppression and cruelty were also brought home to him. Huggins next surrendered the patent for 5000*l.* to Bambridge, who permitted Crown debtors to escape, extorted large sums of money, and loaded debtors with irons and put them into dungeons. The Committee found here instruments of torture which Bambridge had put on the necks of prisoners, to extort fees or bribes; and among other sufferers here was Sir William Rich, confined in a loathsome dungeon and loaded with irons, for some slight offence he had given to Bambridge. Another of his victims, Jacob Mendez Solas, after being seized and fettered, and kept in a sponging-house for a week, was turned into the dungeon, or "Strong Room," a vault where dead bodies were kept until the coroner's inquest passed upon them; it had no chimney or fireplace, and only light through a hole eight inches square; it was neither paved, boarded, nor plastered, and built over the common sewer, close to the prison dunghill: in this wretched cell the poor prisoner was kept, manacled and shackled, for nearly two months.

It is to this Gaol Committee, who exposed these enormities, that Thomson so touchingly alludes in his *Winter:*

> And here can I forget the generous band,
> Who, touched with human woe, redressive searched
> Into the horrors of the gloomy gaol?—
> Unpitied and unheard, where misery moans;
> Where sickness pines; where thirst and hunger burn,
> And poor misfortune feels the lash of vice.

Hogarth painted Bambridge before the Committee: he was tried, but acquitted for want of evidence; he died a few years afterwards by his own hand. In his time, the Prison was divided into Common Side and Master's Side; every prisoner, at his entrance, was forced to pay six shillings to the tipstaff, towards a bowl of punch; he had to bring his own bedding, or hire it of the Warden, or lie on the floor. Prisoners were called pigeons; and it was proved that Bambridge had retained men in prison long after they had been ordered to be discharged, and had even made one man a prisoner by force. Drunken, disorderly persons were then punished by putting them in the stocks; and prisoners attempting to escape were put in a tub at the gate of the prison, by way of public shame. The Committee of 1729 estimated the rents, perquisites, and profits of the wardenship at 4623*l.* 18*s.* 2*d.* per annum. In James I.'s reign, the Warden's fee was 19*l.* 4*s.* 3*d.*; in 1807, 200*l.* a year. A Warden who succeeded in 1758 held the office for sixty-two years.

One Dance, the son of the architect of old Buckingham House and Guy's Hospital, was imprisoned in the Fleet as a debtor, and, in a poem entitled the *Humours of the Fleet*, 1749, has described the inmates of "this poor but merry place," its rackets or wrestle, billiards, backgammon, and whist; the rough justice of drenching disturbers of the peace beneath the pump; the "tip" for the chamberlain to show proper lodgings; the master's fee, 1*l.* 2*s.* 8*d.*, for a decent room; which was sometimes "Mount Scoundrel," wretched quarters on the Common Side, shown to get a fee for better. Dance's book has a frontispiece of the prison-yard: a new-comer treating the gaoler, cook, and others, to drink; racket-playing against the high brick-wall, with *chevaux-de-frise* mountings; and a pump and a *tree* in one corner.

Dance tells of a "wind-up to a day in prison,"—that watchmen repeated, *Who goes out?* from half-past nine till St. Paul's clock struck ten, to give visitors notice to depart; when the last stroke was given, they cried, *All told;* the gates were locked, and nobody suffered to go out upon any account.

Curll's Corinna, Mrs. Thomas, was a prisoner in the Fleet for some time: on her release she took a small lodging in Fleet-street, where she died, February 3, 1730. The notorious Mrs. Cornelys died in the Fleet in 1797. Another eccentric prisoner here was Parson Ford, who figures in Hogarth's Midnight Conversation: he died here in 1731. Parson Keith, of May Fair, was here in 1758; and Robert Lloyd, the poet, and Churchill's friend, in 1764.

A century ago the Prison was considered a nuisance; and, in 1769, it was proposed to remove it to Ely House, Holborn; but the opposition of the inhabitants prevailed. It was then planned to transfer it to St. George's Fields.*

But in the Riots of 1780, the Fleet was destroyed by fire, and the prisoners liberated by the rioters. Most of the papers and records were lost; though there remain scattered books and documents of several centuries back. The Warden had been directed by the Lord Mayor not to make any resistance to the mob, which, as an eye-witness informed the writer of a short history of the Fleet published in 1845, might have been easily dispersed by a few soldiers. The rioters were polite enough to

* It was then also proposed to remove Fleet Market, which had been built over part of the Ditch, to the site of the Prison; and make a street through the Swan Inn, Holborn-bridge, to Turnmill-street.

send notice to the prisoners of the time of their coming; and on being informed that it would be inconvenient, on account of the lateness of the hour, to postpone their visit to the following day. The conflagration here must have been terrible; for Horace Walpole tells us, that his printer beheld three sides of Fleet Market in flames; Barnard's Inn at one end, the Prison at one side, and the distiller's at the other, besides Fetter-lane and Shoe-lane.

After the Riots, the Prison was rebuilt, with stone staircases. It consisted chiefly of one long brick pile, parallel with Farringdon-street; the entrance was by a passage immediately into a court, the whole length of the place on one side, and bounded on the other by a high wall, ending in *chevaux-de-frise.* Passing through the lobby, you entered another court, the whole length of the Prison, sixty yards, and surrounded by lofty walls. In this court was a good racket-ground. The Prison was all one building, in four floors, or "galleries," having passages the whole length of the building, which comprised the chapel, coffee-room, and tap-rooms. There was no "prison allowance," but various donations from the Courts of Exchequer, Chancery, Common Pleas, from the City Companies, and private individuals.

The galleries were ill-lighted, and had almost countless doors, opening into single rooms, 14½ by 12½ feet. The dark and dirty appearance of the passages, and the turmoil of prisoners and visitors passing to and from the rooms; the ceaseless banging of doors, echoing through the vaulted roof,—had a depressing effect upon the nerves, and made one shudder at man's self-imposed suffering. The rooms presented the usually wretched aspect of a debtors'-prison luxury in the dirty-white squalor of the walls, perchance scrawled with the offscourings of a low mind, or vulgarity ill at ease, and exemplifying "want of decency is want of sense." Perchance, too, the light streamed through the begrimed window upon a bed of "London white," which the occupant, in the heyday of dissipation, would have scarcely deemed fit for a pauper; whilst the tattered curtains, the rickety and broken furniture, and "G. R." upon the jambs of the grate, denoted all manner of unrest.

The inmates and stragglers in this house of care presented almost as much variety as a parish crowd. Here might be seen the turbaned debtor, bewrapped in the dirty relics of his flaunting finery; the *ci-devant* man of property, creeping about in rags, and craving to do the offices of the menial; and the woful wife, ministering to cheat sorrow of a smile—yet heart-sick and sore. Ever and anon doors opened, and there came forth the revel-shout and the jolly laugh—the indiscriminate welcome which would have the whole world for a table, and keep it in a roar.

They whom curiosity tempted to stroll thither did not soon forget the rabble rout and their nestling-places. Alack! what strange bedfellows did Debt—a phase of misery—make men acquainted with in the Fleet!

If a prisoner did not wish to go to the Common Side,—a building apart, and to the right of the Master's Side, where he was put, with several other prisoners, into a common room, divided only cabin-fashion, for which he paid nothing,—he had the choice of going down into "Bartholomew Fair," where he paid 1*s.* 3*d.* for the undisturbed use of a room; or up to some of the better apartments, where he paid the same rent, but was subject to "chummage," *i. e.* a fellow-prisoner put into his room, or "chummed upon him;" but who might be got rid of for 4*s.* 6*d.* a week, or more, according to the fulness of the Prison. The latter prisoner would then provide himself with a common lodging, by letting which inmates of the Fleet were known to have accumulated much money.

Out of doors there was a strange indication of recreant waste, vagabondism, and recklessness. Here might be seen the *characterless* characters of the place, in which debtors' prisons were sure to abound. Smokers and other idlers loitered about the steps leading to the racket-ground, where many won who had lamentably failed with the ball of life. Beneath a shed was played skittles—the senseless wooden rumble echoing through the place, though not drowning the roar of the great town outside; and you might see two or three of its church-spires above the iron fringe of the prison-walls. What a painful reflection was called up by the outside roar, in contrast with the bankrupt life within these walls! Then, as if to keep up the mockery, they verged upon the yard of the Belle Sauvage Inn—a place strongly suggestive of locomotive liberty.

The morals of the place seemed incorrigible. Half a century ago, a Parliamentary Committee reported the prevalence of scenes of riot and disorder, and the difficulty of altogether preventing them; and though the Warden had the power of confining those guilty of disorderly behaviour, the punishment did not seem to produce much effect.

Another Fleet abuse remains to be noticed. Marriages were performed in this Prison, previously to 1754; and though not legal and regular, were tacitly recognised as being valid and indissoluble. Many of these weddings were really performed in the Prison-chapel; though the "Fleet parsons" and tavern-keepers in the neighbourhood fitted up a room as a chapel; and most of the taverns near the Fleet kept their own registers. In the *Grub-street Journal* of January 1735, we read: "There are a set of drunken, swearing parsons, with their myrmidons, who wear black coats, and pretend to be clerks and registers of the Fleet, and who ply about Ludgate-hill, pulling and forcing people to some peddling alehouse or brandy-shop, to be married; even on a Sunday, stopping them as they go to church, and almost tearing their clothes off their backs." Pennant says: "In walking along the streets in my youth, on the side next the Prison, I have often been tempted by the question, 'Sir, will you be pleased to walk in and be married?' Along this most lawless space was frequently hung up the sign of a male and female, with hands conjoined, with 'Marriages performed within' written underneath. A dirty fellow invited you. The parson was seen walking before his shop; a squalid, profligate figure, clad in a tattered plaid night-gown, with a fiery face, and ready to couple you for a dram of gin or roll of tobacco."

The indecency of these practices, and the facility they afforded for accomplishing forced and fraudulent marriages, were not the only evils. Marriages could be antedated, without limit, on payment of a fee, or not entered at all. Parties could be married without declaring their names. Women hired temporary husbands at the Fleet, in order that they might be able to plead coverture to an action for debt, or to produce a certificate in case of their being *enceinte.* These hired husbands were provided by the parson for five shillings each; sometimes they were women. And for half-a-guinea a marriage might be registered and certified that never took place.

In the Fleet, the errant Edward Wortley Montague (Lady Mary's son) was married; also Charles Churchill, the poet; and the Hon. H. Fox, son of the first Lord Holland, to the daughter of the Duke of Richmond. In 1702, the Bishop of London interfered, to prevent the scandalous practice, but with little effect; and it was not until the passing of the Act of Parliament, in 1754, that the evil was put an end to: on the day previously (March 24), in one register-book alone, were recorded 217 marriages, the last of the Fleet weddings. In 1821, a collection of the registers, weighing more than a ton, and recording Fleet marriages, was purchased by Government, and deposited in the Bishop of London's Registry, Doctor's Commons: the earliest is dated 1674. They are not now, as formerly, received in evidence: Lord Kenyon considered them admissible in a pedigree case; and Lord Eldon as declarations. Still, they are not altogether useless as matters of record (see *History of the Fleet Marriages,* "The Parsons and their Registers," &c., by John S. Burn).

Above the entrance to the Prison was the figure 9; so that a delicate address, given by the prisoners, was "No. 9 Fleet Market." The front had also, southward, an arched opening into a cell-like room, called "the grate," from the crossed iron-bars at the window. Above was inscribed, "Pray remember the poor prisoners, having no allowance;" a small box was placed at the window-sill, to receive the charity of passengers in the street, while a prisoner within shouted in loudly-suppliant tones the echoing prayer. We have dropped a few pence into this box, and the emphatic *prayer* lingers in our ears. This was a relic of the ancient Prison, corresponding with the "begging at the grate" in some old comedies, as well as with "having part of the box." There was written for this poor-box, in 1812, the following quaint inscription :

> Da obolum insolventibus,
> Qui in hoc carcere, sine pane, sine pecuniâ, sine amicis,
> et oh ! sine libertate,
> Vitam miserrimam trahunt.

There was likewise "the Running Box;" that is, a man running to and fro in the neighbouring streets, shaking a box, and begging the passengers to put money into it for the poor prisoners in the Fleet. In Marcellus Lauron's *Cries of London*, published in 1710, is a representation of such a person, with his cry of "Remember the poor prisoners !" inscribed beneath him. At his back, a capacious covered basket is suspended by leathern straps round his arms for broken victuals ; and he carries in one hand a staff, and in the other a small, round, deep box, with an aperture in the lid for receiving alms in money.

The liberty of the Rules and Day-Rules of the Fleet may be traced to the reign of Richard II., when prisoners were allowed to go at large, by bail, or with a baston (tipstaff), for nights and days together. This license was paid for at 8*d.* per day, and 12*d.* for his keep that shall be with him. These were the Day-Rules. The Rules wherein prisoners were allowed to lodge were enlarged, so as to include the churches of St. Bride and St. Martin, Ludgate ; New Bridge-street, Blackfriars, to the Thames ; Dorset-street and Salisbury-square ; and part of Fleet-street ; Ludgate hill and street, to the entrance to St. Paul's Churchyard ; the Old Bailey, and the lanes and courts in the vicinity : the whole circuit being one mile and a half. Those requiring the Rules (called Rulers) had to provide sureties for keeping the boundaries, and to pay to the Warden a percentage on the amount of debts for which they were detained :

if the Rules were broken, the Warden was responsible. Formerly, the Rules extended only to the London Coffee-house, and from Ludgate-hill to Fleet-lane, so that lodgings were bad, and very dear. The Fleet and the Queen's Bench were the only prisons in the kingdom to which these privileges had been for centuries attached. Penn, the founder of Pennsylvania, was living in the Rules in 1707; Richard Savage, to be secure from his creditors, took a lodging "within the liberties of the Fleet," and here his friends sent him every Monday a guinea. He is now proved to have been an arrant impostor.*

Howel's *Letters*, already mentioned, have had a reflex in our time in Richard Oastler's *Fleet Papers*, "a weekly epistle on public matters," inscribed to Thomas Thornhill, Esq., of Fixby Hall, Yorkshire, whose steward Oastler had been, and at whose suit he was imprisoned here; he was liberated by subscription, February 12, 1844, and has left an interesting account of his imprisonment. Of Oastler, a colossal bronze group, by Philip, has been erected at Bradford, in memory of his advocacy of the Ten-Hours Factory Bill.

At length this pest of a Prison was, in 1842, abolished by Act of Parliament; and its few inmates were drafted to the Queen's Prison. The property, covering nearly an acre of ground, was then purchased of the Government by the Corporation of London for 25,000*l.* It was taken down in 1846, and the materials were sold,—comprising nearly 3,000,000 of bricks, 50 tons of lead, 40,000 feet of paving, &c. It was then proposed to make available the site of the Prison as part of a scheme of a Grand Central Railway Terminus, by Mr. Charles Pearson, the City Solicitor. To this, however, the Corporation demurred; and the ground, after lying almost useless for seventeen years, was sold to the London, Chatham, and Dover Railway Company for the erection of their Ludgate Station.

Thus have we journeyed through the dark history of the Prison of the Fleet. It would be difficult to point to any spot

* See Mr. Moy Thomas's admirable papers in *Notes and Queries*, 2d S., vol. xi.

in the metropolis, save the Tower, whereon crime and infamy of every hue so long held sway; even in its mildest phase, as a Debtors' Prison, it had long been odious. To get rid of such a pestilential place was a most beneficial measure: nevertheless, the teaching by example which its history presents should not be lost sight of in the public gain to be anticipated from the new appropriation of the site—or, in the change from a pool of stagnant life to a centre of boundless civilisation. We remember the piteous cry of "*Pray* remember!" and at the same instant four men in the pillory, within the shade of the Prison, of which "the grate" is the last to disappear: paraphrasing the old Diarist, we behold the change, and bless God.

The transition has been the work of many years. More than a century ago, the benevolent Dr. Fothergill projected the great street from Blackfriars northward to Islington, which we now see partly realised in Farringdon-road. In clearing this portion of the valley of the Fleet, many old and decaying dwellings, some of date anterior to the Fire of London, have been swept away, thus opening from Coppice-row (a name suggestive of rurality) a new view of St. Paul's Cathedral. The moral clearance westward commenced some twenty years ago, with the removal of that infamous rookery of the dangerous classes, Field-lane, with its mart for stolen silk handkerchiefs, purchased from pick-pockets, and well described as "the emporium of petty larceny." Chick-lane was then weeded, and horrifying were the stories of the haunts of Jack Sheppard and Jonathan Wild, which were pointed out here; and the thieves' lodging-houses and taverns, and trap-doors through which unwary visitors had been slipped into the Fleet; whilst bones and fragments of bodies unearthed from the basements disproved the adage, that "dead men tell no tales." These strange sights were nine-day wonders; but they have left impressions which time has strengthened rather than effaced.

FORTY YEARS IN FLEET-STREET.

FLEET* is nearly as applicable to this life-stream of London as it was to the small river which, centuries ago, taking its rise in a hill-side of Hampstead, ran through gardens and orchards into the busy town. We all remember Dr. Johnson's dictum—" Fleet-street has a very animated appearance:" he dwelt upon its borders nearly forty years; and however applicable the observation may have been in Johnson's time, it is threefold characteristic in the present day.

North and south of the confluence of Fleet-street, the hand of change became busy in 1864. In that year, between 700,000 and 800,000 persons entered the City every morning to their daily occupations—20,000 of them in conveyances, involving the daily employment of between 60,000 and 70,000 public carriages. This glut of traffic will, however, be thinned by the railway operations upon the east side of Bridge-street and Farringdon-street. In any consequent rearrangement of the roadway here will, doubtless, be respected the two memorial obelisks: one inscribed with the name of Wilkes, and the year of his mayoralty, 1775; and the other erected in 1839, to the memory of Alderman Waithman, who commenced business as a linendraper, close to this spot, in 1785; was Lord Mayor in 1823-24; and was returned six times to Parliament for the City. He had removed to the corner of Fleet-street and Bridge-street some years before his retirement from business. Latterly, the alderman grew too moderate for his Farringdon-Ward friends, and he was defeated of being Chamberlain; he then withdrew to a pleasure-farm near Reigate, and in this bucolic retirement he passed away. A memorial tablet placed in St. Bride's church states it to have been "his happiness to see that great cause triumphant of which he had been the intrepid advocate from youth to age." Singularly enough, this

* *Fleet*, a small stream; Saxon.—*Nares's Glossary.*

tablet is placed in the vestibule of the church, directly opposite a similar memorial to Mr. Blades, of Ludgate-hill, who was a fine old Tory, and a stanch opponent to Waithman throughout his stormy political career: as in life, so in death, the great leveller has laid them here. In early life, Waithman showed genius for acting, and his success in the character of Macbeth led his friends to press upon him the stage as a profession; but he chose another sphere. He was uncle to John Reeve, the popular comic actor.

Next door but one to Alderman Waithman, at No. 98, Joseph Brasbridge, the silversmith, kept shop. In his eightieth year he wrote his Life, which he entitled *The Fruits of Experience*, full of pleasant gossip about the tavern-clubs, card-parties, and minor gaieties, of St. Bride's. He was more fond of following the hounds than his business, and failure was the ill consequence: he tells of a sporting party of four—that he and his partner became bankrupt; the third, Mr. Smith, became Lord Mayor; and the fourth fell into poverty, and was glad to accept the situation of patrol before the house of his Lordship, whose associate he had been only a few years before. Smith had 100,000*l.* of bad debts on his books, yet died worth one-fourth of that sum. Brasbridge's Toryism made him a troublesome neighbour to Waithman, who denounced the silversmith at Ward meetings; but, by the help of friends, gifts, and loans, he became reëstablished in business, with moderate success.

One of Brasbridge's tavern-haunts was the Globe, in Fleet-street. Among the company was a surgeon who, living on the Surrey side of the Thames (Blackfriars Bridge was not then built), had to take a boat every night, at 3*s.* or 4*s.* expense, and the risk of his life; yet, when the bridge was built, he grumbled at having a penny to pay for crossing it. Other frequenters of the Globe were Archibald Hamilton, "with a mind fit for a lord chancellor;" Carnan, the bookseller, who defeated the Stationers' Company upon the almanac trial; Dunstall, the comedian; the veteran Macklin; Akerman, the keeper of Newgate, who always thought it most prudent not to venture home till daylight; and William Woodfall, the reporter of the Parliamentary debates. Then there was one Glover, a surgeon, who restored to life a man who had been hung in Dublin, and who ever after was a plague to his deliverer. We remember the Globe, a handsomely-appointed tavern, some forty years since; and meeting here the eccentric Hugh Evelyn, who set up a claim upon the Wotton estate of Sir Frederic Evelyn, in Surrey.*

Another of Brasbridge's circles was the Sixpenny Card-Club, at the Queen's Arms, St. Paul's Churchyard: among the members was Henry Baldwyn, who, under the auspices of Bonnel Thornton, Colman the elder, and Garrick, set up the *St. James's Chronicle*, which once had the largest circulation of any evening paper. This worthy newspaper-proprietor was considerate and generous to men of genius: "often," says Brasbridge, "at his hospitable board have I seen needy authors, and others connected with his employment, whose abilities, ill-requited as they might have been by the world in general, were by him always appreciated." Among Brasbridge's acquaintance, also, were—John Walker, shopman to a grocer and chandler in Well-street, Rag-fair, who died worth 200,000*l.*, most assuredly not gained by lending money on doubtful security; and Ben Kenton, brought up at a charity-school, and who realised 300,000*l.*, partly at the Magpie and Crown, in Whitechapel.

* The Globe had other celebrity. Here was held the Robin Hood Club: Oliver Goldsmith and his friends often finished their "Shoemaker's Holiday" by supping at the Globe, where was held a Wednesday Club, for songs, jokes, dramatic imitations, and burlesque parodies. Here a huge "tun of a man" used to delight Goldsmith by singing the jovial "Nottingham Ale." Tom King, the fine gentleman comedian, frequented the Globe; as did Hugh Kelly, who "had written more than he had read;" Glover, above-mentioned, failing in the medical profession, took to the stage, but having succeeded in restoring to life the malefactor who had just been executed, he abandoned the stage, resumed his wig and cane, and came to London to dabble in physic and literature; he gave capital imitations of Garrick, Foote, Colman, Sterne, and others. Another *habitué* was a wealthy pig-butcher, who put himself on too sociable a footing with Goldsmith, when he pledged him with "Come, Noll, here's my service to you, old boy!"

An odd story is told by Brasbridge of a surgeon in Gough-square, who had purchased for dissection the body of a man who had been hung at Tyburn: the servant-girl wishing to take a peep at the defunct, stole up-stairs to the room where the body had been deposited, and was horrified at seeing *him* sitting up, when she ran down-stairs in great terror. The surgeon humanely concealed the resuscitated subject in his house until he could get him conveyed to America. This he did, and outfitted him at his own expense. The man prospered, made a handsome fortune, which he gratefully left, many years after, to his deliverer and benefactor. Brasbridge ultimately retired from business, with a competency, to a cottage at Herne Hill; and his object in writing his *Life* was to show that "a man may be a bankrupt without the smallest imputation on his integrity; that it is never too late to do well; and that honesty, frugality, and industry will invariably, in the long-run, be rewarded with at least decent competency, peace of mind, and the good opinion of all but the envious and malignant."

Nearly opposite the old silversmith's is the shop, No. 106, formerly John Hardham's, the tobacconist, at the Red Lion, who realised here a large fortune by his snuff, "No. 37." Hardham, who was a native of Chichester, began the world in domestic service; he came to London, became fond of the stage, wrote a comedy, which was printed, and thus got introduced to David Garrick, who made him his "numberer" at Drury-Lane Theatre: by a single glance round the house he could tell the receipts. He commenced business in Fleet-street, as tobacconist and snuff-maker; his shop was frequented by dramatists and wits of the theatre, and even by Garrick himself. He next compounded the renowned No. 37 snuff, thought to be named from the number of qualities, growths, and descriptions of the fragrant weed introduced into the snuff: which, by the way, Garrick helped into fashion, by *gagging*, in one of his comedy characters, of the celebrated "37 of John Hardham." The snuff-maker grew rich; he died in 1772, bequeathing some 22,000*l.* to the parish of Chichester, besides many legacies, in cluding ten guineas to Garrick; and "ten pounds for his funeral expenses, for none but vain fools spend more."

In 1824, Nov. 14, some old houses, on the south side of the street, were destroyed by fire; when the opportunity was taken of opening to Bride Church the present architectural avenue, designed by J. P. Papworth: this improvement cost 10,000*l.*, of which Mr. Blades advanced 6000*l.* At the corner, No. 86, was the shop of Tilt and Bogue, the publishers; who, by judgment and integrity, prospered largely: the latter realising a handsome property in a few years; and the former, founding a fortune of 180,000*l.*: here was published the *Curiosities of London*, in 1855, pp. 800, of which 3000 copies were sold, notwithstanding the purchase of the copyright had been declined by reputedly astute publishers. In the above fire, it is believed, was destroyed the house in which Milton lodged, in St. Bride's Churchyard. In the passage westward was a large dining-house, where, some forty years ago, Colton, the author, used to dine, and publicly boast that he wrote the whole of his *Lacon; or, Many Things in Few Words,* upon a small, rickety deal-table, with one pen! Another frequenter of this place was one Webb, a sort of walking newspaper, who was much with the King and Queen of the Sandwich Islands when they visited England, in 1825. In Salisbury-square, adjoining, was the printing-office of Gillett, twice destroyed, in 1805 and 1810, by fire: the premises were rebuilt; and here, in 1814, were burnt 10,000 copies of the Memoir of the notorious Mary Anne Clarke, upon condition of her debts being paid, and an annuity of 400*l.* granted her: the burning occupied three entire days. The premises in the north-west corner of the Square, communicating with the court, No. 76 Fleet-street, was the printing-office of Richardson, the novelist, who wrote here his *Pamela*, and printed his own novels. Oliver Goldsmith was sometime his reader. Richardson was visited here by Hogarth, Dr. Johnson, Dr. Young; Secker, Archbishop of Canterbury; and Mrs. Barbauld, when a playful child. At the opposite corner of the Square are the premises of Peacock and Bampton, and Mansfield, the famous pocket-book makers, whose *Polite Repository* for 1778 is "the patriarch of all pocket-books:" its picturesque engravings have never been surpassed, and their morocco and russia bindings scarcely equalled. In our time, Queen Adelaide and her several maids-of-honour used the *Repository;* George IV. was provided by the firm with a ten-guinea housewife,—an antique-looking pocket-book, with gold-mounted scissors, tweezers, &c.; and Mr. Mansfield relates that, on one occasion, the King took his housewife from his pocket, and handed it round the table to his guests; and next day the firm received orders for twenty-five, "just like the King's."*

Returning to Fleet-street: in Raquet-court is the house of the London Society of Compositors, for use as a library and news-room. The Society appeals to those whose connection with literature is loftier and more remunerative than their own, to contribute copies of their works: we need scarcely add, that any step which tends to the improvement of printers—such as the formation of this library—must redound to the advantage of authors.

Fleet-street has been the cradle of printing, almost from its first introduction: Wynkyn de Worde (assistant of Caxton), at the Golden Sun, Swan, and Falcon, the latter in Falcon-court; the imprint to the *Demaundes Joyous* is as follows:

> "Emprynted at London in Fletestre
> te at the signe of the Swane by
> me Wynkyn de Worde
> In the yere of our
> lorde A M
> CCCCC
> and XI

There, however, exists a book inscribed: "emprynted by me Richarde Pynson at the temple barre of London 1493." To these may be added Rastell, "at the signe of the Starre;" Richard Tottel, the eminent law printer and publisher, "within Temple bar, at the signe of the Hande and Starre," now the house and property of Messrs. Butterworth, who possess all the

* Sketch in the *Bookseller.*

original leases of the same, including Tottel's, in the reign of Henry VIII., to the present time.

The following were also contemporary printers in Fleet-street, viz.: Robert Copland, stationer, printer, bookseller, author, and translator: his sign, in 1515, was the Rose Garland. John Butler lived at the sign of St. John the Evangelist in 1529. Thomas Bertholit, king's printer, dwelt at the Lucretia Romana: he retired from business about 1541. John Bedel, stationer and printer, lived, in 1531, at the sign of Our Lady of Pity. John Waylond, citizen and stationer, lived at the Blue Garland, 1541. Lawrence Andrew, a native of Calais, was a printer at the Golden Press, by Fleet-bridge. Thomas Godfrey, the printer of Chaucer's works, lived near the Temple-bar.

Here, too, we find the nursery of steam-printing; Bensley was the first to aid König, who had applied to German and other Continental printers unsuccessfully. They were joined by Woodfall and Taylor, both printers; and out of their joint exertions grew cylindrical printing, of which Mr. Walter, of the *Times* newspaper, was the first to avail himself, 28th of November 1814; Bensley's inking apparatus was, however, superseded by Cowper's—a very important advance. These details may be too esoteric for the general reader; so that we shall merely add that, soon after the above date, we remember to have seen a large working cylinder-machine, which had been invented by Winch, a printer's joiner, while he was confined in the King's Bench Prison for debt.

Two of the most disastrous fires in Fleet-street were those at the printing-office of S. Hamilton, in Falcon-court, where printing materials, &c., were consumed to the value of 80,000*l.*, in 1803; and at Bensley's, Bolt-court, in 1819, when the costly wood-cuts and printed stock of Dallaway's elaborate *History of the Three Western Rapes of Sussex* were destroyed. This house was the last home of Dr. Johnson, who died here in the back-room of the first-floor, 13th of December 1784: of this room, John Thomas Smith made a drawing just before Mr. Bensley pulled that part of the house down to make way for a staircase. It was to this house, in company with William Maltby, that Samuel Rogers, when a young man, went to see Dr. Johnson, and show him some of his juvenile poems. Rogers knocked at the door, but his heart failed him, and he and his young friend made off without seeking an interview with the dreaded but warm-hearted dictator of the republic of letters. While Dr. Johnson lived in the Court, he is said to have had this prevision of gas-lighting: one evening, from the window of his house, he observed the parish lamplighter ascend a ladder to light one of the glimmering oil-lamps; he had scarcely descended the ladder half-way, when the flame expired; quickly returning, he lifted the cover partially, and, thrusting the end of his torch beneath it, the flame was instantly communicated to the wick by the thick vapour which issued from it. "Ah!" exclaimed the Doctor; "one of these days the streets of London will be *lighted by smoke.*"

In Bolt-court William Cobbett wrote, printed, and published his *Political Register*, and sold Indian-corn. He removed thither from No. 183 Fleet-street, a few doors from St. Dunstan's church, and midway between that and Fetter-lane. Cobbett conducted his *Register* for more than thirty-three years: it bore upon its first page the figure of a gridiron, an emblem of the political martyrdom which he avowed he was prepared to undergo, upon certain conditions. He often threatened to set up a gridiron over his publishing-office, but did not carry his threat into execution. His son, Mr. J. Paul Cobbett, however, states that "a *bona-fide* very large iron gridiron was actually made, ready for publication when required, and probably it is now to be seen (where I saw it about six years ago) on the gable-end of a building in the occupation of the successor of Mr. Tucker, candle manufacturer, an old neighbour of ours at Kensington" (*Catalogue of Mr. J. H. Wilson's Pictorial Records of London, privately printed*). Nearly opposite Cobbett's office, Wright (late Kearsley) kept shop, and published a searching criticism upon Cobbett's *English Grammar*, soon after it appeared.

On the south side of Fleet-street remains, though much

altered, the Bolt-in-Tun Inn, of considerable antiquity; for, in a grant to the White Friars in 1443, it occurs as "*Hospitium vocatum Le Boltenton;*" the sign is an arrow, or *bolt*, partly in a tun. In Whitefriars-street, adjoining, is the Black Lion, a small inn-yard, with the exterior wooden gallery in part remaining.

At the east corner of Peterborough-court was one of the earliest shops for the Instantaneous Light apparatus, "Hertner's Eupyrion" (phosphorus and oxymuriate of matches, to be dipped in sulphuric acid and asbestos), the costly predecessor of the Lucifer-match. Nearly opposite were the works of Jacob Perkins, the engineer of the steam-gun, exhibited at the Adelaide Gallery, Strand; and which the Duke of Wellington truly foretold would never be advantageously employed in warfare.

About midway on the north side lived Thomas Hardy, who was tried with Horne Tooke, in 1794, for treason; he was also one of the three who commenced the London Corresponding Society, and its secretary: in Fleet-street, he kept shop as a bootmaker; he died in his eighty-second year, and is buried in Bunhill Fields, where a monument, some six feet in height, bears a lengthy semi-political inscription.

Johnson's-court, No. 7, was the abode of Dr. Samuel Johnson from 1765 to 1776; and in Gough-square, north, at No. 7, he compiled the greater portion of his *Dictionary*, 1748 to 1758. In Johnson's-court was commenced at No. 11, in 1820, the *John Bull* newspaper, with Theodore Hook for its editor, and William Shackell, the printer, as capitalist. Hook was then living in a small cottage in Somers Town, where he wrote for the newspapers and magazines, to supply the wants of the day. In the spring of 1820, Sir Walter Scott met Hook at dinner, with Terry and Mathews. Terry's account of Theodore and his distresses had much interested Scott, whose warm heart was ever open to the sufferings of a brother author. Shortly after the above meeting, Sir Walter was asked by a nobleman of influence, in the confidence of George IV., if he could find in Edinburgh some fit person to undertake the editorship of a county newspaper. Sir Walter at once suggested Hook, who had already openly opposed the pretensions and partisans of Queen Caroline. For some time Hook heard no more of the county project; but, towards the close of the year, appeared the *John Bull*, with Hook for its editor. The title, it appears, had been preëngaged by Elliston, the comedian, who had projected, with Hook, a paper with that name. Early in the undertaking, many contributions were addressed to *John Bull* from persons of high life, men of acknowledged ability. The main political object of the journal was to meet, by various means of exposure, those hot-headed persons who made themselves ostensibly the champions of Queen Caroline. Alderman Matthew Wood, and Messrs. Brougham and Denman, were the head and front; and the visitors to Brandenburgh House, and the clergymen who introduced the Queen's name into the Liturgy, received the same castigatory attention. This was, to a certain extent, a bold and determined resentment of the numerous attacks on the King by the Radical party, especially by offensive caricatures and doggerel pamphlets, of the virulence of which the reader of the present day can have little idea. *Bull* undoubtedly frightened the Whig aristocracy from the Court of Brandenburgh House, and this influenced the minds of the decorous middle-classes. The Parliamentary speeches and votes of the Whig leaders were also dwarfed in the conflict; and the popularity of the Queen was left to the hurrahs of the multitude.*

The success of the *John Bull* was immediate. The publisher had only provided 750 stamps for the first number; in the sixth week the sale had reached 10,000: the early numbers were more than once reprinted, and some were stereotyped; and later files of the paper realised four and six times the original price. Meanwhile the *Bull*, besides its political satire in quite a new vein, contained a good digest of the week's news; and its treatment of public questions had much of the plain, straightforward character which we associate with the *sobriquet* of *John Bull*. The paper long yielded Hook 2000*l*. a year, and the other proprietors

* In these details our recollection has been greatly aided by Mr. Barham's *Life and Remains of Hook*.

a like sum. Besides the virulent satire on the Queen, it contained a more generally amusing class of papers; such as "Mrs. Ramsbottom's Letters," full of capital things to laugh at, and famous specimens of ludicrous *etourderie*, produced before Thomas Hood appeared in the comic horizon. Still, the death of Queen Caroline modified the profits as well as the pungency of *Bull;* and its puns, attributed to Samuel Rogers, and pellets fired at Grey, Bennett, and Joseph Hume, Humanity Dick Martin, and others, fell short of the attraction of the object with which the paper was originally established. Then the public taste for satire of this kind dropped: the success of *Bull*, as usual in such cases, had brought out imitators; and the second-rate article eventually created disgust at the entire system of personality. Hook continued to edit *John Bull* until his death, in 1841. The paper is to the present day a Conservative organ, ably conducted, and has a good club circulation.*

Among the Fleet-street booksellers of our time, William Hone must be mentioned: he commenced business at No. 55, about the year 1812; and besides publishing a pamphlet in vindication of the ill-fated Eliza Fenning, he took much personal interest in vindication of her innocence. Many are the cases in our criminal history of the extreme danger of convicting for capital offences on presumptive or circumstantial evidence alone; but in no instance, within memory of the present generation, was the public sympathy more intensely, and, as since proved, more justly, excited than in the following case. Elizabeth (Eliza) Fenning, cook in the family of Mr. Olibar Turner, law-stationer, of Chancery-lane, was tried on April 11, 1815, at the Old Bailey, before the Recorder, "that she, on the 21st day of March, feloniously and unlawfully did administer to, and cause to be administered to, Olibar Turner, Robert Gregson Turner, and Charlotte Turner his wife, certain deadly poison (to wit, arsenick), with intent the said persons to kill and murder." There were other counts, varying the offence. Mr. Gurney conducted the prosecution. The poison, it was stated, had been mixed

* *Lives of Wits and Humorists*, ii. 310-315. 1862.

in some yeast dumplings, of which the family, as also Eliza Fenning, had freely partaken at dinner. Although violent sickness and excruciating pain was the result, in no case, fortunately, did death ensue. Of those who suffered the most was Eliza Fenning. Medical evidence proved that a large quantity of arsenic was mixed with the dough from which the dumplings had been made. No counsel in criminal cases being then permitted to address the jury on behalf of the prisoner (except on points of law), poor Eliza Fenning could only assert her innocence, saying: "I am truly innocent of the whole charge; indeed I am! I liked my place; I was very comfortable." The jury in a few minutes returned a verdict of guilty, and the Recorder immediately passed sentence of death.

Had it not been for this calamitous event, in a very few days Eliza Fenning would have been married to one in her own position of life. Her bridal dress was prepared; with girlish pride she had worked a little muslin cap, which she proposed wearing on that joyous occasion. In this bridal dress, and little muslin cap, on the morning of the 25th of July, she followed the Ordinary of Newgate through the gloomy passages of the prison to the platform of death. Here again she firmly denied her guilt; and with the words on her lips, "I am innocent!" her soul passed into eternity.

We quote these details from Mr. Wilson's privately-printed Catalogue: it is added, from a communication made to this gentleman by one acquainted with Mr. Fenning's family: "If my information be correct, Eliza Fenning was as guiltless of the crime for which she suffered as any reader of this note; but some years elapsed before the proof of it was afforded. At length, however, Truth, the daughter of Time, unveiled the mystery. On a bed, in a mean dwelling at Chelmsford, in Essex, lay a man in the throes of death, his strong frame convulsed with inward agony. To those surrounding that bed, and watching his fearful exit from the world, he disclosed that he was the nephew of a Mr. Turner, of Chancery-lane; that many years since, irritated with his uncle and aunt, with whom he resided, for not supplying him with money, he availed himself of the absence, for a few minutes, of the servant-maid from the kitchen, stept into it, and deposited a quantity of powdered arsenic on some dough he found mixed in a pan. Eliza Fenning, he added, was wholly ignorant of these facts. He made no further sign, but, like the rich man in the Testament, 'he died and was buried.' I will not presume to carry the parallel further."

Mr. Hone published a narrative of the above case, with a portrait of the poor girl; this was replied to, and there was much contention upon the case. The medical man who had given evidence on the trial suffered considerably in his practice. She was the last person condemned by the Recorder, Sir John Sylvester.

It appears that the circumstance which gave colour to the case against the accused was, that she had often pressed her mistress to let her make some yeast dumplings, at which she stated herself to be a famous hand. On the 21st of March, the brewer left some yeast, and instead of getting the dough from the baker's, the accused made it herself.

Fleet-street had, for ages, been noted for its sights and shows; and one of its curiosities, which lasted to our time, was Mrs. Salmon's moving Wax-work. It was originally established at the Golden Salmon, St. Martin's, near Aldersgate (*Harl. Ms.*, 5931, British Museum), and delighted the sight-seeing public of the days of Queen Anne, as we gather from the 28th paper of the *Spectator*, April 2, 1711: "It would have been ridiculous for the ingenious Mrs. Salmon to have lived at the sign of the Trout." Her handbill runs: "Mrs. Salmon's Wax-work—Royal Court of England—the moving Wax-work—140 figures as big as life, all made by Mrs. Salmon, who sells all sorts of moulds and glass eyes, and teaches the full art," &c. In what year she removed to Fleet-street is unknown: her collection was shown near the Horn Tavern (now Anderton's), in a house with the sign of the Salmon, which has been engraved by J. T. Smith. Thence the Wax-work was removed to 198 Fleet-street, to a house on the site of the present banking-house of Messrs. Praed & Co. She lived to the age of ninety, when her death was thus announced: "March 1760: Died Mrs. Steers, aged 90, but was generally known by the name of her former husband, Mrs. Salmon. She was famed for making several figures in wax, which have been long shown in Fleet-street." Upon her death, the collection was purchased by Mr. Clark, a surgeon, who lived in Chancery-lane. Mrs. Clark, after the decease of her husband, continued the exhibition in the name of Salmon until the close of 1794, when, the premises occupied by her on the north side of Fleet-street having been purchased by Messrs. Praed & Co. for their banking-house, she removed to No. 17, on the south side, as thus announced in the *Morning Herald* of January 28, 1875:

"The house in which Mrs. Salmon's Wax-work has, for above a century, been exhibited, is pulling down: the figures are removed to the very spacious and handsome apartments at the corner of the Inner-Temple gate, which was once the Palace of Henry Prince of Wales, the eldest son of King James the First, and they are now the residence of many a royal guest. Here are held the courts of Alexander the Great, of King Henry the Eighth, of Caractacus, and the present Duke of York. Happy ingenuity to bring heroes together, maugre the lapse of time! The levées of each of these personages are daily very numerously attended, and we find them all to be of very easy access, since it is insured by a shilling to one of the attendants."

We have already, at pp. 69, 70 of the present volume, pointed out Mrs. Salmon's misdescription, as well as the misinscription upon the house itself. It may, however, be noted that the rich ceiling of the first-floor, and the general style of the rooms, partake of the manner of Inigo Jones, whose first office was that of surveyor to Henry Prince of Wales. Here the Wax-work was exhibited until Mrs. Clark's death, in the year 1812: the figure of Ann Siggs on crutches, at the door, we well recollect, but not the kick which Mother Shipton gave the visitor on going out, and of which J. T. Smith had so vivid an impression.

When the frail establishment was broken up, the wax-folks were sold, it is said, for less than *50l.* Many of the figures were removed to a house at the west corner of Water-lane, and there exhibited for a few pence, by which the proprietor realised a considerable sum. However, one night, in July 1827, some thieves broke open the premises, and stole a sum of money and several articles of wearing-apparel; destroyed some of the figures, stripped part of their clothes, and tore the gold lace and trinkets from others; they then smashed the heads of the figures to pieces, and piled them up until they nearly reached the ceiling: the loss was set down at *150l.* Still, the wax-work, with repairs and additions, lingered here until 1831, when the fine folk—emperors, kings, and princes—were sold under an execution for rent! A short time previously, there appeared in the *Spectator* newspaper this amusing, melting joke upon the exit of the patronymic old lady:

"Mrs. Salmon is no more! She was a mighty lover of death-shows—we believe she married an undertaker, or one of his mutes. She revelled in white crape, wore a cap bordered with coffin-trimmings, slept in a winding-sheet every night of her life, laid on a mattress, under 'a canopy of costly state,' while a shroud served her for a night-dress, and a pall for a coverlid. Her face was like one of her waxen images, and her eyebrows white and thatchy like theirs. She also *waxed* old and infirm—her taper was almost burnt out; and it seemed likely that the funeral pomp which constituted a considerable part of her stock-in-trade would soon be employed to deck her remains. It was on one of those intensely hot days—more than dog-days—in a broiling summer, that the old lady walked into her exhibition-room, to be out of the sun, and for the purposes of meditation,—for she was of a warm constitution, and seriously inclined; whether the mournful tone of her mind or the solemn hues of her dumb regiment affected her fancy, I can't say; but she thought the mutes who attended the lying-in-state of the Princess Amelia looked unusually melancholy, and was surprised at observing a tear upon every cheek—not those of the spectators, but of the performers. She approached, with the corner of her white-lawn apron upraised, to wipe the drops away—they were tears of *wax*. Hence the favourite phrase of Mr. Newman's novelist, 'melted into tears.' Her dummies were in a state of profuse perspiration, and dissolved to the back-bone (generally a mop-stick), while the wax-candles shed burning drops of sympathy. It broke the poor old lady and her heart at once; and it was remarked that not a waxen figure was ever known to hold up its head after."

Rackstrow's Museum, exhibited at No. 197, was a Fleet-street sight of the last century. The house had been, for many years before Rackstrow's time, tenanted by tombstone-cutters: and here it was that Howel, in 1684, saw the huge marble, with an inscription to four of the Oxenham family, each of whom, it was positively stated, died with a bird with a white breast fluttering about the bed: witnesses' names were engraven on the stone, which "was to be sent to a town hard by Exeter, where this happened." Rackstrow was also a statuary, and had Sir Isaac Newton's Head for a sign: his museum consisted of natural and artificial curiosities and anatomical figures; and "the circulation of the blood, shown by a red liquor conveyed through glass tubes, made in imitation of the principal veins and arteries of the human body; the heart and its auricles, and likewise the lungs, are put in their proper motions." *Au reste,* the kind of exhibition is intimated by the announcement, "a proper person attends the ladies." Rackstrow died at his house in Fleet-street, in 1772; and in seven years after, the collection was dispersed by auction. One of the prodigies of the collection was the skeleton of a whale, more than 70 feet long. Donovan, the naturalist, subsequently exhibited here his *London Museum,* which, however, was soon after dispersed as its predecessor had been.

The house afterwards became the office of the *Albion* newspaper, whither Charles Lamb thus humorously describes his removal: "From the office of the *Morning Post,* by change of property in the paper, we were transferred—mortifying exchange!—to the office of the *Albion* newspaper, late Rackstrow's Museum, in Fleet-street. What a transition—from a handsome apartment, from rosewood desks and silver inkstands—to an office—no office, but a *den* rather, but just redeemed from the occupation of dead monsters, of which it seemed redolent—from the centre of loyalty and fashion, to a focus of vulgarity and sedition! Here, in murky closet, inadequate, from its square contents, to the receipt of the two bodies of editor and humble paragraph-maker together at one time, sat, in the discharge of his new editorial functions" (the 'Bigod' of Elia) "the redoubtable John Fenwick.

"F., without a guinea in his pocket, and having left not many in the pockets of his friends whom he might command, had purchased (on tick, doubtless) the whole and sole editorship, proprietorship, with all the rights and titles (such as they were worth) of the *Albion*, from one Lovell; of whom we know nothing, save that he had stood in the pillory for a libel on the Prince of Wales. With this hopeless concern, F. resolutely determined upon pulling down the Government in the first instance, and making both our fortunes by way of corollary. For seven weeks did this infatuated democrat go about borrowing seven-shilling pieces, and lesser coin, to meet the daily demands of the Stamp-Office, which allowed no credit to publications of that side in politics. An outcast from politer breed, we attached our small talents to the forlorn fortunes of our friend. Our occupation was now to write treason. * * * Our cue was now to insinuate, rather than recommend, possible abdications. Blocks, axes, Whitehall tribunals, were covered with flowers of so cunning a periphrasis—as Mr. Bayes says, never naming the *thing* directly—that the keen eye of an Attorney-General was insufficient to detect the lurking snake among them."

But of the four-and-thirty streets, lanes, courts, and alleys leading from Fleet-street, the most notable is Crane-court, eastward of Fetter-lane; though this court does not lead any where, it being a *cul-de-sac*. It was originally named Two

Crane-court. It was rebuilt immediately after the Great Fire of 1666, and contains a few specimens of fine brickwork. The large front house was built by Sir Christopher Wren, and was inhabited by Dr. Edward Brown, an eminent physician, until 1710, when it was purchased, with the "adjoyning little house," by the Royal Society; the President, Sir Isaac Newton, recommending it as being "in the middle of the town, and out of noise." The removal of the Society from Gresham College was, however, strongly objected to, especially in a pamphlet published at the time, and in which the new purchase is thus described: "The approach to it, I confess, is very fair and handsome, through a long court; but then they have no other property in this than in the street before it; and in a heavy rain, a man can hardly escape being thoroughly wet before he can pass through it." The front of the house towards the garden is nearly half as long again as that towards Crane-court. "Upon the ground-floor there is a little hall, and a direct passage from the stairs into the garden, and on each side of it a little room. The stairs are easie, which carry you up to the next floor. Here there is a room fronting the Court, directly over the hall. And towards the garden is the meeting-room, and, at the end, another also fronting the garden. There are three rooms upon the next floor. These are all that are as yet provided for the reception of the Society; except you will have the garrets, a platform of lead over them, and the usual cellars, &c., below, of which they have more and better at Gresham College."

The Society met for the first time in Crane-court on the 8th of November 1710; their library and repository were also removed thither; and thus the College and the Society separated, after being together nearly fifty years. The exterior of the house in Crane-court remains unaltered, though the interior has undergone some changes. "Happily, however," said Mr. Weld, in 1848, "the room in which the Society met is in the same condition as when Newton occupied the presidential chair; and it is impossible to stand in that ancient apartment without feeling the associations connected with those days stealing over the mind." When the Society got settled, by Newton's order, the porter was clothed in a suitable gown, and provided with a staff, surmounted by the Arms of the Society, in silver; and on the meeting-nights, a lamp was hung out over the entrance to the Court from Fleet-street. The repository was built at the rear of the house, and thither the Society's Museum was removed. The Catalogue of its most remarkable rarities fills twenty pages of Hatton's *London;* and it is curious to observe how much it must have propagated error. Thus we find:

"The Quills of a Porcupine, which, on certain occasions, the creature can shoot at the pursuing enemy and erect at pleasure.

"The Flying Squirrel, which, for a good nut-tree, will pass a river on the bark of a tree, erecting his tail for a sail.

"The Leg-bone of an Elephant, brought out of Syria for the thigh-bone of a giant. In winter, when it begins to rain, elephants are mad, and so continue from April to September, chained to some tree, and then become tame again.

"Tortoises, when turned on their backs, will sometimes fetch deep sighs, and shed abundance of tears.

"A Humming-bird and Nest, said to weigh but 12 grains; his feathers are set in gold, and sell at a great rate.

"A Bone, said to be taken out of a Mermaid's head.

"The Largest Whale, liker an island than an animal.

"The White Shark, which sometimes swallows men whole.

"A Siphalter, said with its sucker to fasten on a ship, and stop it under sail.

"A Stag-beetle, whose horns worn in a ring are good against the cramp.

"A Mountain Cabbage: one reported 300 feet high."

Such were a few of the rarities of Dr. Grew's Rarities. Equally curious are the early proceedings of the Society—such as bottling up stags' tears, catching wild ducks by "walking into the river where the ducks are," and then marching out again; and the marvellous cure of the sailor's wooden leg—all which are old-standing jokes, which, however, got the Fellows laughed into improving their Transactions.

Although the philosophers protested against having to walk up Crane-court in a heavy rain to get to their new house—for umbrellas were not in those days—they protracted their stay to seventy-two years; keeping their library in cedar-wood cases, in the adjoining house, No. 8. In 1782, the Society removed to Somerset House, and sold the Crane-court house to the Scottish Hospital and Corporation, who now occupy it. In parting with "the Royals," we reflect how many distinguished men of science—discoverers and improvers—must have walked up this court to attend the Society's Meetings during the long term. And the retrospective interest increases as you ascend the broad stone steps, and pass through the small hall, and up "the stairs somewhat easie," by which the Presidents and Secretaries led the way: we conjure up the short but well-set figure of Newton, with hair abundant and white as silver; the courtly Sir Hans Sloane; and that martyr to gout and glory, Sir Joseph Banks, to whom the "easie" stairs must have been a boon. Upon the Society's removal, most of their older curiosities, Grew's rarities, were transferred to the British Museum, which, in its early days, was a general receptacle for monstrosities and doubtful treasures.

The Royal Society in 1862 attained the two hundredth year of its existence, the royal charter of incorporation being dated April 22, 1662, by Charles II. The second charter is dated 1663. The Society early exercised the privilege of claiming the bodies of criminals executed at Tyburn, which were to be dissected at Gresham College. The experiments made before the Fellows were generally repetitions of researches already made in private. Robert Boyle was so frequently engaged upon these experiments, that he used to write over his street-door, when thus occupied, "Mr. Boyle cannot be spoken with to-day." The first charter, in Latin, has ornamented initials, and a finely-executed portrait of Charles II. in Indian-ink. The charter empowers the president to *wear his hat* while in the chair; and the Fellows addressed the president bare-headed till he made a sign for them to put on their hats—customs now obsolete. The *hat* also formerly played an important part at the Society of Antiquaries; the strict form of admission being by the president or presiding officer placing upon his head a cocked hat, holding the Society's iron-gilt mace in one hand, and with the other welcoming the new Fellow.

The Meeting-room at Crane-court is embellished with a pair of fluted columns, and has an enriched ceiling of finely-carved oak. The walls are hung with paintings, among which are portraits of the Duke of Lauderdale, by Lely; Mary Queen of Scots, by Zucchero; the Earl of Bedford; the Duke of Queensberry; the second Duke of Sutherland; Keith Milnes, Esq.; James, third Duke of Montrose; the Scottish Regalia; and a large whole-length portrait of William IV., painted by Wilkie, and presented by him to the Scottish Hospital—a copy of a portrait which Wilkie painted for the King; its chief local interest is its being the work of a Scottish artist. The Hospital originated in what a writer in *Chambers's Edinburgh Journal* terms "a peculiarity of our Scottish countrymen, which can be set down only on the credit side of their character—their sympathy with each other when they meet as wanderers in foreign countries. Scotland is just a small enough country to cause a certain unity of feeling amongst the people. Wherever they are, they feel that Scotsmen should stand, as their proverb has it, *shoulder to shoulder.* The more distant the clime in which they meet, the more disposed are they to take an interest in each other's welfare."

Elizabeth, we are told, kept down the number of Scotsmen in London to the astonishingly small one of fifty-eight; but with James I. came such a host of traders and craftsmen, many of whom failing to obtain employment, gave rise to, as early as 1613, the institution of the "Scottish Box," a sort of Friendly-Society's treasury, when there were no banks to take charge of money. In 1638, the company, then only twenty, met in Lamb's Conduit-street: in this year, upwards of 300 poor Scotsmen, swept off by the Great Plague of 1665-6, were buried at the expense of the Box; while numbers more were nourished during their sickness, without subjecting the parishes in which they resided to the smallest expense.

In the year 1665, the Box was exalted into the character of a Corporation by a royal charter, the expenses attendant on which were disbursed by gentlemen who, when they met at the Cross Keys, in "Coven Garden," found their receipts to be 116*l.* 8*s.* 5*d.* The character of the times is seen in one of their regulations, which imposed a fine of 2*s.* 6*d.* for every oath used in the course of their quarterly business.

Presents now flocked in. One of the Corporation gave a silver cup; another, an ivory mallet, or hammer, for the chairman; and among the contributors we find Gilbert Burnet (afterwards Bishop) giving 1*l.* half-yearly. In no very Scotsman-like spirit the governors distributed each quarter-day all that had been collected during the preceding interval; but in 1775 a permanent fund was established. The Hospital now distributes about 2200*l.* a year, chiefly in 10*l.* pensions to old people; and the princely bequest of 76,495*l.*, by Mr. W. Kinloch, who had realised a fortune in India, allows of 1800*l.* being given in pensions of 4*l.* to disabled soldiers and sailors. All this is highly honourable to those connected by birth or otherwise with Scotland. The monthly meetings of the Society are preceded by divine service in the chapel, which is in the rear of the house in Crane-court. Twice a year is held a festival, at which large sums are collected. On St. Andrew's-day 1863, Viscount Palmerston presided, with the brilliant results of the addition of 1200*l.* to the hospital fund.

Appended to the account of the Society, already quoted, we find the following "Note by an Englishman:"

"It is not one of the least curious particulars in the history of the Scottish Hospital, that it substantiates by documentary evidence the fact, that Scotsmen who have gone to England occasionally find their way back to their own country. It appears from the books of the Corporation, that in the year ending 30th November 1850, the sum of 30*l.* 16*s.* 6*d.* was spent in 'passages' from London to Leith; and there is actually a corresponding society in Edinburgh to receive the *revenants*, and pass them on to their respective districts."

Crane-court has a few other notabilities. The first house on the right (now rebuilt) was, about a century ago, the scene of an abuse of power so monstrous as to have corrected itself. Here lived Dryden Leach, the printer; who, in 1763, was arrested on a general warrant, upon suspicion of having printed Wilkes's *North Briton*, No. 45: Leach was taken out of his bed in the night, his papers were seized, and even his journeymen and servants were apprehended; the only foundation for the arrest being a hearsay that Wilkes had been seen going into Leach's house. Wilkes had been sent to the Tower for the No. 45; after much litigation he obtained a verdict of 4000*l.*, and Leach 300*l.* damages from three of the King's messengers, who had executed the illegal warrant. Kearsley, the bookseller, of Fleet-street (whom we recollect by his *Tax Tables*), had been taken up for publishing No. 45, when also at Kearsley's were seized the letters of Wilkes, which seemed to fix upon him the writing of the obscene and blasphemous *Essay on Women*, and of which he was convicted in the Court of King's Bench, and expelled the House of Commons. The author of this "indecent patchwork" was not Wilkes, but Thomas Potter, son of the Archbishop of Canterbury.—See Walpole's *George III.*, vol. i. p. 310.

Another house in the court became connected with the history of Warburton and Pope in this fortuitous manner. Late in 1726, Warburton came to London, and, with Theobald, Concanen, and others, banded in a sort of confederacy by their common hostility to Pope, under whose satire they were smarting. Warburton was unfortunate enough to write to Concanen, January 2d, 1726 (that is, 1727), a letter, in which he said that Dryden borrowed for want of leisure, and Pope for want of genius; and which letter, much to the writer's annoyance, was published long afterwards, in 1766, by Akenside, the poet, whom he had offended; the original letter having been discovered, in 1750, by Dr. Gavin Knight, of the British Museum, in fitting up a house in Crane-court, where, it is supposed, Concanen had lodged. This may appear a roundabout story; but the mischief caused by the publication of this letter can scarcely be conceived in our mild seasons of literary controversy, gentlemanly criticism, and quizzing humour: which, however,

> has a moral, and no doubt
> You all have wit enough to find it out.—*Gay.*

The court has long been a sort of nursery for newspapers: here was the office of the *Commercial Chronicle;* and the *Traveller* removed to No. 9 from Fleet-street, and remained until its junction with the *Globe.* In the basement of the house nearly opposite, were printed the early numbers of *Punch; or, the London Charivari.* In No. 10 (Palmer and Clayton's), was first printed the *Illustrated London News*, projected, started, and established, by Herbert Ingram, in the spring of 1842.* Most of the large and lofty offices in the court we owe to the genius of steam-printing.

Here the Society of Arts first met, in apartments over a circulating library; and here the Society awarded its first prize (15*l.*) to Cosway, then a boy of fifteen, and afterwards a fashionable miniature-painter. The circulating library in the court was one of the earliest established in the metropolis: the first was Batho's, about 1740, at No. 132 Strand; in 1770, there were but four.

We are again in Fleet-street, where newspaper histories are thick-coming as fancies: of these we can chronicle but a few. On the north side, in 1817, John Stoddart, having seceded from the *Times*, started an opposition paper, called the *New Times:* it was unsuccessful, and in a short time Stoddart left it; but the journal was continued long after. It was here that first appeared the anecdote of Mr. Upcott, of the London Institution,

* In 1843, a popular, but in this instance a short-sighted, writer said of "illustrated newspapers:" "Some old experienced traders shake their heads, and much question whether one illustrated paper will exist three years longer."

having discovered the Ms. Diary, or Kalendarium, of John Evelyn, brought from a lumber-room at Wotton-place, the seat of the Evelyns, in Surrey, and published in two quarto volumes in 1818. The story travelled through the newspapers of the day; but Upcott, when appealed to as to its truth, replied—though not upon the first application—that it was an after-dinner fabrication, which was seized on by Dr. Stoddart, and forthwith imported into the *New Times*, whence it started upon its journalistic tour. However, the anecdote was related to us at Dorking and at Wotton long before it appeared in print.

Michael Drayton, the poet, is stated by Aubrey, in his *Lives*, to have "lived at the baye-window house, next the east end of St. Dunstan's ch.:" this points to the house of Messrs. Bell and Daldy, the publishers; but the adjoining house is of greater age, and has in one of the rooms a Perpendicular chimney-piece; and an outer attic gallery for viewing processions, &c.; a few years since, it had some good ironwork. The Great Fire of 1666 stopped within three houses of the church, as did also another fire in 1730. If this be not the poet's house, it has noteworthiness of another kind; for here, amid the revolutionary throes of the year 1848, was published the first cheap *daily* newspaper, the *London Telegraph*, at 3*d.*; it was, however, soon brought to a close through the proprietor being thwarted in his printing arrangements.

Nearly opposite, over Falcon-court, at No. 32, inscribed date 1667 upon it, lived John Murray, father and son, booksellers and publishers. Here the latter, in 1807, published Mrs. Rundell's *Domestic Cookery;* in 1809, the *Quarterly Review;* and in 1811, Byron's *Childe Harold;* in 1812, he removed to Albemarle-street. He said once to a friend: "Lord Byron used to come to my shop in Fleet-street, fresh from Angelo's and Jackson's. His great amusement was making thrusts with his stick, in fencer's fashion, at the spruce books, as he called them, which I had arranged upon my shelves. He disordered a row for me in a short time, always hitting the volume he had singled out for the exercise of his skill." Murray added, with a laugh, "I was sometimes, as you will guess, glad to get rid of him." This was related in the *Athenæum*, 1843.

Mr. Murray's letter to Mr. Canning, then Chancellor of the Exchequer, suggesting a periodical by eminent Tories, in opposition to the *Edinburgh Review*, is preserved; he tells Mr. Canning that he is "no adventurer, but a man of some property, inheriting a business that has been established for nearly a century." Hence originated the *Quarterly Review*.

A few doors eastward lived John Major, the publisher of many carefully-annotated and beautifully-embellished works; and best known by his editions of Walton and Cotton on Angling, and Walpole's *Anecdotes*. The first edition of Walton's *Angler* was published near the same spot in 1653, in St. Dunstan's churchyard, at 1*s*. 6*d*.; a copy at Haworth's brought thirteen guineas. Dr. Dibdin calls Major's Walton "an enchantingly decorated and got-up little volume:" yet the producer of these beautiful works had to seek the haven of the Charterhouse.

When the church of St. Dunstan was rebuilt, in 1830-3, the town lost one of its minor wonders. The old church projected some thirty feet farther into the street than the present one; shops with overhanging signs were built against the south and east walls; though previously the churchyard thus built in was a permanent station for booksellers, as appears by many imprints. John Smethick had his shop here, "under the Diall;" as had also Richard Marriott, Walton's publisher; and Lawton Gilliver, at Homer's Head. The clock had a large gilt bracket-dial overhanging Fleet-street, and above it two figures of savages, life-size, carved in wood, and standing beneath a pediment; each figure having in his right hand a club, with which he struck the quarters upon a suspended bell, moving his head at the same time. To see the men strike was a great attraction, and opposite St. Dunstan's was a famous field for pickpockets, who took advantage of the gaping crowd. So it had long been, for Ned Ward, in his *London Spy*, says: "We added to the number of fools, and stood a little, making our ears do penance to please our eyes with the conceited notion of their (the puppets') heads and hands, which moved to and fro with as much deliberate stiffness as the two wooden horologists on St. Dunstan's when they strike the quarters." Cowper thus refers to them in his *Table-Talk:*

> When labour and when dulness, club in hand,
> Like the two figures at St. Dunstan's stand,
> Beating alternately, in measured time,
> The clockwork tintinnabulum of rhyme,
> Exact and regular the sounds will be;
> But such mere quarter-strokes are not for me.

These figures were put up in 1671, and were at first painted the natural colours; Hatton describes them, in 1708, as more admired by many of the populace on Sundays than the most eloquent preacher from the pulpit within. Among those who were struck with the oddity of these figures was the third Marquess of Hertford; when a child, and a good child, his nurse, to reward him, would take him to see *the giants* at St. Dunstan's; and he used to say that, when he grew to be a man, *he would buy those giants.* Many a child of rich parents may have said the same; but in the present case the Marquess kept his word. When the old church was taken down in 1829, Lord Hertford attended the second auction-sale of the materials, and purchased the clock, bells, and figures for 200*l.*: he had them placed at the entrance to the grounds of his villa in the Regent's Park, thence called St. Dunstan's Villa; and here the figures do duty to the present day. At the east end of the church was a statue of Queen Elizabeth, from Ludgate; it was put up in 1766, when the figures of King Lud and his two sons, also from Ludgate, were deposited in the parish bone-house; these statues are said to be the only existing remains of the City gates; the statue of Queen Elizabeth has been placed at the east side of the new church. This was designed by John Shaw,—who, however, died on the twelfth day after the external completion of the edifice; and the interior was finished by his son. It is in the latest Pointed style; the lantern-tower is 130 feet high, and differs from any in the metropolis; but resembles St. Botolph's, Boston; St. Helen's, York; and St. George's, Ramsgate: designed by

Shaw in 1825. St. Dunstan's has eight fine bells from the old church, the sound of which receives effect from the four large upper windows. Over the entrance-porch are sculptured the heads of Tyndale, the Reformer, preacher here; and Dr. Donne, who was once vicar of the parish: they are accredited portraits. The body of the church is of octagon form; the altar-piece has richly-carved oak canopies; above is a magnificent painted window, by Willement, the gift of the Hoare family.

The house westward of the church is a fine specimen of Jacobean street-architecture, by Shaw. Clifford's Inn has been much improved; and Serjeants' Inn, adjoining, was rebuilt by Sir Robert Smirke, 1837-8, except the old dining-hall, which was fitted up as a Court of Exchequer for Equity sittings; the windows have some old armorial glass.

A very peculiar dinner-custom is observed in the Hall, which is believed to be unique. The Society consists of two distinct bodies—"the Principal and Rules," and the junior members, or "Kentish Mess." Each body has its own table: at the conclusion of the dinner, the chairman of the Kentish Mess, first bowing to the Principal of the Inn, takes from the hands of the servitor four small rolls, or loaves of bread, and, without saying a word, he dashes them three several times on the table; he then discharges them to the other end of the table, from whence the bread is removed by a servant in attendance. Solemn silence—broken only by three impressive thumps upon the table—prevails during this strange ceremony, which takes the place of grace after meat in Clifford's Inn Hall; and concerning which, not even the oldest member of the Society is able to give any explanation (*Notes and Queries*, 2d S., No. 4). In No. 7, Mr. Buckton, of Lichfield, says: "Cakes, sacred to Ceres, usually terminated the ancients' feasts; and the rolls at Clifford's Inn may be thrown down as an offering to Ceres, *legifera*, as she first taught mankind the use of laws"—an ingenious but remote probability.

In Clifford's Inn lived Robert Pultock, author of *Peter Wilkins*, "with its Flying Women." Who he was is not known—

probably a barrister without practice; but he wrote an amiable and interesting book (*Leigh Hunt*). *Peter Wilkins* is best known to the present generation by melodrama and pantomime; in the former Keeley made an early impression at Covent-Garden Theatre. Clifford's Inn has a terrace and raised garden, rearward of which is the new Record Office, of late Gothic or Tudoresque style, somewhat of a German character, with massive buttresses and Decorated windows.

The architectural embellishment of Fleet-street West dates from the rebuilding of St. Dunstan's. The Jacobean edifice was next built; in 1832, were taken down some old houses with bay-windows. Button the confectioner's house remained until 1859: it had been in Button's family forty years; in 1750, it was known as the Haunch of Venison, and subsequently as Clifford's Inn Coffee-house. Upon the site will be built an Assurance Office. At the south-east corner of "the greatest legal thoroughfare" has been erected a lofty decorated pile, some 60 feet from the pavement to the cornice; which, and the arch-headed windows, display great taste: the cost about 15,000*l.* The architect, Mr. Knowles, began his professional career in the competition for the new Houses of Parliament. No. 21, nearly opposite, is an Italian pile of the Palladian school, designed by Shaw; and being set back from the street-line, has the sides of the party-walls enriched with decorative masonry and panels of coloured marbles, corresponding in position with windows; the ornaments and ironwork are excellent; the four floors are Tuscan, Doric, Ionic, and Corinthian. No. 29 is another enriched front, of Portland stone, polished granite, and marble, and decorations of fruit and flowers and lions' heads. The old houses, Nos. 14 and 15, with their large bay-windows for enjoying the sights of Fleet-street, have disappeared; and on their site we have the large and lofty Union banking-house, of Portland stone and Italian design; and Groom's, which had been a confectioner's shop for nearly a century, has been rebuilt, with an enriched frontage. Altogether, the recent embellishment of this portion of Fleet-street induces us to hope that ornament as well as convenience may characterise the street-architecture of the metropolis of the Victorian era.

In our conceit about the present must not be omitted veneration of the past. At the south-west corner of Chancery-lane was the picturesque oak-and-plaster house, with the sign of the Harrow, which was taken down in May 1799, to widen the Lane. According to a deed of 1624, Walton lived two doors west of the end of Chancery-lane (or next to the Harrow), where he is stated to have been a linendraper; and that the house was jointly occupied by Isaac Walton and John Mason, hosiers: whence we may conclude that half a shop sufficed for the business of Walton. He removed into Chancery-lane, seven doors higher up, on the left-hand, where, in 1632, he carried on the business of a sempster or milliner; the house was subsequently the Mitre tavern, now rebuilt. Walton "took his place at the Vestry Board, and many a chat must he have enjoyed with Dr. Donne;" he served also as Constable for the Precinct next Temple Bar, and as Overseer: in 1643, he attended the Vestry for the last time, and soon after quitted London, "finding it dangerous for honest men to be there."* Still, Walton kept up his correspondence with his former parish: his several children were baptised in St. Dunstan's; and here, ten years after he had quitted the parish, his *Angler* was published, as already stated. These houses, which were half-timbered, with projecting windows, overhanging storeys, and gabled fronts (see *Curiosities of London*, p. 70, 1854), and some enriched ceilings, have been taken down, and in their places have been erected dwellings with ornate frontages, as well as higher up in the lane. Aubrey tells us that "Cowley was born in Fleet-street, near Chancery-lane. His father was a grocer," &c. Brayley, in his *Surrey*, says, the lower end of Chancery-lane. "As there is no entry of Cowley's baptism in St. Dunstan's Register, Dr. Johnson infers that Cowley's father may have been a sectary. Praise-God Barebones was another worthy of the parish: he was a leather-seller, and possessed a house near Crane-court,

* *The Worthies of St. Dunstan's.* By the Rev. A. B. Suter, A.B. 1856.

with the name of the Lock and Key; we first hear of him as preaching at a conventicle in Fetter-lane, in the year 1641, along with Mr. Green, a felt-maker" (*Worthies of St. Dunstan's*). Then we hear of him as constable, common-councilman, and sitting in "Barebones's Parliament;" and then the tide turning against him: on February 11, 1660, all Fleet-street was in a flare at the downfall of the Parliament; and Pepys tells us, there were fourteen fires between Temple Bar and St. Dunstan's Church; the boys broke Barebones's windows, and then again on the 21st. After this he was not molested, and attended the vestry the year after the Restoration. We last hear of him appealing before the Judges in Clifford's Inn Hall for his house near Crane-court, which had been consumed in the Great Fire: a family named Speight were the tenants; it was rebuilt by Barebones. The "Silver-tongued Bates," appointed vicar in 1652, was very popular: Pepys greatly admired his eloquence, though he had "so low an opinion of the man;" and when he preached his farewell sermon, naughty Samuel had his head turned with ogling a fine lady he had often seen in Gray's Inn Walks. While Baxter was preaching in the old church, and there had been two alarms of its falling, the preacher sat down in the pulpit; when the alarm was over, he resumed his discourse, and said, with equal tact, composure, and eloquence: "We are in the service of God, to prepare ourselves that we may be fearless at the great noise of the dissolving world, when the heavens shall pass away, and the elements melt with fervent heat."

Among the parishioners remembered for their ingenuity were Edward Marshall, Master Mason of England, *temp.* Charles I.; and his son, Joshua Marshall, Master Mason to Charles II., who left money for the daily reading of Divine Service in the church. By him or his father was sculptured the pedestal of the statue of Charles I., at Charing Cross, long attributed to Grinling Gibbons. At the same time lived Henry Jones, of the Inner Temple-lane, clockmaker, who first constructed and sold barometers, by the advice of Lord Keeper Guildford, "because the instruments were rare, and confined to the cabinets of the virtuosi." At the corner of Water-lane, Tompion, the "Father of Clock-makers," and his apprentice, "Honest George Graham," kept shop; "greater benefactors to mankind," says Adam Thomson (himself a watchmaker, by the way), "than thousands whose sculptured urns impudently emblazon merits that never existed." Tompion became a synonym for a first-rate watch; and Graham invented the machine miscalled the Orrery.

Bell-yard, a few doors east of Temple Bar, is a specimen of an old London thoroughfare, which Pope, a century and a quarter ago, called "a filthy old place," which he begged Fortescue, "his counsel learned in the law," to quit: here and there a house-front has a bit of ancient woodwork.

A more notorious spot is Lower Serle's-place, next the Bar, formerly called Shire-lane, from its dividing the City from the Shire; and, in James I.'s time, Rogue-lane. But the place had a higher fame: here lived Sir Charles Sedley; and here his son, Sir Charles Sedley, the dramatic poet, was born, "neere the Globe." Here too lived Elias Ashmole, and here Antony à Wood dined with him. This was at the upper end of the lane, where, at the Trumpet public-house, Isaac Bickerstaff met his Club; hence he led down the lane, into Fleet-street, the deputation of "twaddlers" from the country, to Dick's Coffee-house, which we never enter without remembering the glorious humour of Addison and Steele in the *Tatler*, No. 86. Sir Harry Quickset, Sir Giles Wheelbarrow, and other persons of quality, having reached the Tatler's by appointment, and it being settled that they should "adjourn to some public-house, and enter upon the business," the precedence was attended with much difficulty; when, upon a false alarm of "fire," all ran down as fast as they could, without order or ceremony, and drew up in the street. The *Tatler* proceeds:

"In this order we marched down Sheer-lane, at the upper end of which I lodge. When we came to Temple Bar, Sir Harry and Sir Giles got over, but a run of coaches kept the rest of us on this side of the street; however, we all at last landed, and drew up in very good order before Ben Tooke's shop,* who favoured our rallying with great humanity; from whence we proceeded again, until we came to Dick's Coffee-house, where I designed to carry them. Here we were at our old difficulty, and took up the street upon the same ceremony. We proceeded through the entry, and were so necessarily kept in order by the situation, that we were now got into the coffee-house itself, where, as soon as we had arrived, we repeated our civilities to each other; after which we marched up to the high table, which has an ascent to it enclosed in the middle of the room. The whole house was alarmed at this entry, made up of persons of so much state and rusticity."

The Trumpet public-house lasted to our time; it was changed to the Duke of York sign, but has long disappeared: we remember an old drawing of the Trumpet, by Samuel Ireland, engraved in the *Monthly Magazine.*

In Shire-lane was formed the Kit-Kat Club, about 1700, consisting of thirty-nine distinguished noblemen and gentlemen zealously attached to the House of Hanover; among whom were the Dukes of Somerset, Richmond, Grafton, Devonshire, and Marlborough, and (after the accession of George I.) the Duke of Newcastle; the Earls of Dorset, Sunderland, Manchester, Wharton, and Kingston; Lords Halifax and Somers; Sir Robert Walpole, Vanbrugh, Congreve, Granville, Addison, Garth, Maynwaring, Stepney, and Walsh. The Club is said to have been named from one Cristopher Kat, at whose house it was held, and who was famous for his mutton-pies, which formed a standing dish at the Club suppers. But in the *Spectator*, No. 9, the name is said to have been taken, not from the maker of the pie, but from the pie itself. Thus, in a prologue to a comedy of 1700:

> A Kit-Kat is a supper for a lord;

and Dr. King, in his *Art of Cookery:*

> Immortal made, as Kit-Kat by his pies.

* At the Middle Temple-gate. Ben Tooke was the bookseller of Swift and Pope, and left a considerable estate to his young brother, Andrew Tooke, many years master of the Charterhouse School.

Then comes Ned Ward, with another derivation—from one Cristopher, who lived at the sign of the Cat and Fiddle. Now, the Club had its toasting-glasses, on which were engraved verses in praise of certain ladies, reigning toasts; which gave rise to the well-known epigram:

> Whence deathless Kit-Kat took his name,
> Few critics can unriddle;
> Some say from pastrycook it came,
> And some from Cat and Fiddle.
> From no trim beaus its name it boasts,
> Grey statesmen or green wits,
> But from this pell-mell pack of toasts
> Of old Cats and young Kits.—*Arbuthnot* (?).

However, it is more certain that Jacob Tonson, Secretary to the Club, had the portraits of the several members painted for him by Kneller, each on canvas 36 inches by 28, since known among portrait-painters as "Kit-Kat size." The Club met also at the Flask, Hampstead; and Tonson built at Barn Elms a club-room, round which were hung the portraits, forty-two in number. Tonson left them to his grand-nephew, who died in 1767; the pictures were then removed to the house of his brother, Water-Oakly, near Windsor; and on his death, to the house of Mr. Baker, of Hertingfordbury, where they are stated to remain.*

From being the resort of "a set of wits, in reality the patriots that saved Britain," to a lane of squalid houses, of reputations too various to be repeated, is a sad falling-off,—yet such has been the Shire-lane of our time. We have heard related a few terrible tales of this sad place; one must suffice. In the times of the old parish-watch, upon a winter-night, when a thick coat of snow concealed the grime of the murky alley, a dissipated man strayed into one of its vile haunts: there an altercation arose with the extortionate owner of the house; a fiendish struggle ensued, in which the luckless victim was thrown down a long

* See *A Morning's Walk from London to Kew.* By Sir Richard Phillips. 1817. Pp. 201-208.

flight of stairs, and was taken up at the foot almost lifeless! How to dispose of the body was a small matter for the stronger man, who, waiting for the interval of the watchman's drowsy cry, soon after two o'clock, with some help carried the body a few doors up the lane, and placed it against a neighbour's door, by the pin-head light of a single oil-lamp. Here the corpse was found by the guardian of the night, and conveyed away. Next morning there was some stir in the lane, and suspicion hovered about, not knowing where to alight amidst so many nestling-places of vice and crime. The inquest followed, without pointing to the perpetrator. But many years after, in the vaulted room of a metropolitan debtors' prison, the door of which stood open, there was overheard a volley of recrimination between two men of desperate character, who were caged here for their least offences. In this fierce contention was gathered the above outline of one among many of the dark deeds of Shire-lane.

At some distance from this scene of crime, higher up in the lane, was the sponging-house to which, some forty years since, Theodore Hook was taken under arrest for a Crown debt of 12,000*l*., the amount of his defalcation in the Mauritius case. What little property he possessed was sold, and Hook was locked up here from August until the following Easter, in the house of the sheriff's officer who had arrested him. "It is remarkable," says the account of this affair, "in how many cases a great weight of misery, instead of pressing a man down, incites him to greater efforts. Here was Mr. Hook, the delight of dinner-tables and drawing-rooms, confined in a house in which air and light were almost unknown luxuries; yet in this wretched place the editor of the *John Bull* (see page 211 *ante*), was not only at his usual work, but projecting much more." It was while thus occupied that he became acquainted with Dr. William Maginn, who had come over from Cork to assist in the *Bull*, and a newly-projected literary journal. He was Hook's nightly visitor; two spirits of closer kindred could not have met. Hook left Shire-lane in April 1824, after a banquet, for which he improvised a ballad, in the chorus not sparing himself:

> Let him hang with a curse—this atrocious, pernicious
> Scoundrel, that entered the till at Mauritius.

Hook was then removed to the Rules of the King's Bench (Temple-place), where he worked hard, in addition to the editorship of the *Bull*, in founding his most profitable fame.

The nomenclature of Shire-lane was changed in the hope of getting rid of the name and its bad character together. What a phantasmagoria of gay and grave do its vicissitudes present—in the rich humour of the "twaddlers" at the Tatler's; the Kit-Kat Club over their patronymic pies, toasting the reigning beauties; and the sponging-house life of the brilliant wit, borne down by the demon of debt!

At the corner of the lane, in Fleet-street, at the Angel and Crown, one Mr. Quarrington was robbed by Thomas Carr, attorney, of Elm-court, Temple, and Elizabeth Adams, who were executed at Tyburn, January 18th, 1738. The portrait of Elizabeth Adams was painted and etched by Hogarth (*Mr. Wilson's Catalogue*).

Another criminal thus signalised by Hogarth was Sarah Malcolm, the Temple laundress, aged twenty-two, who, for the murder of three women, was hung in Fleet-street, over against Fetter-lane, March 7, 1733. Malcolm is the rarest of Hogarth's engraved portraits; her printed confession was sold with such rapidity, that as much as twenty guineas is said to have been offered for a single copy (*Romance of the Forum*, by Mr. Serjeant Burke; 2d Series).

No. 135 Fleet-street is the office of the *Daily Telegraph*, the first established of the penny morning newspapers. A century and a quarter ago, we had halfpenny and farthing newspapers sold about the streets, without stamps, in defiance both of the law and the penalty. They were said to be got up by "poor, low wretches," living in obscure parts of the town, or in the Rules of the Fleet; and they were suspected to be supported by persons in power against the opposition papers and publishers. The *Farthing Post* circulated during the years 1740-43: a boy is reading this cheap newspaper in the fourth plate of Hogarth's

Rake's Progress. One of these journals was entitled *All Alive and Merry:* it was a small folio half-sheet, having three columns of letterpress on each side: several specimens may be seen in Dr. Burney's Collection of Newspapers in the British Museum, vol. iii., 1741.

Jacob Tonson, whom we have already mentioned as Secretary of the Kit-Kat Club, commenced business as a bookseller at the Judge's Head, near the Inner Temple-gate, as we gather from the title-page of Dryden's translation of *Virgil*, which he published by subscription in 1697, with one hundred cuts, many engraved by Hollar. Here were feuds between them: in one, the following portrait of the publisher was addressed to him by the poet, with an intimation that he was in the vein to write more:

> With leering looks, bull-faced, and speckled fair,
> With two left legs, and Judas-coloured hair,
> And frozey pores, that taint the ambient air.

This was enough for Tonson, and the breach was healed.

Of Whitefriars, the Precinct of streets, lanes, and alleys, between Whitefriars-street and the Temple, and Fleet-street and the Thames, little that is old, save the name, remains; explaining the disappointment of the old-lady reader whom Sir Walter Scott's *Fortunes of Nigel* sent there purposely to look for the convent of "Carmelites, or White-Friars," founded some six centuries ago. In the Precinct stood three of our early theatres: the Whitefriars, the hall of the monastery; the Salisbury-court, not rebuilt after the Great Fire; and the Duke's, in Dorset-gardens, the site of which is now occupied by the Gas-Works. Whitefriars retained the privileges of sanctuary after the Dissolution, and hence became the asylum of fraudulent debtors, cheats, and gamblers, here protected from arrest: its cant names, Alsatia and Lombard-street, will be remembered. Poets, players, and dancing-masters flocked here; and Hanging Sword-alley, which exists, belongs to this period; as does the assassination of Turner, the fencing-master, in the reign of James I., for which the two assassins were hanged in Fleet-street, opposite Whitefriars-gate; and Lord Sanquhar, who hired them, was hanged in Old Palace-yard. In the Friary House lived Selden; he died here, and was buried in the Temple Church. The finest edition of Selden's works, by Wilkins, 3 vols. folio, was printed in Whitefriars, by Bowyer, father and son, who had for their printing-office the old George Tavern: here the Poems of Lord Byron were first printed; and the premises are now the printing-office of Bradbury and Evans, who maintain the excellence of their predecessors: in the old tavern (a scene in one of Shadwell's comedies) have been printed for twenty years the renowned lucubrations and right merry conceits of our old friend, *Punch*.

We remember the tortuous passage, and its ballad-wall from Temple-lane to Blackfriars: this has long disappeared, and has been followed by the Old Palace of Bridewell, of which King Edward-street is a reminder; Wilderness-lane and Primrose-hill, in the rear of Bridewell site, may be slang names of the Alsatian period.

Temple Bar, which we have just reached, has a dark as well as a bright history. It is ancient compared with some of the houses immediately adjoining it; but the Bar itself is scarcely two centuries old. Yet the present generation has witnessed here the curious ceremony of closing the gates upon the visit of the Sovereign until admission was formally demanded—a custom now dispensed with; we have seen the Bar also clothed in gloomy grandeur with the drapery of death; we have beheld it glittering with emblems of triumph, and decked with the gaiety of the bridal pageant, and the emblems of wedded love. There is much obscurity in the history of the Bar, which, receiving its name from the adjacent Temple, separated the freedom of the City of London from the liberty of the City of Westminster; or, as Hatton states, "the Bar opens not immediately into the City itself (which terminated at Ludgate), but into the liberty or *freedom* thereof;" "which separation," says Strype, "was anciently only posts, rails, and a chain, such as are now at Holborn, Smithfield, and Whitechapel Bars. Afterwards there was a house of timber erected across the street, with a narrow gateway; and an entry, on the south side of it, under the house." This timber gateway is shown in Hollar's seven-sheet Map of London, and has been enlarged in a drawing in Mr. Wilson's valuable collection; it is described in its carefully-prepared Catalogue. The old Bar is also clearly defined in a bird's-eye View of London, within a bordure, inscribed "The Cittie of London," showing the conduits, crosses, and City gates, as they stood about the close of the reign of Queen Elizabeth, 1601.

The entries respecting the Bar in the City records are very incomplete; but Mr. Wilson, after a laborious search, found this the first entry of any matter connected with the Bar:

"1554. I. and II. Philip and Mary. Mr. Chamberlain shall commit the custody of the new gates at Temple Bar to the Cittie's tenants, dwelling nigh unto the said gates; taking, nevertheless, especial order with them for the shutting and opening the same gates at convenient hours."

Wyatt and his followers had, probably, a few months previously, in his ill-contrived rebellion, destroyed or so damaged the old gates in forcing his way into the City, that the civic authorities were compelled to erect new ones, the care of which, by the above resolution, devolved on those of the City's tenants who were living adjacent to them.

It appears that in 1669 the Court of Aldermen and Common Council resolved to rebuild the Bar, on receiving from the Commissioners of Streets and Sewers the sum of 1005*l.* towards the cost. The City had several times been pressed to do this, but had considered the above sum inadequate. The King then sent for the Lord Mayor, when "the Citty's weak state and inability," on account of the great expense of rebuilding public works consumed in the Great Fire, was pleaded; but King Charles insisted upon the Bar being taken down, and he promised, if the 1005*l.* proved insufficient, to supply other funds to complete the work. The destruction was accordingly commenced in 1670, and the present Bar, after the designs of Sir Christopher Wren, was erected.

We need not detail its history, nor how it has lost some sculptured decoration, and almost its inscription; or how the City refused, in 1852, to spend 1500*l.* to restore the Bar as Wren had left it. The display of the heads and limbs of traitors upon the spikes of the pediment was not so revolting nor so unprofitable as might be thought. Walpole writes, August 16, 1746: "I have been this morning at the Tower, and passed under the new heads (Townley and Fletcher) at Temple Bar, where people make a trade of letting spy-glasses at a halfpenny a look." And, in 1825, a person, aged eighty-seven, remembered the above heads being seen with a telescope from Leicester-fields, the ground between which and the Bar was then thinly built over (*J. T. Smith*). The last of the iron poles, or spikes, was not removed from the Bar until the commencement of the present century.* The old oaken gates remain: they were originally shut at night, and guarded by watchmen; and in our time they have been closed in cases of apprehended tumult. Upon the visit of the Sovereign to the City, or the proclamation of a new Sovereign, or of Peace, it was formerly customary to close the Bar, until admission was formally demanded by a herald and trumpeters, when the gates were opened, and the procession admitted; this was done on the Accession of George IV., William IV., and Queen Victoria: on her Majesty's visit in 1837, the City Sword was surrendered to the Queen, and redelivered to the Mayor; but at the Royal visit in 1851, the ceremony was entirely dispensed with. In the plan for the concentration of the Courts of Justice and Law Offices, Temple Bar is specially excepted; its appropriation resting with the Common Council.

Above the gateway, lighted by two semicircular windows, is an apartment, which is held of the City, at an annual rent of

* For "A Narrative of the Historical Occurrences of a Criminal Character associated with the present Bar," see *Temple Bar, the City Golgotha*, by a Member of the Inner Temple; small 4to, 1853. This work has two very interesting views of the Bar, and treats ably of the revolting effects of capital punishments and public executions. In literary history we may also record *Temple Bar* as the title of the popular monthly magazine, commenced December 1, 1860, and now in its fifth year.

50*l.*, by Messrs. Child, the bankers, as a depository for their account-books. Child's is the oldest banking-house in London, and was known by the sign of the Marigold, which is still to be seen within where the cheques are cashed: it bears the motto, "*Ainsi mon ame*," gilt upon a green ground, and of elegant design, in the French taste of the time. The firm was founded in the reign of Charles I., when Francis Child, apprentice to William Wheeler, a goldsmith, whose shop was on the site of the present banking-house, laid the foundation of his fortune by marrying his master's daughter, and thus succeeded to the estate and business. Messrs. Child have the accounts of Nell Gwynne; and among the records of the firm are the accounts of the partner, Alderman Backwell, for the sale of Dunkirk to the French.

Another original bank-sign may be seen, prominent in the ironwork of the window towards the street, at Goslings and Sharpe's, No. 19—namely, three squirrels. Gosling, the founder of the house, is thus mentioned in the Account of "Moneys received and paid for Secret Services of Charles II. and James II., 1679-1688:" "To Richard Bakenham, in full for several parcels of gold and silver lace bought of William Gosling and partners, on 2d May 1674, by the Duchess of Cleveland, for the wedding-clothes of the Lady Sussex and Litchfield, 640*l.* 8*s.*"

The firm of Hoare, No. 37, dates from 1680, at the sign of the Golden Bottle, said to represent the flask carried by the founder of the establishment, when journeying to London, as the story-books say, to seek his fortune. Among the debts of the celebrated Lord Clarendon occurs, "To Mr. Hoare, for plate, 27*l.* 10*s.* 3*d.*" Sir Richard Hoare was Lord Mayor in 1713; and his kinsman was Sheriff in 1740-41, and has left an interesting journal of his shrievalty, which he concludes thus: "After being regaled with sack and walnuts, I returned to my own house in Flete Street, in my private capacity, to my great consolation and comfort." He served as Lord Mayor in 1745, and was very active in the preparations to receive "Bonnie Prince Charlie," which were so formidable as to daunt the Pretender. The old bank-sign, the Golden Leather-bottle, was reserved from the former banking-house—a low-browed building, with a narrow entrance, such as now scarcely exists in London—and was inserted in the spacious stone-fronted edifice, built about thirty-five years since.

Of the old Fleet-street taverns we have but few remains. Child's banking-house nearly occupies the site of the Devil Tavern, the resort of the minor wits of Ben Jonson's family. The well-known verses inscribed over the door of the Apollo Room,

Welcome all who lead or follow, &c.,

are still preserved in the premises at the back of the bank, and likewise the bust of the tutelar deity of the Club; it is of good design, in terra-cotta, covered with black varnish: the contemporary landlord was Sim. Wadlowe, "the King of Skinkers." The club-room was afterwards used for balls and entertainments, and continued to be well frequented. Here we find Swift dining with Garth and Addison; and here Dr. Johnson celebrated the birth of Mrs. Lennox's first literary child, as he called her book, by a whole night spent in festivity. In the supper was "a magnificent hot apple-pye, stuck with bay-leaves," because Mrs. Lennox had written verses. Here Johnson invoked the Muses, and crowned Mrs. L. with laurel; and there was pleasant conversation and harmless mirth, and tea and coffee. About five, Johnson's face shone with meridian splendour, though he had only drunk lemonade. The waiters had all fallen asleep; it was two hours before the bill could be got; and not till near eight did the creaking of the street-door give the signal for departure.

This scene of gaiety is kept in memory by Apollo-court, opposite, and next, eastward, to another olden resort, the Cock Tavern. When the Plague was raging, in 1665, the landlord shut up his house, and retired into the country; and here is preserved one of the farthings referred to in this advertisement: "This is to certify that the master of the Cock and Bottle, commonly called the Cock Alehouse, at Temple Bar, hath dismissed his servants, and shut up his house, for this long vacation, intending (God willing) to return at Michaelmas next; so that all persons whatsoever who may have any accounts with the said master, or *farthings belonging to the said house*, are desired to repair thither before the 8th of this instant, and they shall receive satisfaction." Here, in 1688, Pepys drank, and ate a lobster, and sang mightily merry, with Mrs. Pierce and Mrs. Knipp. The tavern has still a primitive air; the gilt signboard over the passage-door is stated to have been carved by Gibbons. Above the mantelpiece is some carving, at least of the time of James I.; but we remember the entire room similarly carved, and a huge black-and-gilt clock, and settle. The head-waiter of our time lives in the verse of the Laureate—"O plump head-waiter of the Cock!" apostrophises the "Will Waterproof" of the bard, in a reverie wherein he conceives William to have undergone a transition similar to that of Jove's cup-bearer:

> And hence, says he, this halo lives about
> The waiter's hands, that reach
> To each his perfect pint of stout,
> His proper chop to each.
> He looks not with the common breed,
> That with the napkin daily;
> I think he came, like Ganymede,
> From some delightful valley.

And of the redoubtable bird, who is supposed to have perfomned the eagle's part in this abduction, he says:

> The cock was of a larger egg
> Than modern poultry drop,
> Stept forward on a firmer leg,
> And cramm'd a plumper crop.

Nearly opposite is Dick's Coffee-house, now a tavern, called Richard's in 1680: the interior is engraved as a frontispiece to a drama called the *Coffee-house*, by the Rev. James Miller, 1737,—an inadvertence of the engraver, which led to its being intended to hit the landlady, Mrs. Yarrow, and her daughter, who were reigning toasts with the frequenters; when the Templars went in a body to Drury-lane Theatre, and damned the *Coffee-house* irretrievably. Cowper, when he lived in the Temple, was a frequenter of Richard's. The "twaddlers," and the *Tatler*, at Dick's, we have already mentioned.

The Rainbow, No. 15, now a tavern, by the Inner Temple-gate, was the second coffee-house opened in London, and had its token-money, of which there is a specimen halfpenny in the Beaufoy Collection at Guildhall. The house was kept by James Farr, a barber; who, in 1657, was indicted by the inquest of St. Dunstan's, not on account of his making and selling "a sort of liquor called coffee," but for annoying his neighbours, "by evill smells, and for keeping of fire for the most part night and day, whereby his chimney and chamber hath been set on fire, to the great danger and affrightment of his neighbours." However, Farr was not ousted, but remained at the Rainbow, and rose to be a person of eminence and repute in the parish. His token, dated 1666, bears a rainbow based on clouds, to indicate that he and his house had escaped the Great Fire. The house was let off into tenements; for books were printed at this very time "for Samuel Speed, at the sign of the Rainbow, near the Inner Temple-gate, in Fleet-street." The Phœnix Fire Office was established here about 1682. Hatton, in 1708, evidently attributed Farr's nuisance to the coffee itself, saying: "who would have thought London would ever have had 3000 such nuisances, and that coffee would have been (as now) so much drank by the best of quality and physicians."

Mr. Moncrieff, the dramatist, used to tell that about 1780 this house was kept by his grandfather, Alexander Moncrieff, when it retained its original title of "the Rainbow Coffee-house." The old coffee-room had a lofty bay-window at the south end, looking into the Temple; and the room was separated from the kitchen only by a glazed partition; in the bay was the table for the elders. All this has been swept away, and a lofty and spacious saloon, richly gilt and coloured in the Renaissance manner, has been erected upon the site: it is one of the handsomest dining-rooms in the metropolis.

With two Johnsonian links we conclude. The Mitre Tavern, in Fleet-street, was the favourite rendezvous of Dr. Johnson's evening parties, including Goldsmith, Percy, Hawksworth, and Boswell; here was planned the Tour to the Hebrides. Johnson had a strange nervous feeling, which made him uneasy if he had not touched every post between the Mitre and his own lodgings. Chamberlain Clark, who died in 1831, aged ninety-two, was the last surviving of Dr. Johnson's Mitre friends. William Scott (Lord Stowell) also frequented this tavern. Here, in 1640, Lilly met old Will Poole, the astrologer, then living in Ram-alley; the Royal Society Club dined at the Mitre from 1743 to 1750, the Society then meeting in Crane-court. Johnson's Mitre is commonly thought to be the tavern of that sign which still exists in Mitre-court, over against Fetter-lane; and here is shown a cast of Nollekens's bust of Johnson, in confirmation of this house having been his resort. Such was not the case: Boswell distinctly states it to have been "the Mitre Tavern *in Fleet-street;*" Lilly, in his *Life*, specifies "the Mitre Tavern in Fleet-street," where he met Poole; and the Royal Society's Minutes state the Club to have dined at "the Mitre Tavern in Fleet-street;" which Mr. Burn, in his excellent account of the Beaufoy Tokens, explains, was "the house, No. 39 Fleet-street, that Macklin opened in 1788, as the Poet's Gallery; and lastly, Saunders's auction-rooms." It was taken down to enlarge the site for Messrs. Hoares' new banking-house. The now Mitre Tavern, Mitre-court, was originally called Joe's Coffee-house; and, on the shutting up of the old Mitre, in Fleet-street, took its name; this being four years after Johnson's death.

Peele's, at the south-east corner of Fetter-lane, was one of the coffee-houses of the Johnsonian period; and here was long preserved a portrait of Dr. Johnson, on the key-stone of a chimney-piece, stated to have been painted by Sir Joshua Reynolds. The house is referred to in the *Daily Courant* of February 13th, 1722.

CHANGES AT CHARING CROSS.

THAT the confluence of the Strand, Whitehall, and Cockspur-street should have been termed, a century since, the full tide of human existence, is reasonable enough. The opening of Trafalgar-square northward has spoiled the uniformity of the comparison. The name, Charing Cross, is more debatable. The latter part is from the stone cross erected there, 1291-94, to Eleanor, Queen of Edward I.; from which fanciful etymologists traced the name to *Chere Reine* (dear Queen). But the village of Cherringe, Charing, is mentioned in 1260: there are one or two other Charings in England, one in Kent—*ing* means meadow; and Mr. Cunningham conjectures the name to signify Char Meadow. The Rev. A. Dyce (*King Edward I.*, Peele's Works) asks whether it is alluded to here:

> Erect a rich and stately carved cross,
> Whereon her statue shall with glory shine,
> And henceforth see you call it Charing Cross;
> For why? the *chariest* and the choicest queen,
> That ever did delight my royal eyes,
> There dwells in darkness.

This was the last spot at which the Queen's body rested on the way to Westminster Abbey for burial; and minute accounts exist of Charing Cross being built of Caen stone and Dorset marble steps, by Richard and Roger de Crundale; it was highly decorated, and had paintings and metal figures, gilt; besides Eleanor and others, sculptured in Caen stone by Alexander of Abingdon, and modelled by Torel, a goldsmith, probably an Italian. The Cross appears in the Sutherland View, 1543, with only a few houses near it; St. Martin s Church, literally "in the fields;" and Hedge-lane, now Whitcombe-street. In a good map of London of this date we find that Covent Garden then extended to St. Martin's-lane, and the fields behind it reached to the village of St. Giles's. The Haymarket then had a hedge on one side, and a few bushes on the other; hay was sold here, and washerwomen dried their linen upon the grass of the site of the present Opera-house. Neither Pall Mall, St. James's-street, Piccadilly, nor any of the streets in that part of the town, were built; and Westminster was a suburb on the south-west and south sides of St. James's Park. A century later, puritanical bigotry was at its full height; and, April 23, 1643, "by order of the Commission or Committee appointed by the House, the sign of a tavern, *The Golden Cross, at Charing Cross*, was taken down as superstitious and idolatrous." Next followed the Cross itself, which was pulled down in June, July, and August 1647, and knife-hafts were made of some of the stone, or marble. Then the wits had their gibe:

> Undone, undone, the lawyers are,—
>   They wander about the towne,
> Nor can find the way to Westminster,
>   Now Charing Cross is downe.
> At the end of the Strand they make a stand,
>   Swearing they are at a loss,
> And chaffing say, That's not the way,
>   They must go by Charing Cross.
>
> *The Downfalle of Charing Cross.*

Next, regicides were executed "at the said place, where Charing Cross stood." In 1674, was placed here the noble equestrian statue of Charles I., by Le Sœur, which had been cast in 1633, but long lay concealed. A memorandum in the State-Paper Office points to the statue having been originally ordered of Le Sœur by Lord Treasurer Weston, afterwards Earl of Portland, to be set up in his gardens at Roehampton. The stone pedestal, long attributed to Gibbons, is proved by written evidence to be the work of one of the Marshalls, master-mason to the Crown (*see page* 232).

The old story of the horse being without a girth is a fiction; the girth passes over a very strong rein on the right. In 1810, the sword, buckles, and straps fell from the statue; and about the Coronation of Queen Victoria, 1838, the sword (a rapier of Charles's period) was stolen. The George pendent from the ribbon has also been taken away, as denoted by the vacant hole in the metal where the George should hang.

Walpole, we know, speaks of "the commanding, graced figure, and the exquisite form of the horse, as striking to the most practised eye." Dr. Kitchiner says: "The figure and symmetry of the horse is nowhere more perfectly displayed than in this most finished piece of workmanship. Continually, however, in our sight, this *chef-d'œuvre* is not only disregarded but neglected." It is refreshing, therefore, to find these opinions backed by a later critic, as follows: "Although taken soon after Charles's accession, and at a time when sorrow could hardly have been put upon him, yet the character of melancholy is deeply impressed on the countenance. The horse is superb: the action is that which is taught in the *ménage*, the motion of the legs showing the spirit of the animal; yet the action is not that of progressing,—it is a movement that would not communicate motion to the body, but leaves the rider perfectly undisturbed; the bridle falls almost loose upon the neck; nor does the well-taught steed disturb the reverie of thought expressed in the countenance of its master."*

The iron-work has been removed from round the pedestal; let us hope we shall not hear of any further pilfering.

The changes at Charing Cross have been very striking, yet more mismanaged and cavilled at than the "improvements" in any other quarter. We well remember the paved area about St. Martin's Church, with the surrounding labyrinth of courts and alleys, including the Bermudas, Carribbee or Cribbee Islands; and Porridge Island, noted for its cookshops: all which were removed in 1829. One of these thoroughfares was Round-court, leading to the Strand, where, in 1798, one Williams, the keeper of a reading-room, was convicted of lending a newspaper to read, and taking one penny for the use of it, for which, by 29th Geo. III. cap. ix., he was fined 5*l.* Another knot, on the west side of St. Martin's-lane, was cleared away for Trafalgar-square, including Duke's-court, where lived Roger Payne, the

* *Times*, Sept. 1, 1838.

celebrated bookbinder, whose *chef-d'œuvre*, Æschylus, in Lord Spencer's library, cost fifteen guineas binding. Then, at the Mews-gate, lived honest Tom Payne, the bookseller, whose little shop, in the shape of L, was named the Literary Coffee-house, from its knot of literary frequenters. The Royal Mews, with Kent's three stone cupolas, after housing for a time the National Repository, Cross' Menagerie, and the Public Records, was taken down in 1830. The ground was then cleared for the site of the National Gallery, to cost 50,000*l.*, in miserable contrast with 76,000*l.* voted for the Royal Stables at Windsor. The low-built saddler's shop fronting Charing Cross was then removed.* Upon the area in the rear was exhibited, in 1831, the entire skeleton of a Greenland whale, taken off the coast of Belgium in 1827; total length ninety-five feet. The skeleton was raised upon iron supports, and visitors ascended within the ribs by a flight of steps; the age of this whale was estimated by Cuvier at from 900 to 1000 years; it is figured and minutely described in No. 503 of the *Mirror:* the small wits called it "the palace of the Prince of W(h)ales." The National Gallery was built partly with the materials of the Mews; and the beautiful Corinthian columns from Carlton House were used in the portico. The Gallery was not opened until 1838, when "the pie-crust edifice" and its "contemptible closets" were soundly abused; as were also the oyster-shell grottoes, or cupolas, of the wings,—poor imitations of Vanbrugh. Dr. Waagen, at this early period, condemned the great defect in the site—its very small depth; he foresaw that more room would be wanted: meanwhile, the edifice was designated "a handsome front to St. Martin's Workhouse," which now, some six-and-twenty years after, is to be taken down, to make room for the extension of the Gallery.

Next was commenced the erection of the Nelson Column, which occupied from the year 1837 to 1852; in the interim

* "Isaac Barrow, the divine, died 'in a mean lodging at a saddler's near Charing Cross; an old, low, ill-built house, which he had used for several years' (Pope, *Life of Seth Ward*), and still standing at the commencement of the present century" (Cunningham's *Handbook of London*, 2d ed., p. 107)—and somewhat later.

invoking the early humour of *Punch* upon its slow progress with a man and a boy: even now it awaits the four colossal lions to be placed at the angles of the pedestal steps. The site was much objected to; but, in a Parliamentary examination, eight architects and sculptors were in favour of it, and four against it. Chantrey considered it as "the most favourable site that could be found or imagined for any national work of art; its aspect is nearly south, and sufficiently open to give the object placed on that identical spot all the advantage of light and shade that can be desired: to this may be added the advantage of a happy combination of unobtrusive buildings around; but to conceive a national monument worthy of this magnificent site is no easy task." The Square, though planned by Barry, has been, with witless sarcasm, called "an artificial stone-quarry:" its granite capstan-posts are, at least, characteristic; and the terrace is picturesque, as well as serviceable to the effect of the Gallery façade. The Fountains came in for a still larger share of abuse; and the Artesian wells have been alike condemned for their great cost and inefficiency. Altogether, it appears that niggardliness had much to do with these shortcomings; together with a certain fondness for abusing public works, without taking into consideration the amount of money placed at the disposal of those engaged in planning and executing them.

The commemorative sculpture of Trafalgar-square has been equally unfortunate: Baily's statue of Nelson has been likened to a Greenwich pensioner, and the bas-reliefs on the pedestal have been no better treated. The Column was not commenced until three-and-thirty years had elapsed from the day on which were borne in mournful pomp, past this very spot, all that was mortal of him

> Whose sacred splendour, and whose deathless name,
> Shall grace and guard his country's naval fame.

Chantrey's equestrian statue of George IV., to whom western London is so largely indebted for its reconstruction and embellishment, has, however, been commended for its bold and judicious innovation on the old custom of representing horses in statues either curveting or ambling: here it stands still on all four legs. The portrait-statues of Napier and Havelock are interesting memorials of our Indian wars. Dr. Jenner occupied the south-western angle for a time, to be near the College of Physicians; but was soon removed to Kensington Gardens, as a more appropriate spot for the originator of Vaccination.

Stepping eastwards, we are reminded of Canaletto's famous picture of Charing Cross, in the collection at Northumberland House: it was painted about 1746, and shows the houses, with their signs, among which is prominent the Golden Cross; this picture was engraved in 1753. The façade of Northumberland House, as we now see it, was altered in 1749. There is in existence a drawing, by Vertue, of the front, before this alteration: it was purchased at the Strawberry-Hill Sale for the Rev. Dr. Wellesley, and is now in the collection of Mr. J. H. Wilson. The only old portion of Northumberland House is part of the portal.

This end of the West Strand has been handsomely rebuilt. We soon reach the Charing-Cross Hotel and Railway Booking-Offices, which have displaced the luckless Hungerford Market and surrounding houses. The Hotel is a fine example, designed by Mr. E. M. Barry, of a new class of buildings, which promises to become almost as national as the railway itself. An ably-written description of this vast structure has appeared in the *Builder*, No. 1139: we have little space for details, but may briefly state that the interior plan presents many novelties, —as, an ascending room, various lifts and ventilating shafts, and a cistern at the top of the building to contain 17,000 gallons of water, one in the basement for 10,000 gallons, and twelve other cisterns. Then we have a *buffet* and *restaurant*, coffee-room, ladies' coffee-room, reading-room, board-room, meeting-room, smoking-room, and billiard-room, and suites as well as separate bed-rooms, bath-rooms, and sitting-rooms. The beds number about 214. There are five storeys in the Strand front, besides two storeys in the roof; and three storeys below the

Strand. In the fore-court is the picturesque Cross, which we have engraved as the frontispiece to the present volume.

We conclude this occasionally prosaic account of Changes at Charing Cross with a very pleasant ditty with which we were favoured by our excellent friend and brother-antiquary, Thomas Crofton Croker, in the year 1854, shortly before the publication of *Curiosities of London*. All who had the felicity of knowing the amiable writer of this Ballad will feel that this is but one of the many effusions of generous and kindly feeling by which his too short career was characterised: his *gaité de cœur* was boundless.

3 *Gloucester Road, Old Brompton.*

O Mister Timbs—oh, F. S. A.!
  One of five hundred Fellows,
To organise and make us hay
  Who rake, and blow the bellows;
Who do recall things great and small—
  The past, who will make pleasant;
What is pulled down in this our Town
  Your London makes most pleasant.

Imagine thus, in twenty-five
  ('Tis no such mighty hardship),
To think that I was then alive,
  And thinking of the Bardship.
Imagine then, that in my inn
  I was alone and lonely,
And that in hope the wreath to win,
  I wrote this ballad only.

An excellent new Ballad: being entitled, A Lamentation over the Golden Cross, Charing Cross.

Let others prate, in phrases grand,
  Of palaces and squares,
Approving all great George has planned,
  And all Bob Nash prepares;
I joy not in such schemes at all,
  But much bemoan my loss,
When looking up from fair Whitehall
  I'll miss the Golden Cross.

I miss already, with a tear,
  The Mews-gate public-house,
Where many a gallant Grenadier
  Did lustily carouse;
Alas! Macadam's droughty dust
  That honoured spot doth fill,
Where they were wont the ale robust
  In the King's name to swill.

I sorrow when I see the sight
  That hackney-coaches stand
Where once I saw the bayonet bright
  Levelled with steady hand—

That their plebeian noise should now
  Invade the listening ears,
Where once we heard the tow-row-row
  Of British Grenadiers.

As for Tom Bish, my agony
  Of grief for him is past,
Because next year he will not be
  What he was in the last:
For Humdrum here hath won the day,
  And lotteries are done;
And why should Thomas longer stay,
  His occupation gone?*

But not the Mew's-gate house of call,
  Nor yet the barrack-yard,
Nor Bish, foredoomed to hasty fall,
  By House of Commons hard—
Afflict my mind with so much woe,
  Such sorrow manifold,
As the approaching overthrow
  Of Charing's cross of gold.

It stood, last relic, many a year,
  Conspicuous to be seen,
Of Longshanks' sorrow o'er the bier
  Of Eleanor, his queen;
Fanatic hands tore down the Cross,
  Carved out of goodly stone;
And when we mourn the present loss,
  All trace of Nell is gone.

Here once, in days of ancient date,†
  The judges used to call
On palfreys from the Temple-gate,
  Bound for Westminster Hall;
Here venison pasty's savoury fare
  Consoled the learned maw,
And made it valiant to declare
  The oracles of law.

---

* Bish kept his western lottery-office near the Golden Cross.

† The Judges used formerly to breakfast in the pleasant village of Charing Cross, when they rode on palfreys from the Temple, to open the King's Courts at Westminster.

But now, its ancient fame forgot,
  And other whimsies come,
For plans I value not a jot,
  Predestined is its doom.
No more I'll eat the juicy steak,
  Within its boxes pent,
When in the mail my place I take,
  For Bath or Brighton bent.

No more the coaches shall I see
  Come trundling from the yard;
Nor hear the horn blow cheerily,
  By brandy-bibbing guard.
King Charles, I think, must sorrow sore,
  Even were he made of stone,
When left by all his friends of yore
  (Like Tom Moore's rose) alone.

No wonder the triumphant Turk
  O'er Missolonghi treads;
Roasts bishops, and in bloody work
  Snips off some thousand heads!
No wonder that the Crescent gains,
  When we the fact can't gloss,
That we ourselves are at such pains
  To trample down the Cross.

Oh! London won't be London long,
  For 'twill be all pulled down;
And I shall sing a funeral song
  O'er that time-honoured town.
One parting curse I here shall make,
  And then lay down my quill;
Hoping old Nick himself may take
  Bob Nash and Wyatville.

* * * *

'Twas thus I sung in twenty-five,
  And now 'tis fifty-four;
Yet things though altered still survive,
  Some dozen or a score.
The Golden Cross is grown so grand,
  And puts on such an air,
That you must seek it in the Strand,
  And Morley's echoes—"Where?"

The Mews is gone—Trafalgar Square,
  With water squirting up,
And statue (would there were a pair,
  Like saucer and a cup),
With column high, insults the sky,
  Upon ignoble base;
And Art is seen upon this scene
  Out of its proper place.

Alas! alas! for East and North,—
  I'll not expose the rest,
The College, Spy Club, and so forth,
  To Charing Cross the blest:
Where one can't cross without a scud,
  And cabs do make one flutter;
While "Busses" they fling up the mud,
  Or pitch one in the gutter.

Oh! for the golden days of yore—
  We had no railroads then
To make us tunnels dark explore
  By railways and their men;
Where late at night and every morn
  The whistle shrilly sounds,
Instead of musical guard's horn
  Like following up the hounds.

Alas! alas! for chances too;
  All but Art-Union's done,
And there is little chance to woo
  When chances are small fun.
Now for the Turk—we'll do his work
  With bayonet and with ball;
Nor do we care how Russians fare,
  So we have at 'em all.

For wrong or right, we love to fight,
  Whatever may be said:
A Queen we own upon the throne,
  Not like King Charlie dead,
Just stuck up there, at which to stare,
  But living in the Park;
And we'll agree, that long may she
  Enjoy this glorious lark.

So Mr. Timbs—dear F.S.A.—
  Let me no further chatter;
I cannot, if I would, be gay
  About this mighty matter;
And yet to you a debt is due
  For writing and recording;
And may the public take my view,
  Your labour well rewarding. T. Crofton Croker.

The Charing Cross Railway Company, with the view of more closely associating the site of their superb Hotel and Station with the memorable patronymic and historic site, have erected in the Courtyard the handsome Memorial engraved as the Frontispiece to the present volume. This has been designed as a restoration of the Eleanor Cross, and has been a work of considerable difficulty to the architect, Mr. E. M. Barry, A.R.A.; inasmuch as the authorities for the Cross are exceedingly limited. We possess the most minute details of the cost and materials of the sumptuous structure; but of its elevation we have no satisfactory representation. There are three Views of the Cross, but not one of architectural value. There is a rough drawing in the Crowle Collection, in the British Museum, which is described by Pennant, and engraved by Wilkinson; there is another View in the Bodleian Library, at Oxford; and a third in the Library of the Society of Antiquaries. These views are obviously incorrect, and evidently by persons unaccustomed to architecture. But the three above-mentioned drawings agree in the main features, such as number of storeys, figures, sides, &c.; and Pennant describes the Cross as being octagonal on plan, and having eight figures; while Waltham and Northampton have only four each; and Geddington, three. These drawings, with Pennant's description, constitute the principal authority for the Cross here engraved; the details of the design having been left entirely to the architect, and they are in strict accordance with the architecture of the period.

Mr. Wilson, to whose Collection we are indebted for much interesting and out-of-the-way assistance in the course of our *Walks and Talks*, has called attention to the representation of the Cross in the title-page of the scarce quarto, *A Dialogue between the Cross at Cheap and Charing Cross*; which "agrees with the Cross in Aggas's plan;" the latter is, to our thinking, too rude to be depended on. The View in the Bodleian, in the Sutherland London, in 1543, has evidently been followed by Mr. Barry, who has succeeded in designing an elegant Monument; and we must recollect, that Charing Cross, being the last, and in London, was the most sumptuous cross of the entire number.

The Monument has been erected entirely at the expense of the Railway Company. Whatever may be its identity with the ancient Cross, this must be regarded as a very tasteful work.

RAILWAY LONDON:

FROM LONDON BRIDGE TO CHARING CROSS—FROM NEWINGTON TO BLACKFRIARS.

IN no portion of the Metropolis has the Genius of Change wrought so many and such striking changes as in the ancient suburb of Southwark, within the last thirty years. The time to pull down, and the time to build up, and the time to pull down again, have here succeeded each other with rapid, though not noiseless, pace. Little more than thirty years have elapsed since the old High-street of Southwark (the Borough), the narrowest leading thoroughfare into London—with many a gabled and plaster house-front in grimy picturesqueness—was swept away for the southern approach to the new Bridge; this, and the corresponding approach northward, costing a million of money, or twice the cost of the Bridge itself. The Southwark street, though doubled in width, is not unique: the old houses on the east side being only cleared away as far as St. Thomas's Hospital; but the most was made of the fine area gained by this removal. The Hospital was rebuilt in massive style, commencing with the north wing; for the site of which 40,850*l.* was paid, and not considered an extravagant price, though at the rate of 54,855*l.* per acre; and the site of the two houses adjoining, the City purchased of the Hospital at the rate of 69,935*l.* per acre.

We recollect St. Thomas's front of fifty years since,—its huge iron gates and stone piers, with a statuette on each of the latter—a male and female crippled patient. The gates, and the two large houses on each side, were erected by Mr. Guy, at an expense of 3000*l.* The centre of the principal front, in the first quadrangle, was of stone, and a characteristic composition. On the upper story was a clock, under a circular pediment; and beneath was a niche, containing a statuette of Edward VI., with a sceptre in his right hand, and the charter in his left. Lower, in niches on each side, was a man with a crutch, and a sick woman; under them a man with a wooden leg, and a woman with her arm in a sling; and next the Royal arms, and an inscription. Hatton, in 1708, describes the Queen's arms in the pediment, pine-apples and festoons, and the figures of the cripples; besides the figure of Charity between two cripples, on the east side of the court, which had a Tuscan colonnade. After these figures of cripples had been removed from the piers and niches, they were placed in the shrubbery-plots, with grotesque effect.

The second quadrangle, or court, had St. Thomas's Church on the south side; on the east, the Court-room, over a Doric colonnade; and on the north, the Chapel for the use of the patients, where service was performed daily. In the centre of this Court was placed a bronze statue of Edward VI., by Scheemakers, with an inscription, stating it to have been erected by a private gentleman, in 1737. Scheemakers was a Flemish sculptor, who settled, about 1735, for many years in England; so that this statue of King Edward was one of his earliest works executed in this country. It is a very graceful impersonation of the amiable young monarch; and the small pedestal, with his crown laid upon a cushion, is picturesque.

The third court of the Hospital was surrounded by a Tuscan colonnade. In the centre was a statue of Sir Robert Clayton, which Hatton, in 1708, describes as "curiously carved in full proportion, in the habit of Lord Mayor, with a charter in his hand, and standing on a pedestal about 6 feet high, all neatly cut in marble. The pedestal is enriched with Sir Robert's arms, supported by two Cupids," &c. Sir Robert Clayton, "the prodigious rich scrivener," was "the fanatick Lord Mayor" of Dryden's *Religio Laici.* Sir Robert lived in sumptuous state in a house, or palace, in the Old Jewry—a magnificent residence, with a superb banqueting-room of cedar, painted with "The Historie of the Gyants' War." Charles II. once supped here. The fine old place was taken down in 1863.

In rebuilding the west side of the street, the east end of St.

Mary Overie—in magnitude and architectural character the third church in the metropolis—was left open to view, though in the old street arrangement it had been hidden, save the upper portion of the tower, for centuries. The tower is 150 feet in height; and from its roof Hollar drew his celebrated View of London: upon the restoration of the tower, and the rebuilding of the east end of the church, the parishioners expended some 45,000*l*. This is the work of Mr. George Gwilt, F.S.A.—the choir consisting of an enriched gable, with an elaborately-foliated cross on its apex; pinnacled, staircased turrets, with niches at the angles; a new triple Lancet window, and a Catherine-wheel window of extraordinary richness and beauty. Over the vaulting was erected a cast-iron roof covered with copper; the flying buttresses were cased with stone, the aisle-windows built anew, &c.; in all which Mr. Gwilt rigidly adhered to the former work, not only in the general design, but in the minutest details, wherever prototypes could be found. The above is allowed, even in these days of revivalism, to be one of the most conscientious works in the country. It is to be wished that half the praise could be accorded to the transept and nave of the church, restored and rebuilt by less painstaking architects. We must not, however, forget the Lady Chapel at the east end, which, after a stout battle with the iconoclasts who fought for its removal, was restored by public subscription, under the superintendence of Mr. Gwilt and Mr. Cottingham.

The public had scarcely appreciated the fine architectural group we have just sketched, when, at the close of 1836, the opening of the Greenwich Railway—the first complete line from the metropolis—soon threw the locality into a transition state, which has continued to the present hour. The railway companies were the disturbers. The newly-built Grammar School of St. Olave and St. John's was taken down for the enlargement of the terminus; and other clearance was made. In 1861, a railway hotel of imposing dimensions was built adjoining the terminus: it is seven storeys high, and has a Mansard-roof, with dormer windows. We should, however, have noted, that in

1854 was erected, midway in the road, opposite St. Mary Overie's Church, a clock-tower of Gothic design, resembling a market-cross, with a canopied niche; thus adding a picturesque architectural feature to the spot.

The public had long complained of the journey from the railway termini, through the overcrowded streets, to the west end of London occupying nearly as much time as the railway transit from Brighton; when an extension line along the southern bank of the Thames, to cross the river by three bridges, was determined on—one of these bridges being for the Charing Cross extension into Hungerford; another for the Chatham and Dover line into Farringdon-street; and the third, between Southwark and London Bridges, to take a line into Cannon-street, near the Mansion House.

The Charing Cross Company, having determined on their plan of extension from the nest of stations at London Bridge, besought the authorities of St. Thomas's Hospital to sell them a small piece of garden-ground, one-sixteenth of an acre, for 20,000*l.*, which offer was refused. The railway-bill was then in Parliament, and was vigorously opposed by the Hospital; but at last the Company got their Act. Then said the Hospital, "You shall take all our place—all or none; we will not let you have a part only." After long and tedious litigation and arbitration, the Company were compelled to purchase the entire property; the Hospital being removed to Walworth.

The Hospital ground, nearly four acres, is considered to have been obtained cheaply at 74,000*l.* an acre; for it is stated in the *Builder* that the site of the Alliance Bank is rented at 500*l.* per annum; which, when capitalised, is at the rate of 260,000*l.* an acre. Another property has been taken, on a twenty-one years' lease, at an improved rent of 750*l.*, which is at the rate for the freehold of 298,000*l.* per acre. The site of the old Town-hall, taken at 500*l.* a year, the area about 2090 superficial feet, indicates a freehold value of more than 250,000*l.* per acre. It is hoped that eventually the Hospital ground will become the site of buildings worthy of this costly location. When this shall be accomplished, we may look forward to the rebuilding of the east side of the High-street; but then will be swept away the most picturesque relics of old Southwark, including "many fair inns for receipt of travellers—the Spurr. Tabarde. George. Hart, King's Head," &c.

To return to the Railway. Though only a very short extension, and presenting no peculiar engineering difficulties, it has been the most expensive, for its length, ever built. When all is paid up, it will be found to have cost very nearly, if not quite, 1000*l.* sterling per yard. Much of this immense expenditure was no doubt due to the unexpected opposition of the Governors of St. Thomas's Hospital, and the compulsory purchase of the institution, which that opposition necessitated. Much was also lost by the secret of the intended route of the line not being well kept, so that property of little value before the railway came was purchased for a trifling sum, and resold to the Company at an immense premium. This and other causes have swelled the original estimate for the construction of the line to a sum more than four times greater than was at first contemplated. Though called by the general name of the Charing Cross Line, this extension really embraces two distinct schemes, viz. the line from Charing Cross to London Bridge, and the line from Charing Cross to Cannon-street. Yet, though legally distinct, they are practically one; and from the junction at the Borough Market, where the Cannon-street branch diverges across the Thames on a magnificent bridge, both run on the same viaducts to Charing-cross. The line leaves the London Bridge station by a rather sharp curve of little more that 500 feet radius. This quick turn was introduced to propitiate the Governors of St. Thomas's Hospital, and avoid, if possible, the necessity of buying that costly property. The curve, however, was made in vain. Two girder bridges, of immense span and undeniable ugliness, take the line over the approach to London Bridge. A viaduct on iron columns carries it through the Borough Market; and thence the line is continued, with scarcely any curves or inclines, through the poor neighbourhoods lying between the

Borough and Blackfriars, across the Blackfriars-road, and parallel with Stamford-street, to the Waterloo-road, where it makes a junction with the South-Western Station, which it enters by a single line of rails; and so practically brings that large system of lines to Charing-cross, and hereafter to Cannon-street. From this, it continues in almost a straight line across Stamford-street and the Belvedere-road to what was once Hungerford Suspension Bridge, but which has now been converted into one of the strongest and most important railway bridges over the Thames. On this the line is taken over the site of Hungerford Market, where has been erected a magnificent Hotel and Station.

In this line, two miles in length, there are no less than fourteen iron bridges across streets, and some of unusually great span; two iron viaducts on columns; two junctions made with other lines; and two immense railway bridges across the Thames. For the Cannon-street Station, large and newly-built edifices have been taken down; old Dowgate has been mercilessly pulled about.* The bridge here is to be built of wrought-iron plate

* Many years ago, Dr. Wigan, then a surgeon, practised on Dowgate-hill, at the corner of Cloak-lane, and facing the burial-ground of All-Hallows-the-Less, destroyed in the Great Fire, and not rebuilt. Dr. Wigan had long entertained peculiar notions as to the Preëxistence of Souls—when the whole scene around you appears to be reacting after a long interval, and you say, *all this has happened before;* as Lord Lindsay says, "you remember it as some remote and indefinite period of pre-existence; you always know what will come next, and sit spell-bound, in a sort of calm expectancy." Dr. Wigan has well described this sensation in his clever work, *The Duality of the Mind*, adding: "all seems to be *remembered*, and to be now attracting attention for the second time; never is it supposed for the *third* time." After observing that the delusion occurs only when the mind has been exhausted by excitement, the persuasion of the scene being a repetition coming on when the attention has been *roused* by some accidental circumstance, Dr. Wigan explains, "Only one brain has been used in the immediately preceding part of the scene; the other brain has been asleep, or in an analogous state nearly approaching it. When the attention of both brains is roused to the topic, there is the same vague consciousness that the ideas have passed through the mind before which takes place on reperusing the page we have read while thinking on some other subject. The ideas *have* passed through the mind

girders, resting on cast-iron cylinders, similar to those seen now under Hungerford. It is to be laid for no less than five lines of rails; to be thirty-four feet from the water, and sixty-four feet in its extreme width. When this bridge is completed, trains will run backwards and forwards between Charing Cross and London Bridge like shuttles in a loom all day long. The station in Cannon-street will be thirty feet higher, forty feet wider, and one hundred feet longer than the Charing Cross Station and Hotel. They will be in the Italian style, Renaissance, with high roofs and towers at each end of the building.

We have now to deal with another extension—the Chatham and Dover—from the Elephant and Castle to Blackfriars Bridge. The actual length of line is scarcely a mile; but in traffic value to the Company this mile into London is of greater importance than any other ten miles of their way; and is, indeed, only of less importance than the quarter-mile which will take the line across the Thames, and place them in direct communication with the Underground Railway, and through that with all lines running to the north of England. Third-class passengers can now travel in less than four minutes from Blackfriars Bridge to the Elephant and Castle for 1*d.* The cheap line of omnibuses for the same distance is 2*d.*, and take nearly seven times

---

before; and as there was not a sufficient consciousness to fix them in the mind without a renewal, we have no means of knowing the length of time that had elapsed between the faint impression received by the single brain, and the *distinct* impression by the double brain: it may seem to have been many years."

Dr. Wigan often discussed this subject with his friend Dr. Gooch, who took great interest in topics occupying the debatable region between physics and metaphysics; but neither of the Doctors could devise a satisfactory explanation of the above phenomenon. In support of Dr. Wigan's theory, the cause has been referred to "some incongruous action of the double structure of the brain, to which perfect unity of action belongs in a healthy state."—*Things not Generally Known*, 2d Series, p. 150.

Dr. Wigan wrote fluently upon many subjects: he was the "Luke Roden" of the *Illuminated Magazine*, started in 1843, under the editorship of Douglas Jerrold, and illustrated by Ebenezer Landells. In this work, Mr. Tom Taylor, then fresh from Cambridge, first appeared as an author.

the time to accomplish the journey. The line from the Elephant is carried entirely on arches, to enable it to cross the level of the Charing Cross Railway at the Blackfriars-road, and also to enable it to cross the Thames at the level of the new Bridge at Blackfriars. The curves on the line are of as constant occurrence as the bridges that span the streets, which intervene at about every one hundred yards. The stations, which are very numerous, are tastefully relieved by terra-cotta, coloured bricks, tiles, &c. The Bridge at Blackfriars, a magnificent work, was built with such rapidity, that even the casual observer could mark the progress from day to day, the whole occupying but fifteen months. It is constructed with wrought-iron plate girders, resting on cast-iron cylinders; each of the spans is 160 feet long by 16 feet deep, and laid for two lines of rails; two such spans laid side by side form the width of the structure, which is five spans, or nearly 930 feet long. The method of building it was by constructing what is called an American truss —that is, a powerful lattice-work of timber, strengthened with iron tie-rods in every part. This truss is floored at the bottom, and strong enough to bear a load of three tons per lineal foot. Each span is built six times in excess of the strength required to resist the proof strain, calculated at more than four times what the ordinary exigencies of metropolitan railway traffic will ever bring upon it. Provision is made for each span to contract or expand as freely as the weather may require; but the greatest difference between the extreme of summer heat and depth of winter will only make a difference of from two and a half inches to three inches in the length of the entire structure, the foundations of which go twenty-eight feet deep into the London clay. The total weight of the iron in the bridge is 3000 tons, and the exact number of rivets fixed in it is 603,682. Three hundred men and boys were constantly employed on it from the 29th of January to the last day of September—a few days before the time allowed by the contract.

Blackfriars, which the railway now crosses, is a precinct of great historic interest, and is named from the monastery of

Black or Dominican Friars, built in the reign of Edward I., who kept here his charters and records; and Parliaments and other great meetings were held in the church. In 1522, the Emperor Charles V. of Spain was lodged here by Henry VIII.; Henry's divorce from Katherine of Arragon was decided here; and the Parliament which condemned Wolsey assembled at Blackfriars. Of the old Palace and Prison of Bridewell, upon the opposite side of the street, we have already talked; see pp. 31-38. In the Sutherland View of London, in 1543, we see the church of the monastery, with a tower and lofty spire, and the end towards the Fleet river flanked with two turrets. At Hunsdon House, in the Friary, occurred the catastrophe of "the Fatal Vespers," on the anniversary of Gunpowder Plot, 1623, when a Jesuit Father and one hundred of his congregation were killed by the fall of a gallery. Leigh Hunt, in his agreeable book *The Town*, relates this catastrophe to have been regarded by many as a token of the displeasure of Heaven against the Roman-Catholic faith; and to such an extent was the religious animosity carried, that those who were killed "were buried, without either the ceremony of a funeral service, or the decency of a coffin or winding-sheet, in two large pits or trenches, dug, the one in the court before, and the other in the garden behind, the house in which the accident had taken place."

The precinct retained the sanctuary privilege after the Dissolution of the Monasteries; taking advantage of which, Burbage and his fellows, when ejected from the City, built a playhouse in the Blackfriars: Shakspeare was a sharer in 1589. The theatre stood upon part of the present "Playhouse-yard," where was a piece of ground "to turne coaches in;" and there exists an Order in Council for the removal of the coaches in 1653, two years before the theatre was taken down. Hard by is another Shakspearean locality, the site of the house bequeathed by Shakspeare to his daughter, Susannah Hall; the counterpart of the deed of conveyance of which is preserved in the Guildhall Library, with Shakspeare's signature attached. The *very house* was, probably, destroyed in the Great Fire; but was rebuilt upon its proper site, close to the churchyard of St. Andrew-by-the-Wardrobe.

Hard by was the King's Printing-House, then "the completest printing-house in the world." Leigh Hunt observes upon this: "The King's Printer now lives elsewhere; but on the same spot is a house, which may be called the world's printing-house, seeing the enormous multitude of newspapers which the mighty giant of steam daily throws forth out of his iron lap, full of interest to all parts of the globe. We need not say that we allude to the *Times* newspaper. There is no knowing, in this and other instances, what bounds to put to human expectation, when mechanical and intellectual force are thus joined in a common object." And the steam giant has been at work here half a century.

It is not a little singular that this royal monopoly should have been succeeded by the marvellous invention of the printing-machine, and the use of the steam-engine; and this upon a fragment of the Roman wall. To have planted so powerful an engine of civilisation upon this material evidence of the Roman dominion is, indeed, as suggestive of England's greatness as are those vast railway works which are now in progress almost upon the same spot. To the late John Walter is due the merit of having first applied this new and mighty power to the improvement of journalism. At the commencement of the present century he became a joint proprietor, and the exclusive manager, of the *Times*. In the following year, an ingenious compositor, named Thomas Martin, had made the model of a machine for printing, which met with the approval of Mr. Walter, who expended a considerable sum in the attempt to complete the machine; but having exhausted his own funds, and his father, who had hitherto assisted him, having refused him any further aid, the attempt was abandoned. About this time, Kœnig came from Germany, with the contrivance of a printing-machine, with which he had made some progress; and having the coöperation of an ingenious assistant, named Bauer, and the help of three practical printers, who were satisfied as to the feasibility of the improvement, it was patented March 29, 1810, and assigned to the firm of Bensley, Kœnig, Woodfall, and Taylor. Mr. Kœnig states (*Times*, December 8, 1814) that "sheet H of the *New Annual Register* for 1810 was printed by machine, and was, I have no doubt, the first part of a book ever printed by a machine." This and other of Kœnig's machines were worked by hand. Perry, of the *Morning Chronicle*, was applied to, but declined to purchase one. Mr. Walter, however, seeing the invention accomplished, and in full operation, gave an order for two machines, which were to be worked by the power of a steam-engine. Notwithstanding violent opposition from the pressmen, the machines were completed on adjoining premises; and on the 29th of November 1814, the *Times* was printed for the first time by machines worked by steam-power. The scene of this triumph was Printing-House-square; and here, three-and-thirty years after, died John Walter, whose memory is kept green by remembrance of this vast accession of power to journalism which he carried out, as well as by the erection and endowment of a church upon his estate in Berkshire.

Many of the nobility dwelt in Blackfriars precinct: there lived Oliver, the miniature-painter; Jansen, the portrait-painter; and the illustrious Vandyke, whom Charles I. often visited here, coming by water from Whitehall. The great Wall is traced beneath the *Times* office, upon the site of the King's Printing-House; where is a fragment of Roman work, upon which is a Norman or Early English separation; and upon that are the remains of a passage and window, probably of the Blackfriars' monastery.

Ben Jonson lived in the precinct, and he dates his Preface to *Volpone, or the Fox*, "from my house in the Blackfriars;" and here he has laid the scene of the *Alchemist*. The Earl and Countess of Somerset were living here when Sir Thomas Overbury was murdered.

In Water-lane, adjoining, is the Hall of the Apothecaries' Company, built in 1670:

> Nigh where Fleet Ditch descends in sable streams,
> To wash his sooty Naiads in the Thames,
> There stands a structure on a rising hill,
> Where tyros take their freedom out to kill.
>
> Garth's *Dispensary*.

The Apothecaries were with the Grocers until 1617, when they were incorporated as a distinct Company by King James I.: at this time there were 104 apothecaries' shops in the metropolis and its suburbs: they kept shops for the sale of drugs; and it was not till nearly a century later that apothecaries in England, as distinguished from physicians and surgeons, began to act as general practitioners. This encroachment was strongly resisted by the College of Physicians, who, by way of retaliation, in July 1687, established a Dispensary for the sale of medicines to the poor, at prime cost, at their Hall, in Warwick-lane. Hereupon a furious controversy arose; but the tracts issued on both sides are now forgotten, except Garth's *Dispensary* (quoted above), first published in 1697. The apothecaries, however, made good the position they had taken: Addison, in the *Spectator*, No. 195, published in 1711, speaks of the apothecaries as the common medical attendants of the sick, and as performing the functions both of physician and surgeon. By the Act of 10 Anne, 1712, apothecaries were exempted from serving on juries, or ward or parish offices.

Towards the close of the last century chemists and druggists appeared in London, and began to prescribe as well as to dispense medicines; but they were soon checked by the Apothecaries' Company, whose Court of Examiners have, from time to time, greatly improved the standard of the medical education requisite to obtain the diploma for practice as an apothecary. The Hall has no architectural pretension: it has a retail department for the supply of unadulterated medicines.

In Earl-street, upon the site of the present house of the Bible Society, the Translators of the Bible used to meet early in the seventeenth century, and there they reviewed the whole work before it was printed, in 1611.

Before we describe the railway clearance, we should explain that a new street will be made from Blackfriars to the Mansion House, to pass Adel- or Addle-hill, where stood the palace of the Anglo-Saxon kings, erected by Athelstan. It will also pass directly through the garden of the College of Advocates, in Great Knightrider-street and Bennet's-hill, Doctors' Commons. The original house was destroyed in the Great Fire, and rebuilt of brick, in the style that prevailed shortly after: the interior has two quadrangles, containing 140 rooms, exclusive of the basement, the court, dining-room, library, &c., with frontages to Great Knightrider-street and Bennet's-hill; the total area is more than three-quarters of an acre. The library is rich in civil law and history, and originally belonged to Sir John Gibson, Judge of the Prerogative Court, by whose son it was presented to the College; each Bishop also makes it a present at his consecration. Hard by, in Great Carter-lane, stood the Old Bell Inn, whence, in 1598, Richard Quyney directs a letter "To my loving good friend and countryman, Mr. Wm. Shackspeare, deliver thees"—the only letter addressed to Shakspeare known to exist. The original is in the possession of Mr. R. B. Wheler, of Stratford-upon-Avon.

In the railway operations, great part of the east side of New Bridge-street has been removed, including the house built by Mylne, the architect of Blackfriars Bridge, for his private residence. Here has been erected a large Passenger Station, 150 feet in width, for the site of which a newly-built Insurance Office was removed; it was a handsome structure, and cost some 12,000*l.* It is stated that the Railway Company had to pay for this building and for compensation for removal no less than 40,000*l.*, for which they received in return 400*l.* for the old materials of the structure.

The railway is carried upon brick arches, nearly in the direction of the street-line, passing over the new street to the Mansion House; which, and Earl-street, are to be crossed by bridges. The railway then crosses Water-lane, much to the annoyance of the Apothecaries' Company, who contest the right of the engineers to deprive them of light, so requisite for their operations. The objection of the proprietors of the *Times* to the line is thus amusingly told:

"They are closing in upon us on every side, by land and by water, marching, burrowing, flying, swimming, scaling our walls, undermining our foundations, looking in at our windows, like the legion of rats that took Bishop Hatto's tower. Had any one told our citizens thirty years ago, even in those days of reform, that they would live to see a railway crossing Ludgate-hill, they would have set down the prophet as a madman. Our own case is serious. The London, Chatham, and Dover Railway, and the proposed street in connection with the Thames Embankment, contain us within their angle; and as neither the precise direction of each is fixed, nor the breadth of area it may require, we are as it were within the range of an immense pair of scissors, opening and shutting. The railway passes within about fifty yards of us, at an aërial level: and the thoroughfares which constitute our only carriage-approach are to be neatly and substantially arched over. It is gratifying to learn further that the railway, which may be so 'convenient' to us, is expected to be the great trunk-line connecting the North and South of the metropolis, and to dispense entirely with all the goods' traffic passing over all our bridges. For the future, if the hundred acres of goods' stations in our northern suburbs, and the New Cattle Market in Copenhagen Fields, wish to disgorge their contents into similar areas south of the Thames, they will pass, of course by night, between the hours of passenger traffic, over our heads at this office. We are only one among many sufferers, and can claim no pity.

* * * * *

"As for ourselves, we are martyrs without even the compassion that usually solaces the pains of martyrdom. We happen, as we said above, to lie at the very intersection of the grand new communications between the East and West, the North and South, of the metropolis. They are, we are assured, the greatest improvements of the age, and we shall have ample opportunity of knowing the truth of the promise, for we shall hear the passage of every train. However, we submit with a good grace, and hope dukes and their friends will take a lesson from our resignation, remembering that what we suffer is not only for a few months, but every night of the year."

From the Ludgate-hill Station the line runs in a north-easterly direction, passing under Skinner-street, Snow-hill, at a depth of sixteen feet, to a junction with the Metropolitan (Underground) Railway, near Carthusian-street, Smithfield; and there will be also a spur-line from it in a still more easterly direction, to meet the line of the Metropolitan Railway Extension to Finsbury, at a point near the northern extremity of King-street, Smithfield.

The most unpopular of all the works in this line is the Ludgate-hill Viaduct; yet, strange to say, the inhabitants gave evidence in its favour; and the design is identical with that exhibited by the Company, in 1860, before Parliament. The objections are too numerous to detail here: one is, interference with one of the finest architectural views in the metropolis. Coleridge, many years since, complained of the steeple of St. Martin's Church, on Ludgate-hill, constantly getting in the way when you wish to see the dome of St. Paul's:* what would "the odd fish" have said had he lived to see this railway obstruction? It is true that the level of the bridge is low, but it has unquestionably spoiled the view, and its small elevation above the street (18 feet) traffic is an objection of another class.

The street of Ludgate-hill is here only 42 feet wide; but as the Corporation intend, at some future time, to enlarge the thoroughfare, the span is 18 feet wider than the street, or 60 feet. The bridge is composed of five girders of wrought iron, screened from sight by ornamental iron-work, and relieved with

* Coleridge's remark was: "A Mr. H——, a friend of Fox's, who always put himself forward to interpret the great orator's sentiments, and almost took the words out of his mouth, put him in mind of the steeple of St. Martin, on Ludgate-hill, which is constantly getting in the way when you wish to see the dome of St. Paul's."

decorative brackets, and bronze armorial medallions, and handsome gas-lanterns and standards, by which the bridge will be lighted. It carries four lines of rails.

The only alternative of a bridge was tunnelling; the chief difficulty in which was the short distance from the bank of the Thames to the junction of this line with the Metropolitan Railway; and which would have necessitated a very steep gradient. But this was not all. Had the line been carried *under* Ludgate-hill, it would have had to make a slight *détour* for the purpose of easing the ascent, and the cost of constructing it would have been enormously increased. One of the most feasible of the suggestions made in regard to a change of course, and to the construction of a tunnel, involved the destruction of Apothecaries' Hall, the churchyard adjoining it, the *Times* printing-offices, and serious interference with the foundations of St. Martin's Church, the Old Bailey Sessions House, and Newgate Prison; and at the same time precluded the construction of a station at any point between the Metropolitan Railway and the River Thames.

Ludgate, Ludgate Hill and Street, have still associations which no railway innovation or discord of its "blatant beast" can drive out of mind. The old City-gate stood between the London Coffee-house and St. Martin's Church. That it was built by, and named from, King Lud, is mere tradition; more probably, it was named from the Flood, or Flud, which ran into Fleet-river. However, King Lud and his sons got statues here; in those days it was not asked—"Shall King Lud have a statue?" That the Gate was fortified or rebuilt by the Barons leagued against King John, and this with materials from the rich Jews' houses, was proved by a sort of receipt, in Hebrew, found in 1586: "This is the ward of Rabbi Moses, the son of the honourable Rabbi Isaac." Another ornament of the Gate was the statue of Queen Elizabeth, now at St. Dunstan's, Fleet-street. We see Ludgate in jeopardy, in Greffier's picture of the Great Fire. Chamberlayne (1726) describes the Gate as a prison, "only for debtors who are freemen of London,"—a sort of privileged insolvency. Pennant remembered it "a wretched prison for debtors;" and it was taken down when George II. became king. We should not forget the tradition of the handsome Stephen Foster, Lord Mayor in 1454, *begging at the grate* of Ludgate, and attracting the sympathy of a rich widow, who paid the debt for which he was confined, and afterwards married him; as Rowley has dramatised in his *Widow never Vext, or the Widow of Cornhill*, which has delighted many an audience of our own days. Moreover, there is a charge against Dr. Dodd—who had already sins enough to answer for—that he took his *Prison Thoughts* from an old quarto tract of that title, by Thomas Browning, a prisoner in Ludgate, "where poore prisoners are starved amidst copies of their freedom."

In Ludgate-*street*, from the Gate to St. Paul's, at "The Dunciad," Dr. Griffiths published the *Monthly Review*, No. 1, May 1749; and at No. 65 lived John Newbery, for whom Goldsmith wrote *Goody Two Shoes*, a pamphlet on the Cock-lane Ghost, and a *History of England;* and edited the *Public Ledger* newspaper; here, in the self-same shop, Griffith and Farren publish books as fitted for the young folks of these days as Francis Newbery's were for his generation. Next door were the head-quarters of the Society for the Diffusion of Useful Knowledge, the early scene of Mr. Charles Knight's valuable contributions to the commonwealth of literature—the *Penny Magazine* and the *Penny Cyclopædia.* Ave Maria-lane leads to Amen-corner, a sort of world's-end; and to Paternoster-row, where "of making of books there is no end." Stationers' Hall-court, as a matter of course, leads to Stationers' Hall; and at No. 7, the worthy publishers of these *Walks and Talks* keep shop. In the Court is a flourishing sycamore, to cheer the heart of many an overworked Londoner with anticipations of short Saturdays and green fields. When, a few years since, temporary publishing premises were erected upon this spot, a spirit seemed to say: "O Stationers, spare that tree!" the noble sycamore was, accordingly, built round, but not in, and it still flings aloft its picturesque and graceful form, and leaves of refreshing verdure, to gladden the monotony of the Court and relieve the blank architecture of the Hall.

Then, Hill and Street have their Roman history. A barbican, or watch-tower, has been discovered between Ludgate and the Fleet-ditch, being part of the City-wall extension in 1276; a fine fragment of which exists in St. Martin's-court, opposite the Old Bailey. In a bastion of the wall, in 1800, was found a sepulchral monument, in the rear of the London Coffee-house, where it is now preserved. And Wren found, when he was clearing the site for St. Martin's Church, the monument of a Roman soldier, now in the Arundelian Collection. The London Coffee-house was at first advertised as "a Punch House, Dorchester Beer and Welsh Ale Warehouse, where the finest and best old Arrack, Rum, and French Brandy is made into Punch." Ludgate Street and Hill were famous for mercers in Stow's time; and so they continue.

The great historical event of the Hill is, that here stopped the rebellion of Sir Thomas Wyat. In the *Chronicle of the Grey Friars of London*, we read: "And he (Wyat) himself came in at Temple Bar, and soo downe alle Flete-strete, and soo unto the Belle Savage. And then was his trayne (attacked at) the commandment of the Erle of Pembroke, and sartayne of his men slayne. And when he saw that Ludgatte was shutt agayne hym he departed, saynge, 'I have kept towché,' and soo went (back) agayne; and by the Tempulle-barre he was tane, and soo brought by watter unto the (Tower) of London."

Fuller, however, states that Wyat flung himself on a bench opposite the Belle Savage, and began to repent, &c. Here we have mention of the Inn 300 years ago; where dramas were played before a regular theatre was established in this country. Here, in Queen Elizabeth's time, was a School of Defence; and here Banks exhibited the feats of his horse, Marocco, which ascended to the top of St. Paul's, to the delight of "a number of asses," who brayed below. Banks then took his wonderful horse to Paris and Rome: he had better have stayed at home; for both he and his horse, which was shod with silver, were burnt for witchcraft. In the Belle Savage-yard lived Grinling Gibbons, "where," Walpole tells us, "he carved a pot of flowers, which shook surprisingly with the motion of the coaches that passed by." Had the old carver lived here in our time, he might probably have claimed compensation for the interference with his delicate art by the vibration of passing railway trains. The antiquaries were sadly misled by the early signs of this inn: one, *temp.* Henry VI., a bell within a hoop; and another, a savage man standing by a bell; until the *Spectator*, No. 82, read, in an old romance, translated out of the French, an account of a very beautiful woman, who was found in a wilderness, and is called, in the French, *la Belle Sauvage.* Stow added to the mystery by asserting a Mrs. Savage to have given the inn to the Cutlers' Company, which their books disprove. Near this spot lived the famous cobbler whom Steele mentions as a curious instance of pride. He had a wooden figure of a beau of the time, who stood before him in a bending posture, humbly presenting him with his awl, or bristle, or whatever else his employer chose to put in his hand, after the manner of an obsequious servant.

Among the changes we have witnessed, were the clearing away of the Belle Sauvage, one of the last of the coaching-inns, now shouldered by the railway. We miss, too, from the north side of the Hill the picturesque old shop-front of Rundell and Bridge, goldsmiths and diamond jewellers to the Crown, with the sign of two golden salmon, meeting at an angle over the doorway: does there exist any drawing of this famous sign? Here was executed Flaxman's Shield of Achilles, silver-gilt; here was fitted up the imperial crown for the Coronation of George IV., —for the loan of the jewels, Rundell and Bridge are stated by Haydon to have received 7000*l.* The firm also made for George IV. the gigantic silver wine-cooler, now at Windsor Castle; this cooler occupied two years in chasing; it is so large that two men can be seated in it: upon christenings, and great festal occasions, it has been filled with wine, to be served to the guests. Mrs. Rundell wrote the *Art of Cookery* (*Domestic Cookery*), for the conduct of the families of her own daughters; in the edition of 1833 we are told, "the authoress will receive from it no emolument;" yet she ultimately received 2000 guineas. In her preface it is remarked: "we rarely meet with butter properly melted, good toast-and-water, or well-made coffee." This was said thirty years since; how much nearer are we to these desiderata? the well-doing of common things seeming as difficult as *communia proprié dicere.*

In after-years little will be heard of the Milton Hall and Club, established in the large house, No. 35, so brief was the existence of the Association. Here is a clever bust of Milton; the premises are now the publishing-house of Sampson Low, Son, and Co.; and the office of the *Publishers' Circular.*

Another literary association of the Hill is the shop of William Hone, who removed here from the corner of Ship-court, in the Old Bailey, where he published his noted Parodies in 1817; for which he was three times tried and acquitted. On Ludgate-hill, No. 45, Hone published his political satires, with woodcuts by Cruikshank, and his *Every-day Book, Year-Book, Ancient Mysteries,* &c. Hone sat in a second-floor back-room among his black-letter rarities, and odd, out-of-the-way literature: he was a very *heluo librorum.* Southey's eulogium on the *Every-day Book* came too late to benefit the author commercially: the success of Hone's book lay in the vulgar or vernacular character of its contents, and its originality; those who have followed in his wake, with better and more copious materials, have not succeeded, through their attempted refinement where no refinement was required, and where the substitution of one quality for another was not likely to be attended with an advantageous result. Hone's description of the Bartholomew Fair of his time will best illustrate our meaning: we saw much of him at the starting of his *Every-day Book.** In the house,

* Hone was a sceptic; and we are induced to relate the following anecdote to show an improved phase of his mind. He used to tell, that being called to a house in a certain street, in a part of London quite new to him, he had noticed to himself, as he walked along, that he had never been there before. "I was shown," he said, "into a room to wait. On

No. 7, opposite Hone's, was published another successful venture, the *Percy Anecdotes*, the origin of which we have already narrated.

Among the houses lately removed was the former office of the Albion Assurance Company, where its clever actuary, Mr. Frend, wrote nearly a score of annual volumes of *Evening's Amusements*. At the opposite corner of the Hill lodged Olive, "Princess of Cumberland," who delighted to show herself at the first-floor window to the crowd in the street; proud of her

---

looking round, to my astonishment, every thing appeared perfectly familiar to me—I seemed to *recognise* every object. I said to myself, 'What is this? I was never here before, and yet I have seen all this; and if so, there is a very peculiar knot in the shutter.'" He opened the shutter, and found the knot! Now then, thought he, "Here is something I cannot explain on any principle; there must be some power beyond matter." The thought never left him; and it happily led him to doubt the truth of the system of materialistic atheism which, for thirty years of his life, he had adopted. "The strong intimation which the incident seemed to convey to his mind of the independence of the soul of the body gave rise to inquiries, which terminated in his becoming a convert to the truth of the Christian religion." Happy result!

Next to this escape from "the horror of great darkness," the most remarkable fact in this mysterious impression is Hone's proposal, as a test to himself of the reality of the impression, the finding of a certain knot in the wood of the window-shutter,—and that he actually did discover it.

We were well acquainted with Mr. Hone, and give implicit credence to the truth of his account of his conviction. He had hitherto been an almost unvarying sceptic; but, like many sceptics, he appears to have believed what most men doubt; for he asserted that he had seen an apparition!—in his study on Ludgate-hill, if we mistake not.

How descriptive are these lines, by Tennyson, of the above strange sensation!

> 'Moreover, something is, or seems,
> That teaches me with mystic gleams,
> *Like glimpses of forgotten dreams*—
> Of something felt, like something here;
> Of something done, I know not where;
> Such as no language may declare."

The subject has haunted the author of the present volume from his earliest years of thought.—*Things not generally Known*, 2d Series, p. 151.

tall, portly figure, but still prouder of the resemblance of her features to more than one of the members of the Royal family —the object of her defeated hopes, it will be remembered, was revived in one of our law-courts not long since.

To return to the Railway: the cost of the Extension line from Earl-street to West-street, Farringdon-street, is stated at a million of money; a large expenditure, yet duly justified by the importance of the object to be achieved by this last link in the through communication between the railways north and south of the Thames. In availing themselves of this communication, the Great Northern and South-Western Companies have secured for their lines the advantage of a through route and City termini without the vast cost to either company of separate extensions. The whole of the district south of the Thames will thus be brought into immediate connection with the Metropolitan (Underground) Railway system; and, besides the great convenience to the public afforded by trains running direct between the stations north and south of the river, there will be no reason why trains commencing their journey at Farringdon-street should not make the circuit of London, *viâ* King's Cross, Paddington, Kensington, Brixton, Blackfriars, and so return to Farringdon-street again. Further, the whole of the districts of country served by the Great Northern and Midland Railways will be brought into unbroken communication with the southern counties, and with the chief continental ports.

The profitable appropriation of Fleet-valley has been expedited by the formation of the Metropolitan Railway. Ninety years since, the great northern street was first proposed, but did not get beyond paper and print. Nearly forty years ago, the project was revived; when a writer in the *Quarterly Review* said: "We venture to consider this important improvement already secured,—which is, the extension of the great street from Blackfriars Bridge to Clerkenwell, sweeping away Fleet Market, and all that hive of infamy which has swarmed for centuries on Saffron-hill." In 1830, Fleet Market disappeared; the Fleet Prison followed in 1844; but with an interval of nearly twenty years before the Railway was commenced. "Seeing is believing in this matter-of-fact metropolis. The public never know either a convenience or a difficulty till they feel it themselves. Poor Mr. Charles Pearson, and a small host of enthusiasts, toiled, and talked, and wrote, and exhibited plans, for nearly twenty years; and it is only just now, after the death of the chief projector, that the Metropolitan Railway is at work" (*Times*, 1864).

During the excavations, several interesting antiquities were found in and near Fleet-ditch—medalets of old London, they may be called. Thus, there were—a series of silver coins of the reigns of Henry VIII., Mary, Elizabeth, James I., Charles I., and James II.; the sovereign or sceptre unit of James; a coin in tin, struck by James II. for America; also several halfpence and farthings of the same metal, with copper plugs in the centre; numerous leaden money-pieces, impressed with trade-devices, merchants' marks, &c.; a number of spurs and keys of various date, and a dagger presumed to be of the reign of James I.; spoons in pewter and brass, differently marked and lettered, one stamped with the date 1598; objects in leather, comprising jerkins, collars, and shoes of periods ranging from Henry VIII. to James I.; sheaths of daggers and girdle-knives; with many notable varieties of the ink-horn; a series of tradesmen's tokens. These we owe, says Mr. Butterworth, F.S.A., to the preservative qualities of the mud of the Fleet-river, which, however, has much to answer for in a sanitary point of view.

It is hard to imagine "ten or twelve ships, navies, at once" sailing up the Fleet to Holborn-bridge; yet so it is recorded. An anchor has been discovered as high as the present Bagnigge Wells-road; and even, it is said, the remains of a ship, in the bed of this ancient river, near Camden Town.

BLACKFRIARS BRIDGE.

LITTLE more than a century has elapsed since the first stone of this ill-fated Bridge was laid, with much pomp and circumstance, and all sorts of propitiations for its perpetuity; yet, at the moment we write, scarcely one stone remains upon another. This is too short an existence for so handsome a structure as Blackfriars Bridge undoubtedly was; though inferior to the two stone bridges which have been built across the Thames almost within the last half-century. Iron is the favourite material of the great masters of this mechanical age: the old stone bridge at Westminster has been replaced by an iron structure; and at Blackfriars there is to be a similar change of material in that which is to be built in place of the former Bridge.

The history of what can scarcely be called the old Bridge is a troublous one. There had been, for ages, four bridges over the Fleet-river ere the citizens projected the building of a bridge from Blackfriars across the Thames; when it appears to have been rather a matter of accident than of forethought. Labelye, the architect, had been called in to plan the removal of the houses from London Bridge, and to provide for its general repair; when the Committee appointed to investigate his plans ended their discussions with a proposal for building a new bridge at Blackfriars, or rather at Fleet-ditch. To cross the Thames in a boat at this point, at this period, was an expensive and dangerous passage; which, the reader may recollect, cost Mr. Brasbridge's friend, the convivial surgeon, 3*s.* or 4*s.*, after they had sat late over their potations at the Globe, in Fleet-street; besides which, the crossing over was attended with considerable personal danger.

The Corporation, having obtained their Act from Parliament,

set about the choice of an architect; and here their troubles began. Plans were advertised for, when several were sent in: one was by Smeaton, the celebrated engineer; another by Gwyn, who wrote a work on London Improvements. Mylne, a young man of six-and-twenty, fresh from a professional tour abroad, also sent in a design, which was unanimously chosen by the Bridge Committee. Out-of-doors, however, there was considerable opposition, and the question was warmly agitated whether elliptical or semicircular arches were preferable. Mylne had adopted the elliptical arch, Gwyn the semicircular one; the Press took up the matter, and Dr. Johnson, the friend of Gwyn, wrote three several letters in the *Gazetteer*, in opposition to Mylne. Johnson was blamed for his interference; but Boswell defended him in this common-sense manner: "If it should be remarked that this was a controversy which lay quite out of Johnson's way, let it be remembered that, after all, his employing his powers of reasoning and eloquence upon a subject which he had studied on the moment is not more strange than what we often observe in lawyers, who, as *quicquid agunt homines* in the matter of lawsuits, are sometimes obliged to pick up a temporary knowledge of an art or science of which they understood nothing till their brief was delivered, and appear to be so much masters of it." Boswell tells us that it was ungraciously suggested that Johnson's motive for opposing Mylne's scheme might have been his prejudice against him as a native of North Britain; when, in truth, he gave the aid of his able pen to a friend who was one of the candidates; and so far was he from having any illiberal antipathy to Mr. Mylne, that he afterwards lived with that gentleman upon very agreeable terms of acquaintance, and dined with him at his house. Indeed, Mylne had the best of it; for Boswell tells us that Mr. Muller, of Woolwich Academy, "the scholastic father of all the great engineers which this country has employed for forty years, decided the question by declaring clearly in favour of the elliptical arch."

There was, however, a political element in Mylne's success: he had for his friend Paterson, the City Solicitor, both being of the anti-Wilkes' party, and of the same country as Lord Bute, the unpopular first Minister of the Crown. Churchill, in his poem founded on the Cock-lane Ghost, condensed in these withering lines the popular feeling as well against Paterson as Mylne:

What of that Bridge, which, void of sense,
But well supplied with impudence,
Englishmen, knowing not the Guild,
Thought they might have the claim to build;
Till Paterson, as white as milk,
As smooth as oil, as soft as silk,
In solemn manner had decreed,
That, on the other side the Tweed,
Art, born and bred, and fully grown,
Was with one Mylne, a man unknown;
But grace, preferment, and renown
Deserving, just arrived in town:
One Mylne, an artist perfect quite,
Both in his own and country's right,
As fit to make a bridge as he,
With glorious Patavinity,
To build inscriptions, worthy found
To lie for ever underground.

The first pile of the Bridge was driven in the middle of the Thames, June 7, 1760; and the foundation-stone was laid by Sir Thomas Chitty, Lord Mayor, on the 31st of October following. Walpole has this ill-natured note upon the event: "The Lord Mayor laid the first stone of the new Bridge yesterday. There is an inscription on it in honour of Mr. Pitt, which has a very Roman air, though very unclassically expressed: they talk of the contagion of his public spirit. I believe they had not got rid of their panic about mad dogs." A pamphlet was written in ridicule of the inscription. This critical squib was entitled *City Latin*; it went through several editions, and was answered by *Plain English in answer to City Latin*, by a Deputy. Both pamphlets are in the Guildhall Library. Several gold, silver, and copper coins, of the reign of George II., were placed under the stone, with a Silver Medal which had been presented to Mr. Mylne by the Academy of St. Luke; and upon two plates of tin was engraved a Latin inscription, written at the request of the Court of Common Council. As the Latin is very faulty, we give the translation:

"On the last day of October, in the year 1760, and in the beginning of the most auspicious reign of George III., Sir Thomas Chitty, Knight, Lord Mayor, laid the first stone of this Bridge, undertaken by the Common Council of London, amidst the rage of an extensive war, for the public accommodation and ornament of the City; Robert Mylne being the architect. And that there might remain to posterity a monument of this City's affection to the man who, by the strength of his genius, the steadiness of his mind, and a certain kind of happy contagion of his probity and spirit (under the Divine favour and fortunate auspices of George II.), recovered, augmented, and secured the British Empire in Asia, Africa, and America, and restored the ancient reputation and influence of his country amongst the nations, the citizens of London have unanimously voted this Bridge to be inscribed with the name of William Pitt."

On November 19, 1768, the Bridge was made passable as a bridle-way, exactly two years after its reception of foot-passengers; and it was finally and generally opened on Sunday, Nov. 19, 1769. A toll of one halfpenny each on week-days and *one penny on Sundays* was levied, but was very unpopular; for the toll-house was burnt down in the Riots of 1780, when all the account-books were destroyed. "The toll-gates at Blackfriars," says J. T. Smith, "were among the edifices that suffered in the awful No-Popery Riot of Lord George Gordon's followers. They were burned down for the sake of the plunder, as it was supposed there were considerable sums of ready money there, the produce of the tolls. Some lives were lost there; and one man, who was shot, ran howling for thirty or forty yards, and then dropped down dead." Nevertheless, the toll was continued until 1785, when it was redeemed by the Government. Pitt's popularity had remained firm; and, according to the order of Common Council, the bridge was named "Pitt

Bridge." The City approach was named, after him, Chatham-place; one of its streets William-street; and another Earl-street. The name of "Pitt Bridge" was soon dropped; upon which Cunningham remarks: "It was easier, however, in conversation to remember the particular locality of the bridge than the name of the illustrious statesman." Yet, with another Thames bridge the reverse took place: Waterloo Bridge was first called the Strand Bridge. The decline of Pitt's popularity may have had something to do with this; for political fame is less lasting than the names of localities.

The Bridge was erected in ten years and three-quarters, and executed at a cost of 152,640*l.* 3*s.* 10*d.*—163*l.* less than the original estimate, the most creditable fact in its history. This, however, did not include 5830*l.* for altering and filling-up the Fleet-ditch, and 2167*l.*, the cost of the temporary wooden bridge. It was built of Portland stone, and consisted of nine semi-elliptical arches, then first introduced into this country. The piers were decorated by Ionic columns, of several heights and diameters, the line of parapet being a curve: this was the most objectionable feature. The balustrades were handsome; it was our favourite bridge in boyhood, the low parapet and balustrades allowing us to enjoy the Thames sights, which the higher parapets of London and Westminster Bridges prevented.

The approaches to the Bridge were of handsome design. New Bridge-street was designed by Mylne, who also superintended the roadway over the Fleet-ditch: the houses were cleverly planned; and Mylne built one for his private residence, at the corner of Little Bridge-street, having on the exterior a medallion, with the initials R. M., surmounted by Mylne's crest, and the date MDCCLXXX; the walls of the principal rooms bore medallions of classic figures; the house was long the York Hotel, and was taken down in 1863.

Blackfriars Bridge proved a costly failure. Between 1833 and 1840 it was thoroughly repaired by Walker and Burges, engineers, at an expense of 74,000*l.*—it is stated, at a loss to the contractors; the removal of the cornice and balustrades altogether spoiled the architectural character of the bridge. From the footway could be obtained a magnificent view of St. Paul's Cathedral, which our great landscape-painter, Richard Wilson, frequently came here to study. Mylne, the architect, is buried in the Cathedral, of which his bridge afforded so stately a view.

By a return made by the Chamberlain of London to the Court of Common Council in January 1843, the large sum of 100,960*l.* had been expended up to that time in repairing the structure, under a local Act passed in the fourth year of the reign of William IV.; over and above the cost of procuring the Act itself, amounting, with other incidental charges, to about 800*l.*; and according to a subsequent Report of a Committee of the Corporation, 10,520*l.* was spent in repairing one of the arches between June 1850 and January 1856, of which 8620*l.* odd was expended in the eighteen months previous to September 1851. The subsequent expenditure in that way down to the end of 1859 was at the rate of 600*l.* a year. This continual decay of the Bridge bespoke the unfitness of its materials, which Boswell exposed soon after it was built. Sir John Hawkins abused it, as "an edifice in which beauty and symmetry were in vain sought for; by which the citizens of London perpetuate their own disgrace, and subject a whole nation to the reproach of foreigners." This is pretty strong towards the superstructure. Boswell condemns this as unjust and ill-natured censure, and praises the Bridge as a stately, elegant, and airy structure. But Boswell's *amor patriæ* led him too far in favour of Mylne, though he was correct as to the cause of the failure. "*As to the stability of the fabric,*" he says, "the City of London took every precaution to have the best Portland stone for it; but as this is to be found in the quarries belonging to the public, under the direction of the Lords of the Treasury, it so happened that Parliamentary interest, which is often the bane of fair pursuits, thwarted their endeavours. Notwithstanding this disadvantage, it is well known that not only has Blackfriars Bridge never sunk in its foundation or in its arches, which were so much the subject of contest, but any injuries which it has suffered from the effects of severe frosts have been already, in some measure, repaired with sounder stone, and every necessary renewal can be completed at a moderate expense." The fact of importance here is the acknowledgment of the bad quality of the Portland stone: how costly a work the renewals proved, the Chamberlain's accounts best show.

At length, the Court of Common Council resolved to build a new bridge; and the requisite accommodation was provided, this being a lofty tier of scaffolding: as the first temporary bridge we have yet seen over the Thames in London, and for its own intrinsic merits, this is a very simple yet immensely strong contrivance in scaffolding. Its length is 990 feet from wharf to wharf, and it is built in two storeys; the lower one 26 feet wide, the upper story raised 16 feet above this, and consisting of two footways. The lower storey is for the carriage-traffic, the upper for pedestrians, and the four feet extra width of footway given to the latter is to accommodate loungers. This scaffolding, though called a temporary bridge, is in reality a permanent structure, as far as strength is concerned. The lower piles are driven 10 feet into the bed of the river; the staying piles which carry the roadway are only 18 feet from centre to centre longitudinally—those laid transversely are only 7 feet apart: all these, too, are braced together with horizontal and diagonal bracings; and in fact, even as far as the woodwork is concerned, the whole is built of considerably greater strength than ordinary wooden viaducts for railways.

The demolition of a large bridge is, at all times, an operation interesting to witness. In this case, within four months of Blackfriars Bridge being given up to the contractors, all the superincumbent mass of rubble and masonry above the turning of the arches—nearly 20,000 tons in weight—was removed; the centerings fixed beneath the arches; and the work of pulling down the arches themselves begun by the removal of the keystone from the second arch on the Surrey side.

In the *Times* report of the demolition, it is stated that within the above time, the contractors had removed every thing but the actual masonry of the turned arches themselves. The spaces between the springing of the arches and the roadway above appear to have been filled with river-ballast, to judge from the quantity of bones and old-fashioned tobacco-pipes found in it. The work, however, had been every where well performed; though the masonry of the arches was thinner than appeared externally. A clever engraving is extant, which represents the process of building this bridge in 1766; and the aspect which it then wore is almost identically similar with its appearance at this day. If the three-cornered cocked-hats of the labourers were suppressed, and steam-cranes substituted for hand-jacks, this old engraving might pass easily for a picture of the works in 1864. The presence of steam-cranes, however, makes an important and most suggestive alteration. Old Blackfriars Bridge took ten years to build. It was calculated to take less than a year to remove it entirely; and less than two to substitute in its place another double its size, strength, and beauty. In some cases, where the new piers came in the centre of the water-way of the old arches, the work of removal and reconstruction proceeded simultaneously. The scaffolding, which intersected the bridge like a high backbone of timber, was, as the work of demolition proceeded, carried down through the arches into the bed of the river, to form the staging for the erection of the new work.

In the *Illustrated London News*, December 3, 1864, appeared an effective engraving of the demolition, in which the novel steam-cranes are shown travelling upon rails laid along the beams at the top of the scaffolding, and lifting and carrying the largest blocks of stone with unexampled rapidity. At the above season, as the days were short, the men had to work in the evening by the light of naphtha-lamps, which gave a sort of romantic effect to the scene of operation.

There is reason to conclude that the same cause which destroyed Westminster has been fatal to Blackfriars Bridge, namely, the removal of old London Bridge, which so largely increased the downward scour of the ebb-tide. Every bridge then built—that is to say, Vauxhall, Blackfriars, and Westminster—suffered more or less from this cause; and early in the removal of the Bridge was observed an increase in the scour, which disturbed much of the mud, and laid bare the gravel at many parts on the Surrey side.*

In the competition, twelve designs were sent in—one by Mr. Mylne, grandson of the architect of the old bridge; all were noble designs, and showed the advances made in bridge-building in our time. That of Mr. Page was selected as the handsomest and the cheapest, and consisted of only three arches; but this choice was overruled, and ultimately the design of Mr. Joseph Cubitt, with five arches—the centre one 89 feet span—was decided on; the style to be Venetian-Gothic; the cost 265,000*l.* The piers will be of gray granite, and each will have a red-granite column, with bases and capitals of richly-carved white Portland stone: the arches, balustrades, and roadway to be of iron-work, with rich and tasteful ornamentation. With the completion of this beautiful Bridge, every metropolitan bridge across the Thames will have been built within the memory of the seniors of this generation—all within the last forty years; and no less than seven, including railway-bridges, within the last six years.

This increase of Bridges will not add to the effect of the Thames Embankment, now in progress. The Adelphi-terrace, and the river-front of Somerset House, are noble instalments of this grand improvement; and our architects and sculptors have here fine examples, especially in Sir William Chambers's majestic edifice; the sculpture is unrivalled. The Embankment, when completed, will provide a fine street, from 80 to 100 feet in width, between the West-end and the City.

Abridged from the *Times* report.

THE RAISING OF HOLBORN VALLEY.

THE Corporation of London, whose share in the City improvements is often grudgingly allowed, are about to remedy the declivities of Holborn and Snow Hills, by what is, in new phrase, termed "the raising of Holborn Valley." The Holborn side was called "the heavy hill" in Ben Jonson's time; and so it was proved to horseflesh as well as to criminals in the cart *en route* to Tyburn:

> As clever Tom Clinch, while the rabble was bawling,
> Rode stately through Holborn to die of his calling,
> He stopt at the George for a bottle of sack,
> And promised to pay for it when he came back.—*Swift*, 1727.

Taylor, the Water-Poet, says, in his *Travels from London to the Isle of Wight*, 1647:

> We wheel'd the top of the heavy hill
> Called Holborn,
> Up which hath been full many a
> Sinful soul borne.

Tom Brown tells us that an old counsellor in Holborn used every execution-day to turn out his clerks, with this recommendation: "Go, ye young rogues; go to school, and improve."

The Holborn-hill acclivity has, in our times, been modified. In 1842, it varied from 1 in 16½ to 1 in 23. In 1838, Mr. Whishaw, the engineer, assumed the average annual amount of traffic between Fetter-lane and the Old Bailey at "20,000,000 pedestrians, 871,640 equestrians, 157,752 hackney-coaches, 372,470 carts and wagons, 78,876 stages, 82,258 carriages, 135,842 omnibuses, 460,110 chaises and taxed carts, and 354,942 cabs." It is now stated, that upon an average upwards of 4200 vehicles a day go up and down the hills from the low levels. Holborn was paved four centuries and a half ago; yet up to this date no satisfactory remedy for this dangerous portion of one of the oldest thoroughfares of the metropolis had been provided. Various plans have been proposed, by viaducts crossing the Valley of the Fleet and otherwise. Among the plans was that of Alderman Skinner, who built Skinner-street, and proposed to construct a bridge from Snow-hill across the valley to Holborn-hill. To lift the valley 17 feet formed part of Mr. Charles Pearson's plan. And the Improvement Committee have recently received 105 designs, illustrated by 206 drawings and 13 models; from which they have selected such as appear to them to present the leading requirements of the case. They recommend that Holborn-hill and Skinner-street shall be pulled down, and that the viaduct shall cross the valley as nearly as possible over the whole line of road, so as to make a high-level street, commencing on Holborn-hill, near Ely-court; passing Hatton-garden, Ely-rents, Ely-place, and terminating in Skinner-street, near the Old Bailey.

Here is the Improvement more in detail: "The plan provides that the line of improvement from east to west shall commence at or near the Old Bailey, and terminate at a point fifty-five feet beyond the western side of Hatton-garden. The whole of the property on both sides is to be pulled down, and a high-level roadway formed eighty feet wide, with an almost imperceptible gradient. Farringdon-street is to be crossed by a bridge, with a minimum central headway of twenty-one feet. Two new streets are to be laid down, both starting from Farringdon-road, to afford communication for vehicles between the upper and lower levels; the western street to be sixty feet wide, and to start opposite New Market-street, now in course of formation by the Corporation, joining the upper level at Hatton-garden, the gradient being one in forty-five; the eastern street to be fifty feet wide, to start a little north of the bridge over Farringdon-street, to join the upper level at St. Sepulchre's Church, with a gradient of one in forty-five. Farringdon-road is to be widened as far as West-street to the present width of Farringdon-street. To increase the convenience of access on the southern side of the improvement between the high and low levels, it is also proposed that Shoe-lane be carried on to the viaduct. The gradients will be improved in various places."

The improvement will, it is estimated, cost about 575,000*l.*, and require seven years in completion. The pulling down of the houses in Skinner-street was commenced with No. 41, where William Godwin, author of *Caleb Williams*, kept a bookseller's shop, and published his works for young persons under the name of Edward Baldwin. In the lunette over the door was an artificial stone-relief of Æsop narrating his fables to children. Nearly opposite, over against the door of Mr. Beckwith, the gunsmith, No. 58, was hung, in 1816, Cashman the sailor, who, having joined a mob from a Corn-Law meeting in Spa-fields, was tempted to join in plundering Beckwith's shop; and being taken with a gun in his hand, he was tried and condemned to death.

Captain Gronow relates an anecdote of the above meeting, which is very striking. The captain was sent to Spa-fields, with a company of Guards, to occupy the adjoining prison. The leaders of the mob, including Major Cartwright, Henry Hunt, and Gale Jones, got information that the soldiers had orders, above all, to *pick off* the ringleaders, who accordingly soon left, and the meeting dispersed. Several years after this, at the time of the Reform Bill, Hunt was elected Member of Parliament for Preston, and Captain Gronow was elected for Stafford. One evening, in the smoking-room of the House of Commons, the Captain told Hunt, that if any attack had been made upon the prison at Spa-fields, he (Gronow) had given his men orders to pick off Major Cartwright, himself (Hunt), and one or two more. Hunt was perfectly astonished; he became very red, and his eyes seemed to flash fire. "What, sir! do you mean to say that you would have been capable of such an act of barbarity?" "Yes, sir," replied Captain Gronow; "and I almost regret you did not give us the opportunity; for your aim that day was to create a revolution, and you richly deserved the fate which you so marvellously escaped by the cowardice or lukewarmness of your followers."

Among the railway removals in Skinner-street was that of the printing-office of Woodfall and Kinder, in Angel-court. These premises possessed historical interest in connection with Woodfall and the *Letters of Junius*. The office was built by Mr. George Woodfall, father of the above Mr. Woodfall, about fifty years ago; and his edition of *Junius*, in three octavo volumes, was the first book printed there. The Letters first appeared in the *Public Advertiser*, which was printed by the elder Woodfall, grandfather of Mr. Kinder's partner, at his office in Paternoster-row, at the corner of Ivy-lane.

Some old picture-shops in King-street and hereabout remind us of the pleasant anecdote of Vandyke seeing, in a shop on Snow-hill, the picture by Dobson, which led him to seek out the painter in a garret, and recommend him to Charles I. On the death of Vandyke, Dobson was appointed Sergeant-Painter to the King, whom he accompanied to Oxford, where he painted his portrait, that of Prince Rupert, and several of the nobility. Dobson was born in St. Andrew's parish.

The curious may have sought in vain the house of Strudwick, the grocer, at the sign of the Star, on Snow-hill, where his friend, John Bunyan, author of the *Pilgrim's Progress*, died, Aug. 12, 1688. This house, we suspect, was removed in the formation of Skinner-street; in which there is no house old enough to have been Strudwick's. It is described as above on Snow-hill in most accounts; but in the first volume of *The Labours of that most eminent Servant of Christ, Mr. John Bunyan* (London, 1692, folio), he is stated to have died "at his very loving friend's, Mr. Strudwick's, a grocer, at *Holborn Bridge.*"

Many have been the displacements hereabout. We have long missed the old tobacconist on Holborn-hill, who sat with his *pigtail* against the shop window-pane, advertising his business. We have got rid of the pillory, in which, about 1812, we remember to have seen four men undergoing punishment, at Holborn-bridge, handy for the mob to pelt them with the filth, vegetable and animal, of Fleet Market. We have lived to see in the Valley, Holborn Bridge covered up, and an arch unearthed in

1841; Field-lane and its thieves' haunts swept away with the age of bandanas; Fleet Market and the Fleet Prison disappear; and Skinner-street built, to be pulled down, according to the present City plan. We still have the George on Snow-hill, a relic of the time when this hill was the only highway from Holborn Bridge eastward: the house was a carriers' inn at a very early date; and a carved sign-stone of

> St. George that swing'd the dragon,
> And sits on his horseback at mine hoste's door.

Shoe-lane has a blighted and stagnant aspect, and it is hard to imagine the town-house of the Bishop of Bangor, with its garden, lime-trees, and rookery, lingering at the north end of the Lane until 1828. Farringdon Market, though it cost a quarter of a million of money, and its architect studied the best continental markets in his design, is so thinly tenanted, as to make us wish it had another appropriation; and the gloom is not relieved by the recollection that the Market-place covers the burial-ground of St. Andrew's Workhouse, where lies Chatterton.

Journeying onward, through Holborn, we may note a long-desired improvement—the removal of Middle-row, to be shortly effected. In Stow's time, the Row was mostly tenanted by periwig-makers; and the objection to it is almost as old as the periwig: the place was, in our time, redolent of "bear's-grease," if not of bears. At the south-east corner of the Row, opposite the City stone obelisk, denoting the site of Holborn-bars, Sir James Branscomb kept a lottery-office forty years: he had been footman to the Earl of Gainsborough, and was knighted when Sheriff of London and Middlesex, in 1806. Hard by is Staple Inn, traditionally named from having been the hostel of the merchants of the (wool) staple, and an Inn of Chancery since the time of Henry V. The Holborn front is of the reign of James I.: the entrance, with its therms, is striking. The Hall is of later date, but has armorial glass of 1500. We miss the fine old fig-tree, which once covered one side of the Hall, now represented by offshoots. The Terrace, with the Taxing-Master's Offices, completed in 1843, is the purest Jacobean, with frontispiece, arched entrances, and semicircular oriels, finely effective; and the pier and parapet, lodge and gate, are very picturesque. Dr. Johnson removed into Staple Inn from Gough-square, in 1759: his chambers were but scantily furnished. Isaac Reed had chambers at No. 11. "Here, in Reed's chambers," relates Cunningham, "Steevens corrected the proof-sheets of his edition of Shakspeare. He used to leave his house at Hampstead at one in the morning, and walk to Staple Inn: Reed, who went to bed at the usual hour, allowed his facetious fellow-commentator a key to the chambers, so that Steevens stole quietly to his proof-sheets, without, it is said, disturbing the repose of his friend." In 1748, he had lived for a short time at the Golden Anchor, Holborn Bars.

A few doors from the Inn is an old short-stage tavern (up a passage, of course), the resting- and starting-place of the earliest Paddington coach. "The whole of London can now be traversed in half the time it took to reach Holborn Bars, at the beginning of this century, when the road was in the hands of Mr. Miles, his pair-horse coach, and his redoubtable Boy. This coach, and these celebrated characters, were for a long time the only appointed agents of communication between Paddington and the City. The journey to the City was performed by them in something more than three hours: the charge for each outside passenger was two shillings; the insides being expected to pay three. The delivery of parcels on the line added very materially to Mr. Miles's occupation and profit; and Miles's Boy not only told tales, to the great amusement of his master's customers, but gave them some equally amusing variations on an old fiddle, which was his constant travelling-companion, and which he carefully removed from its green-baize covering, to beguile the time at every resting-place on the road."*

In Holborn, the historical inn, the George and Blue Boar, has been taken down, and the Inns-of-Court Hotel erected upon its site. At this inn was intercepted the letter of Charles I., by which Ireton discovered it to be the King's intention to

* *Paddington: Past and Present.* By William Robins. 1853.

destroy him and Cromwell—which discovery brought about Charles's execution. The following are the details: While Cromwell was meditating how he could best "come in" with Charles, one of his spies—of the King's bedchamber—informed him that his final doom was decreed; and that what it was might be found out by intercepting a letter sent from the King to the Queen, wherein he declared what he would do. The letter, he said, was sewed up in the skirt of a saddle, and the bearer of it would come with the saddle upon his head that night to the Blue Boar Inn, in Holborn; for there he was to take horse, and go to Dover with it. This messenger knew nothing of the letter in the saddle; but some persons at Dover did. Cromwell and Ireton, disguised as troopers, taking with them a trusty fellow, went to the inn in Holborn; and this man watched at the wicket, while the troopers continued drinking beer till about ten o'clock, when the sentinel at the gate gave notice that the man with the saddle was come in. Up they got, and, as the man was leading out his horse saddled, they, with drawn swords, declared they were to search all who went in and out there; but, as he looked like an honest man, they would only search his saddle. Upon this they ungirt the saddle, and carried it into the stall where they had been drinking, and left the horseman with the sentinel; then, ripping up one of the skirts of the saddle, they found the letter, and gave back the saddle to the man, who, not knowing what he had done, went away to Dover. They then opened the letter, in which the King told the Queen that he thought he should close with the Scots. Cromwell and Ireton then took horse and went to Windsor; and finding they were not likely to have any tolerable terms from the King, they immediately from that time forward *resolved his ruin.**

It has been proposed to open a thoroughfare from Holborn to Lincoln's-Inn Fields, through Little Turnstile, but has been negatived by the Metropolitan Board of Works on account of the expense, 30,000*l.*, and the more pressing urgency of other works; but the cost is not so great as to outweigh the benefits.

* The Earl of Orrery's *State Letters.*

It is certainly extraordinary that so fine a spot as Lincoln's-Inn Fields should have no thoroughfare to Holborn for carriages. Yet, here of old lived many eminent persons in noble mansions, some of Inigo Jones's work. It was also a place of execution: the pillory was set up here so lately as 1808. The *Turnstiles*, Great and Little, carry us back to "*the fields*," they being placed both for the convenience of foot-passengers and to prevent the straying of cattle, the fields being at that period used for pasturage. Even *New* Turnstile is as old as the Bill of Rights (1688). The well-planted area or garden has often been threatened with an incubus of bricks and mortar: it has only just escaped such a fate; and, as if to commemorate this incident, we have, at the north-west angle of the Fields, one of the most picturesque drinking-fountains in the metropolis.

Across the square (which, by the way, is not so large as the area of the Great Pyramid of Egypt, but many thousand square feet less), a great clearance of old places will be made for the concentration of the Courts of Justice; the site to be within the following limits: "Carey-street, Bell-yard, Fleet-street, Temple Bar, the Strand, Pickett-street, Foregate, the passages or roadways on the north-east side of Clement's Inn, Horseshoe-court, and Yeates's-court, or some of them." The scheme contemplates the removal of a great number of dwelling-houses and other buildings, occupying a site of some celebrity—a sort of theatrical locality of the last and previous centuries. Here, in Clare Market, figured Orator Henley, in his velvet and gold tub, for nearly twenty years. In Gibbon's-court was "the finest playhouse that ever was in England," quoth Pepys. Killigrew's company acted here some time; and in and around the market were several taverns, one of which (the Black Jack), in Portsmouth-street, was the haunt of Joe Miller, and here he uttered his time-honoured jests; he was buried in St. Clement's upper ground, in Portugal-street. Opposite, in Portugal-street, were the last of the Stocks of London, which existed till our time. The old tavern hard by has been the resort of more than one club of Antiquaries. We all remember the removal of the old theatre in Portugal-street, in 1848: and the Grange Inn and old coffee-houses in the neighbourhood, which has been for years in a transition state. This plan of the Law Courts will, doubtless, be more popular than Mr. Barry's design, in 1841, to cover one-third of the area within the rails of Lincoln's-Inn Fields with a great hall, surrounded by twelve courts. Funds were wanting, and the blocking-up of the open space was objected to: in the evidence persons stated they considered this area as their "country walk," and that "they had been *in the country* when they had been round Lincoln's-Inn Fields." We can only say, such persons must have enjoyed a very limited appreciation of rural life.

"Portugal-street," in our time, became a term almost synonymous with debt and something worse; of course we mean the Court for the Relief of Insolvent Debtors. A whole volume could not so well picture the place as Mr. Dickens has sketched it, in these lines, in his *Pickwick Papers:*

"A temple dedicated to the genius of seediness," and "the place of daily refuge of all the shabby-genteel people in London. There are more suits of old clothes in it at one time than will be offered for sale in all Houndsditch in a twelvemonth; and more unwashed skins and grisly beards than all the pumps and shaving-shops between Tyburn and Whitechapel could render decent between sunrise and sunset. There is not a messenger or process-server attached to the Court who wears a coat that was made for him; the very barristers' wigs are ill-powdered, and their curls lack crispness. But the attorneys, who sit below the Commissioners, are, after all, the great curiosities. The professional establishment of the more opulent of these gentlemen consists of a blue bag and a boy. They have no fixed offices, their legal business being transacted in the parlours of public-houses or the yards of prisons, whither they repair in crowds, and canvass for customers after the manner of omnibus-cads. They are of a greasy and mildewed appearance; and if they can be said to have any vices, perhaps drinking and cheating are most conspicuous amongst them."

AN OLD TAVERN IN ST. JAMES'S.

ST. JAMES'S, the metropolis of the Court, has little of antiquity to recommend it to our respect. The old Palace, with its patched-up gatehouse, and a glimpse of Holbein's ceiling through the chapel-window on the right, are the principal olden features; *au reste*, the Palace is of all periods; though the ancient Hospital, which the Palace replaced, was of the Norman times. Little more than a century and a half ago, the parish of St. James's was described as "all the houses and grounds comprehended in a place heretofore called St. James's Fields, and the confines thereof;" and it was not until the reign of Queen Anne that it had acquired the distinction of the Court quarter. St. James's may be said to bear about the same relation to the other portion of western London as the City does to the Metropolis.

St. James's-street dates from 1670, when it was called "the Long Street;" and the best houses, at the upper end, had a terrace-walk before them. The poet Waller lived on the west side from 1660 to 1687; and Pope lodged "next door to ye Golden Ball, on ye second terras." At the south-west end was St. James's Coffee-house, which was taken down in 1806: this will be remembered as the Foreign and Domestic News House of the *Tatler*, and the "fountain-head" of the *Spectator*. Thus early, the street had a sort of literary fashion, favourable to the growth of taverns and clubs; one of the earliest of which, being in all probability *thatched*, was denominated the *Thatched House Tavern*, which did not disappear until the autumn of 1863; when a handsome stone-fronted edifice, named Thatched House Chambers, rose upon the site.

The Tavern had been for nearly two centuries celebrated for its clubs, its large room for public meetings, and its public dinners. It was one of Swift's favourite haunts. In some birthday verses he sings:

> The Deanery-house may well be matched,
> Under correction, with the Thatch'd.

Swift was of a very clubbable nature; and here he was made a member of the Brothers, in his absence. "The end of Our Club," he then says, "is to advance conversation and friendship, and to reward deserving persons with our interest and recommendation; and, if we go on as we began, no other club in this town will be worth talking of." The Dean preferred to call "The Brothers" a Society, and not a Club; and his journal is very full of Brothers Arran and Duplin, Masham and Ormond, Bathurst and Harcourt, Orrery and Jack Hill, and other Tory magnates. Swift tells Stella he entertained here his "Brothers," at the cost of seven guineas. "I staid till eight," he adds, "and then we all went away soberly. The Duke of Ormond's treat, last week, cost 20*l.*, though it was only four dishes, and four without a dessert; and I bespoke it in order to be cheap. Yet I could not prevail to change the house. Lord Treasurer is in a rage with us for being so extravagant; and the wine was not reckoned neither; for that is always brought by him that is president." Swift had much to do with the management of the Club, and was influential; for he writes: "We are now, in all, nine lords and ten commoners. The Duke of Beaufort had the confidence to propose his brother-in-law, the Earl of Danby, to be a member, but I opposed it so warmly that it was waived. Danby is not above twenty, and *we will have no more boys;* and we want but two to make up our number." Afterwards, they shifted their dinner from the Thatched House to the Star and Garter, "on the Pall-mall."

At the Thatched House first met the Dilettanti Society, or, as Walpole describes it, "a club for which the nominal qualification is having been in Italy, and the real one being drunk." The character of the club, however, became changed, the members being persons devoted to art and antiquarian studies: in the club-room were two fine conversation portrait-pieces by Sir

Joshua Reynolds, painted in the manner of Paul Veronese; and a collection of portraits, the earlier ones by Hudson, Reynolds's master. These pictures were hung in the club-room, which faced St. James's-street; it was lit in the evening with wax-lights, in large old glass chandeliers; and the paintings could be seen from the pavement of the street. The Dilettanti is now a publishing Society, as the Roxburgh, the Camden, &c.

To the Thatched House removed, in 1779, from Parsloe's, in St. James's-street, "the Club," from the time of Garrick's death known as "the Literary Club," founded just a century since, at the Turk's Head, in Soho, by Sir Joshua Reynolds and Dr. Johnson. The members were limited to nine, including Reynolds, Johnson, Hawkins, and Burke; and Goldsmith, notwithstanding Hawkins's objection to Oliver as "a mere literary drudge:" the number was increased, but was never to exceed forty. It was originally a club of *authors by profession:* it now numbers few except titled members, which was far from the intention of its founders. The writer of a paper in the *National Review*, No. 8, however, says, complacently enough: "the Club still acknowledges literature as its foundation, and love of literature as the tie which binds together its members, whatever their rank and calling." The title is now changed to "the Johnson Club," and its hundredth anniversary was celebrated at the Clarendon Hotel last year, 1864. Among the members lately deceased were the late Marquis of Lansdowne, Sir George Cornewall Lewis, Mr. N. W. Senior, the political economist; and the Earl of Carlisle.

There is an amusing anecdote of the mention of the tavern in the House of Lords, thus related by Lord Campbell: In the debates on the Regency, a prim Peer, remarkable for his finical delicacy and formal adherence to etiquette, having cited pompously certain resolutions which he said had been passed by a party of noblemen and gentlemen at the Thatched House Tavern, the Lord Chancellor Thurlow, in adverting to these, said, "As to what the noble Lord in the red ribbon told us, he had heard at the alehouse," &c. Lord Thurlow was just the man to demolish such affectation, and Lord Campbell just the author to chronicle such an incident.

The greater part of the Thatched House Tavern was taken down in 1844, and the Conservative Club House now occupies the site. The remaining portion of the tavern has been taken down for the site of the new edifice already mentioned. In the rear, Thatched House-court has also disappeared. Beneath the tavern-front was a range of low-built shops, one of which Tayleure, the actor, kept for the sale of prints. There was a public way to it through the tavern; and we recollect a similar public way through a tavern on the opposite side of the street, to King's-place.

Dipping into Captain Gronow's second series of *Reminiscences,* we find this recollection of the Thatched House Tavern locality: "The most fashionable 'coiffeur' was Rowland, or Rouland, a French *émigré.* His charge for cutting hair was five shillings, and his shop was next door to the Thatched House Tavern, in St. James's-street. He was the inventor of the famous Macassar Oil, and made a large fortune. He came to London with the Bourbons on the breaking out of the French Revolution, and followed them back to France in 1814."

For the site of the Conservative Club was also taken down the house of Elmsley, the bookseller, at the south corner of Little St. James's-street, where Gibbon, the historian, died, January 16, 1794. Elmsley was the over-cautious person who would not enter upon the perilous adventure of publishing the *Decline and Fall,* by which publishers profited ten times the amount paid the author for his copyright. Horace Walpole relates this droll story of Gibbon: "One of those booksellers in Paternoster-row who publish things in numbers went to Gibbon's lodgings in St. James's-street, sent up his name, and was admitted. 'Sir,' said he, 'I am now publishing a *History of England,* done by several good hands: I understand you have a knack at them there things, and should be glad to give you every reasonable encouragement.' As soon as Gibbon had recovered the use of his legs and tongue, which were petrified with surprise, he rang the bell, and desired his servant to show this encourager of learning down-stairs.

In this part of the street lived the famous Betty, often mentioned by Horace Walpole, and whom Mason has introduced in his *Heroic Epistle:*

> And patriot Betty fix her fruit-shop there.

Walpole's mention of her conveys that her shop was a place for gossip: thus, he says of a story much about, "I should scruple repeating it, if Betty and the waiters at Arthur's did not talk of it publicly." Again, "Would you know what officer's upon guard in Betty's fruit-shop?" Her death, August 30, 1797, is thus recorded in the *Gentleman's Magazine* of the time: "Died, aged 67, at her house facing St. James's-street, at the top of Park-place, Mrs. Elizabeth Neale, better known by the name of Betty. She had kept, for many years, a house in St. James's-street, as a fruit-shop, from which she had retired about fourteen years. She had the first preëminence in her occupation, and might be justly called *the Queen of Apple-women.* Her knowledge of families and characters of the last and present age was wonderful. She was a woman of pleasing manners and conversation, and abounding with anecdote and entertainment. Her company was even sought for by the highest of our men of rank and fortune. She was born in the same street in which she ever lived, and used to say she never slept out of it but twice—on a visit to a friend in the country, and at a Windsor installation." No. 7 is, to this day, a fruiterer's shop.

We have long missed, lower in St. James's-street, the large bow-window which Theodore Hook compared to an obese old gentleman in a white waistcoat. Round the corner, in Cleveland-row, Hook lived from 1827 to 1831, in a handsome house, which he furnished at some 2000*l.* or 3000*l.* expense, and by this and other outlays so increased his embarrassments that he had to sell a moiety of his share in the *John*

Bull for 4000*l.* Of the St. James's-street of Hogarth's days we get a glimpse in the background of his picture of "The Rake arrested by Bailiffs;" here the projecting sign and the barber's pole carry us a century back. The Tavern which has just disappeared was nearly the last relic of old St. James's-street, although its memories survive in various clubs; and the "Thatched House" is to be kept in mind by the chambers built upon its site.

The Palace clock has connected with it an odd anecdote, which we received from the late Mr. Vulliamy, of Pall Mall, who, with his family, had been the royal clockmakers since 1743. When the gatehouse was repaired in 1831, the clock was removed, and not put up again, on account of the roof being reported unsafe to carry the weight. The inhabitants of the neighbourhood, missing the clock, memorialised William IV. for the replacement of the timekeeper; and the King, having ascertained its weight, shrewdly inquired how, if the Palace gatehouse-roof were not strong to carry the clock, it was safe for the number of persons occasionally seen upon it to witness processions and the company on drawing-room days. There was no resisting the calculation; the clock was forthwith replaced, and a minute-hand was added, with new dials; the original dials were of wainscot, in a great number of very small pieces, curiously dovetailed together.*

On the west side of the street the eccentric Thomas Wirgman, the Kantesian, as a goldsmith and jeweller, made a considerable fortune, which he squandered as a regenerating philosopher. He had paper made specially for his books, the same sheet consisting of several different colours; and, through his whims, one book of 400 pages cost him 2276*l.* He published a children's grammar of the five senses, which book, he maintained, if adopted in schools, would restore peace and harmony to the earth, and cause virtue every where to replace crime. What an elysium would this make of St. James's!

* *Curiosities of London*, p. 571.

INDEX.

VAUXHALL GARDENS, WALKS AND TALKS IN

REMAINS OF JOHN SELDEN.—(*See page* 73.)

AFTER this page had been printed, the following appeared in the "Column for the Curious," contributed by the Author of *Walks and Talks* to the *Illustrated London News:*

The dust and bones of the learned John Selden have, during the recent repair and restoration of the Temple Church, been "carted away and shot into a dusthole." This desecration, which in enormity equals the dust of Alexander stopping a bunghole, has been detailed in a lengthy letter of condemnation, addressed by "Old Mortality Redivivus," to the *Times*. Opposite the bell-turret, in the burial-ground, the correspondent found a decayed blue flag or slate ledger-stone, inscribed with uncial letters, ending DEN, which slab was once "laid over the earthly remains of one who has ever been considered not only the greatest legal jurist, but most learned luminary of the past, either in his own or any other age." This *find* led to inquiries and evidence, which we have not space to quote, save that the dust and bones of the profound scholar have been ignominiously treated as above; which is very remarkable, seeing that, according to the account of Aubrey, iii. 533, at the time of the interment, no pains seem to have been spared to render their depository secure.' Aubrey tells us:

"His (Selden's) grave was about ten foot deepe or better, walled up a good way with bricks, of which also the bottome was paved, but the sides at the bottome for about two foot high were of black polished marble, wherein his coffin (covered with black bayes) lyeth, and upon that wall of marble was presently lett downe a huge black marble stone of great thickness, with this inscription :—'Hic jacet corpus Johannis Seldeni, qui obiit 30 die Novembris, 1654.' Over this was turned an arch of brick (for the House would not give their ground), and upon that was throwne the earth," &c.

As it is impossible to recover the dust, "Old Mortality Redivivus" suggests that the spot of the interment should be marked by a granite slab, inlaid with brass, inscribed with the simple epitaph which Selden himself wrote; and that "the old monument should be removed from its present dismal abode behind the seats of the Benchers of the Middle Temple to the ambulatory of the Greek Church, where at least may be read, without inconvenience, this simple memorial."

ERRATA.

Page 57, line 11, for "W. Hobart," read *James Hobart.*
" 77, " 13, for "Mansfeld," read *Mansfield.*
" 89, " 24, for "Landor," read *Landon.*
" 164, " 14, for "Foote's Mirror," read *Foote's Minor.*

CPSIA information can be obtained
at www.ICGtesting.com
Printed in the USA
LVHW040026180422
716440LV00005B/405

9 783752 590869